in love with Allie Larkin's quirky and endearing characters and found myself thinking about them long after I turned the last page."

—Ann Mah, author of *The Lost Vintage*

"Poignant and funny, touching and eccentric, *Swimming for Sunlight* is brimming with heart. A gem of a novel that will charm not only dog lovers, but anyone, anywhere who's ever felt a twinge of anxiety. In other words, all of us."

—Tish Cohen, author of *Inside Out Girl* and *Town House*

"A heartfelt and bittersweet ode to taking the long view of life when we fall short of our own expectations, to choosing courage and hope in the face of disappointment and tragedy. This book was just what my soul needed."

—Julia Whelan, author of *My Oxford Year*

ALSO BY ALLIE LARKIN

Stay

Why Can't I Be You

SWIMMING FOR SUNLIGHT

ALLIE LARKIN

ATRIA PAPERBACK

New York   London   Toronto   Sydney   New Delhi

ATRIA
PAPERBACK

An Imprint of Simon & Schuster, Inc.
1230 Avenue of the Americas
New York, NY 10020

First Atria Paperback edition April 2019

ATRIA PAPERBACK and colophon are registered trademarks of Simon & Schuster, Inc.

For information about special discounts for bulk purchases, please contact Simon & Schuster Special Sales at 1-866-506-1949 or business@simonandschuster.com.

The Simon & Schuster Speakers Bureau can bring authors to your live event. For more information or to book an event, contact the Simon & Schuster Speakers Bureau at 1-866-248-3049 or visit our website at www.simonspeakers.com.

Interior design by Jill Putorti

Manufactured in the United States of America

10 9 8 7 6 5 4 3 2 1

Library of Congress Cataloging-in-Publication Data

Names: Larkin, Allie, author.
Title: Swimming for sunlight / Allie Larkin.
Description: New York : Atria, 2019. |
Identifiers: LCCN 2018028792 (print) | LCCN 2018030240 (ebook) |
  ISBN 9781501198496 (eBook) | ISBN 9781501198489 (paperback)
Subjects: | BISAC: FICTION / Contemporary Women. | FICTION / Family Life.
Classification: LCC PS3612.A6485 (ebook) | LCC PS3612.A6485 S95 2019 (print)
  | DDC 813/.6—dc23
LC record available at https://lccn.loc.gov/2018028792

ISBN 978-1-5011-9848-9
ISBN 978-1-5011-9849-6 (ebook)

Praise for

SWIMMING FOR SUNLIGHT

"I loved every page of this beautiful, heartfelt book. Full of compassion, warmth, and charm, Larkin makes a complex story about anxiety and loss and female friendships at all ages feel both effortless and hopeful. I dare you not to hug this book when you finish."

—Julie Buxbaum, *New York Times* bestselling author of *Tell Me Three Things* and *What to Say Next*

"I instantly fell in love with this narrator—who's brave, funny, feisty, tender, and, most of all, relatable. She handles a seismic change in her life with rapier-sharp humor and grace, proving that life's curveballs can be processed with love and laughter—and the often-underestimated power of the companionship and loyalty of animals. Katie's next chapter in life takes us on a wild water park ride, addressing losses in her past, the surfacing of a college flame, and a grandmother you'll wish was your own. Add to this Larkin's descriptive writing—which sparkles on the page—and you have a gem of a novel."

—Lolly Winston, *New York Times* bestselling author of *Good Grief* and *Happiness Sold Separately*

"Allie Larkin knows her characters so well—and loves them so much. Reading *Swimming for Sunlight* is like visiting a real place, spending time with a real and really good friend."

—Rainbow Rowell, #1 *New York Times* bestselling author of *Eleanor & Park*

For Joan Pedzich.
Because of apple juice.
And everything.

PROLOGUE

~~~~~~~~~~

My husband brought a date to our divorce.

To be fair, she didn't come in the actual room. And according to Eric she wasn't a date, she was a *friend*, but it was still bullshit. He knew it and I knew it and I don't think either of us wanted it to be that way, but that's where we were. He was defensive and hurt and mean, and needed to bring his *friend* along to say, *See? You see? Someone loves me. You couldn't, but someone does.* And I was just there. Involuntary processes. Flesh taking up space. Even in that moment, I wanted to be better for him. Give him a better divorce. A satisfying fight, or at least one last burst of kindness to end what we both started with decent intentions. With hope, at least. We didn't get married out of indifference.

His friend sat on a bench in the hallway and pressed at the screen of her phone with the pads of her fingers, long fake nails clicking against the glass. I swore I could hear her from the conference room while Eric's attorney droned on.

"My client requests a divorce be granted on grounds of Irretrievable Breakdown . . ."

Click. Click. Click.

". . . and maintains neither side is at fault . . ."

Click. Click. Click.

". . . furthermore, we expect the fair and equitable division of assets . . ."

Clickity. Click. Click. Click.

I picked at the ragged edge of my thumbnail, bitten down too far, while my attorney, Arnold Troyer: Rochester's Best Divorce Lawyer, responded in sonorous tones, beads of sweat collecting around his sad little horseshoe of brown hair.

I'd pictured Eric's friend many times, imagining a better version of me. Someone more polished, less nervous, who liked listening to Eric curse through Buffalo Bills games on Sunday afternoons, but was otherwise fundamentally the same. I imagined her that way because I wanted to believe if I'd worked a little harder I could've fixed things. If what Eric and I had was close enough to almost work, that meant it had been reasonable to try.

The woman in the hall wasn't a better version of me. She wasn't the same species. Probably not the same phylum. Like there was a special kind of spinal column for women who were born to be trophy wives, and it was so much lighter and thinner than everyone else's. Seeing her made me realize that even if I had worked harder to get better, to be better, to learn the difference between a checkdown and a backward pass, I still wouldn't have been the right person for Eric, the same way he wasn't ever going to be the right person for me.

When we were almost done dividing up assets, Eric's attorney stated that Eric was seeking full custody of my dog.

"Wait! Time-out!" I said, jumping to my feet, making a T with my hands.

"There's no time-out in divorce, Katie," Eric said, turning his wrist to check a watch I'd never seen before: big and silver with an unmarked blue face.

"Whatever. Sidebar," I said, tugging at Arnold Troyer's sleeve. Arnold grabbed his files and allowed me to drag him to the hallway. Once we were out of earshot from Eric's bottle blond friend, I took a deep breath and said, "Bark is all I want."

"What is Bark?"

"Barkimedes. My dog. I told you. Eric can have everything else, but I need my dog."

"Let's not be rash," Arnold said, wiping his nose with a folded paper towel he'd pulled from his pocket. "Perhaps, if you'd be willing to share custody—"

"No! Eric hates Bark. He's only doing this to pick at me. To prove a point he doesn't have to prove. I get it. I know why he cheated. I know I was a shit wife. I just want my dog."

Arnold thumbed through my file. "Is this dog a purebred? Show dog? Can we assign a cash value?"

"Does your best friend have a cash value?" I asked, my voice getting froggy as my throat tightened.

Arnold sighed, mopping at his head with the same paper towel. "I like to tell my clients not to lose sight of the forest for the trees."

"I don't want the forest," I shouted, and then, surprised by the echo of my voice in the hall, I tried to take it down to a whisper, "or the house, or the stupid blender his mom gave us, or the baby clothes I bought too soon, or the ugly couch he probably screwed her on." I pointed down the hall to the friend, who was still clicking away on her phone. "I want Bark and I want to start over. And I think it's all he wants too; it's just that this—this is the worst part of it."

Eric needed to justify himself. The cheater doesn't get to feel like they've been wronged, and that lack of acknowledgment was making him reckless, like a kid coloring on the walls in permanent ink. He cheated. I checked out. Neither of us was right, but I checked out long before he cheated. This was him, embarrassed, hurt, broken, saying, *Look at what you made me do! Pay for what you made me do! React to me for fuck's sake!*

I wiped tears from my chin with my sleeve.

Arnold reached into his pocket and handed me another paper towel folded into four. I wondered if he sat around at night folding paper towels so he could have them at the ready. Why didn't he carry tissues or a handkerchief like a normal person?

Arnold watched me while I blotted my eyes. His face softened. He leaned in close. "Is this really what you want?"

I nodded. *Okay, Eric. I'm reacting. This is the end, and I'm fighting.*

"Alright," Arnold said, pulling his files to his chest. "Go to the ladies' room, calm down, splash some water on your face. I'll see what I can do."

"Thank you." I blew my nose. It echoed.

"If I can get you more, I'll get you more, but if all else fails we take the dog and call it a win."

I ran down the hall, the high heels I almost never wore punctuating my retreat. In the bathroom, I ran cold water on my wrists and tried not to picture what it would feel like to hand Bark's leash over to Eric.

I loved that dog from the second I saw him on the shelter website. He had a face like a German Shepherd, the bat ears of a Boston Terrier, and fluffy Chow fur that was spotted and dappled like a Border Collie. One of his eyes was the richest caramel brown, and the other was a clear bright blue. I needed desperately to save someone, and there he was—Dog 2357—waiting for rescue.

I made Eric drive us all the way to Syracuse to adopt him. We got there just in time. Bark was scheduled to be put down the next day.

Because he was from Syracuse, I thought naming him Barkimedes was hysterical. Eric didn't get it. He wanted to name him Jeter. Plus, Bark ate the back of the passenger seat in Eric's brand new BMW when we made a pit stop at a gas station on the way home, so right off the bat, Eric was not a Bark fan. It went downhill from there.

For all intents and purposes, Bark was my dog. Every morning I sat on the floor next to his bowl of kibble and drank my coffee with his ribs pressed against mine because it was the only way he'd eat his breakfast. I was the one who knew which patches of floor he was afraid of, and that you couldn't use the stove without first closing him safely in the bedroom with three toys and his favorite blanket, and that when we went to work, he needed the radio tuned to NPR so he could listen to *All Things Considered* and feel less alone.

Eric didn't know these things. He didn't bother to learn. He didn't take me seriously when I told him how Bark needed us to act around him. So the one time I left them alone to go to Florida for a funeral, I came back to find shirts shredded, a section of the rug chewed away, and a dog who probably hadn't eaten in four days, cowering in a corner while a basketball game blared on the radio.

I had to believe that Eric was only posturing and he wasn't really going to take my dog. And I had to believe that Arnold Troyer: Rochester's Best Divorce Lawyer was at least slightly competent.

I dried my hands and smoothed my hair.

My phone buzzed.

A text from my grandmother: *Over yet?*

I wrote back: *Almost.*

Hallelujah!

I smiled and typed: *Nan! So smug!*

Grab freedom by the balls!

I laughed and looked in the mirror and stood up straight as if Nan had told me to. My cheeks were flushed and my eyes were starting to swell, but when I walked back down the hallway, I clacked my high heels against the marble floor like a statement.

Eric's friend was still sitting on the bench outside the conference room. She had begun to wilt, eyeliner pooling under her eyes.

Suddenly, I felt sorry for her. If Arnold Troyer did his job, I would walk away with Bark, but she'd still be stuck with a cheater who clipped his toenails at the kitchen table and talked to his mother on the phone every single day.

"I'm Katie, Eric's ex," I said, reaching out my hand to shake hers.

She didn't introduce herself, only mumbled *hello* in a voice that was softer than I expected. Her hand was cold and boney. There were rhinestones glued to her nails.

"He should be done soon," I said, and then blurted out, "Nice to meet you."

Nice to meet you. And it played in my head when I sat next to Arnold and signed by the *X*'s. Nice to meet you, woman who facilitated my husband's escape from what I'd previously thought was a lifelong thing. Woman who left your hair clip in my living room like you were marking your territory. Woman who gave me the push I needed to start over. It's nice to meet you.

CHAPTER ONE

"That's the coffee shop I like," I said, pointing out the window as I drove. "And that's where I went to high school." I turned onto Nan's palm-tree-lined street of Florida ranch houses, each with a postage stamp yard and a kidney-shaped pool. "Ooh, Mrs. Cohen lost her flamingos!" The healthy flock of plastic birds had dwindled to three, and only one of them wore sunglasses now. "Times have changed, my friend."

I looked behind me. Barkimedes had jammed all eighty pounds of himself into the tiny bit of backseat floor space, shoving his head as far as he could under the passenger seat.

"You're going to like Nan." My voice was raw and throaty from narrating the entire trip from Rochester, New York, to Port St. Lucie, Florida, in a futile attempt to keep Bark calm. I'd done some crying too. "Or maybe you won't like Nan, because it's you. But I think you should try. Please, Bark?"

We rounded the bend and there was Nan's house. The crown of thorns I'd planted by the front path was tall and unwieldy. Dandelions dotted the lawn. I worried these were signs of Nan's bursitis acting up again. She hadn't mentioned it on the phone. But that was Nan. She didn't complain. She *tsk*ed and moved on.

I caught a flash of motion across the picture window in the living room, and slowed the car to get a better look.

There was a man in Nan's living room. Not one of her ancient, shrinking neighbors. A large man. Hulking. Standing close enough to the window that I could see the outline of his enormous shoulders through the sheer curtains. And then I couldn't see him at all. A nervous rabbit heartbeat took over my chest.

I threw the car into park at the curb, leaving it running for the AC. "I'll be right back, Bark," I whispered, ducking out of the driver's seat, pushing the door closed quietly behind me. The air was too thick, too warm. Crouching low, I tiptoed toward the house. I thought about banging on the window or yelling at the top of my lungs so that man would know I was aware of him. Maybe he would stop, afraid. Run out the back door, leaving Nan safe. But what if my yelling turned things? What if he was peacefully stealing Nan's valuables, and my yelling pushed him into a hostage situation? Did he have a knife? A gun? I used my sleeve to push the thorny plants out of the way so I could peek in the window.

He was on top of Nan, pinning her to the floor. I fought the urge to scream. My eyes watered. Thorns snagged my bare legs as I ran to the front door. I wanted to kill him, and in my rage, it felt possible, like those women who lift cars to save their babies.

I slowly turned the knob and pushed the door open, stepping out of my flip-flops so they wouldn't smack against the tile. That man was so much bigger than me. I needed the element of surprise. Adrenaline spiked in my veins, blood dripped from one of the scratches on my leg. I grabbed the knockoff Ming Dynasty vase of dried flowers by the door, raising it over my head slowly so he wouldn't catch movement from the corner of his eye. Holding my breath, I snuck toward them.

When my toes hit the living room carpet, I heard Nan giggle. The man wasn't forcing himself on her. She wrapped her bare arm around his bulging bicep, her naked knee pressed to his chest.

I backed from the room, still holding the vase in the air, dried flowers falling to the floor. My heart stuck in nervous rabbit time.

"Kaitlyn!" Nan called. "What in the world?"

"Oh, no," I said, closing my eyes. "I'm going to go . . . I'm not judging— Good for you, Nan . . . Ooh, vitality and wow . . ."

"Oh, lord, sweetie! What is wrong with you?"

I opened my eyes. The muscled man had moved aside. Nan was sitting on the floor dressed in running shorts and a tank top. Instead of her comforting, pillowy folds of flesh, she was lean and wiry. She'd abandoned her yellowed bubbles of permed hair for a short white pixie cut that made her blue eyes shocking and sprightly.

"Wow," I said, trying to make sense of this new version of Nan. "You look—"

"I owe it to this fellow." She patted the bicep. "Billy, this is my granddaughter, Katie."

"I've heard so much about you," Billy said, grinning.

I tucked the vase in my armpit so I could shake his hand.

"Nice to— I'm sorry, I thought— I thought that . . ."

"Katie, we were stretching," Nan said flatly. She jumped up from the floor with a surprising amount of vigor, took the vase from me, returning it to its place, and gave me a bear hug.

"It was like a piece of me was missing," she said, kissing my cheek. She picked a dried strawflower from my hair and pointed to my leg. "Let's get that cleaned up before you make a mess of everything."

I nodded.

"Thank you, Billy!" Nan said. "Same Bat-time?"

"Same Bat-channel," Billy said, smiling as he let himself out.

Nan led me to the bathroom. I sat on the lid of the toilet and she cleaned my leg with a cotton ball soaked in witch hazel, blowing on it to dull the sting.

Now that I knew she was okay, my heartbeat steadied, and my eyes filled with tears. Every bad thing that could have happened cycled through my brain in vivid detail. Billy the Intruder, with a sneer on his lips, gun in hand. Nan crying in a heap on the floor, her face battered and bruised. Worse. It could have been worse than that. Even though I knew there had never been any danger, I couldn't stop the movie in my head.

"Still such a baby," Nan said, smiling. "You always cried over cuts and scrapes."

I tried to focus on Nan's not-broken nose, her bruise-free cheeks. "I thought he was hurting you," I said, stifling a sob.

"I know, sweetie." Nan brushed hair from my face and kissed my forehead, saying the words she'd said to me a million times when I was a child: "It's not always the worst-case scenario."

It could be, was my constant reply, but now I kept it to myself. I didn't want her to know that I wasn't any better. That maybe I was worse.

Nan returned the witch hazel back to the medicine cabinet and threw the band-aid papers in the trash. Her arms were strong and sinewy. No signs of bursitis.

"Did you have a good drive?" she asked.

"Crap! My car is running! I have to get Bark!"

Nan followed me outside.

As we approached the car, I couldn't see Bark through the window. "Maybe I should do this myself?"

"Well, let me help you with your bags, at least," Nan said.

"We can get them later," I whispered, hoping Nan would bring her volume down.

"Nonsense. I'll help you now."

"With Bark, things need to be a certain way."

"He's a dog. You tell him how things are. He'll deal with it." Nan reached for the door handle. Bark sprung from his hiding place, growling and gnashing his teeth.

"Holy crow!" Nan said, stepping back. "Pop the trunk, I'll grab your suitcase." She tried to act like she wasn't rattled, but as I climbed in the car to calm Bark, I saw her press her hand to her heart and take a deep breath.

Bark wouldn't ever bite her. At least I didn't think he would. He wasn't mean, just scared. I scratched his chest until he settled to a grumbling growl. Then I climbed into the driver's seat to grab the butter knife from the door pocket.

My ancient Honda Civic had served me nobly for a hundred and seventy thousand miles, but these days, it needed sweet-talking.

"Right back, Barky. Promise." I hit the trunk release and ran around to jimmy the latch with the knife. Nan watched silently. In the trunk there were two laundry baskets of clothes and an array of odds and ends shoved in plastic grocery bags from Wegmans.

"Eric got the suitcases," I said, slipping the butter knife into my back pocket.

"Goodness," Nan said. "When will the rest of your stuff get here?"

"You're looking at it." I could have taken more from the house when I left. I should have. But Eric hovered as I packed, ready to argue over what was his and what was mine. The resolve I'd mustered to get through our divorce proceedings was crumbling, and I needed out before I broke in front of him. He couldn't argue over my ratty old sweaters, or the endless collection of t-shirts from shows at the Rochester Regional Theatre, where I'd been assistant costume designer. He had no claim on the small stack of my father's books, or the lap quilt Nan's friend Bunny made me when I left for college. Almost everything else felt like set dressing for a life that didn't belong to me.

I knew it was rash to leave so much. Stupid. Heartbreaking, when I realized my sewing machine was in the mix of what I left behind. Bark and I were already in Pennsylvania when that loss dawned on me. Too late to turn around.

Nan stared, mouth slack.

"It's no big deal," I said, wiping sweat from my upper lip. "Don't worry about it."

"Are you at least getting a nice fat alimony check?" Nan asked, reaching for one of my green plastic laundry baskets.

"It's not like that."

Nan rested the basket on the bumper. The plastic was cracked at the handle. "Kaitlyn, what the hell? Eric was the one cheating, but he gets the house? His fancy car? Everything?"

"*Allegedly* cheating. He never admitted to it. I never caught him in any act," I said. And it was true. I hadn't seen anything other than circumstantial evidence. I found the infamous hair clip in the cushions of our couch. He came home smelling like perfume I didn't wear. It was cliché. Embarrassing. I didn't want to talk about it.

The car sputtered and stalled.

"I'm out of gas," I said. "Can you go inside so I can get Bark out of the car before it gets hot? I'll grab the rest later."

"Kaitlyn." Nan lifted the laundry basket again. It wasn't even full. "How did Eric get everything? What did you get?"

"Bark," I said, blinking to keep tears at bay.

Nan nodded solemnly and carried the basket to the house, but I knew she'd insist on having a talk about it later.

I climbed in the car with Bark.

"Okay, baby," I whispered. "I need you to do something for me."

He licked my chin.

"We're going to leave the car now."

I wrapped his ThunderShirt around his belly to help him feel safe, and reached, slowly, to the front seat to grab his leash, letting him smell it before clipping it to his collar. When I opened the door and got out of the car, Bark inched to the edge of the seat, legs shaking, fighting to be brave.

"Come on, Barky," I said, crouching. "You can do this!" I wished I had someone coaxing me into the world the way I did for Bark. Sometimes, I wished I had a ThunderShirt.

Bark stepped out of the car, and we made the trek to the house, a few steps at a time, so he could sniff things and gather courage. When we got inside, Nan walked into the foyer a little too fast and said, "What is he wearing?" a little too loud.

Bark flashed me a pained look and darted away, yanking his leash from my hand. He ran down the hallway, feet skittering on the tile like a cartoon dog.

"It's a compression garment!" I called, running after Bark.

Nan followed. I wished she wouldn't, but she was kind enough to take us in. I couldn't tell her what to do.

Bark ran to my old room and hid under the bed, his feathery tail and fluffy butt sticking out from under the ruffled bed skirt. Maybe it still smelled like me on that microscopic level only dogs can detect.

When Nan drove me to college freshman year, she promised my room would be waiting for me whenever I needed to come home. She said the same thing when Eric and I got married, which was possibly a heavy-handed hint, but I was five years younger and thought she was merely trying extra hard to say parental things because no one else would.

She'd made good on her promise. All my childhood belongings were right where I'd left them: unicorn bookends on the old pine desk, petal pink comforter smoothed across the white-washed wicker bed, a Lisa Frank poster of a panda wearing over-alls tacked to the wall above the headboard.

"Compression garment?" Nan said. "Does he think he's fat?"

"He's not fat," I said. "It puts pressure on certain points to make him feel secure."

"Mmm-hmm." Nan raised an eyebrow, trying and failing to hide her amusement. "He's beautiful, Kay. At least the bit of him I can see."

"He's a good boy. He's just had a rough time of it." I knelt on the floor and stuck my head under the bed skirt. Bark pressed his nose to my nose. His caramel-colored eye looked sad and soulful. The blue one looked scared. I scratched behind his ear. "You'll be fine," I said, breathing his warm doggy breath, feeling the clench in my chest let go.

"This is a sight," Nan said, laughing. "Two butts. Where's the camera? It's a Christmas card picture!"

"No pictures, please." I wriggled out from under the bed and dialed the purple clock radio to NPR. "He'll be okay. We should let him get acclimated."

"And how about you?" Nan asked, putting her arm around me while we walked to the kitchen. "How can we get you accli-mated? A stroll to stretch your legs? A shower? I made cookies." She pulled the head off the blue pelican cookie jar we painted together when I was nine, offering me his hollow belly filled with her famous double chocolate macadamia nut cookies.

They were still warm. I grabbed two. I hadn't eaten much more than potato chips and peanut M&M's since Bark and I left Rochester. Bark was afraid of drive-thru windows and I didn't want to leave him in the car a second longer than nec-essary.

I shoved a cookie in my mouth. It had the texture of shred-ded cardboard, and something tasted off, like maybe the butter had spoiled. I avoided chewing while I inspected the other one. It looked normal: chocolaty brown, flecked with macadamia nuts.

"What is this?" I asked, with my mouth full, trying to decide if I should spit it out.

"Double carob macadamia nut," Nan said. "I used soy flour instead of wheat, and applesauce instead of butter. High protein, low fat, and you can barely taste the difference!"

My saliva was turning the cookie to paste. I gagged.

"Are you alright, Kay?"

"Milk?" I said. "Please."

Nan poured me a glass. I took a gulp to wash the cookie down. It tasted like pureed grass clippings.

"It's hemp milk," Nan said.

"Sure is." I tried to smile.

"Well, you enjoy. I need to shower." She did a move that was half jog, half cha-cha as she made her way across the kitchen. "Billy and I really worked it today."

As soon as I heard the shower running, I threw the extra cookie down the garbage disposal, dumped the hemp milk, and tipped my head under the faucet to wash the remnants of horror from my mouth.

The fridge was no better. The old white Pyrex container that was always a reliable source of lasagna or mashed potatoes held grilled tofu and steamed asparagus. Even the blue roosters on the front looked disappointed. There was no Cool Whip, no peppermint patties hidden in the door rack, no rocky road ice cream in the freezer. I wanted fried chicken and real cookies and a squishy hug from Nan. I wanted things to be the way they'd always been, so I could forget I'd ever left. I settled on a tiny tub of chocolate soy yogurt and sat on the kitchen floor to mourn my failed marriage and the death of comfort food.

Staring at Nan's fridge magnets, I spooned yogurt into my mouth. It wasn't good, but at least it was chocolate.

One of the magnets had a picture of Betty Boop in pink leg warmers saying, "Nothing tastes as good as fit feels!"

"You lie," I yelled, pointing my spoon at her. "Lasagna is better." Betty stared back at me with fishbowl eyes. I chased the yogurt with half a dozen martini olives and hoped their presence in the fridge meant Nan hadn't nixed real drinks in favor of wheat grass shooters.

"Helloooo," a squeaky soprano voice called from the foyer. It was Ruth, Nan's next-door neighbor.

There hadn't been a knock. No ring of the doorbell. There never was. "Anybody hooooome?" Ruth called.

I raced toward my room.

"Helloooo," Nan sang back, rushing down the hallway to dump her soggy towel in the laundry room. "Make yourself comfortable. Be right theeerrre." Her hair was still wet, dripping on the collar of her neon pink t-shirt, but she'd applied a fresh coat of Persian Melon lipstick and given her cheeks a good pinch.

"What did you do?" I whispered.

"Everyone wants to see you," she said, winking.

"I just got here!"

"That's how welcome home parties work, Kay."

"I'm not even settled," I hissed, panic tightening my throat. I loved Nan's friends. It was like having an enclave of grandparents in the most wonderful way, but also in the awkward-personal-question, not-so-gentle-nagging kinds of ways. No one in their right mind wants to walk into a room full of Grammys and Pop Pops heavy with the news that since the last visit she's struggled with infertility, gotten divorced, moved back home, and isn't game for being set up with that nice young doctor they see for their trick knee.

"Settle!" Nan said, giving me a gentle shove toward my room. "We're not stopping you. Everyone will be here for hours."

I tried to keep the groan inside my head, but I think Nan heard it anyway, and when I marched down the hall, it felt like teenager déjà vu.

Bark was curled up on the bed next to my old teddy bear. He raised his eyebrows when I walked in the room, guilty.

"It's alright, buddy. You can have Mr. Waffles." I sat on the bed and picked up the bear. It was already soaking wet.

Bark licked things when he got nervous. It drove Eric crazy. Admittedly, it was gross to sit on a cold damp spot on the couch or step on a patch of rug Bark had carefully groomed, but I understood the impulse. I'd been a thumbsucker and a nailbiter as a kid. When anyone shamed me about my self-soothing be-haviors, it made me need them more, so I didn't see the point in scolding Bark.

I moved the bear to the foot of the bed, away from my pillows. Bark gave me a longing look.

"You can have it," I said. "Just down here, okay?"

Bark inched toward the end of the bed, but I was sure soggy Mr. Waffles would be back on my pillow as soon as I looked away.

I flopped next to him and stared at the smiley face sticker Nan stuck to the ceiling to cheer me up on my first day in this room.

Two years after my dad died, when my mom was bored of being my mom and wanted to move both of us to Costa Rica to live with a man she met on a wine tasting tour, Nan flew up from Florida to make an issue of it. "You can do whatever you want with yourself, but you'll have to fight me for the kid," she said, making tight fists with her hands. I wasn't sure if she was proposing a legal battle or a brawl. I don't know about court, but Nan would have beaten my mom to a pulp if they took it to the backyard.

In the end they let me choose. I was terrified picking Nan would crush my mother, but I only knew the Spanish I'd learned from *Sesame Street*, and I felt better around Nan. My mother made me nervous *before* my dad died. After, it was worse. She either paid me too much attention, or looked past me, like I didn't exist. I never knew what to steel myself for. Nan was the same all the time, and she always tried to be nice, even when she didn't understand me.

So I moved to Florida, to the bright little bedroom Nan decorated with flowers and ruffles. I drank Shirley Temples while Nan and her neighbors had "martoonis." I learned to play canasta, macramé plant hangers from nylon rope, and identify popular songs in Muzak form.

I shouldn't have worried about my mother. She seemed relieved to walk away from the constant reminder she'd picked the almost expired fruit at the market. She'd tell me I had my father's eyes, and it was an accusation, not a compliment. After Nan took on the burden of me, my mother was finally free to be with the mustachioed wine tour man, and then to follow her next great love to an ecovillage in Nicaragua, then move to Morocco with some guy she met at a beach volleyball tournament. At first, she called every Sunday. All she wanted to hear was that I was happy, healthy, and doing well in school. I tried to be the girl she wanted me to be, but then Nan would get on the phone, spilling beans about the bronchitis I couldn't shake, or my problems with long division. She'd beg my mom to plan visits that never happened. Eventually, the phone calls stopped coming, letters turned to postcards, and then the postcards stopped too. For the most part, it was easier. One less person I had to pretend for.

To be fair, it must have been really hard to lose your husband at the ripe old age of thirty-one, left with a nine-year-old kid to raise by yourself, without the luxury of being able to blame some trashy *friend* in a courtroom hallway for the whole mess.

I lay on the bed next to Bark while he sucked on Mr. Waffles's ear. Someone fired up the stereo in the living room and the shouts of *helloooo* grew louder as more neighbors arrived. Bark hadn't peed since we'd trekked into the woods behind a gas station in Midway, Georgia, to find him adequate privacy. I knew if I didn't take him out immediately, there wouldn't be another chance until well after midnight.

My room had a sliding glass door to the screened-in patio. I peeked from behind the curtain to make sure no one was there. The sun had set, and the pool lights were on, casting creepy webs of light across the water. The plan was to go from my room to the nearby screen door and out into the darkness of the back-yard before anyone saw us. But as soon as we got to the patio, I smelled cigar smoke and knew Nan's friend Lester Sam was already wandering around the yard, like he always did at her parties. There was no way Bark would do his business with an audience.

The patio had another screen door, leading to a small patch of grass on the other side, but we'd have to go past the pool to get there. I grabbed Bark's collar and tried to walk toward the other door, but looking at the water gave me the same kind of wobbly-kneed feeling I got at the top of a Ferris wheel. I started thinking about Bark falling in. Bark sinking below the surface. Tendrils of dappled fur at the bottom of the pool, waving like seagrass. I wanted to hug the ground to make sure it wasn't moving, like it could tilt at any moment and send us careening into the water.

I told myself if I took one step, the next would be easier, but I couldn't move my legs at all. My toes felt numb, like the blood in my veins had stopped flowing and my nerves were no longer connected to my brain.

Bark whined and nudged my arm.

"Okay," I whispered, "we're okay," and the spell I was under started to crack. I looked away from the pool and took a deep breath. The patio had inset garden beds along the edge where I'd planted bromeliads and miniature palms during my last summer home from college. I led Bark toward them, away from the pool. My legs still felt like rubber, but they moved.

"Do you have to pee?" I asked, and waited while he paced in the dirt until he found an acceptable spot behind a concrete mermaid statue. He still squatted like a puppy, even though he was over a year old. The mermaid was new. The red canistropsis he desecrated was not.

When he was done, we ran to my room like the ground was hot lava and there were monsters lurking in the dark. I slid the glass door closed and shut the curtains. Bark jumped on the bed, burrowing under the comforter. I wanted to climb under the covers with him and be done with the world for the night, but I knew eventually Nan would come find me, and she'd be disappointed if she thought I didn't want to go to her party at all.

"Are you going to be okay in here, Barky?" I asked, and saw his tail wag under the blanket. "I won't be gone long. Promise."

On my way out, I caught a glimpse of myself in the pink-framed princess mirror on the back of my bedroom door. I didn't look like a child pretending to be an adult anymore. I looked like an actual adult, and what troubled me was that the new lines on my face were all carved into my forehead. No crow's feet, no laugh lines. Worry was all I had to show for the last five years. Worry and Bark.

CHAPTER TWO

I snuck to the edge of the living room and sat on the floor in the shadows of the hallway, like I had so many times as a child, sneaking around in my nightgown to watch everyone after I'd been sent to bed. Happy chatter. Ice cubes clinking in the good rocks glasses. Dean Martin on the record player. The warm yellow glow of the dimmed lights creating a barrier against the night. I'd watched Nan and her friends to learn how to be a person, trying to absorb all of it: the way to hold a martini glass, how to touch someone's arm when they said something funny. It made me an anachronism. Manners and gestures from another era, figures of speech that didn't make sense to other kids, who spent their free time playing soccer or going to Girl Scout meetings. I don't know if I would have been a wallflower anyway; if I watched because that's who I already was, or if watching made it so.

I spotted Nan's next-door neighbor Ruth as she handed a drink to her behind-the-fence neighbor, Marta. They were both wearing the same hot pink t-shirt as Nan. In the hallway, I'd only noticed the front of Nan's shirt, but now I could see that on the back was the silhouette of a mermaid posed like the figure on a trucker's mud flap. There were at least a dozen women wearing the same shirt. They all looked so fit and fabulous that I wondered if some of the ladies who weren't familiar were actually old friends in new shape, but I didn't want to stare and risk someone noticing me. I felt like all the words I'd ever learned were stuck in a small dark place in my chest. The idea of polite conversation was painful.

Marta chatted up Althea, who lived one street over, and taught me how to change the oil in my car before I left for college, "because there are things a woman needs to know, Kay, and it's our job to teach each other!" Althea was the director of the Port St. Lucie library, and everyone always teased her about being young. She was sixty-four.

The men, as always, were few and far between. Lester would probably stay on the lawn smoking his cigar for most of the night. Jack "Call me Uncle Jackie" Mitchell, in his half-buttoned Hawaiian shirt, was laughing too loud at one of Ruth's jokes, slapping her on the back hard enough to throw her off balance.

Isaac Birnbaum sat in the blue wing chair at the far corner of the living room, scotch in hand, bewildered. He was still wearing his blue windbreaker and it was close enough to the color of the chair to look like an attempt at camouflage. Isaac showed up to all of Nan's parties, but his wife had been such a talker that he'd never had to get comfortable with party chatter. In high school, I worked for him at his tailor shop during summers and after school. I loved the comfortable silence he allowed. Once, we spent an entire Saturday sewing hems without ever exchanging more than a smile.

The ottoman next to Isaac was open. If I cut through the kitchen and went in the other entrance to the living room, I might be able to sit next to him without fanfare. We could be invisible together, and later, when Nan nagged me about being antisocial, I could honestly say, "I was there the whole time!"

I started to make my move. A shriek came from the crowd.

"Oh my god!" A tiny woman charged at me, her shock of dyed

auburn hair was short and spiky. The sea of pink shirts parted to make way. "I thought I saw a pretty little face over there!"

It wasn't until she leaned in to kiss my cheek that I realized it was Bitsie. It was the scent of Bitsie I recognized. Jean Nate and baby powder. Her flabby underarm "angel wings," as she called them, were gone. She was sleek and toned, except for a charming little pouch under her chin.

"You look amazing!" I said.

"Billy!" she said breathlessly. "But I'm not having an affair with him either." Bitsie laughed and her face sunk into the folds of her neck like a turtle. I'd always loved the way she didn't care how laughter made her look. She laughed with her whole self in a way I wished I could. She'd been a pediatric intensive care nurse until she retired at sixty-five, and she'd seen so many sad things that when there was joy to be had, she was all in.

I wondered if it was Nan or Billy who told her about my grand entrance.

"I never seem to get used to you all grown up," Bitsie said, reaching up to mess my hair. "I still can't believe you didn't invite me to your wedding!"

Eric and I were married at city hall on a Wednesday.

"Sorry," I whispered. "No one was invited." I'd assumed Nan told her friends why I was back. I didn't want to have to say the words: *I am divorced.*

"I'm going to be at your next one," Bitsie said, like it was fact. "With bells on. No excuses. And if you pick a dud, I will shout my objections." She winked at me.

"Where were you last time?" I asked, slipping into the old rhythm of our banter. "I could have used a warning."

"You only get warnings the second time. You have to make mistakes on your own first." Bitsie leaned in close. "I was married once before, you know. To a man," she whispered. "Us divorcées have to stick together." She looped her arm into mine and called out, "Somebody get this girl a martooni!"

Suddenly, I felt settled. I could handle a party if Bitsie was my wingman. I watched her pour gin and vermouth into Nan's old silver shaker.

"Dirty?"

I nodded, and she added a dash of olive juice to the mix, before giving it the briefest of jiggles. Her freckled hands were steady when she poured. She passed me a too-full glass and ushered me to the loveseat for a chat.

"Seriously, how are ya, kiddo?" she asked. "I barely saw you last time you were here."

"I'm sorry," I said, "I should have spent more time—"

"It meant a lot that you came home for the funeral." Bitsie patted my back the way you might comfort a baby. "I know how hard that was for you."

"How are you?" I asked, embarrassed I'd made any of it about me. She was the one mourning the most. I came home for her wife's funeral with every intention of being a person she could lean on, the kind who sets out platters of cold cuts and does the dishes at the end of the night. But the smell of embalming fluid at the wake got to me in the worst way, and I never even made it to the funeral. I never made it past the lobby of the funeral home. I told Nan it was a stomach flu, but she knew it wasn't that kind of sick. I walked six miles home in stiff, sweaty ballet flats to get away from that smell. The blister holes in my heels took weeks to mend and left scars.

"I'm so sorry," I said. "I'm so sorry she's gone."

"I still wake up every day thinking Bunny is going to be there." Bitsie's smile was sad and sweet. "I'm scared someday I'll wake up and already know she isn't, and that's when she'll really be gone."

I set my martini on the coffee table and grabbed her hand. She squeezed mine back.

"If that happens," I said, "I'll come over early and bang pans in the kitchen and sing the 'Good Morning' song so you can lie in bed and pretend."

Bitsie laughed. "She loved you so much, you know."

The tears happened fast, splashing on my shirt. Bitsie pressed her forehead to mine.

"I loved her," I whispered. I couldn't even find words for the extent. Bitsie was Nan's best friend from all the way back when they were teenagers. Bunny always made me feel like I was her friend, like Nan was over to visit Bitsie and I was there to visit her. She kept me from being a kid in tow. She made me feel important.

"Bun always wanted you to have her sewing machine."

"I couldn't . . ."

"Why don't you take her whole sewing room? You still have a key, right? Come over tomorrow. I have a project for you."

"What are you old biddies carrying on about?" Nan called from across the room, dancing over to us. "Get up! Get up! It's a party, for Christ's sake!" I used my leg muscles to stand while Nan went through the motions of pulling me to my feet. She gave a little shimmy and bumped her hip to mine. She was at least two drinks in. "Isn't my granddaughter gorgeous?" she said to Bitsie as she squeezed my cheeks, forcing a fish face.

"Gorgeous!" Bitsie said. "You know, Billy is single!"

"I do know!" Nan said.

"Oh, what a beautiful couple!" Bitsie shouted, giving me an exaggerated wink.

"You're both the worst!" I said, smiling. "The absolute worst. And I love you." My glass was almost empty, and it had been a long time since I'd had anything stiffer than chardonnay. I kissed them both and went to the kitchen for a glass of water before anyone could hand me another martooni.

CHAPTER THREE

It was almost one o'clock when the last of Nan's friends filed out the front door, leaving lipstick marks on our cheeks.

"What's with all the pink t-shirts?" I asked as I helped Nan hand wash martini glasses.

Nan took the next clean glass from me, drying it with a dishcloth. "Bitsie and I started an exercise group. We decided it was about time we were mermaids again, so we're teaching the others."

"You were dancers, right?" I asked, remembering a yellowed black-and-white photo I'd seen when I was little: Nan and Bitsie, young and glamorous, in matching seashell tops, applying lipstick side by side at a dressing room mirror.

"No, Kay, we were mermaids. Underwater." She put down the glass and walked out of the room.

I froze, remembering how Homer Lampert used to come for drinks on Fridays and tell us crazy tales about his days at sea. At first they were old sailor stories. A girl in every port. An epic bender in Bora-Bora. But over time, his tales grew more fanciful. Sirens and sea creatures. A fierce battle with an octopus I was fairly certain came from *20,000 Leagues Under the Sea*. One time he asked me what a girl like me was doing in a place like this, as if he were still a twenty-year-old boy in a sailor suit.

We all took care of Homer as long as we could, trading shifts watching war movies with him on his tiny old Zenith. The first time I drove without Nan in the car was to take Homer to his doctor's appointment.

I liked when it was my turn. I'd bring my homework with me, but I always ended up doing it on the bus the next morning so I could listen to Homer's stories. The way he lived in his mind and shared it with us, the way he got to be young again even though his bones were old and brittle, was sad and awful and beautiful at the same time.

I cried the day Nan called Homer's daughter in Oklahoma City, after he slipped out on Bitsie's watch and tried to swim in the water trap at the golf course. I helped Nan pack up Homer's things and finally got to see pictures of him as a sailor: young, smiling, strong enough to wrestle an octopus.

When his daughter came, tight-lipped and unamused by Homer's new penchant for racy jokes, we moved martooni night to Tuesday so he could join us one last time. We toasted to Homer and Homer toasted to the sea, and then he left with his daughter the next morning. Landlocked for the rest of his life.

A few weeks later his daughter called Nan to say that Homer had a stroke and passed away. We all felt awful. We could have kept taking care of him until the end. He would have been happier with the family he had with us than the one in Oklahoma.

I placed the martini glass in the sink and held on to the counter to steady myself. Bitsie and I would make a list of who to ask for help watching Nan. Maybe Billy could continue her training so she could keep her body fit even if her mind . . . I gasped for air.

Nan walked in carrying a big black photo album and dropped it on the kitchen table with a smack, sending dust from the pages. She flipped the cover open. "Look!" she said. I joined her at the table, hands at my sides so she wouldn't see them shake.

There she was: a mermaid. Smiling wide, bubbles escaping from her nose, her long blond hair curling around her face in weightless tendrils.

I sat across from her, trying to catch my breath. I didn't understand, but at least it was a real memory, not made-up. She had a fin.

Nan turned the book to face me and flipped the page. "And here's Bitsie, and remember my friend Bernadette?" She pointed to a photo of two identically dressed brunettes underwater, their arms around a man in an old-fashioned diver's suit. She turned the page again and pointed to more mermaids. "Audrey, and Hannah, and Woo Woo."

"Woo Woo?" My hands stopped shaking.

"Her name was LouEllen, but underwater it sounded like 'Woo Woo.'"

"Nan, what is all this?" I asked, pointing to LouEllen's picture. I'd never even seen the album before.

"It was a mermaid show at a roadside attraction shack off Highway One, and we were the stars. The Caloosahatchee Mermaids."

"Mermaid show?"

Nan grinned, nodding. "There were dozens in Florida back then. Entertainment on the way to someplace else. Mermaid shows, alligator wrestlers, fortune-tellers, mystics. There was something at almost every exit." She turned the page and touched a picture of her young face. "Mr. Crozier, the owner, built a huge tank with windows for a dolphin show. But then he couldn't get dolphins, so he got us girls instead." She laughed. "We weren't the only mermaid show, and we certainly weren't the biggest. But I like to think we were the best."

She flipped the page to another picture: Nan and Bitsie, arms around each other, blowing bubble kisses toward the camera.

"Why did you stop?"

She shook her head. "Your grandfather was embarrassed. Like he'd started dating a gypsy or a burlesque star. Swimming around and breathing from tubes, having people see me in a shell bra . . . He convinced me it was something to be ashamed of. But now"—she smiled and her blue eyes sparkled—"now I look back and I'm amazed at myself. At all us girls. We were strong. It took guts for us to do what we did. It took skill and practice."

"Where did they all end up?" I asked.

"I don't know," Nan said. "Bernadette was in West Palm Beach until she passed away, but the others . . . they got married and moved on. We used to send Christmas cards, but eventually they came back without forwarding addresses." She sighed, and I realized how close she was to crying. "I still miss Woo Woo. Me and Bitsie and Woo, we were a team. The three of us rented a teeny-tiny studio apartment and slept on camping cots. We were so broke. But it was the most fun I've ever had." She touched a photo of Bitsie pulling off a bathing cap to shake out her hair. "I miss swimming like that. Mermaid class isn't quite the same."

I stared at a picture of Nan underwater, arm curled like Rosie the Riveter, looking straight at the camera, offering up a dare.

"We could look for Woo Woo," I said. "On Facebook. I'll set up my old computer tomorrow so we can search."

"I can do it on my cell phone, I think," Nan said, pulling her phone from her pocket, holding down the home button until it chimed. "Siri, open the Facebook."

She handed me her phone with the blue Facebook sign-in on the screen. "Now what?"

"Do you have an account?" I asked.

"Can't I just look?"

"You need an account."

"I don't want an account. I just want to see if Woo Woo is there."

"Fine," I said, typing my log-in into her phone because mine was almost out of battery power.

"Is she there?" Nan asked before my account finished loading.

"Well, I can't type 'Woo Woo' into Facebook and find her!"

"LouEllen Griggs," Nan said. "LouEllen is one word. Capital *L*, capital *E*."

"Do you think she has a married name?"

"That *is* her married name," Nan said. "Her maiden name was Welsh."

"Woo Woo Welsh?"

"Pretty great, huh?" Nan smiled.

I typed LouEllen Griggs into the search bar. "Where did she last live?"

"Atlanta."

"There's a Lorna Griggs," I said, pointing to a photo of a woman with salt-and-pepper hair and a sweet smile. "Atlanta, Georgia. But she's only fifty-three."

"That's her daughter. Let me see!" She pulled her folding reading glasses from her pocket and squinted through them. "It's so tiny."

"Here," I said. "Let me see." I flipped through Lorna's pictures until I saw a family photo, with a dozen people in matching white shirts and blue jeans. An elegant woman with fluffy ivory hair sat in a chair in front, Lorna's hands on her shoulders.

I pinched and spread my fingers across the screen to zoom in. "Is that . . . Woo Woo?" I asked, still awkward with the nickname.

"That *is* her, isn't it?" Nan took the phone from me, tipping the screen from side to side like it might give her a better view.

"I'll go dig up my old computer—"

"Oh, this is silly. She has her own life. And it's late anyway! Past our bedtime." She waved the idea away with her hand, but I could see the wanting in her eyes.

Before we went to bed, I ran to the car to get the rest of my things.

"You know," Nan said, following me to help, even though I told her I didn't need it, "liquor stores will usually give you boxes if you ask." She grabbed several plastic Wegmans bags with each hand.

"Bark is afraid of cardboard," I told her as we walked back to the house. I slid all my bags to my left arm so I could lock the front door behind us. They weren't heavy.

"Bark is lucky to have you." Nan handed me her bags when we got to my bedroom door. "I can't say many other people would be so patient."

"I'm lucky to have Bark."

Nan put her arm around my shoulder and hugged me close, kissing my forehead. "Goodnight, sweetheart. I'm so glad you're home."

"Me too," I said. "It was like a piece of me was missing."

"Did I ever tell you you're my favorite grandkid?" Nan grinned. My dad was her only child, and I was his. A stale joke, but one of her favorites, and there was comfort in the familiarity.

The powdery scent of her perfume stayed with me as she shuffled down the hall to her room.

I shoved the bags in my closet and climbed into bed. Bark snuck under the covers, resting his head on my pillow. He sighed in my ear.

When I was four or five, my dad took me to the Catskill Game Farm and I got to feed a goat pellets from a gumball machine. His warm breath and the whiskers on his chin tickled my hand. I felt it in my head, the same wonderful tingle across my scalp that I got when someone drew me a picture or braided my hair—a buzz of closeness and attention. I remember seeing a video my dad took that day. I was squealing with joy. "He's eating the food! He's eating the food, Dad!" The camera got closer and then shook when my dad dropped more pellets into my chubby palm, again and again, the smell of alfalfa sweeter each time as they warmed in his hand. I could hear him laugh, breath crackling against the camera's microphone. "He's eating the food, Dad!" And we were both so happy.

Sometimes, I'd watch Bark do normal dog things and think, *He's playing with the toy! He's drinking the water! He's eating the food!* It was the same magic, if I let myself slow down enough to notice it.

Bark yawned and stretched, then he tucked his nose under my chin, and I felt the tightness at my temples dissolve.

CHAPTER FOUR

At five thirty a.m., Bark jumped out of bed growling. Someone was knocking at the front door.

"It's fine. It's fine, Barky," I whispered, trying to calm myself too. Bark on the defense didn't make for a pleasant wake-up call. I told myself it was just a neighbor and that Nan would get the door, but then the knocking turned to pounding, and the urgency of it sent my thoughts racing through a roll call of everyone we knew, and every emergency they could have.

Bark followed as I stumbled to the foyer. When I looked out the window, there was Bitsie, standing on the front step, in a pink chenille bathrobe and yellow duck slippers, a full pot of coffee in hand. Smiling. Perfectly fine.

"Well, aren't you lovely," she said as I let her in.

Bark skittered back to my room. I could hear Nan's shower running.

"I just woke up."

"You don't say." Bitsie grinned. "Why's the door locked?"

"That's what this latch is for." I turned the deadbolt. "You're supposed to use it." Nan never locked the door, and it drove me crazy.

"You know, for a young kid, you really are an old fuddy-duddy." Bitsie kissed my cheek and padded to the kitchen.

"How'd you get here?" I asked, following.

"Walked," Bitsie said. "Like always."

"Like *that*?" Bunny wouldn't have let her leave the house in a robe.

"Nothing they haven't seen before." Bitsie got three mugs from the cabinet and set them on the counter, pouring coffee in two.

"We have coffee," I said, pointing to the percolator. Nan always had the pot going by five.

"Kiddo, that swill your grandmother makes is not coffee." Bitsie handed me a mug. "Shade-grown Costa Rican."

I took a sip. She wasn't wrong. Her coffee was always better than Nan's.

"Isn't everyone supposed to be at your house?" I asked, worried the other ladies were on their way. The neighborhood migrated around food. Breakfast was usually at Bitsie's. Marta could get a nice lunch spread going. Ruth made borscht on Sundays. Althea did Taco Night. Nan was the one everyone went to for drinks and finger food.

"Trying to get rid of me?" Bitsie said with a wry smile.

"Just wondering what I'm in for."

Bitsie laughed. "Only me. We have mermaid class at six thirty."

"*You* I don't ever mind," I said, nudging my shoulder against hers. "Even though it's early."

We sat at the counter, sipping in silence. The curtains were still drawn, so we stared at the fabric. I wondered if Bitsie was counting magnolia blossoms too.

Finally, she said, "Nan's making me co-chair the community center fundraiser."

"Ah." I tapped her slipper with my foot. "She can force you to meet with her, but she can't make you put on real shoes."

"See. You get me." She sighed. "I'm tired of bake sales. Bunny did that stuff, not me."

We heard the whine of the pipes as Nan shut off the shower.

Bitsie dropped her voice to a murmur. "No one is going to want whatever kale-carrot-seaweed thing she decides to call a muffin."

I could tell by the sadness in her eyes, her real worry was that Nan would make her fill in for what was missing. It was a reasonable fear.

She chugged her coffee, poured more. "I'm being such a bitch."

I squeezed her arm. "You're just blowing off steam. I know how much you love her."

"I like you being an adult," Bitsie said, refilling my mug like I'd earned more coffee. "You're doing it well."

"Twenty-seven, divorced, living with my grandmother. I think that's failing."

"You're figuring it out. That's the success. To know there's something to figure."

"I feel defeated." It was easy to talk to Bitsie. Maybe because she was blunt with me. Maybe because I used to tell Bunny everything.

"I felt that way after my divorce," Bitsie said. "You pictured your life one way. Now it's going somewhere else. You have to recalibrate."

"How?" It wasn't like I had a baseline of normal to get back to. My life had always felt like it was being pulled along by bent bicycle gears turning out of sync with their chain.

"I went to nursing school," Bitsie said.

I laughed. "I don't think I'd be good at nursing."

Bitsie laughed too. "I don't think you would either. What I mean is, I found my purpose. You'll find yours. You knew enough to get out. Celebrate that."

I thought about the hair clip in the couch; black plastic

pocked with hair-spray residue. "I'm not sure I ever would have left him. If he hadn't—" My face flushed. I didn't know how much Nan had told her. "He cheated."

"So, he did you a favor," Bitsie said, getting up, the heads of her duck slippers bobbing as she walked to the cabinet.

"I don't want to pretend he did something altruistic," I blurted out, remembering the crinkle of butcher paper beneath me as I sat on the exam table in my gynecologist's office and had to ask for STI testing from the same doctor who'd seen me through both miscarriages. "I don't want to give him that."

Bitsie looked over her shoulder, light in her eyes. "Good. Don't." She grabbed two glasses and walked her ducks to the fridge for water.

"All that time I could have been figuring out what to do with myself."

She handed me a glass of water and sat down. "I know you feel like you already made the big choices, but you're just starting, kiddo. What do you want?"

I figured it was a rhetorical question, and I smiled politely, but she asked again, "What do you want?"

"I don't know." I searched my mind for things normal people are supposed to want, but all I could come up with was one of those blenders that can even blend a cell phone.

"Horseshit," Bitsie said. "You *know*."

"Then what is it?"

"I'm old, but I'm not Obi-Wan. It's your own damn job to figure it out."

"Who's Obi-Wan?" Nan called from the hallway.

"No one, Nannette," Bitsie said. "It's fine."

Nan bustled into the kitchen, wearing a sleeveless denim shirtdress belted at her now-tiny waist. I was shocked all over again by her muscular legs.

She pointed to Bitsie's pot. "I made coffee already. You didn't have to—"

"Mine's better." Bitsie poured Nan a cup.

"So I was thinking bake sale," Nan said, grabbing the carton of hemp milk.

"I know you were thinking bake sale." Bitsie winked at me. "I was thinking calendar."

"Calendar?" Nan shook the carton with vigor and poured some in her coffee.

"Remember we watched that movie about those British ladies?"

"Bits! I am not posing nude! Who wants a calendar of this?" Nan pushed at the teeny flap of skin under her arm.

"Firstly, we're gorgeous! People should see what real women look like." Bitsie shook her head like a model, but her short spiky hair didn't move.

"What people?" Nan asked.

"People," Bitsie said. "Everyone. Secondly, I wasn't talking about a nudie calendar. I'm thinking mermaids. All of us from class in tails and seashells. It'll be so much better than muffins."

"Muffins are easier." Nan dumped her pot of coffee into the sink.

"Oh, what else are we doing with our time?" Bitsie said. "Let's have some fun!" She shielded her mouth with her hand, loud-whispering to Nan, "I think we know someone who could make costumes."

I looked into my coffee cup, unsure of what to say.

"I don't know, Bits," Nan said. "Katie just got back. That's a lot to ask of her."

"We can even shoot underwater!" Bitsie shouted.

Nan stared at me. My stomach wobbled. I used my thumb to smudge away a coffee stain on the counter. Nan didn't usually leave me space to say no. I wondered if she thought I'd let everyone down.

"Material is expensive," Nan said, sipping her coffee. "We're raising money, not spending it."

"Come on. If the ladies don't have to bake and they get a mermaid costume out of the deal, they'll be happy to chip in . . ."

"A lot of us are on fixed incomes."

". . . plus, this lady gets portfolio pictures. Two birds!" Bitsie said, pitching an imaginary stone at me.

"I won't even make you bake," Nan said, pouring more hemp milk in her coffee. "But it's just easier."

They kept arguing. I lost focus. My mind spun through the ways I could fail, like a film sequence in my head, playing behind what was real. Seams splitting. Silver crepe from Nan's unraveling tail caught in the pool filter, holding her below the surface. Chlorine and blue tiles. Sunlight hitting her too-still body. I went back to counting the magnolias on the curtains. Twenty-seven on one panel. Twenty-five on the other. It always drove me crazy. I started my count again and included the slivers of flowers cut off at the edges, to see if I could find a false sense of even.

"What do you think, kid?" Bitsie said, nudging my arm.

I shook my head, like the motion might make the bad thoughts disappear. Bitsie looked disappointed, so I switched to a nod. "Whatever you want to do," I said, trying to smile. I chugged the rest of my coffee and stood up. "I have to take Bark out."

CHAPTER FIVE

After Bark did his business, I snuck to the garage. I knew that in all likelihood Nan would talk Bitsie into a bake sale, and they'd forget about the calendar, but the divorce and the packing and the drive had frayed my nerves. I couldn't stop the swirling thoughts in my head. Sometimes, I could wear out my fight-or-flight feelings by actually fleeing. Even fake escape could dull the itch.

My old bike hung from a hook in the rafters. I dragged a step stool over and lifted it down. Arms straining, knees shaking. It never used to seem so hard.

I found the red plastic fuel tank from the lawn mower and strapped it to my bike basket.

Nan poked her head in the garage. "Breakfast," she said.

"I'm going to ride to the gas station."

"I can take you after mermaid class."

I could tell by the careful, even tone of her voice she didn't want me to leave.

"It's okay," I said, a little too loudly. I used the corner of my *Chorus Line* t-shirt to wipe dust off the handlebars so I wouldn't have to make eye contact. I couldn't bear the thought of Nan poking at my anxiety, trying to fix it for me.

Nan remedies usually made things worse. When I was a kid,

she sent me to school with an extra lunch bag to breathe into if I started feeling that choking panic in my chest, as if pulling a paper bag out in the middle of class wouldn't be humiliating. She prescribed a shot of sherry for a cold, and served me strong black coffee for asthma attacks, even though it kept me up all night, grinding my teeth. She told me to toughen up, like it was a helpful mantra. She always meant well, but she expected her remedies to solve everything, and it was hard to disappoint her when I wasn't magically better. The best way to manage any sort of ailment around Nan was to avoid her until I could act normal again.

"I could use the bike ride," I said, as calmly as possible.

"Alright." Nan hit the garage door opener like she was releasing me. "Bike safely."

My brakes were way too soft to be safe, and the rusty chain slipped off the gears twice before I even got out of the neighborhood. By the time I made it to the QwickStop, I was covered in bicycle grease and sweat. I clamped my arms at my sides, hoping no one would notice the pit stains, and lugged the gas can in with me to prepay. Powerball was up to eighty million, so the line at the register was epic. I grabbed a cup of coffee and waited.

Every time I started to get nervous about Bark and how long I'd been gone, the line moved up and it seemed silly to abandon my post. Plus, I'd been drinking my coffee. I had to pay for it.

I was three people from the register when I heard: "Katie? Holy crap!"

I turned and came face-to-shoulder with Mo, my best friend from grade school. She hugged me, knocking the gas can into my knees and her collarbone into my chin. I didn't have hands free to hug her back. I tried my best to keep my coffee cup level. She finally pulled away, crinkling her tanned nose. "I'm so sorry I missed your welcome home party! I had to work." Her hair was past her shoulders now, streaked white by the sun.

"Yeah, it was a good party!" I said quietly, turning to assert my place in line.

Of course, she was still around. She'd inherited her grandparents' house after they died. And, of course, Nan invited her. Nan and Mo were their own mutual admiration society.

When I moved in with Nan, Maureen Jacobs was the only friend I had who was actually my age. She lived with her grandparents too.

Wherever Mo's dad ended up was a big secret, and Nan and I were the only people in the neighborhood who knew that her mom was in jail. Everyone else thought Mo's mom was doing outreach work overseas, but in reality, she'd been nabbed at a bus station with a brick of cocaine in her purse. Sometimes, Mo's uncle sent coconut husk key chains and cowrie shell bracelets when he went on fancy vacations, and Mo took them to show-and-tell saying they were from the village where her mom was vaccinating sick babies. I wasn't going to rat her out. She didn't tell people I saw my dad die. But what the other kids did know was that we lived with old people, we didn't have real parents, and we were both kind of weird.

"It's nice to see you," I said, because it really was. Even though I was feeling like I wanted to hide from the world, maybe I didn't need to hide from Mo. Maybe we could still be weird together. "Did you get taller?"

"Hysterical!" Mo said, still at top volume. The other people in line stared. Everything about Mo was a little more intense than everyone else's everything. She was wearing dangerously threadbare cutoffs, and a short-sleeve button-up shirt peppered with tiny blue sailboats. She bought all her clothes at yard sales and consignment shops, and since she was so tall, she mostly wore men's clothes. We used to joke that her style could be described as "dead guy chic."

"So how long are you staying?" she asked.

"Not sure yet."

"Is Eric with you?"

"No Eric. Just me." I was surprised she remembered Eric's name. Mo wasn't a phone person. She didn't write letters. I'm not sure she even owned a computer. So when I was gone, I was gone. I stopped being part of her life and vice versa. It wasn't angry or awkward or mean. It simply was. I kept to myself during my marriage anyway. Even Nan had a hard time getting me on the phone. I think deep down I knew marrying Eric was the wrong choice, and if I talked too long with the people I loved, they'd figure it out.

"Have you encountered the cookie situation yet?" Mo whispered.

"What the hell is up with that?" I asked.

"All the ladies are on this health kick, which is great for them, right? But it sucks for those of us who would like a real damn cookie sometimes." Mo glanced at my brown linen shorts, and I felt instantly frumpy. I hoped she didn't notice the way they strained at the button.

Mo did not look like she ever ate cookies.

"When do you have to head home to the hubby?" Mo asked, reaching down to scratch a bug bite on her thin, tanned ankle.

"We're divorced," I said. I didn't want to lie to her. "I'm here for a bit."

"So you're back to prowling! We'll have to go out soon." She held up her fists and rocked her shoulders back and forth. She was the worst dancer, but it didn't matter. You couldn't look away.

"It just happened," I said, shifting my weight from one leg to the other. "Prowling might not be the right word. Recovering, maybe."

"Hysterical!" Mo slapped my arm, hard enough for it to sting.

"I'm surprised Nan didn't tell you."

Mo gave me her wide, prank-pulling grin. "She did. I wanted to see if *you'd* tell me."

This was the kind of shit we pulled on each other when we were kids. Once, she spent an entire day with a Mr. Yuk sticker on her back. She repaid me by smearing peanut butter between the pages of my math book. And I loved her for it, because even though we were only a club of two, it was still great to belong.

"Asshole." I smiled at her. I was up to the counter now, and the guy at the register gave me a dirty look. "Not you! This one." I nodded toward Mo.

"Brat," Mo said. She leaned in to kiss my cheek. "I'll come get you at Nan's. We'll prowl!"

CHAPTER SIX

~~~~~~

When I got home, Bark greeted me at the door, tongue out, tail wagging, like a normal dog. Nan followed, carrying Bark's stuffed blue monster, Murray. "We were playing catch," she said, grinning.

"In the house?" I said in mock horror. Nan had always been after Mo about catch being an outside game.

Bark jumped up, pulling Murray from Nan's hand. She let him.

"Your friend is a good catcher," she said to me, giving Bark a head scratch. He dropped the toy and yelped at her until she picked it up and threw.

Bark caught Murray in his teeth, shaking his head like a madman.

"Why aren't you at mermaid class?" I asked.

"Bitsie can handle it," Nan said. "It's your first morning back."

"You don't have to miss class for me."

"I missed *you*," she said. "Do you want breakfast? There's scrambled tofu."

"I'm good." I willed my stomach not to growl. I should have bought a donut at the gas station. Tofu Nan was going to require new survival strategies.

Nan was staring at me. It's possible she was only trying to assess my feelings about tofu, but I worried she wanted to have a talk about Eric and everything I gave up. I crouched to play tug with Bark, avoiding her gaze.

Bark growled, pulling Murray away, only to shove him right back into my hands to keep the game going.

Nan took an audible breath like she was about to say something of great importance.

"Hey," I said before she could get a word in, "should we look for your mermaid friends on Facebook? I'll go find my computer."

"Oh, you don't have to—"

"It'll be fun," I said, letting Bark win. "I'd like to see your friends."

"I don't think we have internet, Kay," Nan said, pulling her phone from her pocket. "I'll just use this. You can read the small print for me."

I pointed to the wifi signal on her screen. "That says you do. Unless you're piggybacking on Ruth's service."

"Ruth still has a flip phone," Nan whispered gravely.

"Did someone come over and set up wifi for you?" I asked. "Is there a box with a flashing light and an antenna?"

"Oh! Yes!" Nan said. "Over by the TV. I thought that was the cable."

"Who set it up?"

"The guy from the company, I guess."

"You don't remember?"

"I'm not getting dementia, Kay," Nan said.

I would have worried, but the corners of her mouth quivered. It was her tell. I don't know why she was lying about wifi, but she absolutely was.

I dug my laptop out of the closet and set it up in my bedroom on the desk that had been my father's before it was mine. While

I watched the update bar inch toward black, I traced my finger around the smiley face carved into the soft pine. As a kid, I pretended my father knew I'd have his desk someday and he left me the carving as a message.

My computer ran like someone spilled molasses in the gears, but it did work. When it finished updating, I found Lorna Griggs on Facebook again and called to Nan. She sat on the bed behind me and watched as I clicked through Lorna's profile. There was an album of pictures from the weekend before. A party on someone's deck.

"That's Woo Woo!" Nan pointed to the woman with the fluffy white hair sitting on a lounge chair, a chubby baby in her lap. They were clapping together, laughing, and the lines of their smiles had a sweet sameness.

"She looks so good!" Nan held her hand to her mouth. "She looks so good, Kay." Her eyes teared. "I worried. She was my favorite after Bitsie."

"Should we send her daughter a message?" I asked.

Nan's eyes lit up. "Yes."

I typed what Nan said, verbatim. She told Woo Woo about my dad dying, raising me, that she felt blessed to have me and Bark home. She talked about the swimming class she taught with Bitsie, describing every routine they did. Then she asked a million questions. "Do you still swim?" all the way to "Who is that beautiful cherub on your lap?"

I thought about suggesting we send a short note first, but the way she wanted her friend to know her again was vulnerable and pure. It would have been wrong to edit her love letter.

"Now what?" Nan asked after I hit send.

"Now we wait."

Nan stared at the screen like she expected something to happen right away.

"Should we look for the others?" I asked.

Nan's phone chimed. She glanced at the screen and smiled. "Shoot! I have to— I have errands," she said, standing up, tucking her phone in her pocket.

"Oh, okay," I said, waiting for more of an explanation. Nan usually overshared every detail of her day with anyone in her presence.

"Not sure when I'll be back. Couple hours?" She didn't volunteer anything else. Just kissed me on the cheek and said, "Go to Bitsie's later, okay? She was hoping you could finish the set of curtains Bunny . . . Bunny was working on. Do you mind?"

Before I could even answer, Nan was out the door.

I knew I should finish unpacking, but Bark was sprawled across my unmade bed, snoring. I pulled the laptop power cord as far as it would go and climbed back into bed next to him. He snuggled into my side as I scrolled through my Facebook feed.

Normally, I avoided Facebook. Other people's pictures had the capacity to gut me, even when they seemed benign. A high school friend celebrating her mom's birthday. A meme that said, *Repost this if your dad is your best friend.* Babies. So many babies.

I hated being saddened by other people's joy, but the more I tried to deny my sadness, the worse it would hit when it eventually did. A feed full of Father's Day posts could mess me up for a week. Pictures of happy daughters and dads, arms around each other, beaming. The dads all had gray hair, deep lines on their faces. My father was thirty-two when he died. He never got to age. Twenty-seven is not that far from thirty-two. The idea of life ending in a few years would start to echo in my brain, getting louder until all I could think about was dying before I'd gotten any of the things I wanted. Soon, I'd be sobbing in a bathroom stall at the theatre with no idea what hit me until I connected the dots back to those happy pictures.

But today was not a holiday or a milestone, and my feed seemed low on babies. Some guy I barely knew from high school was waxing philosophical about bacon. Political rant from one side. Political rant from the other. Vacation pictures. Everyone seemed to be on vacation. I wasn't interested in any of it. I wanted to see Luca.

There weren't any posts from him in my feed, so I typed *Luca Pelayo* into the search bar. We were already Facebook friends, but after he accepted my request years ago, we'd said nothing to each other. Merely friending him felt disloyal to my marriage. A scarlet *A*, even if it was lowercase. Messaging would have felt like too large a transgression, and he'd never reached out to me. We only had six mutual friends from Ithaca College. There wasn't enough crossover in our lives to run into each other unintentionally, online or otherwise.

In his profile picture he was red-nosed, breath forming a cloud, snow in his hair. The caption read: *Sundance*. It was from three years ago, when *New Durango* won best documentary. His film was about a boy named Marco growing up in foster care after his mother was deported. The same thing happened to Luca when he was in fifth grade.

At Ithaca, Luca studied TV production. He wanted to run cameras and sound for a news station, but after graduation, when his foster mom took Marco in, she begged Luca to help her tell his story, and as he did, he told his own. I went to see *New Durango* by myself at The Little Theatre in Rochester the night it opened, and sobbed into my popcorn. It was beautiful and poignant and perfect.

I'd seen his profile picture before, done the full stalk when I first friended him, but this time I wasn't overwhelmed by guilt. I was free to zoom in, study his face for signs that he'd changed too much from the person I'd known, so I could click away and put him out of my mind. But then I noticed that the black wool scarf around his neck was the one I'd knitted for him in college. A complicated herringbone stitch I'd taught myself from a library book. I combed his page, looking for anything familiar in his pictures, any other sign that maybe Luca missed me the way I missed him.

He didn't use Facebook much. The most recent post on his page was a photo someone tagged him in. Messy chin-length hair pushed behind his ears as he balanced a handheld camera on his shoulder. Captioned: *The director in action.* Most of his photos were shots other people posted. On set. At an awards presentation. Backstage before his interview on *The Daily Show*, headphones on his ears in a radio booth with Ari Shapiro.

His own posts were few and far between. Pretty, but impersonal. A sunset from three months ago. A macro shot of frayed shoelaces. The U-shaped arches of a saguaro cactus silhouetted against a starry sky. I looked at every photo, waiting for my old computer to load them, one at a time, blurry, then clear. None had anything to do with me. No more signs. But he still had the scarf. He'd worn it to something important. Did it mean he still cared about me? Or did he like the scarf enough to divorce me from its history? "This old thing? Some silly girl made it. I can't remember her name! Cathy? Kerry?"

I went back to look at the photo of Luca in his scarf, the sweet curve of his mouth resting on the cusp of a smile.

When I closed my laptop, Bark woke, jumping at the noise. "It's okay, buddy," I said, prying my legs out from under him. He yawned and wiggled back to a comfortable position as soon as I got out of bed.

In the drawer of my desk, way in the back, I still had the braided leather bracelet Luca made me. He'd swiped snaps from the costume shop to finish it, and told me to close my eyes while he fastened it on my wrist. That bracelet was not divorced of memories of Luca. I knew that every single moment we'd shared could come to life if I stared at it long enough.

I wrapped the bracelet around my wrist, holding my arm against my ribs to keep it in place while I pushed the sides of the snap together until they clicked.

CHAPTER SEVEN

I let myself in. Bunny's collection of antique glass fishing floats still hung in the entryway window, casting splashes of blue and green light against the walls. I expected to hear her voice. I wanted her to rush in from the kitchen and hug me.

"Hey, Bits!" I shouted when I couldn't stand the silence anymore. "It's me!"

"Hey, kiddo!" Bitsie yelled back. "I'm in here." I headed toward her voice and found her in the den, under the oak desk in the corner, mumbling to herself.

"So if this goes there, then that goes . . . Where the fuck does that go?" She backed out, holding a power cable. "Where does this belong?" she asked.

"The printer?"

"I think so. It came loose when I was dusting, but now I can't find the right whatsit for the doohickey."

"Here," I said, scooting under the desk, "I'll take a look for the whatsit."

Bitsie laughed and handed me the cord. "Thank you! I spent all morning writing a letter that won't print."

"Who are you writing to?" I asked, pressing my cheek to the wall so I could thread the cable up behind the desk.

"My congressperson."

"About what?"

"My opinion. I write to him every week," Bitsie said, like it was the most normal thing in the world. I knew Bitsie had marched for women's liberation, gay liberation, marriage equality, and health care reform. On the wall in her reading room were framed pages of her FBI file, from back when the government couldn't figure out if women's rights activists were a threat to society. But for some reason, I hadn't understood the texture of her conviction. The continuity of it.

"Every week?" I pushed the cable through the gap.

"How's he supposed to know how to represent me if he doesn't know what I think?" Bitsie said, grabbing my elbow to help me up. "You don't write your representatives?"

"I haven't," I said, and felt suddenly ashamed. I was an eager voter, I signed petitions for causes I cared about, but I'd never gone beyond that.

"Democracy works best when we speak up," Bitsie said.

I pulled the printer away from the wall and got the wire plugged into the correct whatsit. "There you go," I said.

"Will it print?"

"Where's your letter? Let's see."

Bitsie leaned over the desk and pushed the mouse around slowly, until she found the window with the letter. She hit print, and we could hear the paper queuing up.

"Thank you, sweetie!" She raised her hand for a high five. I slapped it. "Here to sew?"

"Yeah," I said, hoping my jitters weren't apparent.

"It's just some curtains. You can figure it out, right?" Bitsie walked me to Bunny's sewing room, but she stopped at the door. "I'll let you go in on your own," she said, eyes damp, and I realized she probably hadn't been in the room since it happened. I wasn't sure if I could handle going in either, but I felt like Bitsie needed me to, like she knew the room needed company.

"I'll come see you before I go," I said, giving her shoulder a squeeze.

"You better, kiddo," she said.

I opened the door. It still creaked. Once, I told Bunny I'd bring over some WD-40 to fix it. "I don't know why we're all so concerned with dulling the music of life," she said, waving my offer away.

Nan told me that Bitsie came home from Publix and found Bunny, fallen from her chair, draped in the pale blue chambray she'd been sewing into curtains. The fabric lay across her worktable. I picked it up, and it smelled like the rosewater she dabbed on her wrists every morning.

I found a sketch on the back of an envelope with measurements written out. Bunny's careful pencil strokes made a rectangle with a Greek key pattern at the border and an *X* in the middle. A few yards of natural colored linen were folded neatly next to the machine. When I unfolded the fabric, a plastic template shaped like an anchor fell out, and I understood what she'd wanted the curtains to be.

At Bunny's wake, all I could think about was the moment right before they closed the casket on my dad. I couldn't bear the idea of not kissing him goodbye one last time, so I ran over to hug his body. Too solid, like he'd been filled with cement. I kissed his forehead, and the cold shocked me. No blood running under his skin. I knew he was dead. I understood what dead meant. But it was only a concept until that moment. He was a skeleton. He wasn't anything more than bones hiding in flesh. The thick makeup they'd painted on his face lingered on my lips no matter how hard I tried to wipe it off.

Nothing about that memory faded with time. It hovered at

the edges, ready to hijack my mind. So I couldn't say goodbye to Bunny. I couldn't bear to see her body, still and cold. When I went back to Rochester, I tried to erase the fact that her funeral even happened. To keep Bunny alive. In my mind, this whole time, she'd been in her sewing room, making things.

Her unfinished curtains were the worst kind of proof. I swished the chambray between my fingers and fought to keep the feeling of ChapStick on my lips from turning into something it wasn't.

I rolled up my sleeves and flipped on the record player. Patsy Cline was halfway through "She's Got You." I smiled. We both loved that song. But when Patsy sang the refrain about the memory of her love not letting her go, I realized this was probably the album Bunny listened to last. Who turned the record player off? Bitsie? Nan? One of the paramedics? I could see everything that must have happened in my head, like I was sitting in the corner, powerless to help. Patsy wailing, Bunny falling to the floor. Bitsie's screams; sobbing while she called Nan. Stiffness setting into Bunny's graceful fingers. The wait for the coroner when the paramedics couldn't revive her.

They said she didn't have pain. Aneurysm. Instant, Nan told me. The fallen fabric, pins in her sleeve for ready access, it was obvious she was in the middle of her project. She hadn't stopped to nurse a headache.

I heard Bitsie slide the door to the patio. Could she hear the music? Was it making her remember? I switched the record for Ella Fitzgerald, and the images in my mind switched over too.

The opening chords of "Blue Skies." Bunny helping me sew my prom dress. Teal organza. Sequins everywhere. We tried to scat like Ella. With most people I was too embarrassed to be goofy, but in Bunny's sewing room, I felt like the person I was supposed to be.

I sewed the rod pockets to the tops of Bunny's curtains, and pressed them carefully on the ironing board, using the spray can of Niagara Sizing to make them stiff and smooth. I sewed tubes of bias-cut linen for the appliqué border, but I could only find a few pins in Bunny's stuffed strawberry cushion.

She had Royal Dansk butter cookie tins stacked on the shelves on the wall. No labels to mark them, so I opened each one. They still smelled sweet. Buttons, ribbons, scrap squares, zippers—each organized in their own tin. Bunny used to save the pretzel-shaped cookies for me. The kind with sugar that looked like salt. I swore they tasted better than all the other shapes.

No pins. The stack of tins on the next shelf housed her sewing machine feet, upholstery piping, and a vast collection of silk thread for embroidery.

There were three tins on top of the oak bookcase. I opened the first one. It was full of pretzel-shaped cookies in their white pleated paper cups. The other two tins were the same. She kept saving them. For me.

I sat on the floor and hugged the stack of tins to my chest. When I left, I assumed I stopped mattering, but there were so many cookies' worth of thinking about me. I ate one, crunching sugar crystals between my teeth while I listened to Ella sing about poor Miss Otis. Three whole tins was too long for me to have stayed away. I wished I'd had the chance to tell Bunny how much she meant to me.

I slid down to lie next to the spot where she left us. I knew it was terrible, but it felt good to lie there, eating Bunny's pretzel-shaped cookies, pretending her spirit was still in the room.

The same way my brain could imagine the most horrible scenarios in vivid Technicolor—Nan getting attacked by an intruder, Bark drowning in the pool, Eric twisted and tortured in a car accident when he was late coming home—I could imagine good scenes too, even impossible ones.

I closed my eyes.

"Do you still enjoy sewing?" Imaginary Bunny asked sweetly. Without pressure. Without poking at the fact that I'd thrown my dreams away on a bad marriage.

"I think I do," I said.

"Would you mind helping me?" she asked. "With the curtains?"

"Of course." I said. "Happy to."

Bunny was the one who taught me how to sew. The sewing machine I left in Rochester was my twelfth-birthday gift from Bunny and Bitsie. She'd encouraged me to dream about big things. I was going to move to Manhattan to be a costume designer at the Metropolitan Opera. My father took me to New York City to see *Carmen* the year before he died, and all I could think about for weeks after was that beautiful red dress. When Carmen was on stage in that dress, it was impossible to look anywhere else. I wanted to be the person who designed that kind of spectacle, who imagined it and made it so. Bunny made me feel like it wasn't past my reach.

"What are the curtains for?" I asked. I never even applied for an internship at the Met. I was too scared to fail, and Eric was a great excuse for not even trying.

"They're for Bitsie's reading room," Imaginary Bunny said. "To match those throw pillows she likes."

"You be the art director, I'll be the hands," I told her. It's what she said to me when she helped sew costumes for three seasons of plays by the St. Lucie Senior Citizen Thespian Brigade so I'd have a portfolio of work for college.

"Come back again tomorrow?" she asked.

I nodded.

"You can bring your dog." She smiled, the beautiful creases around her eyes amplifying her warmth. If anyone else offered the same, I'd make excuses about how Bark wasn't that kind of a dog. But Bark would have loved Bunny. She would have quieted the unrest in him the same way she had for me.

There was a knock at the door. I opened my eyes, and Bunny was gone. Bitsie came in, stunned when she saw me lying on the floor.

"I am so sorry," I shrieked, jumping to my feet. My heart pounded too hard. The room went black until my balance steadied.

Bitsie's eyes welled up.

I hugged her. "I am so sorry."

"Oh, honey," she said, hugging me hard. "I should have known this wasn't good for you."

"No," I said. "It was. It is."

"We can move her sewing machine to the living room. Or Nan's house. Or you don't have to finish the curtains."

"I do have to," I said, tears dripping from my chin. "I need this." I wanted to make those curtains for Bunny. Like penance for being gone. Like a tribute. "I never got to say goodbye."

"Okay." Bitsie nodded. "Okay. But if it stops being alright, you let me know."

I could see the tremble in her cheek. The fear in her eyes. She was working hard to pretend she wasn't unnerved.

"Coffee?" she asked. "I need coffee."

I worried she'd have a difficult time looking at me, that maybe I'd traumatized her, but Bitsie set up the coffee maker and chatted away about mermaid class, like nothing had happened.

"It's basically water aerobics," she said, pouring soy milk in the little cow pitcher. "We don't have breathing tubes. Or tails. But it's nice to dance in the water again."

"I could make you a tail," I said, the words coming before they had time to bounce around my brain. "Even if Nan insists on a bake sale. I could just make you a tail." I expected her to say no. That she wouldn't want to trouble me. That they were only in it for the exercise, and don't be silly.

"Could you?" she said, her face so suddenly bright.

"I can try." I'd made her sad, but maybe I could make her happy too.

We sat at the kitchen table, drank our coffee, sketched mermaid tails on napkins, and I started to feel like making a mermaid calendar might be something I could handle.

CHAPTER EIGHT

When I got home, Bark was curled up on the couch in the den with Nan, watching a PBS documentary about raccoons. He jumped over the coffee table to say hi when he saw me, tail wagging.

"Whoa, buddy!" I said, crouching to scratch his head.

"Did you know he watches TV?" Nan asked.

"Yeah. He loves PBS cartoons. The funny voices."

"He's quite taken with these raccoons."

I wrapped my arms around his neck and let him lick my face. "Do you like raccoons? Do you like Nan?"

I sat on the couch next to Nan. Bark jumped up to wedge himself between us, resting his head on my lap. I ran my fingers through the downy fur behind his ears.

Then a car door slammed. Footsteps. Bark leapt off the couch, the hair on the back of his neck standing straight up. My face got cold and sweaty at the same time. Bark growled. The handle to the front door turned. He barked rapid-fire, charging. I jumped to my feet, heart in my throat.

Mo walked in carrying an armload of brown paper bags. "Oh, aren't you a goofball," she said.

Bark downgraded to a grumble. Looked at me and back at Mo, then gave her one last defiant woof before hiding behind the wing chair.

"Tough guy," Mo said.

"Don't you knock?" I asked, my body still electric, unstable, even though the threat was nil.

"Kaitlyn!" Nan said.

"Nan knew I was on the way." Mo dropped the bags on the table, oblivious to my snap.

Nan gave me a hard stare and said, "Thank you for bringing dinner, Maureen. That's so nice of you."

"Yeah," I said, feeling like a little kid being reminded of my manners. "Thanks, Mo."

Mo handed me a takeout box. "Boiled veggie dumplings, right?" she said.

"Yeah." I smiled. It was my standing order growing up. "Thanks."

"I still think they taste like Play-Doh-wrapped broccoli."

"They do," I said. "But I like it."

"You didn't have to do this," Nan said as Mo handed her what looked like steamed broccoli and tofu. She always used to get egg rolls and fried rice.

"You cook for me all the time." Mo plopped on the couch with her carton of General Tso's and a plastic fork. She was long ago forbidden from using chopsticks in the living room, after Nan found a desiccated piece of chicken stuck to one of the curtains.

I felt a sudden pang of jealousy. What if, in the time I'd been gone, my grandmother started liking my friend better than me? What if my friend liked my grandmother better than me? My adrenaline was still wonky. I stood there, holding my dumplings, trying not to cry.

"Come on, Kay." Mo patted the couch for me to sit. "What are we watching?"

"Raccoons," Nan said.

"I've got one who hangs around my garbage can. Did I tell you? He's bigger than Mrs. Cohen's Beagle!"

I sat between them and ate my dumplings, tearing off tiny pieces with my chopsticks to make them last, the way I did when I was a kid and Mo would come over to watch *The Wonderful World of Disney* with me and Nan.

When the documentary voice began discussing the feces-borne diseases raccoons introduce to neighborhoods, Nan looked at Mo and said, "We need to evict your friend."

Mo shivered. "I'm done." She dropped her container on the coffee table, then scrambled to shove a coaster under it. She wasn't suffering a loss of appetite. Her container was empty. She'd even eaten the hot peppers.

Bark snuck out from behind the wing chair, staying low, testing the waters. When no one made any rash moves, he turned around three times, flopping on the floor with a thunk and a sigh.

"Hysterical," Mo said in a loud whisper. "He's like a crabby old man."

Bark shot her a wary look before resting his head on his paws to watch the raccoons raid a dumpster.

My heart gave way to normal time. I was almost comfortable.

"You done?" Mo asked, leaning over to peek in my container.

"Are you in a hurry?"

"Two-for-one beers at Sal's until nine."

The idea of going anywhere was overwhelming. "I don't think—"

"You're going," Mo said.

"I hear you're prowling tonight," Nan said, waving chopsticks at me, amused.

"Want to come with?" Mo asked.

"I think I'm okay right here." Nan patted the couch. "Bark will keep me company."

"Come on," Mo said as I dropped the last bit of dumpling in my mouth. "Let's get you purdied up." She grabbed my arm and yanked me off the couch before I could finish chewing.

"God, your clothes are awful!" Mo picked through my closet. She was wearing a faded pineapple print Hawaiian shirt.

"You look like you're going to a Jimmy Buffett concert," I said.

"Ooh, I want margaritas. Let's go to Los Tacos."

I groaned. Me and Mo and tequila were a bad recipe.

She pointed to four sets of black leggings folded over hangers, a black turtleneck hung over each one. "This is interesting. Are you a cat burglar?"

"Work clothes," I said, "for backstage."

She held up a black cotton sweater with holes in the elbows. "Did you actually move this here?"

I laughed, nodding. I hated my clothes too. I never felt like I could spend money on myself. I didn't make much as a costume assistant. My income was limited because Eric's job dictated our location, and there weren't many theatres to choose from in Rochester. I did all the housework, even though I spent as much time at work as he did, but since my salary didn't even come close to paying half of our expenses, none of what I earned felt like mine. Instead of trying to sum out the complex equation of his earnings and my sacrifice, I avoided all talk of money because I was so embarrassed by my meager paychecks. Eric felt entitled to buy himself a BMW, but I stressed over dropping twenty bucks on a new pair of sneakers. So aside from work clothes, all I had were a few pairs of shorts, some jeans that didn't fit, and an endless stack of t-shirts from shows I'd costumed.

Bark sat on the bed, watching Mo with full attention. Every

so often, Mo offered him her hand on the sly, purposely avoiding eye contact. Each time, Bark inched a little closer to get a better sniff.

Mo held up an extra-large tie-dyed t-shirt from *Hair*. "Really, Kay?"

"Who died and left you *that* shirt?" I asked.

"My grandfather," Mo said, eyes big and sad.

"I'm sorry!"

"I'm kidding!" She shoved my shoulder.

Bark growled.

"It's okay," I whispered to him.

"Although . . ." Mo's face turned red. "I think this was one of Ruth's husband's shirts."

I winced and laughed. "We're horrible."

Bark sighed at just the right moment.

"He's not a fan of our humor," I said.

Mo was already on to the next thing. "I'll be right back," she called and ran down the hall full speed.

I heard her say something to Nan. Bark stared at the doorway, ears straining to listen. Nan said, "Oh, of course. Right there!" And then Mo ran back, bare feet thudding against the carpet.

"Here!" she said, throwing a dress at my face. She wasn't even out of breath.

The dress was a simple sleeveless wrap. Black. Clingy. Basically my size.

"So my grandmother dresses better than I do?"

"Yup."

"It's weird if I dress up and you don't."

"It's not about dressing up. I feel awesome in these," Mo said, pointing to her seersucker Bermuda shorts, "but I don't think you feel awesome in that."

I was wearing my too-tight brown linen shorts again, and a

t-shirt from a production of *The Music Man*. For that show, my boss, Edith, actually let me design costumes for the Pick-a-Little Ladies, but at the last minute insisted we use her designs instead. I was essentially wrapped in bad feelings.

I grabbed the dress.

Bark flopped on his side, still watching Mo. His brows wiggled as he tracked her movements, but his eyes drooped toward sleep.

I took my shirt off.

"Did your boobs get bigger?" Mo asked, staring at my ugly beige bra. There was a patch of thread pulls on the left cup from an unfortunate washing machine meeting with the Velcro closure of Eric's bathing suit. How long would it be before Eric was erased from my daily life?

"My everything got bigger," I said, slipping into the dress. "Two years on fertility drugs, only to find out he was cheating." As soon as the words landed I wanted to put them back, so Mo wouldn't witness my seeping anger.

"You had a whole big, serious, grown-up life while you were gone, huh?"

I nodded. I wanted to tell her about the babies I'd lost, and the dull loneliness I couldn't bury, but I didn't know how to start.

"I think you look gorgeous," Mo said. "And fuck him."

I tied the dress sash and shimmied out of my shorts.

"Lose the bra." Mo pointed to where it stuck out at the neckline. "It's Florida. We've got the perkiest pairs for miles."

I threaded my bra through the sleeve hole and threw it at the trash can. It missed. But I resolved to chuck it later, instead of putting it away.

"Ready?" Mo asked.

"No. But you're not letting me off the hook, are you?"

"Absolutely not." Mo planted a kiss on the top of my head. "Hey, I'm sorry you went through all that. I'm sorry I wasn't— we weren't—in touch."

"We are now," I said, giving her arm a squeeze.

When we were about to leave, Nan shuffled to the door in her nightgown and slippers, camera dangling from her wrist. "Ooh! Fits you perfectly, Kay," she said, smoothing the stretch of fabric across my back. "Let me get a picture."

"We're not going to prom. We're getting margaritas."

"It's your first night out as a single lady!" Nan looked through the viewfinder, waving for me to stand closer to Mo. "These are the things we want to remember."

I groaned.

"Indulge me," Nan said.

Mo held her arms out like the Hulk, fists clenched, the muscles in her neck straining. "Come on, Kay! For posterity!"

I rested my hands on my hips, like Wonder Woman. As the flash flared, maybe I did feel a little more powerful.

Nan palmed a lipstick and forty dollars into my hand.

"Nan!" I said. "I'm fine."

"I want to." She winked. "It's good to have you back."

CHAPTER NINE

~~~~~~~~~~~

"Let's get a jump start," Mo said, ordering two tequila shots as soon as we walked in. I hadn't been to a bar in a long time. We didn't even get carded.

"I don't have much of a tolerance anymore," I said.

"All the more reason."

The bartender slid our shots and a rocks glass full of lime slices across the shiny bar. Behind him a giant marlin hung on the wall, body arched like it was about to jump. I hoped it was fake, but I couldn't tell, and the thought of such a grand fish ending up on the wall in a dive bar made me sad.

"And a couple of your finest margaritas!" Mo shouted. She eyed the top shelf bottles. "Well, maybe not your *finest*. They're still margaritas, you know? A couple of your most middling margaritas!"

The bartender laughed. "Celebrating?"

"Hell yes." Mo tipped her head in my direction. "This one is a free woman!"

"Congratulations." He leaned against the bar. "Jail?"

"Marriage," Mo said.

"Same difference," I said, willing myself to participate.

The bartender laughed again, way harder than necessary.

Mo nudged me with her elbow when he turned away to make

our drinks. She raised an eyebrow. He was kind of cute. Tall. Thin. Tan. Blond.

I smiled and shook my head. I met Eric in college and we hung out until we melded into a couple. The idea of dating with intention, as an adult, was terrifying. Or was Mo thinking of some kind of backroom hookup? Was that a thing people did? Was it something she did? It occurred to me that it was probably something my husband had done.

"Bottoms up," Mo said, licking her hand.

I gave the back of mine a quick lick, trying not to think about the doorknob I'd touched on the way in and all the other people who'd touched it.

Mo grabbed the shaker on the bar and sprinkled salt on our hands.

We clinked glasses, licked salt, downed the shots, and stuck lime wedges in our mouths. Mo smiled at me, green rind covering her teeth.

The sparkle in her eyes reminded me of the grade school cafeteria. "Oh, man! Look!" she'd shout, like something urgent was happening, and then she'd open her mouth to show me chewed sandwich. I was mortified when we got to high school and she was still playing see-food. I wanted the cool girls to invite me to sleepover parties. I was desperate to get some guy named Dave from my algebra class to notice me. And there was Mo, with a mouth full of egg salad. Now I couldn't remember Dave's last name, and those girls share one bland, expressionless face in my memory, but Mo was still trying to make me laugh. I smiled wide, showing her my lime.

The bartender came back with our margaritas. "Nice," he said, pointing to my mouth. "These are on me. Happy freedom."

I spit my rind into a napkin. "Thank you."

"Thank you!" Mo said, grinning green, her words muffled.

The bartender winked at us before turning his attention to a guy at the end of the bar drinking beer from a glass cowboy boot.

"How old do you think he is?" I asked Mo, gesturing to the bartender. I honestly couldn't tell if he was older or younger than me.

Mo spit her lime into her hand. "Oooh. Do you like him?"

"I'm just curious. I feel like I was stuck in a bomb shelter for the past five years. Everything's a little off, you know?"

"I totally know," Mo said. "When Gran died, I had to keep Pops going. Getting him to appointments. Every med had a different schedule. He was always confused. And the whole time I'm fighting to keep him alive, he's saying he wishes he'd gone when Gran did. It was so sad and consuming, and when it was over I was like, 'Wait! What year is it?' I honestly didn't know."

"I'm so sorry I didn't come back for—"

"I get it, Kay. I know death is a loaded thing for you."

My cheeks burned, but Mo put her hand on my arm.

"I didn't even want to talk to anybody at his funeral. I didn't want to spend one more second taking care of another person." She took a huge gulp of margarita. "I got the flowers you sent."

Nan must have sent them for me. Pops died three weeks after my first miscarriage. I wasn't even human then. It was strange to realize during that time, other life was happening. Other sadness. My pain wasn't special or separate. There was odd comfort in that.

"Being a grown-up fucking sucks," Mo said, downing the rest of her margarita. She winced, like it gave her brain freeze.

"Let's be kids again," I said, even though being a kid hadn't been all that great for either of us.

Mo tapped her hand on the bar to call the bartender over. "We're switching to Jäger."

"Gross," I said.

"That's what kids do, right?" Mo grinned.

We switched right back to margaritas after that shot. And then Mo had a beer. We talked and laughed and stopped caring that the bartender was cute. Mo told me about her job as a lifeguard, and I felt better about my underachievement, until she told me about the project she was working on for the Port St. Lucie Arts Council.

"They commissioned five huge metal animals," she said. "I made an ant that's about yea high." She held her hand to shoulder height. "Then there's a shark, and a jellyfish, a sea turtle. I'm working on a manatee now."

"That's amazing!" I hoped none of my jealousy was leaking out. I was so proud of her.

"I didn't do any art until after Pops died," Mo said, like she knew what I needed to hear. "I had to get to the end of that, and then I could start."

She laughed. "Actually, not true. I had to get to the end of that and then wallow for six months before I could even think about taking over Pop's garage for my own work. Then I cried for a week. Then I started so small. I made a bunch of arachnid paperweights out of Pop's old nails and bolts. I sold them at the flea market and felt like a hack, and did it anyway."

She looked at me. "The wallowing was important. I can see that from here. I needed the time I needed. But when I was in it, I felt awful about myself every single day."

"Did Nan tell you to give me a pep talk?"

"Yeah." Mo flashed a toothy, sheepish smile.

"Thank you."

"She's worried about you."

"I'm okay."

Mo rolled the edges of the soggy label on her beer bottle. "She said you seem kind of jumpy again."

"Not again," I said, staring at the marlin behind the bar so I didn't have to look at her. The blue stripes across his body were too perfectly spaced for him to be real. "More like still."

"Really? I mean, you've had times—"

"When I was better at hiding it."

"Aw, I'm sorry, Kay," Mo said. "I can't imagine that feels good."

"Yeah, not so much."

"Pops went on Zoloft after Gran died."

"I did that," I said. "I went off it when we were trying. And then . . . it didn't help enough. It made everything feel . . . thick."

"Maybe Nan has some weird tea that will fix it," Mo said. "Like wind nettle tincture, or sunburned newt juice."

"I don't think anything is ever going to fix it," I said, leaning against the bar, resting my forehead in my hand.

"So," Mo said, "we'll live around it." She got up and grabbed my wrist. "Come on."

There was a jukebox in the corner, the kind that looks old-fashioned but isn't. She dug a couple of quarters from her pocket and picked out songs. It wasn't a dancing kind of place, but Mo didn't care.

Her first song was "Brown Eyed Girl." Mo sang loud, her voice raspy and off-key. "Come on, Kay!" she shouted, and held her hand out to me. I let her spin me around. When she was satisfied that I would keep dancing, she let go and grabbed the boot beer guy off his stool. "Dance with me!"

His girlfriend seemed annoyed at being abandoned, so I offered her my hand. She was light on her feet, and I copied her moves, stepping right then left. We swung our hands. And I wasn't faking it, I was having fun.

She started singing, and I did too, like it was a love song to myself. Pretty soon, the whole bar was singing the *sha las*. Mo had her hands in the air and she was spinning and spinning, and to be honest, everything else was spinning too. The bartender cut in, his hand at my waist. He could really dance. I stepped out of my flip-flops so I could keep up. He dipped me, and I laughed so hard.

"I'm John," he said when the song was over. But I didn't care. It didn't matter. It wasn't about him. I wasn't ready for that. But I was ready for me, and my friend, and living around the bad stuff, so I said, "Hey, John, we'll have another round," and went to sing "Sweet Caroline" with Mo.

Neither of us were in any condition to drive when John announced last call. Mo ordered a cab. We sat at the bar while we waited.

"I can drive you to pick up your car tomorrow," I said.

Mo waved the offer away. "I'll take my jog in this direction."

"It's far."

"It's about 10K total." Mo shrugged. "I've done it before. I come here with the kids from work sometimes."

John was wiping down the bar. His face went pale. "Please tell me they aren't actual kids," he said.

"No," Mo said with mock earnestness. "They are all adults and upstanding citizens."

I watched out the window for our cab. The sky flashed yellow in the distance. I felt the static in my bloodstream.

"Oh, man," John said. "They can't come back here."

Mo shrugged. "They all have convincing IDs at least."

A rumble. Fat drops of rain slapped the window hard, then harder. I wanted to be home with Bark, breathing his doggy breath, huddled together under the blankets.

"You alright, Kay?" Mo asked, grabbing my arm.

"Yeah, yeah. Fine." I forced a smile.

John and Mo chatted. Mo's hand stayed on my arm. She meant it to be comforting, but I felt trapped. I didn't want anyone to touch me. I couldn't pay attention to what they were saying. Everything was slow, heavy, until the cab lights shone in the window and it was time to go. Mo took my hand and we made a run for it.

"Southeast Dolphin Road," Mo told the cabdriver.

"No," I said, "your house is on the way to Nan's. We'll drop you off first." I gave the driver Mo's address. The air was thick with the bleachy smell of ozone. I shut my eyes, nausea growing.

"Are you alright, Kay?" Mo asked again.

"Yeah, yeah," I said, making a tent over the bridge of my nose with my hands, trying to rebreathe the air.

"You look like you're going to hurl."

"Hey!" the driver yelled, slowing the car. "No puking in my cab!"

"I'm fine," I said, eyes tearing. I wanted to be alone so badly.

"She didn't even have that much to drink," Mo said, waving her hand to tell him to speed up again. "She doesn't like storms."

I was surprised Mo knew. I thought I'd always done a good job covering on that count.

Mo put her arm around me. "A car is the safest place to be in lightning. Rubber tires."

I nodded, but it wasn't the storm I was scared of, it was all the things the sound of thunder churned up in my brain.

"I can go home with you," Mo said. "It's been a long time since I've crashed on the pullout in Nan's spare room."

"I'm fine." I didn't want Mo to come home with me. There was only so much longer I could hold it together, and I wanted to be far away from everyone when I fell apart.

CHAPTER TEN

~~~~~~

Bark raced down the hall to greet me when I got home, stepping on my flip-flops as I stepped out of them. His ThunderShirt was on upside down. Nan had tried at least.

The light over the stove was still on. She'd left a plate of awful cookies on the counter. I wouldn't have wanted good cookies either.

I pulled the curtains to the patio closed slowly so they wouldn't squeak, trying not to look outside. But then I did. Hard rain splashed the pool water, flashing silver with every lightning strike. I flexed my hands, trying to get the charged feeling in my fingers to stop. Deep breaths couldn't slow my heartbeat.

Bark whined, tail curling between his legs.

I sat on the floor and leaned over to press my cheek against the cold tile, running my finger along the grout line, trying to cling to the details of my surroundings. Cold floor. Magnolias on the curtains. The hum of the refrigerator. The light over the stove. A stray Cheerio under one of the kitchen stools. *I am here. I am here. I'm here.* I couldn't keep my throat from tightening. I couldn't hold the present in my mind. Cold flesh. Dark water. Wet wood. Formaldehyde. Lightning. Thunder. Lightning. The stinging in my nose. A puddle of tears.

Bark lay down with a thud, pressing his side to my side, shaking. Another flash of lightning leaked through the space under the curtain, a clap of thunder shook the house. The storm was right over us.

My father loved to swim in the calm moments right before a storm. Eyes bright and reckless, he'd dare me to race him, and we'd try to get in as many laps from shore to dock as we could before the first rumble.

"You'll get electrocuted!" my mother would say, scolding him.

"We're fine, Jan. Faster than lightning." He'd wink at me, and it would make her fume. She never stopped us. She was as enchanted by him as I was.

It was the second time we'd been swimming that spring. We put the dock out the weekend before. Exactly two hundred feet from shore, like always. Beginning of May, and the water was still too cold for the neighbors. We'd had snow on Easter. But that day was balmy and humid. The air felt close, and both of us were itchy in the way only swimming could fix. My father and I craved movement. My mother didn't understand. She spent summers on the deck reading Agatha Christie in the shade of a floppy black sun hat.

She'd gone to the grocery store, so she wasn't there to complain. The weather report said thunderstorms in early evening. The clouds were rolling in.

"Race ya!" I shouted, and ran across the sand into the water.

He ran after me. Slower than usual. In my nine-year-old mind I had become superhero fast. I'd grown two inches over winter. The world had different parameters. Maybe I could win.

I cupped my hands, pulling with my arms, kicking with strength, breathing hard when I tipped my head from side to side, heartbeat loud in my ears. I remember that I was happy.

The water churned around us, my father right behind me. We made our own waves.

A few feet from the dock, I heard his voice. A shout. I thought he was playing. Trying to get me to stop so he could win. I swam even faster and scurried up the ladder to the dock. "I beat you," I yelled, and looked into the water. He wasn't swimming. Head back, face bobbing barely at the surface.

I wanted to shout, but my brain couldn't remember how to make sound. He cried out. Not words, only noise. Staccato. Horrible. I leapt back in. The surface of the water stung my belly.

Pulling him to the dock was difficult. They always talk about weightlessness in water, but with my arm hooked in his armpit, all my kicking and paddling barely made a difference. I could feel his limbs moving. Trying to help. He was still with me. Still fighting. I couldn't have pushed him up on the dock myself, so I know he must have been conscious, but I can't remember seeing life in his eyes ever again.

Sometimes, I think about that moment, when his body collapsed on the dock, and the water dripped from us, raining through the wooden slats. I play it over and over in my mind, hoping I'll remember his expression. A spark of life. Like maybe there's a hidden answer. Maybe in his last moments he looked at me with so much love and adoration that remembering will bring me peace, the way those discoveries fix everything in movies.

He didn't have final words. Whatever he said last happened on the beach. Too common to remember. He was reading the paper when I called out my challenge. I don't know what he said right before. Sports scores? The punch line to a *Peanuts* cartoon?

Entire days, probably months of my life, if I added up the time, have been spent trying to figure out what he said before I shouted, "Race ya!"

I knew CPR. An EMT came to our school and taught us on limbless dummies. I could barely catch my own breath, but I tried to breathe for my father, choking between puffs. I pushed at his chest as hard as I could, but it barely moved. I threw my whole body against his.

I expected him to cough up water and come back to life, the way people did on TV. Any minute he would sit up. Any minute. I had to keep going.

But he didn't. The thunder rumbled. "We have to swim back," I told him. Of course, he didn't answer. I wasn't sure if I had the right spot on his wrist to check his pulse. I checked mine and then tried to find the same place on him, but there was nothing to tell me if I was right or wrong.

"Come in!" I heard my mother and looked to the shore. She was standing on the beach. "Come in!" she yelled again, swooping her arm, looking at the sky. "Quick!"

I stared at her. My limbs heavy. Mouth dry.

She kept screaming. I stared. She screamed louder.

I finally found the air to shout, "He's dead," and I realized he must have been gone the whole time I'd been doing CPR. His skin was cold. I tried again anyway.

By the time the police boat got to us, I could see lightning above the tree line, way in the distance. My mother didn't ride out in the boat to get me. A big cop with a stern voice pulled me from my father and handed me to an officer in the boat, the way you pass off a baby. Their hands scratched my wet skin. The officer wrapped me in a silver blanket. I remember the crinkle of it against my bare shoulders, the way it didn't absorb water. The officer wouldn't let me cover my face with it. "It's like a plastic bag," he said gently. "You'll suffocate." He had red hair and acne scars. His eyes were bloodshot.

I screamed when he took me away, leaving my father and the

big officer on the dock. They had to wait for the coroner, he said, as if it would make it easier for me to leave. I knew what a coroner was. I could tell the officer was sorry to say it.

At the shore, Mrs. Cowell, from next door, was trying to get my mother to drink a glass of water.

I sat in the sand and watched the dock as the sky got darker, and the rain started. The rumbles grew. I used the foil blanket like a poncho. Fat raindrops made crinkling sounds.

The boat went back for the other officer, to take him to shore until the storm stopped, but they couldn't move my father without the coroner. No one made me come in from the lightning. I watched it light up the lake. My father would have loved his view.

An ambulance came for my mother. She wouldn't stop screaming, and then she passed out. I didn't try to help. I felt like I should, but the neighbors were fussing over her, and I couldn't get my legs to move. After the lightning stopped, the police boat took the coroner to the dock. Floodlights and photograph flashes, and I watched them push my father to one side to get the body bag underneath. His body didn't move like a body. He was a thing now, not a person. The black plastic blocked the light for a moment as they laid it down. Dark and then bright again. The officers and the coroner were solemn silhouettes. The dock dipped low in the water under their weight.

I stayed at the Cowells' that night. My mother stayed at the hospital. "Sometimes, grown-ups need medicine when they get a shock like that," Mr. Cowell told me. Mrs. Cowell made me a stack of grilled cheese sandwiches I couldn't eat. We didn't know them well. I'd never even been in their kitchen before. There was a shiny green frog figurine on the table, with a hole at the top of his head to hold toothpicks.

I think I stayed at the Cowells' for a few days, but I can't remember being there after that first night. The blankets in their guest room smelled like mothballs.

Mrs. Cowell bought me a black dress for the funeral, and my mother was mad instead of grateful, because she thought it was tacky when children wore black. I was grateful. I wanted to mourn the right way. I wanted to do all the things that were supposed to be done, because I had messed up everything else. I wasn't strong enough to press his chest in. At least I could show how much I missed him.

I wanted to be his big brave girl, but when the pallbearers carried the casket into the church, I cried so hard I started to choke. Nan scooped me up in her arms, and I spent the entire service on her lap, like an infant, head to her chest, so I could hear her heartbeat.

After the funeral, before my mother sold the lake house, I swam to the dock every day to lie in the spot where he died so I could try to imagine what he'd felt as he was leaving. So I could feel like maybe he was still there. I'd watch the clouds and talk to them, telling them what they looked like. I was too timid to talk to my dad, but I hoped somehow, wherever he was, he'd overhear me say, "You look like an ice cream cone. You look like a dragon." And he'd smile, because I was right.

My mother hated it. Sometimes, she'd beg me not to swim, promising trips to the movies, butterscotch sundaes, video games. Sometimes she'd yell and scream. But as soon as I got to the water, she stopped trying. It was scary to have that power over her—to get my way without consequence. I swam well into fall, every day after school, in my t-shirt and underpants so I didn't have to go in the house when the school bus dropped me off. In early November, she sold the house and moved us to a condo. I would have kept swimming until the shore iced up. I didn't even feel the cold.

It was only after we left the lake, when I couldn't feel the weight of the water and lie on the dock in my father's spot, that the fear started. I'd lie awake at night, staring at the ceiling, trying hard not to think about blue-black water lapping against the dock, the depths where he could have disappeared. The kids at school made fun of me for falling asleep at my desk.

Once, in college, I went to the library and looked up the newspaper from that day, hoping to unearth a memory. The *Peanuts* cartoon didn't have words.

"Kay!" Nan shouted when she found me and Bark huddled together on the floor. "Come on. Get up!" She helped me to my feet.

I sobbed into her shoulder. "I'm sorry. I'm sorry."

"Don't do this. You're not alone. Don't do this alone." She wiped my face with a dish towel and made me drink a glass of water.

We slept in her bed. Bark snuggled between Nan and me. They fell asleep fast. I rubbed strands of my hair between my fingers and tried to see the ceiling in the dark. The storm drifted away, further and further, until I was sure the rumbling I heard was only in my head. Finally, in tune with the rhythm of their breathing, my heart slowed.

CHAPTER ELEVEN

I didn't hear Nan get up. What finally woke me was the sound of Ruth howling on the patio. Actually howling. Like a wolf, but if a wolf could howl with a Bronx accent. And then I heard lots of laughter.

Bark looked at me like he wanted an explanation.

"I don't know," I told him. "Sometimes Ruth howls."

He stared into my eyes to assess my concern level, then rested his head on the pillow with a sigh. My eyelids felt thick and swollen. I rolled on my back and stared at the ceiling, listening to the chatter, even though I couldn't hear the words. I rubbed my temples, hoping to clear my head. I was still wearing the bracelet Luca gave me years ago. The leather was cracked, browning at the edges, but it looked good on my wrist, like something missing replaced.

Bark nudged me with his nose, gently at first, then with more force, trying to push me out of bed. I wanted to stay put until Nan's friends left, but he licked my face and whined.

"Okay," I said. "I get it. Okay."

I ran Bark to the front yard to pee so he wouldn't have to face the crowd on the patio. He sniffed the entire perimeter of the yard before settling on the perfect spot, but right as he was about to go, a car drove by and scared him, and he had to go through the entire process all over again.

When we got back inside, Althea's arching laughter echoed through the house. Bark's legs shook. His feet slipped on the tiles. I unclipped his leash and let him run to my room.

"Katie, we're out here!" Nan called, like I might not know otherwise.

The sliding glass door in the kitchen was open. Nan, Marta, Ruth, and Althea were at the patio table drinking coffee, a basket of muffins in front of them. I tried not to look at the pool. I was still wearing Nan's black dress, now stretched out of shape and covered in dog fur.

"Look what the cat dragged in," Ruth said, tearing open a Sweet'N Low packet for her coffee. When I was a kid, I used to ask her which cat.

"Kaitlyn went out with Maureen last night," Nan said.

Althea gave me a sympathetic smile. "I've been there. Drink water."

I wondered if she meant she'd been there in a general way, or if she'd actually gone drinking with Mo.

Nan pulled out the empty chair next to her for me to sit down. On a good day, when my brain felt steady and my skin was thick, I could probably manage breakfast on the patio. But I was still struggling to shed the thoughts that flooded my brain during the storm. Sitting by the pool to chat with the ladies would be like squeezing a lemon with a hand covered in paper cuts. I pretended not to notice Nan's gesture, and rummaged around the cabinets looking for cereal instead.

"Where's Bitsie?" I asked, because it seemed more polite than questioning why everyone was at our house.

"Bits sleeps in on Fridays," Nan said.

"Is she okay?" The only cereal I could find was Grape-Nuts. I gave up and poured myself a cup of coffee. I leaned against the counter in the kitchen, still in conversation range, but once they got talking amongst themselves again, I could sneak away.

"Bitsie's fine. She stays up late watching *How to Get Away with Murder*." Nan pointed to the muffins on the table.

I shook my head. There was probably some kind of weird ingredient: alfalfa, or bean curd, or broccoli.

"I tell her to record it, but she won't," Althea said.

"Not after that one time." Nan shot Ruth a look.

"How was I supposed to know she hadn't watched it yet?" Ruth said, holding her hand to her heart.

Marta shook her head. "I don't watch. Too violent."

"You think everything's too violent," Ruth said.

The coffee was hot, but I drank fast, my eyes tearing.

"I hear you're making us mermaid costumes, Kay," Marta said.

"A bake sale makes more sense." Nan studied my face as she spoke. I knew I was puffy and tearstained.

"But this is more fun, Nannette!" Ruth said, shimmying her shoulders. "Live a little!"

"I think it's a lot of hassle for a silly thing," Nan said.

Ruth took a quick breath like she was about to say something, but held it instead. She folded her empty Sweet'N Low packet into halves until the paper wouldn't bend anymore.

Nan stared into her coffee cup and let the silence get awkward.

"Kate, why don't you bring that pup of yours out here to say hi?" Althea asked.

"He's kind of shy. It's probably not the best—"

"It's fine!" Ruth said. "We don't bite."

Marta shook her head. I couldn't tell if she was agreeing with Ruth or protesting.

"Maybe I can help," Althea said. "I spent a lot of time working with Jax after Sam died." Althea's husband, Sam, had been a cop. Jax was his K-9. When I was a kid, Sam let me stand on his feet at Nan's parties, and we'd dance like I had with my dad. He died in an on-duty car accident when I was in high school.

"The ladies would love to meet Bark," Nan said, pushing the change in subject.

I could so clearly imagine Bark, panicked by too many new people at once, backing into the pool. "He doesn't know how to swim. The patio—"

"Oh, Kay." Nan sighed. "Dogs can swim. You don't have to teach them."

"That's not true," I said, but no one heard me.

"He's cooped up in that room," Nan said. "Let him out!"

I hated the implication that I was mistreating him. He wasn't cooped up, he was hiding. And it wasn't for lack of care or work or training that he was the way he was. He'd been afraid of his own name when I got him. The shelter paperwork had him listed as "Lucky," but when we called him that, he backed away, ears flat against his head. I'd spent months with treats always in my pocket, conditioning him to learn his new name. I trained him to sit and shake, lie down, and come when called. I'd even taught him hand gesture commands. Now, as long as he wasn't scared by something else, he did everything I asked, perfectly. He'd come so far, but he still wasn't one of those dogs who could run into the middle of a group of strangers, tail wagging.

"I had so much fun playing catch with him yesterday. He's lovely," Nan said with the same kind of exuberant pride Marta had when she talked about her granddaughter's dance classes.

I didn't want to argue with Nan in front of her friends. Not after I'd been so much to deal with the night before. I felt like I had to show her I was a normal person with a normal dog. I wanted her to have something she could brag about.

My stomach wobbled as I walked down the hall to get Bark.

He was sprawled across the bed using Mr. Waffles as a pillow. Maybe I was wrong and Nan was right and he'd be fine.

"Come on, buddy," I said in a high voice, trying to sound excited. I jogged toward the doorway.

He didn't budge.

"Do you want a treat?" I asked, grabbing a handful of Zuke's from the bag on my dresser.

His left ear turned in my direction.

"Treat?"

He sighed.

I kissed his head. He took a treat from my hand. I backed away from the bed.

"Do you want another one?"

He strained his neck to reach for it. I backed away. He jumped off the bed. I opened the curtains and slid the door to the patio open. He stepped outside. As I closed the door behind him, he saw the ladies, and the hair on the back of his neck went up. I felt like a traitor.

"*Row-rawooo! Row-rawoo-oo-oo!*" His strange howl went from low to high, squeaking as it rose, like an angry prepubescent boy. He backed into the glass.

Marta covered her face with her hands, terrified.

"Oh, you have a lot to say, don't you?" Ruth said in a fake pouty voice.

Althea gave me a look. She knew this was more than Bark being chatty. She got up from her chair, but hunched over as she walked in a careful, winding route toward Bark. "Hey, buddy," she said, avoiding eye contact. "It's okay." When she got close, she crouched low, putting her hand out. He backed into the glass again, legs trembling. "It's okay, bud, I won't push it." Althea stepped away.

Bark sniffed the air, like maybe he was interested in Althea now that she was retreating, but then Ruth shouted, "Does he need a biscuit? Maybe he needs a biscuit!"

"*Rowoooo!*" Bark shouted back at her. He turned, scratching frantically at the sliding door.

Nan's face flushed. She was probably mortified. I remember getting an earful once when I cried at a cocktail party because I was overtired and I tripped on the carpet and got rug burn on my knee. "We have *people*," Nan whispered when she escorted me to my bedroom. The lecture I got was gentle, but I remember feeling ashamed for my tears and the gasps from guests who were trying to enjoy their martoonis and finger food without eleven-year-old drama. I was too big a girl to cry in public like that.

Bark was having a similar breakdown. Everything was new, and then there were more strangers. He had feelings about it, and I didn't want to tell him to hush. It wasn't his fault.

"Why don't we give him a biscuit?" Ruth said again. "Or a muffin!" She ripped off a chunk of muffin and stood up. Bark gave up scratching at the door and stared at me, panicked, like he was begging me to help, and unsure if I would.

Althea looked at Ruth and shook her head.

I slid my bedroom door open and Bark rushed back in.

"Aw," Ruth said, like someone had let her balloon go. "Well, you come have a muffin, at least." She waved the same piece of muffin at me.

"You know, I was going to go for a run before I ate," I said, desperate to check on Bark.

"Oh! Go! Go!" Ruth said. "Get your move on!"

Althea shook her head again, but Ruth was oblivious.

"Be careful!" Marta said.

I slipped into my room, slid the door shut, and closed the curtains.

"*Row-rawooo!*" Bark stood on the bed and howled, like he

was saying, *How could you?* He flopped over with a frustrated sigh.

"I'm so sorry," I said, lying down, wrapping myself around him. "I shouldn't have done that. I won't ever do it again." I scratched behind his ears. Kissed the smooth fur on his forehead.

Eventually, he licked my chin.

"I love you too," I told him.

When he seemed mostly calm, I got up and changed into shorts. The ladies were still chatting on the patio. I had to at least pretend to run.

CHAPTER TWELVE

Even though I hadn't exercised in any consistent way for the entirety of my marriage, I'd hoped my muscles had excellent memory and I'd magically get back to running without the awkward walk/jog stage. I started off strong, tearing down Southeast Dolphin Road at what felt like a respectable pace. It was only five houses' worth of distance, but I was crushing it, even with a hangover.

I stopped to wait for a car so I could cross the street, and when I tried to pick up speed again it was agony. My body had warmed up and was telling me to fuck off. My fat hurt; thighs swooshing and crashing with every step. Muscle memory counts for jack shit when everything jiggles. I ran harder than my lungs could handle and stopped at the end of each street, holding the stitch in my side, gasping for air, until I had enough breath to take off again. The sweat made my skin itch. When I scratched my legs, welts appeared in the marks my nails left.

I saw Mo from across the street, sprinting like a gazelle in short shorts and a sports bra, unaffected by all the tequila.

"Kay!" she shouted. "Do you want to run together?"

I shook my head. She crossed the street in a few graceful strides.

"How come you stopped?" she asked.

I shook my head again.

"Are you okay?" Her abs were tan and taut. She wasn't even breathing hard.

"I'm . . ." Gasp. "Doing . . ." Gasp. "Interval training," I said, hoping she'd allow me some dignity by pretending to believe me.

She laughed. "You look like you're about to pass out. Come on! Run with me."

"Then I *will* pass out."

"Hysterical!" she said, shoving my sweaty arm. She wiped her hand on her shorts and started jogging. "So fun last night," she called over her shoulder. "We need to do that again soon!" Then she was a blur, turning the corner.

I looped back on Carnation Road, doing a slow jog that was more like a limp. By the time I'd gotten to Bitsie's house, I was flat-out walking.

Bitsie was outside in Bunny's floppy straw hat, watering plants. "Look what the cat hacked up!" she shouted.

"Sometimes people say nice things," I yelled. "Like 'Hi' or 'Good morning.'"

Bitsie laughed. "How 'bout 'Coffee!'"

"Nicest thing I ever heard."

She handed me the hose. "This one, and then that one," she said, pointing at Bunny's rosebushes.

I watered until the ground was damp, but not soggy, like Bunny taught me. I used to house-sit for them when they went out of town. Bunny had a morning garden routine that took the better part of an hour. It was strange to think of Bitsie taking over. She wasn't usually patient in that way, but the roses were still vibrant.

Bitsie came out with two mugs of coffee and handed me one. We sat on the stoop. I tried not to scratch my legs.

"I told Bun we should go with native plants," Bitsie said.

"Less work. Less water. And here I am, watering these roses by hand every morning because she swore the sprinkler flooded the roots." She leaned over to sniff one of the orange Gypsy roses, pulling the bloom toward her. "They're worth the work, aren't they?" She held the stem for a moment longer, like she was holding hands with the rosebush.

"Bunny told me the work was the whole point."

Bitsie smiled. "That sounds like Bunny." She took a sip of coffee. "Ladies at your place?"

I nodded.

"I need one morning off, you know?"

I raised my eyebrows.

"Oh, don't look shocked," she said. "You know you have a limit too. That's what this is, right?" She gestured to my shorts.

It was funny to hear her admit she had the same need for retreat, although it made sense when I thought about it. Bitsie was always the one to volunteer to run to the store for a forgotten stick of butter, to mind the roux that needed stirring in the kitchen, or rock someone's fussy grandbaby to sleep in the other room. But when she was on, she was on. The life of the party. I'd always assumed it was effortless.

"There's a name for what we are, Kay," Bitsie said, clinking her coffee mug against mine.

"Yeah?"

"Introverts. Such a beautiful term, isn't it? When I was your age, they called it 'weird.'"

"Have you been reading internet memes?" I asked, laughing.

"I don't know what that is." She shook her head. "Bunny bought me a book about introverts. It made me realize that it's okay to take some space when you need it."

"You, though? You're so . . ."

"Loud?" she said.

"I was going to say 'loquacious.'"

"Don't pull your fancy college words on me!" She nudged my shoulder with hers.

"Fine. Loud," I said, nudging back.

"There was a lot of pressure to have personality when I was younger. My mother used to tell me, 'You'll never be pretty, but you can be charming.'"

"That's terrible!"

"I know!" she said, swirling the coffee around in her mug. "And she meant it to be hopeful. Like I could still find a way to be okay."

"I think you're beautiful," I said. No one else's eyes sparkled quite so brightly.

"I've got a beak like a toucan and a neck like a turtle," Bitsie said, "so the charm must be working on you."

"Oh, Bits!"

"I never had my own kids, of course," Bitsie said, "but I think every mother should believe her little girl is the most beautiful being in the whole wide world." She tapped my knee. "And then she should tell her she's smart, funny, and kind, instead."

I forced a smile, remembering my mother telling me it was too bad I'd inherited my father's cleft chin. "It's weird on a girl," she said, smoothing foundation on my face before the third grade play. It was the tiniest cleft. Barely even noticeable. Gone, once I gained a little weight when I hit puberty, but her attention to it made me feel like I was walking around with the Grand Canyon right there at the end of my face. Every picture through fifth grade has me chin in hand, like a serious 1980s businessman.

"What are you thinking when your face gets like that?" Bitsie asked.

"Like what?"

"Beautiful. And smart, and funny, and kind, of course. But faraway. Like you're gone."

"Something my mom said about my chin being weird."

"Good lord! You were a stunning child. Those big brown eyes. You charmed the heck out of all of us, and you barely even said a word. I don't know how anyone could have looked at that sad little face and tried to break your heart."

"It was just a stupid thing about my chin," I said, pulling a baby dandelion sprout from the dirt, slowly, so the root wouldn't break.

"I heard how she talked to you, kiddo. After your dad died, when she brought you to visit. It wasn't nice things she said."

I broke the stem of the dandelion and sniffed it. Bitsie was right. I remembered the disgusted sighs when I didn't move quickly enough if my mother asked me to do something. The glares I'd get across the dinner table for nothing in particular. After my father died, she got more and more annoyed with me. Nothing I said or did would make it better. At least not in any reliable way. But it didn't stop me from trying. Again and again, until she was gone.

"I think," Bitsie said, "sometimes mothers attack when they feel raw about the parts of themselves they don't like."

"Maybe," I said, twisting the two pieces of dandelion together. The white sap made my fingers sticky.

Bitsie smiled at me. "Hey, did you see all of Bunny's fabric in the sewing room?"

"Yeah."

"You should have it."

"Oh no," I whispered. It felt like too much to take. Those fabrics were the remainders of Bunny's life story. "I could make you clothes. I saw a pretty sundress pattern in her files, and she has some nice ginghams."

"No," Bitsie said, tapping Bunny's hat. "This is one thing. I can wear it at home. And sometimes I sleep in one of her shirts, but those are messy nights." She sighed. "If I tried to wear her clothes to Publix, I'd end up wailing in the produce aisle."

I felt that way about my dad's old shirts. They lived in a box in Nan's attic.

"Same with her fabric," Bitsie said. "I remember all the times she dragged me to the store and labored over which print to choose. They look like her. I can't go around wearing memories and expect myself to act like a normal human being."

"We can leave it all right where it is," I said. "I don't need to—"

"Bunny would want you to have her fabric," Bitsie said. "I am certain of it. Make yourself something. That's what I'd like. To see her memories spread around."

"If I do and it's not okay, you promise you'll tell me?"

"Promise," she said, and squeezed my arm. "You coming to sew today?"

"Yeah." I stood up. "I think I can get those curtains done and hung this afternoon." I crumpled the dandelion remains in my hand. "And maybe we can talk about your tail." I laughed as soon as I said it.

"My tail is worth talking about!" Bitsie said, laughing too.

"Thanks for the coffee." I handed her my empty mug.

"You can hide over here any time you want."

"Thank you," I said, thinking Friday morning jogs would have to become a regular thing.

"Don't tell them I'm awake yet!" Bitsie called when I was half-way down the driveway.

I carried the dandelion on my jog back to Nan's and threw it in the garbage can in the garage so there was no way its offspring could invade Bunny's roses.

CHAPTER THIRTEEN

~~~~~~~

"Maybe you should take Bark for a walk?" Nan called from the den. The other ladies were gone. Nan had her feather duster out and Bark watched warily as she fluttered it across the coffee table.

The words "maybe you should" gave me the same knee-jerk feelings of rebellion they always used to.

"He's fine," I muttered. Bark did the loud yawn thing dogs do when they're feeling awkward about a situation. "The trainer I worked with in Rochester gave me obedience exercises. She said they're enough mental stimulation to keep him happy while I build up his confidence."

"Dogs need more than mental stimulation, Kay. They need to move their bodies. Everyone does." Nan pumped her arms like a power walker. "He has too much pent-up energy. Althea said getting Jax into a regular exercise routine—"

"He can't handle it!" I said too loudly. I looked away. The ugly clay chicken I made in pottery class in fifth grade was still on display on the bookshelf. It felt wrong to yell at the keeper of my artifacts.

"I think he can!" Nan said. "After Ruth and Marta left, Althea got him to sit and shake and walk next to her nicely down the hallway. He was fine."

"It's not— He's different outside," I said, frustrated. Bark had good manners when everything was quiet. I hated that Nan and Althea thought they understood him just because he sat for a treat in the house.

The day after Eric and I brought Bark home from the shelter, I tried taking him for a walk. An unleashed Schnauzer from two doors down ran at us and bit Bark on the nose. There was blood. Enough to scare me. I was shaking when I brought him back to the house. Eric insisted the scratch was small and it wasn't a big deal, but it was a big deal to me. An even bigger deal to Bark. It was a struggle to get him to go for walks at all after that.

Once, I got him halfway around the block, only to have him freak out over a plastic grocery bag blowing down the sidewalk like a tumbleweed. He hooked his tail between his legs and refused to take another step, no matter how much I pleaded. I had to carry him home, stopping every few feet to catch my breath and adjust my grip on his trembling body. I thought we'd never make it. And that was midday when everyone was at work, and there wasn't another dog in sight. When he did see a dog, the hair on the back of his neck stood up. He'd growl and lunge, neighbors watching, horrified.

"Well, have you tried?" Nan asked, like she was offering a new and novel idea.

"Yes, I have," I said, hearing the sharpness in my voice, unable to pull it back. I'd tried everything. The kind of collar that fits over his nose. Positive praise. Pretending to be the pack leader. Fearful Furry Friend classes. A trainer who came to the house. Prozac. An enzyme I bought from the touchy-feely natural foods store that was supposed to be "bioidentical" to calming proteins in breast milk. A contraption you plug into the wall that radiates relaxing scents. A special CD of music for dogs. But none of it fixed Bark. I may as well have taught him to breathe into a paper bag.

"I'm supposed to take him outside when there aren't any dogs around and give him a treat when he looks at something scary," I told Nan.

"What's scary outside?"

"Everything."

Nan shook her head like she thought the whole situation was ridiculous.

"He needs exercise, Kay," Nan said.

"We *do* exercise."

Nan looked at me like she wanted a bigger answer.

I caved. "We dance," I mumbled.

"What?"

"We dance. I put on music and we kind of dance around." Late at night, when Eric wasn't home, when I'd had a glass or two of wine, Bark and I would have a dance party. I don't remember how I discovered that if I jumped, Bark would too, but it became my favorite moment of the day. We'd play music videos on YouTube and bounce around the living room like our pants were on fire. Bark yelped and wagged his tail. He'd scramble to get Murray the Monster and toss him in the air. I danced until my asthma flared up, then I'd crash on the couch with Bark, both of us panting.

"Fine," Nan said. "Let's dance." She opened the cabinet under the stereo and flipped through her records.

I'd spent so much time on the floor in front of that cabinet as a kid. I knew each record by the color of the spine. Nan had her parents' modest collection of big band hits, my father's classic rock, grandfather's classical, her own Motown and jazz, and the random '80s and '90s albums she'd bought for me at yard sales.

Nan chose an album. She set the record needle, and the playful piccolo from "The Tears of a Clown" came through the speakers. "You always liked this one."

"I can dance with him while you're out," I said. It wasn't something I wanted to do in front of another human being.

"Don't be silly. I want to see this dog dance." Nan started doing small jumps from one side to the other, crossing her arms in front of her, falling into the beat. "Come on! Do the pony!"

I felt the prickle of awkwardness in my skin. Bark stared at me. I did the dumb step-touch thing that I called dancing in junior high, shaking my shoulders ever so slightly. Bark wagged his tail.

"He's not dancing," Nan said, grape-vining toward me, waving her arms. Her hands looked like the flapping wings of a dove. She had a grace I did not inherit. Bark shifted his attention to her. His tail wagged slower, but it was still wagging.

"He does get into it," I said. "But—everything is new."

"This isn't enough exercise for him," Nan said.

The carnival theme played again and the song opened up to the triumph of horns. I jumped straight in the air and spun around. Bark yelped. I jumped higher, kicking my legs. Bark jumped with me. I skipped from one side of the room to the other and he followed, prancing along. I forgot about Nan, and embarrassment, and everything else. It was me and Bark and Smokey Robinson.

As we leapt across the carpet again, Nan stopped dancing and put her hands on her knees, like maybe she was having some kind of heart episode.

I stopped mid-skip, almost sliding into the wall. "Are you okay?" I yelled, heart thumping, out of breath.

She looked up, tears streaming down her face.

"Oh my god! Oh my god!" I shouted. My voice sounded like it was coming from someone else.

"That is the most ridiculous thing I've ever seen!" Nan said, gasping for air, laughing.

I wanted to sneak behind the blue wing chair and press my cheek against the soft velour, like I did as a kid when I no longer wanted to be a part of the action.

Nan must have seen the horror on my face because she grabbed my arm. "It's good," she said, her laughter winding down. "It's really good. I've never seen you like that." She hugged me. I didn't hug back. "Oh, sweetie. No, it's good. He's so joyful when you dance."

I nodded. Still craving the shelter of the wing chair while my adult mind came to the realization that everyone must have known where I was hiding when I did that.

"How did this start?" Nan asked.

"I don't know," I said. "Home alone. Wine. Cyndi Lauper."

Nan nodded, like it made perfect sense. She crouched. Bark ran over and licked her face. "You are a very good boy, aren't you?" She scratched his ear. "And you take good care of my granddaughter."

She went to the cabinet, to the section of records she'd bought for me, and started "Girls Just Want to Have Fun." "I always loved this one," she said, slapping her hands to her thighs. "Come on, Bark!"

And we danced again.

CHAPTER FOURTEEN

Nan headed to Marta's for lunch. Bark sat by the door after she left like he was hoping she'd come right back.

"Did Nan leave?" I asked.

He tipped his head to the side, considering the question.

After I showered, I raided Nan's closet and found a white cap-sleeved sweater. I paired it with my navy blue capris—which were the only nice pants that still fit me—shoved my too-big feet into a pair of Nan's navy flats, and slipped her chunky red Bakelite necklace over my head. It was a bit on-the-nose nautical, but it looked purposeful. Plus, the sweater hung long and was thick enough to hide a multitude of sins. Older women are much kinder in the ways they dress themselves.

I knew Nan would willingly allow me the use of anything in her closet, but I didn't want to admit that I hadn't managed to keep myself in presentable clothes. I also knew if I told Nan I was looking for a job, she'd start in about how I didn't have to do that right away and I was welcome to stay with her for as long as I wanted, and goodness gracious, sometimes it's okay to let someone take care of you. But I needed to keep my hands busy, to have a paycheck and a purpose. And I had to make sure I wasn't more of a burden to Nan than I'd already been.

*   *   *

I stopped at the bakery next to the tailor shop to pick up a half-dozen madeleines and two cups of Earl Grey.

My nerves were out of control. It was ridiculous to be afraid. If Isaac said no, I could go home, put Nan's clothes back, and climb into bed like I hadn't even tried. But I'd loved working in Isaac's shop. All through high school, I "made my bones," as he said, hemming pants and fitting wedding dresses. I hoped going back to work for him might be like hitting restart, but it was hard for me to want things.

The bell on the door jangled when I stepped inside.

"Hi, Isaac," I said when he appeared through the curtain from the back room.

He greeted me with a huge smile.

I handed him a cup and the bag of cookies. "We didn't get to talk at Nan's party, and I wanted to say hi." I hated having an ulterior motive. I'm not sure I would have come by otherwise. I never knew how to put myself in another person's path without a reason, even when I wanted to.

"Wonderful!" Isaac said. His eyes lit up when he looked in the bag. "My favorite!"

He sat on the stool behind the counter, gesturing to the stepladder. I took a seat. We held our paper cups and ate cookies as if chewing required full attention. Without the job question hanging over my head, it would have been a comfortable silence. I decided to bail on the mission. The stress was keeping me from enjoying my time with him.

"So," Isaac said, then paused like he was waiting for the translation of what he wanted to say. "You have come home."

Isaac's parents fled Germany to Denmark, where he was born. He was raised in Copenhagen until his family moved to New

York when he was fourteen. His English was perfect, but I think maybe he had to filter what he wanted to say through Danish to German and back before his thoughts came out clearly in English. I always wondered if that's why he was so quiet, or if he would have been quiet in his native tongue too.

"Yes. I'm home." The words formed a lump in my throat.

"Your grandmother is so happy," Isaac said, taking a sip of his tea. "She must be . . . happy . . . of course."

"I hope so. I'm happy she'll have me back."

"She always will," Isaac said, smiling.

"How have you been?" I asked, like I was reading lines from a script of polite conversation.

Isaac stretched his fingers, then clenched them, head wobbling from side to side.

"Arthritis?" I asked.

"Yes. I don't want to quit, but my doctor says it might soon be time."

I couldn't figure out how to ask for help, but I had no qualms offering. "Need a hand?"

He nodded quickly, relief in his face. "Could you start Sunday?"

"I could," I said, trying not to laugh at how easy it was. Everything else in my life felt complicated.

"Wedding party, and the bride . . ." He winced. She was probably a talker. Most people took their cues from Isaac. Customers whispered their requests. But every so often, someone kept going at high intensity, and I'd see on Isaac's face that it chipped away at him. I could handle it a little better than Isaac could, but I understood.

"What time?" I asked.

"Ten a.m."

"I'll be here."

He patted the counter. "Good, good," he said, and gave me a warm grin. "Your grandmother's necklace looks pretty on you."

"I borrowed it," I said. "Don't rat me out."

"Oh, I'm sure she wouldn't mind."

After we finished our tea, we went to the back room so Isaac could show me the dresses we'd be fitting. The bride's gown was a strapless A-line drowned in sloppy tulle ruffles.

I looked at Isaac.

"I know," he said, like he could read my thoughts. He showed me the rack of bridesmaid dresses. Nine of them. Each one a slightly different style, all in a horrid shade of mint green. Uneven stitching. Crooked straps. The boning in the strapless one showed where it shouldn't.

"She ordered them from a store on the internet," Isaac said in disbelief.

"At least none of those girls are going to want to wear them again," I said. "I can't think they'll last much past the day."

"I hate working on bad work."

"Me too," I said, thinking of all the time I spent in the costume shop at the theatre, fixing Edith's mistakes after she went home.

"Well," Isaac said, "we'll do the best we can do. As always."

It shocked me how hard I fell for the belonging in those words. He studied my face while I tried not to cry.

"Good, good," he said, zipping up the last garment bag. "We'll do what we can." There was a bend in his voice. Like maybe it meant something to him too.

After I left Isaac's, I stopped home to change and went to Bitsie's house to sew. I needed presentable clothes for work.

CHAPTER FIFTEEN

~~~~~~~~~~

Bark ran to greet me at the door when I got home from sewing at Bitsie's, Murray clutched in his teeth, tail wagging so hard his whole back end swayed. His body language was different from the way he greeted me in Rochester. I felt different about coming home too. Even though Nan could drive me crazy, I didn't have to steel myself to see her, the way I did with Eric.

"Bark!" I said. "Are you a happy boy?" He pushed his head against my leg and then ran back to the kitchen, looking over his shoulder like he wanted me to follow. The air smelled of roasted garlic.

Nan was in the kitchen mashing potatoes. Something in the oven had a rich, meaty smell.

"Did you make meat loaf?" I asked.

"Well, it's lentil loaf," Nan said, and paused like she was waiting for me to complain.

"It smells amazing." I gave her a kiss on the cheek. "You didn't have to do that!"

"I thought it would be nice for us to have a good meal together."

"I don't want to make work for you," I said.

"Nonsense." Nan dumped heaping spoonfuls of mashed potatoes on two plates.

"Thank you. I appreciate it. And Bark looks happy."

"We danced in the living room. I hope that's okay."

I thought of them jumping around together and felt a twinge behind my nose. "Of course!" I said. Maybe this was all we needed.

Nan sliced the lentil loaf and ladled salad dressing over a plate of asparagus. I set the table. Chet Baker played on the stereo. Nan had the windows open and the night breeze smelled like gardenias and fresh cut grass.

After we sat down to eat, Nan said, "Last night, when I found you on the floor . . . Does that happen a lot, Kay?"

My heart clenched and released with too much force, leaving me woozy. Was that what this dinner was? A chance to make me a captive audience so she could poke? I shook my head.

"I'm sorry," Nan said firmly. "I think we have to discuss this." It was the same voice she used when I was a kid and needed a shot at the doctor's office.

"I can't," I whispered, throat tight.

Nan reached across the table and patted my arm. "I'm here to help," she said, and I know she believed it. She would listen with the best intentions, but then she'd tell me why I shouldn't worry about the things I worried about, as if that was the solution. I'd be stuck holding my worries closer so she could feel like she'd fixed me. Later, when the exhaustion of trying so hard got the best of me, I'd fall apart again, and feel that much worse for letting her down.

"I'll be okay," I said, wishing I believed it. "There's been a lot of change. I'll settle in."

Nan kept her hand on my arm and ate her dinner without talking. My stomach felt twisty and fragile. I pushed food around my plate, trying to make it look like I'd eaten a respectable amount.

When we cleared the table, Nan had a faraway look in her eyes.

"Maybe Woo Woo's daughter wrote back," I said, wrapping up the rest of the lentil loaf. "We should check."

"You go," Nan said. "I'll finish up here."

"I can help you. You made dinner, you shouldn't have to clean up too."

"Oh, sweetie. It's fine," she said with a sigh.

I logged in to Facebook. The first thing in my feed was a post saying Eric's relationship status had changed to divorced. Sixteen people liked it.

He had a new profile picture, taken on the pier at Ontario Beach Park. Sun about to set. Windburned cheeks. Eyes bright. He looked like the person he'd been when we first started dating senior year of college. He looked hopeful.

I had a flash of memory: A few months after my first miscarriage, Eric came home to find me crumpled in a heap on the kitchen floor. Shirt soaked. My tears had formed an actual puddle. He picked me up, helped me into a chair, snapping into full-efficiency mode. "Drink this, hon," he said, handing me a glass of cool water. He wiped my face with the back of his hand and brushed my hair out of the way to plant a kiss on my forehead. "It's okay." His voice was solid and kind. "We'll try again. This one wasn't meant to be." But when he mopped my tears from the floor, he worked his jaw hard, pain flashing in his eyes, and I knew he was thinking about how much a person had to cry to soak a dish towel.

The imaginings that undid me that day were stuck in my mind. Ready to surface if I wasn't careful. Our tiny baby floating on her back in the lake, water lapping against her chubby cheeks, clouds gathering above.

Eric left to throw the dish towel in the laundry room. I bit the inside of my cheek until I tasted blood, using the pain to snap me from my haze. When I took a sip of water, blood seeped into the glass. I gulped the water down so he wouldn't see—so hard and fast I thought my throat would split.

"Feeling better," Eric said when he came back. Not a question. What he needed from me.

I burped and nodded, fighting like hell to smile, lips closed to hide the blood. Eric ordered pizza and I fell asleep on the couch with my head in his lap while he watched *SportsCenter*. It was the first time I'd slept in days.

That wasn't the last time he had to pick me up. Not even close. Sometimes, my brain would get stuck on the memory of the green ceramic frog on the Cowells' kitchen table. I couldn't stop thinking about the toothpicks in his head, the way the glaze pooled at the indents on his webbed feet, and that would be enough to ruin me. The stale toast scent of the Cowells' kitchen would flood my brain. Then it would all come back. Blue-black water. The crinkle of a silver blanket. My mother's screams. The patterned red carpet at the funeral home. Waxy makeup on my lips. Later, the memory of the new crying jag would become a thought I couldn't get unstuck from—fear attaching to fear— like an ever-growing net.

I didn't know how to explain why I was falling apart to Eric. Why I couldn't make dinner, or ask how his day was, or be his lover, or his wife, or even a friend. *I thought about a frog and then I thought about everything*. It didn't make sense to me either. I held hope that Eric would suddenly understand and he'd forgive me, or I'd understand well enough to tell him what was wrong, or even that I'd just get better.

Did I kill his hope? Did his friend bring it back? I hovered over the likes on his status to see who was cheering Eric's freedom:

twelve guys I recognized from his team at work, two friends he'd
known since high school, someone named Nikki Rogers, and his
mother. These people were dinging and donging over the witch
being dead, and I was the witch. It hurt my feelings in a sharp,
strange way, and then the fact that it hurt my feelings hurt my
feelings even more. My hand shook on the mouse pad.

I clicked on Nikki Rogers. She was the friend from the hallway. The girl with the fake nails. I'd avoided learning her name,
and she didn't volunteer it when we met. In her profile picture,
she wore aviator sunglasses and red lipstick, her too-white smile
wide and charming. Her arms wrapped around someone's neck,
riding piggyback, his head bowed toward the camera so all that
could be seen of him was an ear and short brown hair. I knew
who he was. I didn't even have to look closely for the small swath
of silver at his temple.

I clicked the picture. It was two years old. I heard Nan's footsteps in the hall and prayed she'd walk away. A rush of adrenaline
left me clammy. I dropped my head between my knees.

"Are you okay?" she called from the doorway.

"Two years," I said, bursting into tears. I didn't want to tell her,
but I couldn't keep it in. "That's him. With her. Two years ago."

"What a . . . dickhead!" Nan shouted.

"I am so stupid." Two years. I was pregnant the first time.
After so much work, so many hormones. That was before hope
felt dangerous. It was summer in that picture. Fall when I lost
her. Did he tell himself he would stop when the baby came? I
didn't even think we were unhappy back then.

"Oh, Kay!" Nan wrapped her arms around my shoulders.
"He's a snake. How were you supposed to know? He hid it well."

"Maybe he didn't. Maybe I didn't see."

"You were in pain."

"I wasn't paying attention. I drove him away." Nan's hug

pressed my shoulders into the wooden knobs on the chair back. It hurt.

"He wasn't worth keeping," she said. "He's proven that. Does it matter when he proved it? You're no more or less divorced than you were before."

Nan let go of my shoulders and sat on the edge of the bed next to Bark. "I lost a baby once. Before your father. Sometimes the whole day would pass, and I couldn't even begin to tell you how. Your grandfather would come home from work and I'd be in the living room, staring at a book. I hadn't turned a single page the whole time he'd been gone."

Bark shoved his head under Nan's hand. She scratched behind his ears. "Your grandfather had his flaws, but he didn't take advantage of the fact that I wasn't paying attention. At least as far as I knew."

I was only five when Gramps died, but I remembered that he was always after me about elbows on the table, and minding my p's and q's. I couldn't picture Gramps having a "friend." He seemed like someone who'd have found the very thought unseemly.

"I didn't know you had a miscarriage," I said. "Why didn't you tell me?" When she'd caught me on the phone in tears, she'd said, "Time heals all wounds," as if she had nothing of substance to offer. I'd spent days staring too. I didn't know other people lost time in grief that way. I'd seen it as my personal failing.

"I didn't want to trouble you with my sadness," Nan said, leaning over to wipe tears from my cheek with her sleeve. "And I didn't know what to say. The only thing that made it better was having your father." She closed her eyes for a moment, the pause she always took when she wanted to keep her emotions under control. "I think I leaned too hard because of it. He was my band-aid, instead of just a child. But I don't know how you're supposed to reconcile that loss without someone new to fill it. It has to be excruciating."

"I don't think he felt like a band-aid. He loved you so much," I said, smiling through my tears. "He worshipped you. It drove my mom crazy."

Nan smiled and squeezed my knee. "When we lost your father," she said, "I wouldn't have been okay without you."

I smiled back, even though I didn't see how it could be true. I knew how much stress I brought with me when I moved in, and I knew I was doing it all over again.

"*You* have me," Nan said, "and Bark." She took a quick breath, held it for a moment. "Don't you forget that." It didn't feel like a platitude. It felt like a promise.

"Thank you," I whispered, and ran my finger over my dad's smiley face carving on the desk.

"Alright," Nan said, slapping her hand on her thigh. "Let's Facebook-stalk—is that the right term?"

I laughed. "Yes." I wondered where she'd heard it.

"Let's Facebook-stalk this Nikki person and get it out of our systems."

I felt weird about the idea of doing this with Nan. This wasn't the way our relationship worked. "That's okay. I shouldn't—"

"I know you're going to do it anyway. Anyone would. Let's make a pity party out of it." Nan went to the kitchen and came back with two wine glasses and a bottle of Pinot Grigio. She poured for us. "Cheers." She tipped her glass in the direction of Eric's head on my computer screen. "Good riddance to bad rubbish."

"Cheers," I said, even though it wasn't so simple. I wished I knew how to separate Eric's moments of kindness from the lies. He wasn't all bad rubbish.

"Okay," Nan said, taking a gulp of wine. "Let's go."

I went back to Nikki's page. At the top was a photo album dated yesterday. There she was, in front of my house, her perfect blond ponytail sticking out the back of a Rochester Red Wings cap. She held a cardboard box, posing like it was a catalog shoot. The caption read: *Moving Innnnn!*

"Why does it surprise me?" I asked, my voice wobbling. "Of course, she was going to move in with him!"

"It's okay that this hurts," Nan said, rubbing her hand in circles between my shoulder blades. "Anyone would be hurt by this. It's hurtful."

There was a photo of Nikki in ripped jeans painting my kitchen cabinets with chalkboard paint. In the next, she'd written *Love Lives Here* in swooping chalk letters on the pantry door.

"She's trying too hard," Nan said. "Insecurity on display."

I chugged wine.

A photo of every throw pillow I'd ever sewed piled in the middle of the living room, even the vintage Liberty of London prints I'd scavenged from my favorite antique store. *Bonfire at my place?*

Nikki draped over my favorite reading chair, pointing to the standing pendant lamp I'd always loved. *Does anyone want this ugly?*

I had taken pride in the way I'd decorated our home. The major choices were mostly Eric's. Eggshell walls. The notorious couch. Beige tile in the kitchen. All concessions on my part. But the warmth of our home came from my effort. I could justify spending money that way because I was thrifty and clever, and Eric, if he noticed the pillows or the yard sale chair I'd slipcovered, seemed impressed I'd created something. It made me feel like I was contributing. And there she was, mocking my work. Did Eric feel that way too? Had he been humoring me because he felt guilty? *Look at this woman with her ugly pillows! So stupid that she actually believes I had to work late.* Shame bubbled beneath my skin.

"They deserve each other," Nan said. "How can you ever be secure in a relationship you started with a married man?"

I knew there was truth in her words, but the result was the same to me. "I can't tell if this is making it better or worse," I said, forcing a laugh. It sounded hollow. "She's horrible. And now I miss my lamp."

"It's a beautiful lamp," Nan said, and I could tell she felt awkward too. She didn't know what to say, or how we were supposed to feel. There was no greeting card sentiment for this moment, but she was trying anyway.

I clicked to the next picture: Eric, fast asleep in our bed, under a comforter I didn't recognize.

"He has a very strange nose," Nan said, pouring more wine in my glass. "Like it belongs to someone else's face."

I laughed so hard I snorted.

We went through every single picture of Nikki. She was a cheerleader in high school. A sorority girl in college. She fell hard for skinny jeans and tall boots. Had a shag haircut three years ago and pulled it off. A face full of makeup and a pageant girl smile in every single photo. I did not want to be her. She was wired so differently from me that her existence looked exhausting. And I didn't want to be with someone who would choose her over me, but it felt strange to let go of my home and my husband and everything I'd thought my life was going to be.

"I want to see your page," Nan said when we'd finally reached the end of Nikki's.

I clicked over to my profile. Thankfully, I'd kept my name when I married Eric, so I was still an Ellis, like my father and Nan.

"You need a new picture!" Nan said, pointing to the photo of me and Eric at Niagara Falls last year. "Here!" She handed me her phone. "Take a selfie of us." It was funny to hear her say "selfie." It hadn't even been a word when I moved to Rochester.

She leaned toward Bark. I knelt in front of them and snapped the picture just as Bark licked my face. It was a little blurry. My eyes were closed, nose scrunched up. Our wine glasses caught glare from the overhead light. But I was smiling, and Nan was smiling. Even Bark looked happy.

I handed the phone to Nan. "We're so pretty!" she said, and scratched Bark's ears. "Yes, you're so pretty too, Barky." Bark licked her cheek. He'd warmed up to Nan more in a couple of days than he had to Eric in a whole year.

"So"—Nan pointed to my laptop—"how do we get this picture there?"

I was still signed in to Facebook on her phone, so I uploaded it directly, and then refreshed the page on my laptop so she could see us on the bigger screen.

"Amazing," Nan said in a hushed voice. "This is a lovely program." She clinked her wine glass to mine. "To new beginnings."

"New beginnings," I said.

"Nothing from Woo?" she asked.

"Not yet."

The disappointment on her face was clear.

"Her daughter might not check Facebook every day," I said.

Nan drank the rest of her wine in one gulp. "Maybe she doesn't remember me. It was a long time ago."

"I'm sure she remembers," I said, making a little wish in my head for a nice answer soon. "It's almost eleven. Maybe tomorrow."

"Way past my bedtime!" Nan stood up. "Are you okay?"

I nodded.

"You come get me if you're not." She kissed the top of my head.

"This helped, Nan," I said. "Really." And I did feel more steady. I wasn't only saying it to make her feel better.

Bark followed Nan down the hall to her room, and then came running back, tail wagging, like he was proud he'd led her to her destination safely.

Before I went to bed, I clicked on Luca's page. Three hours before, he'd posted a photo of a live oak tree draped with Spanish moss and ivy, blue sky in the space between the crooked branches. The silver moss, glowing in streaks of sunlight, had a sway like long hair caught in a breeze. No description. No location tag. But I could imagine Luca stopping in his tracks at the sight of that tree, standing for a moment in silence to absorb its beauty before he took the picture.

CHAPTER SIXTEEN

Luca slept in my bed a lot in college. It started the night we met. I saw him at a theatre party, leaning against the wall. He looked as overwhelmed as I felt. I leaned next to him. "Do you want pretzels?" I asked, holding out a red Solo cup I'd filled in the kitchen. It was a brave act for me. I wasn't usually so bold, but something about him felt safe.

"Sure," he said quietly, color coming to his cheeks as he grabbed a pretzel from the cup. Just one. Quick smile. The shy thing was surprising coming from someone like him. He was pretty. Heart-shaped face, even brow, a deep bow to his pink lips. The sparkle in his dark brown eyes was warm, pleading. A look that said, *Be careful with me*. I couldn't believe I was the only one swooning. I think maybe there's a bell curve to beautiful and people can't handle beauty too far past the arch.

We ate pretzels together, backs pressed to the wall, watching people. Some girl in a cape started dancing, and Luca nudged me gently, so we'd both be watching the same action. It reminded me of being a little kid at the playground, how another kid could show up and use your shovel in the sandbox, and suddenly you were playing together. I shared my snack, and now we were friends.

When we finished the pretzels, he took the cup from me and

went into the kitchen. "Someone spilled beer in the pretzel bag," he said when he came back with potato chips.

"Thanks," I said, flashing a smile. The top button of his gray Henley was loose, hanging on the thread. I wanted to fix it for him.

We resumed our leaning and watching, not talking, but not necessarily avoiding talking. It was more connection than I'd had through half a semester of chitchat and icebreakers. I worried it was an illusion of the night—the Brigadoon of feeling—and the next time I saw him, he'd ask me what my major was, and it would feel like every other human interaction.

As the party was winding down, he said, "Can I walk you home?" I said yes, and hoped he was asking because he didn't want the connection to end either.

When we got back to my dorm, after a long walk of shuffling feet and "Look at the moon!" and breathing hard into the cold air to see whose breath made more fog, I said, "Do you want to watch a movie?" Because my roommate was never home anyway. It was so late that most of the lights were off on my floor. I hated that feeling of being the last person awake. In my sleepy head, it always translated to being the last person alive, like the rapture happened and I was the only one left. By morning, it felt silly, but at night, the hollow dark left me panicked. It happened often. I fought sleep, then I was up too late and I couldn't keep the panic away. In comparison, inviting this boy I just met up to my room seemed sane. Smart, even. In case of the rapture, or any other disaster my mind could conjure, there'd be two of us.

We sat very still on the floor of my room and watched *Roman Holiday*. One of my favorites, and he'd never seen it. I stifled yawns. I didn't want to give him an excuse to leave. And then it was so late it was almost morning, and I was certain we were the last people awake in my dorm.

"You could stay," I said, which didn't feel bold. It felt comfortable to suggest to this boy I'd just met and had barely talked to. He was already important to me.

We cuddled in my bed. He rested his head in the crook of my neck, and I almost cried. It felt like breathing after holding my breath for too long. I slept soundly for the first time since my father died.

After that, lying in bed, holding each other, was just a thing we did. Night after night, until he felt like another limb.

CHAPTER SEVENTEEN

The next afternoon, Nan was out with Bitsie, and I was lying on the couch with Bark watching HGTV when Mo walked in unannounced and flopped down next to us. She was so blasé about it that Bark didn't even bother to howl. He watched her intently across my lap.

"I like this show," Mo said, and that was it for two episodes. We watched people hunt for houses the way we used to be cartoon zombies after school, and the normalcy of having her in my space felt like a craving fulfilled. I'd forgotten that Mo cracked her ankles compulsively, but my elbow headed to her ribs every time she did it. And like well-rehearsed choreography, Mo elbowed back, shooting me a narrowed glance that made me think of her at eleven years old, with a Ramona Quimby haircut and scraped-up knees.

The couple on the second episode chose the wrong house. The one they should have picked was cosmetically challenged but had a nicer yard. Mo clapped her hand to her forehead. "That's not the way I'd go," she said, shaking her head in disbelief as the closing credits rolled. "Does Nan have beer?"

She didn't wait for an answer. She got up and went into the kitchen, coming back with two bottles. We sat on the front step to drink them. Bark stayed inside. I could hear him whining behind the door for a moment, but then the scratch of his nails on the tile faded away. He probably went to find Murray and take a nap on the bed.

"I think we need a thing," I said, because I wanted to hold myself accountable to spending time with her. I didn't want our friendship to wither again if she got too busy or I got too sad.

"A thing?" Mo picked at the label on her beer, curling the corner away from the bottle.

"I don't know. Like something we do together on a regular basis. A tradition."

"Like happy hour?"

I knew making a habit of drinking with Mo wouldn't do good things for me. "More like a craft. Or class. Karate, maybe?"

Mo laughed, and I was certain she was picturing me attempting a side kick. "Marta teaches stained glass on Tuesday nights at the senior center," she said.

"We're not seniors."

"Marta doesn't care! I've gone a few times, it's kind of cool, but I'm so used to working with metal. I broke a lot of glass." She gulped her beer. "You could come over. I could teach you how to weld."

"Welding?" I picked at the label on my beer bottle.

"Sure, why not?" Mo burped and then shook her head like she was trying to escape it. "I could use help. And you're careful. Careful is good." She set her empty bottle next to the step and stood, wiping her hand on her jeans.

"Now?" I asked. I'd mostly been talking in hypothetical terms. I wanted to feel like I was searching for purpose—in small installments—and then go back to lying on the couch.

"Bring Bark."

"I don't know. It's noisy, right?"

"He'll be okay," Mo said. "We won't do anything too crazy."

I picked up Mo's bottle and went inside to leave a note for Nan. Bark ran to me, tail wagging. I hoped he'd magically act like a normal dog and we'd go to Mo's house and have a good night and everything would be fine. But when I tried to clip his leash to his collar, he sprinted back to my room to hide under the bed.

"Hey, Barky," I called, following. "Come here!"

He backed out, tail curled to his belly, ears flat.

"Oh, buddy! It'll be okay."

He let me clip the leash on this time, but he lagged behind as we walked down the hall.

I opened the front door. He took one look at Mo and froze.

"You just saw her," I said. But to Bark, outside-the-house Mo was a totally different person from inside-the-house Mo. I kept walking, but he stood perfectly still, staring. I gave his leash a tug. He let out a frustrated whine that almost sounded like *I can't!*

"Hey, Bark," Mo said in a soft, high voice. His ears perked. "We're buddies, remember?" She leaned forward to pet him, but he cowered. "Okay. I get it. I know. It's hard." She sat on the step with her back to Bark and put one hand as far behind her as it would reach. Bark stretched his neck to smell the air and then inched slowly toward her.

"Good boy," I whispered.

He gave her hand a quick sniff, then recoiled like she might attack.

Mo sat perfectly still, back straight.

Bark sniffed her arm again and then licked it.

Mo shrugged her shoulders ever so slightly. "Aw, did I get a kiss?"

Bark stepped away, then tried again. This time, he sat next to Mo, staring at her. Mo turned her head toward him slowly. When she looked at Bark, he looked away. When she looked away, he turned to watch her. But then a motorcycle roared down the street, exhaust popping as it passed. Bark skittered into the house, pulling the leash from my hand, running down the hall and out of sight.

"Poor pup!" Mo said. "Should we make sure he's alright and go on our own?"

I nodded, relieved she understood.

"Baby steps," she said. "We'll keep trying."

"Something always happens, right when he's making progress. And he's so—I know you can't tell, but he's sweet. It's sad when he can't show it."

"I can tell," Mo said. "He wears his heart on his face."

We brought Bark some treats. He even took one from Mo, gingerly, with his teeth instead of his tongue. He backed away and jumped on the bed to eat it, watching her, like maybe there'd been a mistake and she might want it back.

"Okay, Barky," I said, scratching behind his ears. "We won't be gone long." He looked up, mid-chew, eyes sad. I kissed his forehead and we left before I could decide I didn't want to leave the house either.

We walked to Mo's. Her grandfather's wood-sided Roadmaster wagon was parked in the driveway, next to her grandmother's beige Cutlass, and it felt like Gran and Pops could be in the house, doing a crossword together at the kitchen table. I wondered if Mo ever drove those cars, or if she didn't even notice them anymore, the same way it's easy to stop seeing a Christmas tree in the living room once you've made it to mid-January. Things ignored become part of the landscape so quickly.

Mo's white 1976 Beetle was at the curb. In high school, she taught herself to rebuild the engine from a library book.

Mo punched the code into the garage keypad. "It's F-U-C-K," she said as we waited for the door to rise. "If you ever need to get in."

I laughed.

"I kept forgetting the last code. But you don't forget 'fuck.'"

"True."

Wedged diagonally across the two-car garage was the puzzle-piece vertebrae of a creature waiting to come to life. Two pieces of rebar attached it to a pedestal surrounded by strips of metal stretched and twisted like kelp.

"He's going to be a manatee," Mo said, running her hand along the arching spine. "I'll wrap strands of metal around him so it will look like he's made from a huge wad of twine."

I nodded, even though I couldn't quite picture it. "Like this one," she said, shoving a postcard in my hand. It was a shark, formed from bands of metal swirled around a frame. Abstract and alive. Mo's car was in the picture, for scale. It looked like a windup toy.

"You can keep that," she said, pointing to the postcard. "I had a ton printed up." She shoved her hands in her pockets. "The manatee won't be as big. I wanted to make the foundation at home. It's hard to work in another space. By the time I'm done lifeguarding, it's dark, and all the warehouses are in crappy parts of town. I'm a wuss about that."

It surprised me. I'd always seen Mo as fearless.

"Are you going to run out of room?" I asked.

"I should have made him a little smaller. But I might be able to work in the driveway if the neighbors don't complain. I have to be careful I don't sacrifice the form because my shop is too small. It's easy to make choices that make things convenient."

"So, how can I help?" I asked, avoiding a greater philosophical discussion. Seeing Mo's work made me even more embarrassed by how little I had to show for myself.

"How dirty do you want to get?"

I looked at my worn jeans and a t-shirt from a nightmare production of *Dames at Sea*. "As dirty as necessary."

Mo got us beers from Pop's mini fridge, prying the tops off with a nail half-hammered in the wall. "Here," she said, handing me one.

She showed me pictures of manatees in motion and several angles of skeletons. "See how their ribs are shaped? Like, they get wider and then thinner, there's almost a twist here," she said, pointing. She gave me a sheepish smile. "I know most people won't look between the cracks to see inside, but it matters to me."

"I get it," I said. It's the way I used to feel about my own work. Even the details that couldn't be easily seen added up to something greater. It's why, back in school, I stitched silver stars into Ophelia's dress for *Hamlet*, and learned to tat lace to make Queen Elizabeth's collar for *Mary Stuart* more authentic.

Mo reached toward the back of her workbench, threw me a pair of yellow suede gloves, and pointed to her grandfather's old work boots on the floor. "Those will be big, but you can't wear flip-flops. You'll lose a toe."

I stepped into them, barefoot, trying not to think about it too much.

"I want to keep the patina on the ribs." She pointed to a stack of rusty rebar, cut to size, numbered with grease pencil. "If you can lay them out in order, I'll get the gear together."

I organized rebar while Mo pushed a large piece of curved steel to the driveway on a dolly. She set up shop lamps, and then wheeled an oxyacetylene torch outside.

We worked well into the night, listening to Pop's Johnny Cash records crackling on the old Philco player. Mo used the torch to heat rebar and we bent each piece around the mold. Then she heated the ends and we pounded the metal with mallets to form the strange paddle shape of manatee ribs. The rebar was heavy. Rust streaked my arms, sweat dripped in my eyes, but there was satisfaction in changing the shape of steel. We got through twelve ribs before we took a break for dinner.

Mo mixed Easy Mac in mismatched bowls of questionable cleanliness, cooking them in an ancient microwave at the end of Pop's workbench. While we waited for the beep, I stepped back to peek under the bench.

"It's still there," Mo said, grinning. "Go ahead."

I got down on my hands and knees, crawled under the bench, and pushed the wood pallet door out of the way. The opening through the cinder block was smaller than I remembered and made me feel a little claustrophobic, but I climbed through anyway. Felt around for the switch. The lone bare bulb still worked. I wondered if Mo had replaced it.

During the Cold War, Pop built a false wall in the garage to make a bomb shelter behind it. He never got around to making an actual door, and it wasn't underground. I think he built it more because he could than because he thought it would save his family from a Cuban missile, but when we were kids, Mo and I honestly believed it was the safest place in the world. Inside there were two army-issue cots and a few rolled-up sleeping mats. Expired cans of corn and peaches older than me and Mo were lined up neatly on the shelves, covered in dust. Crank radio. Bucket latrine. Two steel drums labeled DRINKING WATER that Mo and I would sit on, pretending they were bar stools at a saloon when we played Wild West.

The air was stale and damp, and the smell of it made me think of my Powerpuff sleeping bag, and the times Mo and I camped out in our secret fortress.

"Want to eat in there?" Mo called from the outside.

"Yeah." I pushed on the cot to hear the canvas squeak against the frame, like it had when Mo tossed and turned in her sleep. I loved that sound because it meant she was right there, arm's length away, if I needed her.

Mo passed the bowls of mac and cheese to me through the door before she crawled in. "Man, I haven't been in here in ages," she said when she stood, taking up so much more space than she used to.

We sat on the water drums to eat. Our feet touched the ground now. I was hungry enough to convince myself the microwave heat killed anything gross on the dishes. We ate fast, without talking. When we'd finished our food, Mo pulled one of the manatee skeleton pictures from her pocket to show me how much we'd done.

"Most of the ribs have a similar angle, but we'll need to bend the last few by hand. Maybe adjust these. Then we can attach them all." She yawned and blinked. "Maybe we should stop here, before we get overtired."

I yawned too.

"I hope you didn't hate this," Mo said, eyebrows raised, like she was worried.

"Are you kidding?" I asked. Her face fell. "No! I mean are you kidding in the good way. I had so much fun."

"Really?" Mo said. "Because it was great to have your help. And just . . . you."

She put her arm around my shoulder and gave me a sideways hug.

"Whooo!" She fanned her hand in front of her face as she pulled away. "Is that you or me?"

We both sniffed our pits. "Me," I said at the same time as she said, "Totally me."

I laughed.

"Hysterical!"

When we crawled back into the garage, Mo helped me up and slapped me on the back. "Hit the showers, Ellis!"

I stepped out of Pop's boots and back into my flip-flops. "You too, Jacobs," I said.

Mo wrinkled her nose. "You can't pull that off. The sports thing? No."

"Shut up," I said, laughing as I walked away. "I know it."

"Careful walking home."

"Don't trip walking up the driveway."

"Shut up," she said, pretending to trip.

"Love you, Mo," I called over my shoulder, like we used to when we were kids.

"Love you, Kay!" she shouted back.

CHAPTER EIGHTEEN

Bark ran too fast to greet me and slid across the tile floor into my legs. He righted himself and jumped on me.

"Buddy! Look at you go!" I said, surprised the loss of traction hadn't left him terrified. I bent to kiss his head and he licked my chin. He smelled like clean laundry.

"Where's Nan?" I dropped my voice to a whisper. "Shoot, is she sleeping?"

Bark pushed his head into my hand for an ear scratch. I listened for signs of Nan. No TV chatter in her bedroom. The lights were off in the living room, and in the kitchen only the light over the stove was on. I found a note taped to the fridge: *Back later, leftovers. XO*

In the fridge, another note, taped to a CorningWare dish, said, *Eat me.*

Polenta. And more asparagus. I was tired of my pee smelling weird, but after hauling all that rebar, Mo's mac and cheese wasn't cutting it. I heated the food in the microwave and got Bark's dinner ready.

Bark hopped behind me as I carried both dishes to my room. He was chowing down before I even got the bowl to the floor. No need to sit next to him. "Are you hungry, Barky?" I asked, but he was too busy eating to pay me any mind. I sat at my desk and opened my laptop, shoveling food in my face while I waited for my portfolio pictures from college to load.

In the time I'd spent working for Edith at the theatre in Rochester, I'd stopped believing in myself. Whenever she told me my designs wouldn't work it felt like jealous bullshit, but I couldn't bring myself to challenge her. She was a staple of the community. Everyone in Rochester knew Edith. No one knew Edith's second-in-command. It didn't matter that her work was stale, that she didn't care about historical accuracy or craftsmanship. She'd reuse dresses with 1890s puffy gigot sleeves for a 1940s play, instead of putting an hour or two into alterations. Those things didn't matter to her, but costuming is completely in the details. I always wanted to work for a better end, but Edith didn't, and eventually, I started seeing limitations instead of possibilities. Every time I dredged up my feelings of defiance, she'd knock me down. It was easier to lose faith in my own work than carry the anger. If I believed I wasn't very good I didn't have to think about all the ways I'd cheated myself.

I opened the first set of my old portfolio photos. Titania's costume for *A Midsummer Night's Dream* looked like it was made of moonlight, the bodice wrapped in gunmetal blue silk ribbons trailing in uneven lengths over a skirt I'd sculpted from layers of icy organza on top of deep indigo shantung. The top fabric was pulled close in places, gathered in others, so the dress had an amorphous, magical feel. I stared at the photos of the actress in final dress rehearsal and felt awe for my work, like it came from a different version of me. That designer was brilliant. I'd let her down.

In theory a person could work at the Metropolitan Opera and have a family, but the elements of reality didn't click together for me that way. I chose Eric and his steady job in Rochester and our house with the nice big yard for kids to play in, on a tree-lined street in a good school district. I chose wrong. Eric wasn't worth the compromises. We didn't get to have those kids. And now, when I thought of moving to New York City and starting over, fighting for an apprenticeship, sharing a studio apartment with a Craigslist roommate, it made me tired. I couldn't go back to being someone who was full of hope and low on expectations. My last bit of durability had worn away. In the absence of a family, in the absence of a big dream, I had no idea what to do with myself. I used to have promise, and I squandered it.

I clicked on a picture of Titania with Oberon. I'd woven fresh bay laurel leaves into his crown before every show, and his moss-covered vest was actually alive.

"Hey, Kay," Nan called, walking down the hall to my room. Bark woke from a solid snooze and yelped. We hadn't heard Nan's car pull into the garage. "You got dinner?"

"Yeah, thank you," I said, shame twisting like I'd been caught doing something perverse.

"What happened to you?" she said, and I almost spewed all of my feelings about who I could have been, where I'd lost the narrative, but then she wrinkled her nose and I remembered how grimy I was.

"I helped Mo with her manatee."

"That's good," she said in a clipped voice, like she was trying not to let her excitement spill out. "To do art. That's a nice thing."

"Mo's art," I said. "But, yeah, it was fun."

"You'll shower before you go to bed?" she said, like I was still a little kid in need of nudging.

"Yeah, Nan," I said, trying to keep my tone in check.

She licked her finger and wiped at a spot on my cheek.

"I'm going to clean up," I said. "Promise. I got sidetracked."

Nan looked at my computer screen and pointed to Titania.

"I'm so happy I flew in for that show. When that actress walked on stage in your dress, the whole audience gasped."

I tried to settle the swirl of pride and disappointment into something I could manage.

"You are so full of talent," Nan said. Present tense. Like it still existed. She ruffled my hair and then looked at her hand, covered with rust.

"Shower!" she said.

I marched to the bathroom to clean up before she could complain again.

Under the stream of hot water, my mind wandered to mermaids. High-waisted tails with sequins and barnacles, 1950s tops studded with fake pearls. Pinup girl spirit ripened to something stronger.

I raced from the shower, suds in my hair. There was an old notebook and a few colored pencils in the top drawer of my desk. I sat there in my wet towel and sketched until the mermaids on the page looked like the ones in my head.

Before I went to bed, I signed in to Facebook. Quickly, so I wouldn't lose my nerve, I hit the message button on Luca's profile.

Hi, I wrote, and hit enter, sending before I meant to. I scrambled to figure out if I could delete it, but then Facebook told me my message had been read. I waited for a response, staring at the screen until I was too cold to stay in my wet towel. I closed my laptop and went to bed, dozing and waking over and over. At three a.m., I finally caved and checked Facebook on my phone. No message.

CHAPTER NINETEEN

"So where are you headed all dressed up?" Nan asked, catching me in the foyer before I left for work the next morning.

I was wearing a simple linen shift dress I'd made from Bunny's fabric. I'd pulled my hair into a neat low knot and brushed mascara on my lashes. No lipstick. Lipstick around fabric, especially wedding dress fabric, was asking for trouble.

"I got my old job back," I said. "At Isaac's." I knew it was ridiculous that I hadn't told Nan, but when I'd thought about telling her, the texture of the conversation I imagined we'd have grated against my nerves. She'd say it was nice, or she'd say it was unnecessary, and under all of it, I would see her worries about me.

"I know." Nan grinned.

"Then why'd you ask where I was going?"

"I wanted to see if *you'd* tell me." She leaned against the wall and folded her arms across her chest, pleased with herself.

"You're worse than Mo!"

"She learned that trick from me," Nan said.

"How'd you even find out?" Isaac was not a hub of gossip, and I hadn't told anyone else.

"I ran into Isaac at Publix."

"And pried it out of him?"

"Something like that."

"I wanted to be productive," I said, steeling myself for Nan's response.

But she said, "Isaac is relieved to have you back." She reached out to smooth a hair behind my ear. "It will be good for both of you, I think. It's fortifying to be around kindness."

"Thank you," I said, relieved she approved.

"You look great. Did you make that?"

I nodded.

"Such a gift," she said.

I kissed her on the cheek, gave Bark a good scratch, and hurried off to work.

Isaac had cookies and a cup of Earl Grey waiting for me. "Happy first day," he said, smiling.

I leaned in to give him a one-armed hug, and we both blushed. We sat behind the counter together.

"Have you been busy?" I asked.

Isaac nodded. We sipped our tea.

After a long silence, he said, "I had a young man who helped me for a while. Oh, he is a funny boy!" Isaac's face fought a devilish smile. "He likes rap music. And I got to like some of it, if you can believe. That Macklemore fellow seems like a good kid."

I tried not to laugh.

"Have you heard Macklemore?" Isaac asked.

"I have," I said, trying to picture some kid taking over Isaac's sound system, swapping out Bing Crosby for YouTube videos.

"That one about the thrift store is clever," Isaac said, smiling. "But Artemis left for college last year. And I haven't—I didn't want to get a new kid's hopes up with a job if I couldn't stick around." He flexed his fingers. They didn't straighten all the way anymore. "I don't want to get your hopes up either, of course, but it's different. You could do all of this without me."

I saw my own sadness reflected in his face. Except for Mo, the people I loved were so much older, and sometimes that was excruciating. I knew from my father that youth did not provide guarantees, but old age did. Isaac, Nan, Bitsie, and all their friends weren't going to get younger. Neither was I.

"Artemis will be home for spring break, I think," Isaac said. "I hope you'll get to meet him."

"Me too. If you like him, I'm sure I will."

The bridal party showed up twenty minutes later in a flurry of up-talking and selfies.

"It's so old-school in here," one of the bridesmaids cooed, taking a photo of the giant copper scissors on the wall behind the register.

The scissors weren't old. Mo made them for Isaac when we were in high school. It was her first commissioned work. Isaac paid her two hundred dollars plus materials and had a party for the big reveal.

"Don't you love it?" Marissa, the bride, said. "I love it."

Isaac's face flushed. He gave me a conspiratorial look, eyebrows low, already overwhelmed.

"Wow," I said, smiling wide. "There sure are a lot of you! So here's the plan. Let's get your fitting done first, Marissa. There's a wonderful bakery next door, if you ladies would like to grab a snack."

The tall bridesmaid pulled out her phone. "It's only a three on Yelp," she said, sighing, and all nine of them followed us behind the curtain, filling the fitting room with noise and body heat. Isaac looked like he wanted to hide under one of the sewing tables.

"Brittany!" Marissa called from the changing room. The shortest of them jumped to attention and pushed through the curtains. "No!" Marissa shouted. "Other Brittany!"

The redhead got up and made her way over. There was some breathy discussion, and then both Brittanys came out of the dressing room giggling.

When I helped the bride step up on the tailor stand, her breath reeked of whiskey. As Isaac began pinning the dress, I ran next door and bought two dozen madeleines for the wedding party to soak up some of the booze. I'd find a clever way to add the cost to the bill.

After they left, Isaac and I split a pizza, eating on the back step to keep the grease away from the clothes. It felt like living in a memory. Evening closing in on the streetlights, air thick with the clean malt scent of dinner rolls in the oven at the bakery next door. Isaac's perfect posture and the monogrammed handkerchief spread across his lap like a napkin. Being home now that Bunny was gone made me want to memorize everything so I could keep this meal with Isaac, and all the ones before it, forever vibrant in my mind.

"I forgot!" Isaac said after finishing his first slice. He went inside and came back with a bottle of cabernet and two coffee mugs. "To celebrate!"

He handed me the mugs and pulled a corkscrew from his jacket pocket. The cork didn't give easily. His hands shook.

"Here," I said, resting the mugs on the step next to me. I took the bottle and pulled the cork, handing the bottle back so he could do us the honor of pouring.

Then he clinked his mug to mine. "Welcome home."

"Thank you," I said, taking a sip. It was good wine. An old bottle. Something he'd been saving.

"Was it hard for you today?" he asked. "Wedding work?"

"It was actually fine." I liked that his question would have made it safe for me to admit if it hadn't been. "Even with all the chaos, those girls were sweet. Excited. That's a nice thing, isn't it?"

Isaac nodded. "That is nice."

"Maybe I can be sad for me, and happy love is out there. Right?"

"I think that's true," Isaac said, drawing his bushy white brows together as he considered it.

"Do you have a hard time doing wedding work?" I asked.

"I did," he said, taking another slice of pizza from the box.

"After Freda died?"

"Before." Isaac took a deep breath. "Freda and I were not very happy."

"I'm so sorry," I said, feeling bad that I didn't have the skill to ask questions as kindly as Isaac did.

But he didn't seem to mind. He talked like he was happy to free the memories. "We married because it made sense. Her father knew my father. She did well in school and so did I. It was a suitable match, and that was the most we believed we should want. But she always felt a little like a stranger. We were on the same ship, but we wanted to steer it in different directions." He paused like he needed to collect more words. "Sometimes, when a groom came in to get his wedding suit fitted, he'd have this way about him. This joy. It was hard to see that and then go home to feel out of place."

I didn't know what to say. I took a sip of wine and kept my eyes on Isaac. I wanted him to feel comfortable telling me.

He looked at me carefully. "We get second chances," he said.

"Do you think there's such a thing as real love?" I asked, buoyed by the wine, but also because I wanted to know what he thought. "Not true love like a fairy tale. But real, like you belong?"

Isaac nodded. "I wish I'd looked for it sooner."

"It's not too late," I said. "You're a good catch."

Isaac smiled and took a sip of his wine. "This is a good bottle," he said, and I felt foolish for talking so deep.

"It is good. Thank you."

"Keep trying," Isaac said, giving me a look so hopeful, I found myself fighting tears. "For belonging."

I nodded.

"Don't tell your grandmother about the pizza. She'd kill me for feeding you cheese."

I touched my hand to my heart and held it up. "I won't. Swear."

"I don't eat like this anymore," he said. "But I got nostalgic. Like old times, huh?"

His white hair glowed gold in the parking lot lights. Chipped coffee mugs. His impeccably polished shoes. Grease stains on the pizza box. I would remember everything.

"Yes," I said. "It is."

CHAPTER TWENTY

After dinner, Isaac dropped me at Nan's. I could have used the walk home, but he insisted.

"Dinner's almost ready," Nan called from the kitchen when I walked in the door.

Bark ran to greet me, holding a stuffed elephant in his mouth. He threw it in the air, pouncing as it hit the ground. I hoped he hadn't co-opted a toy that Marta's granddaughter left behind.

"Is Bark supposed to have this?" I asked, walking into the kitchen. Bark followed with the elephant.

"I bought it for him," Nan said. "So I could wash that blue thing."

"Murray," I said.

"Murray smells like old socks." Nan pulled a tray of potato wedges from the oven. "I felt bad taking it away without giving him something else to play with."

"You don't have to buy him toys," I said.

Bark shook his head, elephant still clutched in his teeth, like he was trying to knock it senseless.

"I wanted to," Nan said. "Look how happy he is!"

"Thank you. That was really nice of you."

"Hungry?"

"I ate already."

"You know," Nan said with a sigh, "you could tell me when you're not going to eat dinner at home."

"I'm sorry." My cheeks flushed. I'd said the exact same thing to Eric in the exact same tone a zillion times over. "Isaac ordered food, and I—"

"Oh." Nan softened. "That's nice. He's such a kind man."

"He is."

"What did he order?" she asked, sprinkling nutritional yeast seasoning over the potatoes.

"Salads," I said. "They were good." And then I went to my room to check Facebook before Nan could ask any more questions.

No messages from Luca or Woo Woo.

In a fit of self-destruction, I checked Nikki's page. She was ruining my hardwood floors. I'd spent weeks liberating the living room from yellow shag and overzealous carpet tacking, sanding every inch with a small orbit sander, because I was afraid of renting a full-sized one. I stained and sealed the wood with all the windows open in forty-degree weather. And Nikki was using wall paint to apply a black chevron pattern over my pristine finish. She hadn't even sanded down the gloss. The paint feathered under the tape like lipstick on a smoker. Her lines were crooked and they would peel and scratch in no time. But there she was, red handkerchief tied in her hair, smiling at the camera Eric must have been holding.

My new project!

And all her friends were cheering her on in the comments.

Yur so crafty! And *Come do my floors when ur done!*

Nikki wasn't going to cry about imperfection or obsess over what she could have done better. She exuded a level of pride over her job done poorly that I didn't allow myself for even my most careful work. I'd never been more jealous of a person in my entire life, and it wasn't because she stole my husband, it was because I wished I could let go like she could.

A message alert appeared on the screen. My heart jumped with good nerves. Luca! I held my breath and clicked.

It was from Lorna Griggs.

Hi, Katie! My mother was thrilled to hear from you and your grandmother. Thank you for tracking us down. I'm passing along her message:

Dear Nannette,

How wonderful to hear from you, old friend! I saw the picture of you and your granddaughter and it made my heart swell. She looks so much like you did back when we swam together. I am happy that more of your spirit is in the world.

I'm doing quite well. I live near Lorna. She's my oldest of three daughters. I have two grandsons, four granddaughters, and a great-granddaughter. Hank longed for a boy and then relished having girls. Each one had a special hold over him.

Hank passed away five years ago. The day after Christmas. It's hard to get left behind, isn't it? I feel like I'm supposed to say polite things about the weather and my new home, but you were my best friend and we never made small talk, so I want you to know that I miss you. It hurts to lose Hank and feel unmoored. I want to talk to you about the grace and pain and beauty of age. I want to know what happened to your son, and to tell you that all my sympathy is yours. When I taught my grandchildren how to swim, I told them about you and Bitsie and our adventures underwater. You are a character to them, like Alice in Wonderland, and I hope maybe now they will get to meet you. Please

send Bitsie my love. I'm jealous that you live right down the street
from each other. Let's not fall out of touch again. I never stopped
thinking of things I wanted to tell you.
Love,
Woo Woo

Tears stung my eyes. I wished I'd grown up imagining Woo
Woo as a character in a magical tale and that Nan had felt free
to keep the memory of this great friendship part of her everyday
life. I knew why Nan never talked about it, why she seemed so
against Bitsie's calendar idea: we tried not to talk about water.
But I didn't want her to lose any more history because of me.

I heard Nan chatting on the phone in the kitchen, so I copied
the message and texted it to her.

Then, even though he hadn't written back, I wrote to Luca
again: *Hey, if you were going to take pictures in a swimming pool*
and needed high-res images, what kind of camera would you use?

I hit enter as a reflex and my words were sent. My heart
fluttered. I should have at least asked how he was. Told him I
loved his documentary, and that I missed sitting on the floor of
my dorm room with him, splitting a Buffalo chicken calzone,
watching *Saturday Night Live*, while all the cool kids were out
at parties.

I quickly wrote, *Hope all is well with you.*

And then accidentally hit enter.

Maybe we can catch up soon.

Enter. Damn!

Katie.

I stared at the screen feeling a flush of awkwardness, hoping
kind words about being happy to hear from me would appear
under mine.

Nothing happened.

"Kay!" Nan rushed in, eyes filled with tears. "Did you read it?"
I nodded.

"Can we write back right now?"

After we'd sent Woo Woo an epically long reply, I opened my sketchbook to the mermaid drawings and handed it to Nan.

"Goodness, Kay," she said, flipping the pages. "These are beautiful!" She held her hand over her mouth, eyes welling up. "This one even looks like Bitsie!"

"What if we did the calendar?" I asked, ignoring the uncomfortable clench of my heart.

"Oh, I don't think so," Nan said, but I could see the wanting in her eyes. "It sounds like an awful lot of work, and I wouldn't—"

"I can handle it. Costuming shows for the theatre was way more work than this."

"It's not just the work—"

"I could even make a costume for Woo Woo, and we could find a photographer in Atlanta to take her picture." I took a deep breath. "What if we tried to find the other mermaids?"

Nan squeezed my arm. "Are you really sure?"

"I am," I said, giving her my most convincing smile. "I want to."

"Okay. Okay." She pointed at my computer. "Audrey Mitchell."

I typed the name into Facebook. "That might be a hard one," I said. "Mitchell is such a common—" Audrey Mitchell McClintock popped up on the screen. She had her own profile.

"She always was quick to the uptake," Nan said, leaning forward to get a better view. "Look at her! She's beautiful!"

Audrey had snow white hair in a long side braid, and a purple silk scarf tied around her neck. She smiled at the camera like she knew her angles. Her eyes were kind. She lived in Chicago. Her husband was still alive. Both retired. Lots of travel pictures. Lots of children.

"They have a nice life, don't they?" Nan said, and I wondered if she wished for more than she had; a partner to adventure with, a herd of children, grandchildren, and great-grandchildren to fill a farm table. But there was no hint of envy in the message she dictated for Audrey, and I hoped that maybe envy was a thing to outgrow, like baby teeth and menstruation.

"Okay," Nan said when we sent off that message. "Hannah Whitfield."

I couldn't find anyone named Hannah Whitfield who was even close to the right age. "The name Hannah got popular again," I told Nan.

"Funny how these things come back in fashion—Wait!" She grabbed my arm. "Novak! She married a man named Novak. She sent me the wedding invitation, but it was in California, and Gramps didn't want to go."

I couldn't find a Hannah Novak on Facebook, but when I Googled, her husband's website came up. Patrick Novak was a senator from Baltimore.

"Oh my goodness." Nan pointed at the screen. There was a picture of Hannah standing next to Barbara Bush. We couldn't find recent photos, but there was a glut from twenty years ago. Hannah and her husband had met everyone from Mick Jagger to Stephen Hawking.

"I can't find an email address for her," I said. "But I can write to his office, and see if someone will get us in touch."

"Oh, no," Nan said, smiling. "I think maybe—she'd think it was silly. Let's not bother her."

"Are you sure?"

"Completely," she said, but there was sadness in her voice. Maybe it was hard to see someone you knew go so far beyond your own experience. Maybe she worried she hadn't meant as much to Hannah as Hannah meant to her. "I'm going to go read Woo Woo's email again." She kissed my head and left. Bark followed. Nan had started carrying treats in her pocket.

I emailed Hannah's husband's office anyway. I didn't say anything about mermaids, just that I was the granddaughter of an old friend who would love to be in touch.

Mo never used her Facebook account. She had a blurry profile picture and a post from 2008 that said, *Alright, guys, I'm here!* No other posts.

I climbed into bed with my phone and sent her a text instead: *You're a wonderful friend. Thank you.*

A few minutes later, she wrote back: *Are you dying? :)*

Of sarcasm.

You're the best friend I've ever had, she wrote. *I'm happy you're home.*

I sent her a heart symbol. She sent me an alien head.

Jogging tomorrow? she asked.

Yes, but not with you.

Ha! Then: *Sleep tight.*

I sent her a moon.

She sent me a poop.

CHAPTER TWENTY-ONE

〜〜〜〜〜〜〜

Isaac and I had a full morning. A man came in with an armload of his father's suits to be tailored for himself. He kept his head down, weepy, as he explained that his father had recently passed away.

Isaac asked me to do the fitting. "It's hard for men to cry in front of other men," he whispered. I kept my voice sweet and my words sparse, handing our customer tissues before he had to ask. Isaac took the first suit as soon as I finished marking it, and got to work immediately, so the suit was done before I even finished fitting the rest.

"I thought it would be too sad," Isaac said after the man left, "to walk in with his father's clothes and walk out with nothing."

Nan was right. It was good to be around Isaac's kindness. Eric always complained that I was too thin-skinned, but Isaac made me feel like sensitivity could be a strength.

When I checked my phone at noon, I had three texts from Mo.

Help me with Morty tonight?

The manatee. I call him Morty.

I'll feed you.

I called Nan while I walked to the deli to grab sandwiches for me and Isaac.

"I'm working at Mo's tonight. I'll have dinner there."

"Thank you for letting me know," Nan said, trying her best to sound breezy.

"Say it."

"What?" she asked with fake innocence.

"Say it."

"See, was that so hard?" she said in a whoosh of air and words.

"Unbearably exhausting."

Nan laughed.

"If only I could . . . Find. The. Strength. To go on. Maybe you should bring me dinner."

"Goodness, you're just like your father!" Nan said, her laugh winding to a beautiful sigh.

Part of me hated that my father was on my mind when he hadn't been, but I loved that she thought I was like him. From her it was a compliment.

"Tell Maureen I want to come see the manatee one of these days."

"Stop by tonight," I said.

"Not tonight. I have to go out."

"So you weren't going to make dinner anyway?"

Nan laughed again. "Nope."

After work, I stopped home to change. Nan was already gone. Bark didn't greet me at the door.

"Bark?" I called, waiting for the scratch of his nails against the tile. Silence. I ran down the hall, picturing Bark lying dead on the floor in my room. He wasn't there. He wasn't in Nan's room, where he could have eaten hand lotion and choked on his own vomit, or the laundry room where he could have knocked the ironing board over on himself, the living room where he might be tangled in the curtains, or the garage, where he could lick dripping motor oil.

I ran to the patio and stood at the edge of the pool, carefully scanning from one end to the other and back again, slowly, because sometimes things look warped underwater, and I needed to make absolutely sure he wasn't there.

Had he gotten out? I ran through the house again, screaming, "Bark! Bark!" Fear tight in my throat. I could barely breathe. I threw open the front door to look for him outside, and there he was, on a leash I didn't recognize. Althea held the other end. She'd been about to open the door. Shocked to see me.

"Where was he?" I asked, my voice strained. "I don't know how he got out!"

"I'm sorry, Katie," Althea said. "I assumed Nan told you I was coming to walk Bark."

"Nobody told me! He was just gone!" I sobbed.

"I'm going to run Bark to your room so he doesn't get upset," she said, scooting past me, Bark gladly following.

My brain was still racing through every scenario that could lead to Bark's death. I pictured him limp, spirit gone, no way to get him back, and my body reacted as if it were true. That heartbeat again. So loud. Blood electric under my skin. All of me boiling, about to burst.

"How could you do that?" I screamed when Althea came back. "How could you take him?"

She didn't even flinch. "I'm so sorry, Kay," she said slowly, softly. "I thought you knew."

"I thought he was gone. I thought—" I was gasping for air. My heart felt dangerous. "How could you take him?"

"Alright, Katie," Althea said. "Why don't you sit on the floor. Right where you are. Okay?"

"I don't want to sit!" I said, pacing. My skin felt wrong. Like it was too tight on my body. Too many nerves at the surface.

"Do you want me to help you calm down?"

"I want you to not take my dog!" I knew I was behaving horribly, and I couldn't stop. I couldn't stop moving. My heart, my heart, too loud in my ears. Muscles twitching. I didn't want her to watch me. "Please go!"

"I don't want to leave you, Kaitlyn."

"Go," I said, crying hard, covering my face like it would somehow be less embarrassing if she couldn't see my tears anymore.

"Do you want me to call Nan?"

I shook my head. "Just go."

After she left, I ran to my room. Bark jumped off the bed to greet me, whining until I got down to face level with him. He licked the tears from my chin frantically.

"I'm sorry, I'm sorry, I'm sorry," I said. I wished that Althea could hear my apology too.

CHAPTER TWENTY-TWO

〜〜〜〜〜〜〜

Mo showed up five minutes later, letting herself in. "Hey, hey!" she called from the foyer. I heard her footsteps coming down the hall and wiped my face with my hand. She walked into my room without knocking.

"I'm fine," I said.

"Well, you sure do look fine," she said, sitting next to me. "I think mascara is supposed to go *on* your eyelashes." She gestured to under her eyes. "You've got a thing happening. Like a football player."

I pulled a pillow over my head. Mo pulled it off.

"Althea took Bark—"

"Yeah, I heard."

"God, you can't take a shit around here without—"

"You took a shit too? I didn't hear that part," Mo said, grinning.

I socked her in the face with my pillow and then hugged it to my chest like armor. "I thought Bark was dead. I'm so embarrassed. I thought he was—"

"Did you think he drowned?" Mo asked.

"Shut up."

"You still don't go near water, do you?"

"Shut up."

"You're the only person I know who lives in Florida and doesn't go to the beach."

I turned on my side, away from her. My mind was still cycling through awful thoughts. I wished I could be a normal human being, but in the absence of that, I wished I could hide my abnormality better.

Mo flopped on her back next to me. "I'm not—I'm only trying to tell you that I get what's going on."

I didn't say anything.

Mo was quiet for a long time. "Okay, look," she said finally. "I'm not leaving you alone. You can come help me at my shop, or I'll sit here and stare at you." She leaned over me, making moony eyes. I refused to laugh.

On the walk to her house, Mo bumped her arm against my shoulder and said, "You know, after Pops died, I'd wake up in the middle of the night terrified he might stop breathing. I totally forgot. I'd run into the living room, and he wasn't there and his hospice bed was gone. I felt like a crazy person."

"But it stopped. You don't still do that, right?" I said automatically, before the horror of what she'd gone through set in. I hated that I hadn't been there to sleep on the couch so I could hug her when she raced in and the realization hit.

"Yeah," Mo said. "It stopped eventually."

"That's maybe the difference between you and a crazy person," I said.

Mo put her arm around my shoulder. It made it harder for both of us to walk. Her lankiness, my lack of lank.

"I don't think you're crazy," she said.

I worried she was wrong.

We turned the corner and I could see Morty in her driveway, his finished skeleton all lit up with shop lights.

"Is there something that could help you?" she asked. "Not fix, I know, but help."

"Like what?" I said a little too sharply.

We walked up the driveway. Mo's mask and gloves were on the ground next to Morty. The garage door was open. She must have run out the second Althea called.

"Like a therapist—"

I shook my head. I didn't want to tell a stranger everything that had happened to me. I didn't even want to talk about it with people I knew.

Mo broke away to pick up her gloves. "I mean, you got divorced," she said, her voice barely a mumble. "Aren't you supposed to go to therapy for that?"

I was still raging with adrenaline. It felt like her words were scraping at my skin. I wished she'd stop talking.

"Divorce isn't a mental condition," I said, grabbing my gloves from the workbench.

"Well . . ." Mo sighed. "I mean, for the other stuff too."

"Like what?" I hoped if I pushed back, she'd let it drop. Mo was tougher than me about most things, but she couldn't handle feeling like we were having a real fight. "What stuff?"

"Everything," Mo said, pink splotches creeping up her neck. She was supposed to mumble, "Never mind." That was the way we worked.

"Like what?"

"You pulled your dead father out of the water," Mo said, her face turning red. "Maybe there's someone who knows how to help you handle that."

"He wasn't—" I didn't finish. It wouldn't help my case, but

my father was still alive when I pulled him out. He had to be, and the distinction mattered to me, even though I didn't understand why.

"I think, maybe . . . I mean, sad stuff kind of . . . builds, and we've been to more than our share of funerals," Mo said. "I think you, especially, were, like, mired in death. That can't be good."

She was remembering wrong. Nan couldn't handle the way I cried when she took me to funerals. I mostly stayed home by myself, watching the clock until it was time to walk over and meet Nan at the house of the person hosting the reception after the cemetery. We'd fill up on cold cuts and potato salad so Nan wouldn't have to make dinner that night, because who feels like cooking when their friend just died?

"I don't want to talk about— Are we going to do this?" I hated being a jerk to Mo, and that shame made me feel even more volatile. I shoved my bare feet into Pops's gross boots, tying the laces hard.

"I didn't mean to upset you," Mo said. "I don't— I'm not good at this."

"I'm not upset!" The agitated whine in my voice reminded me of the sound Bark made when I closed a door between us.

We were mostly quiet while we worked. I held strands of metal in place while Mo heated and bent them over and over, wrapping Morty's skeleton. The immediacy of Mo's torch flame and the work of my muscles slowed the frantic thoughts in my brain until I could poke at them one at a time, fighting to think the sensible truth instead. Althea wasn't mad. Bark was home safe. Mo was just trying to help. No one was hurt.

"I like you no matter what you do," Mo said when we were almost done with the layer, her words muffled by her mask.

"I like you sometimes," I said, cracking a smile she couldn't see under my mask.

She laughed.

"Morty looks good," I told her.

"Yeah," Mo said. "He's getting there."

My phone rang. I pulled a glove off with my armpit, flipped up my mask, and answered one-handed without looking at the screen. Nan was the only person who ever called me.

I didn't want to talk to Nan, but I didn't want to make her worry about me either. "Hey, I'm still at Mo's. We're disgusting."

"Thanks for sharing," a male voice said, amused.

"I'm sorry. I thought you were my grandmother."

"No one's ever said that to me before."

I recognized the gentle rhythm of his speech. "Oh my god! Luca?"

Mo lifted her mask and made a kissy face. I stuck my tongue out at her.

"Yeah," Luca said. I could hear the smile in his voice. "I got your note. What are you photographing underwater? Wait. How are you? That's the first question, right? How many years? Five?"

"Almost six." I tried balancing the phone with my shoulder so I could hold the next bit of metal in place, but the mask was not cooperating. Mo waved me away. "Hey, I loved your movie. I saw it in the theatre," I said to Luca, eager to keep the conversation off of me.

"Thank you! My mom, uh, Carla," he said, like maybe I'd forgotten the difference between his mom and his mother, "called yesterday to tell me Marco got into Cornell's agricultural engineering program!"

"That's amazing!" I said, taking my mask off all the way. I walked down the driveway, my feet slipping around in Pop's boots as they clomped against the cement.

In Luca's film, Carla helps Marco plant a container garden. He measures the plants each morning. "They're growing! They're growing!" His eyes are full of wonder as he runs into the kitchen to tell Carla: "Four millimeters since yesterday." The too-short hem of Marco's pants shows how he's also growing. Luca was subtle with it, but seeing Marco changing and thriving while his mother sits in a holding facility in Texas tugged heartstrings.

"So, you're with Mo?" Luca asked as I clomped back up the driveway.

"Yeah," I said. "I'm helping her weld stuff."

"Hi, Luca!" Mo yelled.

"Mo says hi."

Luca laughed. "I heard! Visiting Nan?"

"Um, kind of."

"It must be nice to get out of winter sometimes."

"Yeah." And then, instead of letting the conversation drag out to the eventual result, I just said it: "Eric and I got divorced, so I'm staying with Nan until I figure things out."

"Oh, wow. I'm sorry, Kay. That's got to be hard." Luca's voice was kind, sincere. I couldn't read anything beyond that.

"It was for the best." I watched Mo inspect the work we'd done so far. "It's good to be home."

"Well, I mean, who could resist Nan's cookies?"

"Oh, no, Luca," I said, relieved for the shift in subject. "Things have changed."

Mo opened two beers and handed one over, giving me the thumbs-up to keep talking. She was a Luca fan. He always came home with me for spring break. The three of us spent late nights playing poker and getting into Nan's schnapps. Mo took him to the beach when I would beg off with a made-up headache.

I told Luca about Mo's manatee, Nan's health kick, the mermaids, and the calendar.

"It's probably crazy," I said.

"Crazy in the best way. Better than a bake sale, right?" The familiar music in his voice made my heart swell in a way that felt like relief.

"Right," I said. "It will keep us busy at least."

"So you're going to shoot underwater?"

"Nan and Bitsie want to." I picked at a rough spot at the edge of my thumbnail with the nail of my index finger. "But I'm starting to rethink. I mean, shooting on dry land would be easier, right?"

I'd promised Nan I could handle it, but I was still hoping for a Hail Mary; for someone to say it was impossible, or champion a vision for mermaids on deck chairs that the ladies wouldn't be able to resist. Even if I got someone else to take the pictures, I'd need to be there to style the mermaids, and the idea of watching them in the water made my stomach twist.

"Oh, no," Luca said. "It's totally doable." He rattled off the kind of camera he would use, lenses, and lighting options. I tried to scribble it all down on a scrap of cardboard with one of Mo's grease pencils.

"Is this stuff I can rent?" I asked, wondering how much it would cost. Maybe that would be the obstacle I needed.

"I have a friend in Orlando who would probably loan you that stuff if I ask nicely."

"Really?" I paced, swinging one foot in front of the other. Heel hitting toe, other heel to toe, repeat.

"It's for a good cause," Luca said.

We chatted a little longer and then, with every ounce of restraint I had, I said, "Hey, I think Mo's ready for next steps on this project, so I should go." I could have stayed on the phone listening to him breathe. I was usually bad at being the person to hang up. I'd let conversations grow strange and laborious when maybe the other person was trying to say goodbye. I wanted to do everything right with Luca. Every little thing.

"I'll talk to my friend," Luca said. "Call you tomorrow?"

"Good," I said, trying to push down the welling excitement. "Thank you." We would talk again tomorrow. We were back in touch, and it didn't carry the awkwardness I'd feared.

"Good," he said. "I missed you."

"Me too." I could almost feel his arms around me, his breath warm on my ear. I wondered if he was thinking of that perfect little world we used to exist in together.

"Alright," he said. "Bye for now."

"Bye."

"I ordered Da Vinci's," Mo said when I walked back into the garage.

"Mushroom and anchovy?" I asked, amused to be eating pizza two nights in a row. Nan would be horrified.

"What's the point of anything else?"

We were on our third beers, but because we'd been working and busy and eating pizza, I didn't feel totaled.

"He's the one I wanted," I said, as if we were already in the middle of a conversation about Luca.

"Did you two ever?" Mo made a circle with her thumb and index finger, pointing at it with her other index finger.

I laughed, spitting beer. "Once."

"That's it? Was it bad?"

"I liked him too much," I said, finally admitting something to myself I'd never quite let through. "The stakes were too high. I made a mess of it." I peeled the label off my beer bottle and stuck it to Mo's arm. "I'm pretty fucked up."

"Oh, come on," Mo said. "We didn't drink that much!"

"No, I mean, in general. He's a good guy and I'm not—I don't think I'm the best person."

Mo put her arm around me. Her armpits were ripe. "Don't put yourself down. And don't put everyone else on such a high pedestal."

"You don't know him like I do," I said. "He's incredible. And then, deep down . . . he's even more incredible."

She pulled the damp beer label off her arm and stuck it to my cheek. "I think you make the world out to be extra scary in the name of keeping yourself safe." Mo took a swig of her beer and burped loud.

"You get annoyingly philosophical when you're drunk now," I said, wiping the label from my face. "You used to tell fart jokes."

"I'm coming to terms with my brilliance." She gulped air. "A-B-C-D-E-F-G," she burped, making it all the way through to *Z* in two gulps' worth of belches.

"No burp talking!" I yelled, calling out the old rules of our friendship. I was not allowed to sing show tunes in her presence and she wasn't allowed to burp talk in mine.

"Come on! Try it. Try. It." Mo tipped my beer bottle toward my mouth and spilled it down my shirt.

"Jerk," I said, like it even mattered. I was covered in rust and black oily gunk and metal shavings.

"Thanks for the help tonight," she said, clinking her bottle to mine.

"It's really good," I said, surveying what we'd done. Morty had a full layer of metal rope wrapped like skin over his skeleton. "And thanks for coming to get me."

"Anytime," she said.

I started singing the "Thank You Very Much" song from *Scrooge: The Musical* in my worst cockney accent.

"That doesn't even sound like a real song," Mo said. "You made that up."

I shook my head, and sang louder, hitting the trite rhymes with extra enthusiasm.

Mo shoved my shoulder, hard enough to knock me off balance.

"I talked to Althea," Nan said as soon as I walked in the door like she'd been waiting to pounce.

Bark rushed over too. I bent down to kiss his head. He licked my face.

"You could have told me," I said, hauling myself up on my sore knees.

"Well, I never know what you're going to be alright with," Nan said, a snip in her voice.

"You can *ask* me."

"Althea is happy to walk Bark!" Nan said. "It's good for him."

"I'm not even objecting to that. I'm objecting to— It scared the shit out of me, Nan!"

Nan clucked. "So tightly wound," she said. "Maybe you should come to my meditation class at the senior—"

"You know what? Do what you want." My voice was too sharp, but I was tired of being told what would fix me. "You're going to anyway, right? Do whatever you want. Just— If Althea takes him, leave a note or something, okay?" I went to my room to avoid saying anything worse.

Before bed, I checked Luca's Facebook page. He'd posted a picture of himself with his arm around Marco, captioned: *This guy got into Cornell!* I hit like, and put my phone down before I could get stuck in a web of Nikki photos again.

CHAPTER TWENTY-THREE

I knew Luca for months before he ever mentioned his foster mom.

Over dinner once, telling a story about carving pumpkins for Halloween, he said, "My mom—foster mom—one year she got a pumpkin so big she couldn't lift it herself, so we were trying to carry it together, but she tripped and we dropped it off the back porch. *Splat!*" He laughed hard, not self-conscious of the fact that it wasn't as funny to someone who hadn't been there.

I liked seeing him lost in a good memory. I was curious, but he didn't explain further and I wasn't sure if it was more polite to ask or take it in stride. I'd never met someone in foster care before. At least not that I knew of.

Months later, in bed—we'd had beers—he snuggled into me and shared the story of how his mother came across the border to give birth so he could be American. He didn't call her his birth mother. She was still his mother. His foster mom was mom. "My mother, *my mother*, she came here to have me. Left her whole family for me, and she worked so hard. She scrubbed floors in office buildings at night while all the workers were home, and cleaned houses during the day while all the people were at work. She slept twice a day. Two short naps, and she made sure we always ate dinner together." I could hear his heartbeat. Too loud. Too fast.

"When my mother worked," he said, "I stayed with a lady in our building who took care of a couple of kids like me. We called her Titi, but she wasn't really my aunt. She was okay. She wasn't nice. She wasn't mean. And then my mother would rush in with a flood of kisses and all her perfume and I'd feel so much better, you know? So much better." He threaded his fingers between mine and pulled my arm across his body. "My mother had a broken taillight. She got stopped by a cop on her way home from cleaning offices."

He told me like he was repeating a well-worn story, the same way I could calmly report the details of my father's death if I had to. I squeezed his hand, desperately hoping something had saved her, even though I knew if it had, Luca wouldn't have a foster mom.

"Her license was Mexican," Luca said. "Expired. She was too scared to cross the border to renew it, worried she wouldn't get us back here." He took a deep breath, ragged. "She spent a month in a detention center. Titi said she couldn't keep me, so a social worker picked me up at school and took me to my foster mom's house. Carla had other kids like me. American kids who didn't have American parents. She spent days on the phone trying to find my mother. They don't tell you things. You have to fight for answers. I was eleven. I didn't know how to fight." His tears soaked through my sweater, pooling at my collarbone.

"Have you— Is your mother okay?" I asked, wrapping my arm around him tighter.

"They sent her to Mexico eventually. But we didn't know if she was okay for months. I was so scared. At least when she got to Mexico, we could talk again. She sent phone cards in the mail. She'd sing me songs and tell stories and make me promise that I wouldn't forget how to speak Spanish so I would always be able to call her on Sundays. I still call. Every week. But she can't visit me. And she won't let me go to Durango. She says if it was safe, we would have stayed there."

"I'm so sorry," I said. "I'm so sorry that happened to you."

"I'm not like the other kids here," he said. "It's all so heavy in my heart."

I hugged him hard. I felt like we belonged together.

CHAPTER TWENTY-FOUR

The next day when I got home from work, Bark wasn't there. Nan left a sticky note on the table by the front door where his leash had been: *He's with me.*

I knew she was at Althea's for Taco Night, and I knew I was invited, but I couldn't make myself go. I needed to apologize to Althea, and I didn't want to do it with everyone there. I made myself a bowl of oatmeal and went to my room to eat it. It was too quiet without Bark. The air felt too still. I turned on the TV and flipped channels until I saw black and white. *The Ghost and Mrs. Muir.* I'd seen it so many times that it felt like an old friend chatting in the background.

I dug a tape measure from my desk drawer and took measurements of myself. I was bigger than Nan and Bitsie, but I only needed rough numbers to order supplies for a prototype tail. I sketched and calculated.

I wanted to go for time-period authentic, but Bitsie told me the stiff lamé of their original tails left welts on their legs at the flex points. She said it like a point of pride—how tough they were—but I wanted them to have full range of motion. Spandex would look flimsy, but other fabrics wouldn't flex, or they'd hold water and sag. Latex was too expensive, silicone too. Even though neoprene has been around since the thirties, it didn't scream sixties to me, but performance-wise it made the most sense. I was only planning to order enough to make one tail as a sample, but I found a closeout deal on thirty yards of mustard yellow neoprene that was cheaper than buying four yards of a normal color. It was hideous, but a decent base to paint over.

Bitsie told me the mermaids in the show used two fins bound by the tail, but the way they had to position their feet made her hips ache as a twenty-year-old. I ordered a monofin from a scuba shop. It had a funny rounded edge. I'd have to make an extra insert to shape it correctly, but it was a good place to start.

I started a Pinterest board of kitschy inspiration: mermaid wall hangings, matchbooks, ashtrays, soap dishes, Valentine cards. I used the pictures for inspiration and sketched for hours, fine-tuning my ideas. I didn't even notice that *The Ghost and Mrs. Muir* turned into *Key Largo*, until I looked up and saw Humphrey Bogart where I'd been expecting Rex Harrison.

I fell asleep, pencil in hand, and woke to Bark pouncing on me. I knew it was Bark almost instantly, but there was a time delay between instinct and reason. I screamed.

Bark jumped off the bed, howling. Eyes narrowed, ego wounded.

"It's us, Katie," Nan said, running down the hall to my room.

"I know," I said.

Nan sighed. I used to scream the same way when she woke me up for school in the morning. Bark wasn't used to it because we always fell asleep together. If he woke me, it was small movements, a gentle easing from sleep to wake as I left my nightmares behind.

"I'm sorry, Bark," I said, reaching my hand out to scratch his ear. He grumbled and kept his distance. I didn't even ask how he did at Althea's house. I wanted him to be okay, but the fact that he seemed better without me hurt.

"Wow," Nan said, pulling a Bark-crumpled sketch from the bed. "You've been busy."

"Yeah," I said. "Here." I rifled through the sketches, trying to move my hands quickly enough so she wouldn't notice they were still shaking. "This is what I'm thinking for you."

"Kay," Nan said, and her face softened to joy. "It's perfect!"

"I'm sorry. About last night."

I thought maybe she'd apologize for sending Bark with Althea without telling me, but she said, "I know, dear," and kissed me on the forehead.

After I took Bark to pee and fed him dinner, he forgave me for screaming. We cuddled up to watch TV, but the movie was over, replaced by an infomercial for a contraption that made perfect eggs in the microwave. I hadn't realized it was so late. Taco Night was usually over by nine.

Bark started snoring as soon as his head hit the pillow. But I had more ideas. I sketched until the dark outside faded to lighter blue, and then I finally put my work aside and tried to sleep.

CHAPTER TWENTY-FIVE

I'd used Bitsie's address for the neoprene order, but I forgot to tell her.

"Uh, kiddo?" she asked when I got to her house to work on the tail prototype. "Did you order this giant box of baby poop colored scuba fabric?"

"Nope," I said, working my poker face.

"Smart-ass."

"I'm going to paint it. I swear."

"Good. Because it is ug-ly."

Before we got down to business, I showed Bitsie my Pinterest board of mermaid inspiration.

"Oh my gosh," she said, pointing to a picture I'd pinned of a cherub-faced porcelain mermaid holding a shell full of flowers. "My mother had that vase." She put her hand over her mouth and stared at the screen, haunted. "So strange to see it."

"Not good strange, huh?" I said.

"My father broke it." Bitsie flashed a sad smile, and I could tell the vase wasn't broken by accident. "But it used to be on the table in the kitchen, and she'd fill it with carnations. I thought it was so beautiful." She stroked her wedding ring with her thumb absentmindedly, like she was checking it was still in place. "I wonder if that's what started my love of mermaids."

"I like the color palette," I said awkwardly, not knowing what else to say.

"I'd forgotten all about that vase," Bitsie said. "What a riot." Her eyes were still sad.

"You okay?"

"I read somewhere that memories don't adjust for perspective. The visceral ones—that hit like a flash—they trick you. I don't feel like a seventy-five-year-old woman looking at that vase. I feel like a six-year-old."

I squeezed her arm. When the memories of the day my father died flashed in my brain, it was like video recorded in that moment. Nothing faded. Nothing changed.

"It's all in there." Bitsie pointed to her head. "We can't always get it out or keep it in when we want to."

"I'm sorry, for triggering—"

"Oh, no, no, no!" Bitsie said, messing up my hair. "I think it's good sometimes to stir up the muck in an old noggin. It reminds me how long I've been here to see things."

"What color carnations?"

"Huh?"

"What color carnations did your mom like to put in that vase?"

"Red," she said, smiling. "Always red."

"That's the palette I was thinking about. That turquoise, like her tail, and then a bright red with bluish tones. And the rest of the colors to fit that scheme."

"My mother had excellent taste," Bitsie said, nodding. "She liked things to be beautiful."

I remembered what she'd said about her mother telling her she'd never be pretty. "I'm going to turn you into the most gorgeous mermaid," I said.

Bitsie put her arm around my shoulder and squeezed. "Thanks, kiddo." She looked at the picture of the mermaid vase again. "My mother didn't have a lot of say in her life." She nodded, like she was trying to coax forward the right perspective. "Not like I did either. That was our narrative then. We waited to be chosen, hoping we'd like the life we got. My mother got a shitty consolation prize. Mine was better, but not quite right until I had more say."

"I sort of felt like that." When Eric asked me to marry him, it was like I'd passed a test. I'd pretended to be normal skillfully enough to go on to the next level. "The thing I liked best about Eric was that he wanted me." I sighed. "And then, he didn't."

"But you had a say. Even if you didn't exercise it." Bitsie smiled at me kindly. "When I was your age, if I didn't have my father or husband cosign, I couldn't get a bank account."

"Wait! Really?" It sounded like an ancient rule that might have been true for Bitsie's grandmother, not something that could have been so recent.

"We've come a long way, baby," Bitsie said dryly. "We used to need men to exist in the world."

"I sort of understood the oppression, but I always thought of that time period as pretty dresses and making canapés for dinner parties, and fun Donna Reed stuff." It hit me that my understanding of Nan and Bitsie's lives came from movies I watched on AMC.

"Sure," Bitsie said. "The fun kind of oppression. Ha!" Her laugh was one loud staccato bark.

"So this isn't right." I pointed to the screen. "When you see this stuff, it makes you kind of claustrophobic, huh?" I took a deep breath. *Work over ego. Work over ego.* It was my mantra in college to fight the frantic feeling that fuels the urge to throw good work after bad. These costumes were supposed to make Nan and Bitsie happy. They weren't worth anything if they didn't. But no one likes being wrong, and it takes time for feelings to adjust. That's why an artist needs an honor code. *Work over ego.*

Bitsie paused for a moment, then said, "I think there's joy in honoring where we came from. But I want to celebrate who we are now."

"What does that look like?" It was a question my favorite design teacher in college always asked.

"I don't know. But I think you'll get there," Bitsie said, smiling. "Do you have to know to start the tail? I mean, a tail is a tail is a tail, right?"

"True." No matter what we did, the mermaids were going to have tails. We had engineering work to figure out. "You ready to help?"

"Bunny always got annoyed with me when I tried to help her. I'm not good at straight lines."

I laughed.

"That's not a gay joke," Bitsie said, grinning.

"I was remembering when you tried to teach me how to play hopscotch. Nan saw the board you drew on the driveway and thought I did it and wanted the school to do extra testing on me."

"Holy crap!" Bitsie said, laughing. "I forgot about that."

"I'll do all the cutting," I told her. "You be my model."

Bitsie put one hand behind her head and jutted out her hip. "Dah-ling, I'd be delighted," she said in a funny husky voice.

I traced her figure in the living room so she wouldn't have to lie on the floor in Bunny's room. I told her there wasn't enough space in there.

"It's too quiet in here," she said when we'd finished making Bitsie-shaped markings on the neoprene. "I can't listen to Bunny's records and I don't even remember what I liked that wasn't hers, so it's always too quiet."

I handed her my phone, and she looked through my music while I pinned fabric.

"Oh! I love this song!" she yelped, and turned up the sound.

"Barracuda" by Heart blared at us, tinny on the phone speaker. I laughed. "Good choice."

"I think we should do a number to this," she said, shaking her hips.

I watched Bitsie dance and tried to figure out what a mermaid dancing to "Barracuda" should wear.

Eventually, she settled in to help me pin the fabric together. When we'd placed the last pins, I tried to pick up the tail, and we discovered she'd pinned her side to the carpet.

I laughed, but her face fell. "See? This is why Bunny never let me help."

"You have helped me. I needed the moral support."

"You've always been a sweet one, Kay," Bitsie said, patting my cheek.

I repinned her section as fast as I could so it wouldn't look like much of a setback.

Three hours later, with minimal trial and error, we had a rough approximation of a tail. Bitsie tried it on over her black and white polka dot tankini, her legs threaded through the slit I'd made in the back so she could still walk once she put the costume on. In the water, legs in place, the neoprene would overlap and stay closed.

"You look like a million bucks," I said.

"Only a million?" Bitsie asked, holding one hand up, the other out to the side, like a game show hostess. "This tail alone knocks it up to at least two point five. If we ignore the color."

I laughed. "You're right. You look like three million bucks. Four, once I paint it."

"Let's try it out!" Bitsie said.

Panic hit like lightning, sharp and low in my belly.

"I can't," I told her, collecting my stuff. "I have to feed Bark."

She could see the terror in my eyes. I knew she could.

"Oh, honey, wait!" she said. "Let's have a cup of tea."

"No, no. I know you want to try it out. I'll send Nan over. Don't test it without her, okay?"

"Why don't we go out and get a milkshake?"

"I'm sorry, Bits," I said, willing myself to make eye contact. "I need to go home."

"Yeah. Yeah. I get it."

"Promise me you won't get in the pool with that tail until Nan gets here?"

Bitsie shrugged. "I'll wait." But I wasn't sure if that was a false promise.

CHAPTER TWENTY-SIX

〜〜〜〜〜〜〜〜〜〜〜

I called Nan the second I stepped outside. She didn't pick up, so I ran all the way home. Her car was in the driveway.

Bark ran to greet me, tail wagging, Murray in his mouth.

"Hello?" I called. "Nan?"

I heard her talking to someone in her bedroom. Was she on the phone? I picked up the house line but got a dial tone. I tried her cell phone again.

Then I heard a male voice.

I blushed. She wasn't expecting me back so soon.

"Kay?" Nan called from her room.

"Yeah," I said. I wanted to leave again, let her have her space, but I didn't want Bitsie to try out the tail alone.

"Is everything okay?"

"Yeah. Are *you* okay?" I yelled.

"Bitsie called," Nan shouted, and I realized Bitsie had been tasked with keeping me busy. That's why she was trying to get me to go for a milkshake.

"It's okay," I heard Nan whisper. "It's okay."

Nan came down the hall, hair a bit messy, lipstick freshly applied.

"Do you have a houseguest?" I whispered.

She smiled sheepishly, her cheeks trembling.

"It's okay that you do," I said. "It's a good thing, right?"

She nodded, tears in her eyes.

"Then you don't need to cry." I hugged her.

"I'm so embarrassed," Nan said. "I loved your grandfather."

"I know," I said, rubbing her back in small circles the way she did for me as a kid. "I think this is good, Nan."

She pulled away and looked at me. "You do?"

"Of course!" I was more shocked that she thought anyone would be upset about her moving on from a man who'd died twenty-two years ago.

"At first, it didn't seem like anything to mention," she said. "In case it didn't work out. Then you—when you lost the baby again, I didn't think that was the time. And then you got divorced—I didn't want to go flaunting—plus, I didn't know if you would have a problem with me being with someone other than your Gramps. Or you'd think it was ridiculous. An old woman with a boyfriend."

"I can't believe you thought it was a problem! I'm so sorry." I hoped I hadn't done or said something that might have made her think it was. "I want you to have someone you love."

"I do," Nan said. "I love him. I'm quite sure of that now."

"Can I meet him?" I asked, shaky in my limbs. I worried if she'd hidden him this whole time, he might not be good for her, the same way I'd kept Eric and Nan apart as much as possible.

Then Isaac walked in and I broke down in tears.

"Oh," Nan said, rushing to hug me. "I knew this would be weird! I'm so sorry."

I struggled to get enough composure to say something thoughtful, but it wasn't coming, so I shouted, "Happy tears! Happy tears!"

Isaac smiled. I smiled back.

"You are a ridiculous woman," I said to Nan, "to think I'd be anything other than thrilled."

Nan left to help Bitsie test her tail. Isaac made coffee for the both of us from a bag of good stuff he kept hidden in a cabinet over the refrigerator. He assembled Nan's ancient percolator with ease, completely comfortable in her kitchen. He'd probably been the one to set up the wifi.

We took our coffee to the dining room and I spread my sketches out on the table.

"Well, now," Isaac said, beaming, "you have done a lovely job." I felt like a little kid showing off my artwork. It was weird, maybe, but it was good.

"I'm still stuck," I told him, explaining as much as I could about why my original plans wouldn't work, without giving away what Bitsie told me in confidence.

"Being stuck is a part of the process, right?" Isaac asked. "Work is better for the struggle."

That night, Isaac ate dinner with us at the small kitchen table that was usually just for me and Nan. Nan lit a votive candle. She served some sort of strange millet dish that Isaac seemed to enjoy. We exchanged shy smiles, and talked about Bitsie and the tail.

"It's better than the ones we had, Kay," Nan said breathlessly. "So much better. And I love the overlap you did in the back."

"It's a great safety feature," Isaac said, nodding.

Nan looked at him quizzically.

"I saw it on her sketches. I like the way the dorsal fin hides the overlap."

"It looks amazing in person," Nan said, spooning more millet on Isaac's plate even though he hadn't asked for seconds.

"You taught me that trick, Isaac," I said. "Embellishment to hide a seam."

Isaac blushed. "I think—" he said, and then cleared his throat. "I think I can get some fabric donated."

"Really?"

"I know a few people," he said, grinning.

"That would be lovely," Nan said.

When we finished eating, Nan stood up, stacking Isaac's empty plate on her own. Isaac narrowed his eyebrows, giving her a mock-stern look. She sat down again and let him clear the table. He whistled while he did the dishes.

I made a pot of tea as an excuse to extend the moment a little longer. It was the exact kind of family dinner I'd dreamed about since my dad died. It amazed me that someone else's love story could make me feel a little more complete.

Isaac went home after tea. I didn't know how to tell them it wouldn't bother me if he stayed. Maybe that wasn't their agreement. Maybe it would put Nan on the spot.

After Nan went to bed, I called Bitsie.

"I can't believe you knew this whole time."

"Best acting of my life, kid." She laughed. "Hey, the tail works great."

"Nan said!"

"It's so much better than what we used to have!" She sighed. "Also, kid, I needed that. The whole project. The day with you."

"Me too," I told her. "And we've barely even started."

"I know!" she said, her voice full of glee.

CHAPTER TWENTY-SEVEN

The conversation I'd planned to have with Nan about how I was fine with Isaac sleeping over probably didn't need to happen. I got home from work the next night to a note that said, *Bowling with Bitsie. Staying at Isaac's. XO Nan.*

Luca hadn't called. Not hearing from him meant I could honestly say I didn't know how to get equipment and we'd have to take photos on solid ground. But I was disappointed anyway. I wanted more of him. I wanted him to want more of me. I made a concerted effort to stay away from Facebook. The risk of sending him a dopey late-night message was too high.

Nan and Bitsie wanted to start shooting for the calendar in a few weeks. At the theatre in Rochester, costumes were my only job. Now I was committed to working at Isaac's full-time and helping Mo two nights a week, and I felt a little frantic about all there was to do. I decided to take full advantage of the night alone.

"Okay, Bark," I said. "What music should we listen to?"

Bark got excited, like maybe he knew the word *music*. I didn't want him to think we were going to dance in the living room and not make it happen, so we started my brainstorming session with a good jump around to "Barracuda." If Bitsie loved that song, maybe there was something in it that would send me in the right direction.

I flailed around the room, Bark following in a goofy gallop.

Rock and Roll Mermaids? Sharp barracuda teeth? Long hair like Ann and Nancy Wilson? Should these mermaids have long hair? Nan and Bitsie looked great with their spiky pixie cuts, and I didn't want to shove them into the image of youth normally attached to mermaids. I'd never seen a depiction of an old mermaid. Were they were supposed to be eternally young like vampires? Did they have a short life span? Whatever the standing myth was, it had to change. These mermaids were about wisdom, not youth.

When the song was over, I scribbled *Wisdom!* in my notebook and underlined it. But *wisdom* brought to mind flowing gray Earth Mother hair, muted pinks and purples. It wasn't the right word. I crossed it out and wrote *Vitality! Strength! Joy!* and something clicked in my head. I always felt self-conscious doing artsy-fartsy, free-thought stuff, but I never got anywhere without it. If I failed to do the inspiration work, I usually got stuck later in the process. The design started to feel false, and moving forward would get harder and harder, like I had to drag along the weight of all the wrong choices that snowballed from the first one. It was more productive to do the amorphous creative thought work first, even if it felt silly.

I sat on the couch with Nan's mermaid photo album, flipping through the pages. There was a picture of the ladies in dresses and high heels. Hannah's A-line dress had bold circles along the hem, like bubbles. Woo Woo had a string of oversized fake pearls. Nan's hair was in an actual beehive, and Bitsie wore a checkered trapeze dress that showed off her skinny legs.

The picture made me think of the B-52s video for "Love Shack." My dad had a bunch of their cassette tapes in his car. I thought the deadpan way Fred Schneider spoke lyrics was hysterical, so sometimes my dad spoke the words to other songs to make me laugh.

I remembered being in his old station wagon while he cranked up the Rolling Stones, chasing Mick Jagger singing "Wild Horses" with Fred Schneider–style Sprechgesang. We were driving home from mini golf. I had a chocolate soft serve cone dripping down my arm faster than I could finish it. I laughed so hard it hurt. I'm not sure how old I was, but I remember in that moment, it occurred to me that my father was having fun beyond trying to keep me entertained. He enjoyed my amusement, liked being the source of it. It was the first time I saw him as a person, not just my dad.

I smiled, and felt warmth in my chest. It was one of the rare times I'd been stuck in a good memory of my father. I mostly thought of the last one. But maybe, if I tried, I could get comfortable remembering him. I closed my eyes and worked to picture everything I could about what it felt like to be in that car with him. The sting when I crinkled my sunburned nose. Sticky hands. Sparkly purple flip-flops on my dirty feet. The sun was low in the sky, cotton candy clouds turning pink as it set.

I remembered the click and whir when I put *Cosmic Thing* in the tape deck. We sang along to "Love Shack" with the windows down, my hair whipping into my ice cream. There's no way I had any idea what the words meant, but I understood the joy.

I remembered my dad's deep voice. Faded red t-shirt. Tan arms. Scratched Wayfarers. He popped the rest of his ice cream cone in his mouth and handed me his napkin. "You're a mess," he said, grinning, like I was a great masterpiece of summer. I think he took the long way home. I think he didn't want the moment to end either.

I played the video for "Love Shack" on my phone and got goose bumps. I was on the right path. The video set was a mishmash of diner details and thrift store finds, shabby and loud. Because of the eclectic feel, there was no expectation of time-period accuracy. I watched Kate Pierson jump and shimmy in an orange-fringed onesie and decided she would be my muse. Bitsie needed fringe, not shells. Nan needed shimmering splendor. They would not be demure. These were not mermaids sitting on a rock waiting for a sailor to come by. They were basking in their own strength.

I looked up the B-52s and found a current picture of Kate Pierson in a shiny purple bodysuit, her hair Raggedy Ann red. I pinned it to my mermaid board on Pinterest. Maybe, if I kept the budget tight, I could get my hands on some photogenic wigs.

I stayed up into the morning hours, colored pencils strewn across the coffee table, bowl of popcorn eaten down to the kernels on the floor next to me. Bark lay on my feet, snoring. It didn't seem worth it to wake him for bed, so I slept on the couch.

I woke to the sound of the front door opening, and covered my face with a throw pillow so Nan would leave me to sleep. Bark ran to the door, howling. I thought as soon as he figured out that it was Nan he'd settle down, but his howls grew in intensity.

"Bark!" I yelled. "Here!" But he didn't come back. He growled. "Geez," I shouted, getting up from the couch. The light hurt my eyes. I hadn't even been drinking. It was the lack of sleep. Not enough water. I'd forgotten to eat anything besides popcorn.

"Get off me!" someone said, only it sounded more like "Geddowffme!"

"Ruth?" I rubbed my eyes, stumbling into the foyer. Ruth had her back pressed to the front door like she was about to be attacked.

Bark was six or seven feet away from her, and just as scared as she was.

"Get him off me!" she yelled.

"He's not *on* you." I grabbed Bark's collar anyway.

"How did you get in?"

She held up her key chain.

"Nan's not here," I said, unsure if it was okay to say she was at Isaac's.

"Well, I'm meeting her here," Ruth said, crossing her arms like I might attempt to forcibly remove her from the house. "We're going to the farmers' market."

"Cool," I said. "I'm sure she'll be back soon, then." I wondered if I could sneak off to bed.

"Is there coffee?" she asked.

I wanted to say, "If you make it," but I went into the kitchen to set up the percolator. She followed, opening the door to the patio without asking. I knew it wasn't fair to be grumpy about it. She wouldn't have asked Nan either. Nan wouldn't have expected her to.

Ruth was brusque with everyone, but I felt it acutely. She had boys. Five of them. Her husband had been an army sergeant. She didn't have time for my soft spots.

Once, when Nan bought me a frilly new comforter set, she told Ruth I woke up saying, "I feel like a princess."

Ruth said, "She *is* a princess," in a tone that made me sure it was an insult, even though Nan took it as a compliment.

Bark stayed by my side, staring Ruth down while I scooped coffee into the percolator.

Ruth claimed her usual seat at the patio table. I grabbed a soy yogurt from the fridge and sat with her while I waited. I hated sitting on the patio, but I didn't want to be rude. And I didn't want to hear a monologue about how her youngest son, Joey, used to have antisocial behavior, but her husband wouldn't stand for it, so Joey got over it. She was always going on about

Joey, and how he was better than everyone else. I wasn't sure if I should feel sorry for her other boys, or if it was better because she was too busy fussing over Joey to bother them.

Bark rested his head on the table to stare at Ruth.

"That dog is strange," she said.

I gave her a half smile and went back to my gross yogurt. The good thing about Ruth was that it didn't matter if I answered when she talked.

"My son Joey has a Mastiff," she said. "Best-behaved dog I've ever seen. But, you know, Joey put the work in."

I held my tongue. I ate my yogurt. The words I wanted to say bubbled in my veins.

"You can't just let a dog do whatever they want," she said. "You have to take them to obedience class. And you have to get a good one to begin with. From a breeder. Not a junkyard dog."

I was about to hit my boiling point when I heard the front door open.

Bark ran to the door, but didn't howl, happy to see Nan.

"Yes! Really!" Nan said into her phone. "Bitsie lives right down the street— Well, you should— You should move here too—" She waved at Ruth. Covering the speaker on her phone, she grinned at me and said, "You're such a stinker!"

I sniffed my armpit. Nan laughed, but I wasn't sure if it was at me or the person on the line. She walked away, phone to her ear.

Thankfully, Ruth had moved on from the Mastiff. "Joey's got a watch that hooks up to his phone," she said. "Like Dick Tracy." She held her wrist to chin level. "Just like Dick Tracy!"

From the other room, I heard Nan's cocktail party laugh, rich and arching like church bells.

"You know," Ruth said, pointing at me, "I like your hair that length. It's good on you."

"Thank you," I said, thrown. That was the thing about Ruth,

she wasn't always mean, and when she was nice, I felt like a jerk for writing her off.

Ruth beamed like she'd bestowed magic upon me; an awkward smile that showed all her teeth. It occurred to me that I didn't actually like her. She was loud and rude, and despite all her bluster, she bruised easily if someone disagreed with her. I'd never felt like I was allowed to pass that kind of judgment on an adult. Adults were fixed entities, and it had been my job to keep up, fit in, be quiet and good and nice enough for them to want me around. But now I was an adult, and Ruth made me uncomfortable. She wasn't my friend, she was Nan's, and I'd never made any kind of choice about spending time with her. I didn't hate her, but I didn't like her, and maybe that meant I could stop caring about whether she liked me.

Nan joined us, done with her call. "That was my old friend Hannah." She squeezed my shoulder again. "And I think this one here had something to do with that."

I worried maybe I'd done the wrong thing, but she sat next to me, smiling, and said, "Oh, Kay, thank you. It was lovely to hear her voice again." To Ruth, she said, "She's a senator's wife! Patrick Novak from Maryland."

"Fancy!" Ruth said, fanning herself. "Must be nice."

I thought I saw a hint of irritation flash on Nan's face.

CHAPTER TWENTY-EIGHT

〰〰〰〰〰〰

Isaac was sheepish when I got to work. I wanted to tell him I was fine with Nan spending the night at his place, but I couldn't think of how to word it so it wouldn't sound like I was giving him permission. Instead, I put my best effort into acting like everything was normal, and eventually, our awkwardness faded.

Isaac played Mos Def for most of the morning. After we finished the orders, he helped me work out the details for Nan's costume.

When I got home, Nan and Bitsie were in the living room, shouting. Nan had Woo Woo on FaceTime on her phone, and Bitsie had Audrey on hers. They'd swiped my computer, and a woman I assumed to be Hannah was on that screen. Bark was wedged between Nan and Bitsie on the couch, whipping his head back and forth, trying to figure out which one he should watch. It was so much chaos that none of them heard me come in.

"I think there's a better way to do this," I said. The three of them looked up. Bark jumped off the couch to greet me.

"It's working fine," Nan said, holding up Woo Woo to Bitsie's phone so she could say hi to Audrey.

"Look at you!" Audrey said to Woo. The volume was turned all the way up to static on both phones. "This is amazing!"

Bitsie chimed in, smushing my computer into the mix. "Audrey! It's Hannah!" I don't know if they could even see each other, but Audrey and Hannah let out shrieks of excitement. They didn't have a high expectation of clarity from these magic moving picture phones.

I laughed. Nan and Bitsie turned the phones and computer to face me.

"Oh my god!" Audrey shouted. "Is that your granddaughter, Nannette?"

"Yes!" Nan said, turning the phone back to look at it.

"She's a grown woman!" Audrey said.

"She has your nose," Hannah said, nodding.

"Hi! Thank you," I said, feeling a bit dazed. It was strange to see them in action after studying the pictures of their mermaid days so carefully.

"Tell them what you need," Nan said.

"I need you to send me your measurements so I can make the costumes. I'll show you where to measure. And then we can talk through the photo requirements." I still had my tape measure from work in my pocket. I pulled it out and measured my hips, waist, and bust in the fake kind of way a flight attendant gestures through the motions of putting the oxygen mask on yourself first.

"Why don't we come there for fittings?" Woo Woo said.

"Well, since this is for a fundraiser, we thought it would make sense to keep costs down by doing it this way," I said. "I don't think it will be hard to get someone to measure you. Do you have a local tailor—"

"Pish," Woo said. "I want to see you ladies!"

"That would be much more fun!" Hannah said.

The conversation derailed into possible travel plans and who could stay where. I went to the kitchen to make myself a cup of tea. When I got back, Nan was asking Hannah about the political accuracy of *Scandal*. Audrey and Woo Woo were holding up photos of grandbabies while Bitsie made a fuss over their chubby little toes. There was no jumping back in.

A few hours later, I got a Facebook message from Audrey.

Please tell the others I can't make it. I'm starting chemo this week. It was so nice to see their faces. I hope you'll send pictures.

I wrote back, *Of course.* And added a heart. I'd break the news to Nan later, once the excitement died down.

CHAPTER TWENTY-NINE

~~~~~~~

We had two separate bridal parties at the shop the next day. In between, Isaac helped me figure out a plan for Bitsie's fringe mermaid top. We worked out a prototype with some leftover cotton jersey and bra pads, and brainstormed better fabrics for the real thing. I kept expecting to feel awkward about constructing a bra with my grandmother's boyfriend, but it wasn't strange at all. It was Isaac. We were both well versed in all manner of bodies and the ways to cover them.

The second bride's gown was a work of art, handed down from her mother. Raw silk, impeccably draped. Perfect stitching. It was heaven to work on such a lush creation.

Spending time with Isaac had new meaning. I watched the way he offered a hand to the bride as she stepped down from the tailor stand. He had a box of tissues at the ready for her mother when she saw her daughter in the dress. These gestures were not new to me, but they carried greater weight because I knew Nan was receiving his kindness and care too.

When I got home, there was a red pickup truck parked on the street in front of the house. I kicked my shoes off in the foyer and dropped my keys on the table. Nan and Bitsie were in the kitchen using their company voices. I took a breath to steel myself.

"And then," Bitsie shrieked, "he put it back on the plate! Like nothing happened!"

Nan laughed. There was male laughter too. But it wasn't Isaac or Lester or Uncle Jackie. It was a younger voice, clearer. I hoped against hope it was Bunny's son, Chuckie. He was sweet to Bitsie, and didn't require anything of me. That would be the best-case scenario. Most of the other scenarios involved a cocktail party, but Chuckie was quiet like me, and people actually listened to his preferences.

Bark snuck over, bringing Murray to me. I gave Murray a squeak and passed him back. Bark wagged his tail so hard his entire backside wiggled. He followed me to the kitchen. The owner of the male voice had his back to me. Brown hair, not gray. But he was shorter than Chuck, and thin.

Bark flopped on the carpet in the hallway and gave me a look that seemed to say, *This is as far as I go.* He dropped Murray, resting his chin on top of him, like a portable pillow. I gave Bark's head a scratch before heading into the kitchen.

"Oh, there she is," Nan said.

The guy turned around.

It was Luca.

Right there. In the kitchen. Smiling at me. My knees wobbled. I stepped back. *Don't cry, don't cry, don't cry,* I thought, willing myself to keep it together, mostly winning.

"Hey, Kay," Luca said, standing up.

I'd been wearing the leather bracelet he'd made me in college since I found it in my desk. I slipped it off behind my back and shoved it in my pocket.

Luca hugged me and I felt like I was hovering above us watching. Did I smell? Did I have lint in my hair? Was my fly open? I worried he'd feel me shaking if I let him hug me too hard.

He didn't smell like Old Spice anymore, just bright and soapy with a hint of musk.

"When did you get here?" I asked. "How?" I didn't know what question I should be asking. There was a part of me that wanted to hear "I came because I've lived without you for too long and I don't want to go another second." There was another part of me that wanted to run, fast and hard to the street, away, away, away.

"Nan and I did a little messaging," Luca said. "I was in Savannah working on a friend's project. But we wrapped yesterday, so I came to help figure out this whole mermaid thing." He grinned. "I hope that's okay."

"Of course," I said, the quake in my voice obvious. I shot Nan a look. She was still signed in to my Facebook account on her phone. That's how this happened. She smiled at me, oblivious to any hint of transgression. I knew if I called her on it, she'd say it wasn't any different from me emailing Hannah. But as far as I knew, Nan had never been madly in love with Hannah.

Luca kissed my cheek. "It's so good to see you."

His hair was different. Short on the sides and messy on top in a way that left me wondering if it was the result of a lot of work, or none at all. He had the same familiar scruff on his chin, and his brown eyes still held the brightness that made my heart swell.

"Kay!" Bitsie said. "Show him your sketches!"

I laughed. "Oh, hey, how were the last six years? Want to see my sketches?"

Luca laughed too.

"We were telling him all about your designs," Nan said. "But I didn't want to go in your room to get them."

"So you have *some* boundaries," I said, trying to make my voice sound like I was telling a joke.

"In case you had nudie pictures in that sketchbook," Bitsie said, talking over me. Luca laughed politely, and I could tell it was a joke that had already been made at least once.

"You know, I just got home from work. I'm going to take a minute to get settled." I looked at Luca. "You're okay?"

"I've been promised a martooni," he said. "I'll be fine."

In my room, I twisted my frizzed-out hair into a bun that looked casual, but neater than it would look otherwise. I bit at my lips to puff them up and added a fresh coat of mascara over what I was already wearing. I sprayed perfume at my pits, grabbed my sketchbook, and went back out. It took five minutes tops, but it didn't matter.

"Did you fall asleep in there?" Nan asked. Cocktail Party Nan had a comment for everything.

"Yeah," I said, so glad I hadn't excused myself to use the bathroom, because she was known to make the same joke.

Luca was watching me and it was hard not to feel self-conscious. Did I look too different? Not different enough?

Nan poured gin in the shaker. "None for me," I said.

Bitsie pressed the back of her hand to my forehead. "Are you okay?"

"Yeah. Isaac and I have the wedding party from hell tomorrow. I can't be hung over."

Nan smiled. "I heard about that mother of the bride."

"She gets upset every step of the way, but when we suggest she go elsewhere, she insists we're the best."

"Did I come at a bad time?" Luca asked.

"No, no. I have to put in a couple hours in the morning, but I think I can be back around noon. Is that okay?" As soon as I said it, I felt awkward. Maybe it was presumptuous of me to assume he wanted to spend time together. Maybe he only came to help Nan.

"We'll keep him entertained," Bitsie said.

I made myself a cup of peppermint tea and sat with them while they drank their martoonis. Bitsie asked Luca a million questions about the film he'd made and the one he'd been helping with in Savannah. I struggled to find things to say, and did a lot of smiling and nodding instead. In my mind, I was rewriting our history, imagining where Luca and I would be if I hadn't ended up with Eric. Would I be traveling with him on his whirlwind of filmmaking, or would he never have made his documentary? Would I have held him back?

In a small, dark crevice in my brain, there was a sweet little alternate world where, after college, Luca and I moved to a tiny studio in a prewar walk-up in New York City, while I worked my way from intern to assistant to designer at the Metropolitan Opera costume shop, and Luca ran the cameras at the local news like he'd planned. We ate ramen noodles for dinner and had a favorite rock to picnic on in Central Park, and stayed best friends, on top of being in love. Luca would have felt like a family of my own no matter what.

"I am not too proud to say that Robert Redford is still a very handsome man," Luca said, answering a question I hadn't even heard Nan ask.

Luca was sitting so close that I could feel the vibrations of his voice in my chest. His hand was right there in his lap. I wanted to grab it, hook my fingers into his, feel his skin against mine.

"Well," Nan said, "I am not a single woman anymore. So I guess I shouldn't even be asking." She smiled and then launched into the story of her romance with Isaac, something that under any other circumstances I'd be interested in hearing. Instead, I was lost in thoughts of that other world where Luca and I never parted. I didn't want to find my way back.

*   *   *

Nan made vegan sushi for dinner. She and Bitsie rolled rice and seaweed around strips of cucumber and roasted red pepper.

Luca and I sat in the living room on the couch, side by side, looking at my sketches. Bark eyed Luca suspiciously across my lap.

"These are great, Kay." Luca's arm brushed against mine every time he turned a page. "I love the retro, but new, feeling." He laughed. "And that even looks like Bitsie."

"Thank you. The fabrics they used to use—those costumes were dangerous, I think."

"Nan said Bitsie's tail looks amazing in the water."

"I haven't gotten to see it in action yet. I was busy . . . working with Isaac."

Luca looked at me. I thought maybe he'd picked up on the lie, but then he said, "It's great to see your face again."

I smiled. "It's great to see yours."

There was a quiet moment, staring. I thought we might kiss, even though it would be totally inappropriate. It had been too long. Too much had happened. I didn't know anything about him now, beyond his documentary work. He never had relationship information on his Facebook page. But that look seemed like proof that I meant the same to him that he did to me. Or maybe the moment was only in my head.

He moved closer. Bark yawned. I laughed.

"He's not sure if we're going to be friends," Luca said.

"He's sitting closer to you than he does to most strangers."

"Is that a sign he likes me, or he thinks you might need protection?"

"Here," I said, digging into my pocket. I handed him a few pieces of dog jerky bits.

He held his hand flat, offering the treats to Bark.

Bark leaned across me to sniff Luca's hand, then stepped over me, smelling Luca's cheek with authority.

Luca smiled and said, "This is kinda weird," trying not to move his face too much.

Bark licked Luca's cheek and then swooped in and took the treats from his hand in a quick dip of his head. He flopped down between us, his weight pushing us farther apart.

Luca scratched Bark behind his ears.

"That was a quick warm up," I said.

"We did have a pretty good greeting before you got here. He barked like he was reading me a rundown of house rules."

I laughed.

"He's quite smart, isn't he?"

"Yeah."

"It's hard to be smart," Luca said. "To notice everything. Isn't it?"

My memory flashed to that college party, the two of us, sharing pretzels in a red Solo cup, people-watching together.

CHAPTER THIRTY

Nan served the veggie rolls piled high on a platter, carrying it to the coffee table in the living room. When Bark jumped off the couch to sniff out the food situation, Nan blocked him with her knee. Normal dog behavior. So un-Bark.

Bitsie came in carrying a stack of plates and a fistful of chopsticks.

"That's a lot of food," I said, and felt the same sinking feeling I got as a kid. I knew what was happening.

The doorbell rang. Bark yelped and ran to the foyer, ready to read the riot act to the new visitor, but it was Isaac, so Bark jumped up and tried to lick his face instead. I was surprised by Bark's exuberance, but Isaac didn't seem to mind. "I had a dog years ago," Isaac said, stooping to scratch Bark's chin.

Marta and Ruth arrived soon after. Nan had convinced Luca to screen *New Durango* for them.

"Althea has Bikram," Ruth announced to no one in particular, and I hated that I felt relieved. The apology I owed sat heavy in my mind. I worried maybe Althea hadn't come because she didn't like me anymore.

"I told her hot yoga is bad news," Marta said, shaking her head. "I read an article. She'll ruin her knees."

Isaac and Luca got Luca's laptop hooked up to the television.

Nan brought extra chairs from the kitchen. Ruth dimmed the lights and closed the curtains, which made it hard to see the sushi. We all ended up eating with our fingers.

Ruth and Marta applauded when they saw Luca's name appear on the screen. Bitsie whistled with her fingers in her mouth. Next to me, I knew Luca was blushing. I couldn't see it, but I knew. He still felt like an extension of me. I was his annex, he was mine, and our link wasn't broken.

In the documentary, Luca's foster mom, Carla, calls to ask him to film, recording herself making the call with her camcorder, to get him started. She has a new boy coming. He's twelve, only slightly older than Luca had been. "I'm tired," she says. "I'm tired of our children hurting so much. I'm tired of watching families disintegrating. They have the love—that's the hardest part. You're supposed to want what's best for your kids. That's what these parents are doing. We are failing them."

Luca brings his camera to the police station when they pick up Marco, who's wide-eyed and full of fear. While he follows Marco's story, Luca tells his own, saying the things Marco doesn't know how to say yet.

Carla fights so hard. Phone calls. Legal aid. A mountain of immigration law books piled on her kitchen table.

"She's a superhero," Luca says with tearful awe, turning the camera on himself to talk about her.

There are stacks of little-kid clothes in the closet in Luca's old room. "This used to be my shirt," he says, handing a green turtleneck to Marco. "I liked to pretend I was a Ninja Turtle when I wore it." Marco flashes a smile that disappears quickly.

In the next scene, Carla has the camera. Luca and Marco are asleep in the beat-up red race car bed, a copy of Harry Potter open on Luca's chest, Marco snug in the crook of his arm. You can hear Carla crying.

Luca goes to visit his mother. "*Cariño.*" She holds his face in her hands. "*No deberías estar aquí.* You shouldn't be here," she says through sobs, and she hugs him. It's a death grip hug.

"Mamá, I can come see you," Luca says. "It's allowed. I'm allowed."

But her fear is not laws. It's the violence in Durango. She wants him safe. Away.

They don't get Marco's mother back. Luca brings a cameraman with him to Texas to visit her.

The detention center looks like a city of dome tents. Beds stacked on beds, people stacked on people. If Marco's mother says she wants to return to Mexico, they'll send her there, but she wants to fight to stay with her son, so she's stuck in detention with fewer rights than an actual prisoner. Everyone is looking for a loophole. There isn't one.

When Luca interviews her, you can see the yellow ghost of a bruise across her cheek. She won't talk about how it got there.

As they leave the detention facility, the cameraman catches Luca turning his head away to wipe tears from his eyes.

"Are you okay, man?" a voice says softly from behind the camera.

"I wanted to take her with me," Luca whispers. He slips sunglasses on his face and walks out of the shot.

I tried not to watch Luca watching himself, but I couldn't help sneaking glances. He didn't look at the screen much. He stroked the downy fur behind Bark's ears. Bark seemed happy to let him.

In the last scene of the film, Marco and Luca are on the patio at Carla's house, pulling weeds from Marco's container gardens. Vegetables growing strong and tall.

"Here," Marco says, handing Luca a tomato. "Taste it." He's so proud that it almost eclipses the constant sadness in his eyes.

Luca takes a bite, juice spurting everywhere.

Marco laughs. "It's good, right?"

"Amazing," Luca says.

"Yeah." Marco twists his body away and then back. "You're my brother, right?" he asks. "You'll be my brother, okay?"

"If you'll be mine," Luca says.

"Yeah." Marco nods. "Yeah, I will." He picks a tomato for himself and takes a bite.

The credits roll.

Luca shifted his weight on the couch cushion next to me. It must have been awkward to show people all your pain in Technicolor. He'd done it so many times now. I wondered if it got easier, or if the awkwardness was something that ebbed and flowed. I wondered if he could predict it. Was it harder with people he knew? Easier with strangers?

Bitsie started clapping, and everyone joined her. Nan raised the lights. Ruth's eyes were red. Marta was still crying. Isaac fussed with the cuff of his shirt.

"It was even better seeing it a second time," Nan said, coming over to give Luca a hug. She'd seen it in the theatre when it first came out. "I'm so proud of you."

He soaked up her words. I knew what that kind of needy felt like, and I was glad Nan could give him some nurturing.

"My mother lives in San Miguel de Allende now," Luca told her. "I bought her a house in Valle del Maiz. She runs a bed and breakfast."

Nan kissed him on the forehead. "You're a good son," she said.

"You should visit her sometime. She knows all about you. All the times you let me stay here. She would love to have you. It's a beautiful city. Very safe."

"I would love that," Nan said.

Luca beamed.

Eventually, everyone left and Nan went to bed. Luca and I brushed our teeth in the bathroom, making silly faces at each other in the mirror, the way we used to in my dorm. I still hadn't come close to figuring out the right things to say to him. I'd never been my best with words. He nudged me with his elbow. I nudged him back. He hugged me, toothbrush still in his mouth. A long, tight embrace. I couldn't breathe well through my nose, and my mouth was full of toothpaste, but I didn't want it to end. I felt like I'd rather suffocate than have him let go.

Finally, he broke away and spit in the sink. I did too. We cupped our hands under the running water to rinse our mouths.

"I missed you so much," he said, making eye contact in the mirror. It was easier that way. When we looked at each other for real, it was too much.

"Me too," I said. I wanted him to climb into bed with me, to sleep the way we used to. And for a moment, I thought that's what would happen. He kissed my cheek. I watched him in the mirror as he did. He was thinner, a new sharpness to his jawline.

"Goodnight," he said. And then he left.

I heard him walk down the hallway to the guest room, where he always used to stay when he came home with me. When I went out to the hall, I noticed he hadn't closed the door all the way. Before I could decide if that was a sign, he turned out the light.

In my room, Bark was sprawled across the bed. My body too lit up to sleep, I lay on my back in the tiny spot Bark left me, and stared at the ceiling, trying not to think about the open door.

I'm sure all our friends in college thought Luca and I were having sex long before it happened. For most of our friendship, I felt like we were bear cubs playing together. Rolling around. Cuddling at night for warmth. We kept a line of innocence. What I needed from Luca was bigger than sex, and I was too scared to upset the balance.

When senior year started, the pressure of a deadline changed everything. We would not be in this bubble together by accident anymore. If we were going to stay together, we'd have to make choices, and the weight of those choices pushed at curiosities I hadn't let myself indulge. I started noticing the trail of hair he revealed when he raised his arms to stretch, his shirt lifting away from his pants. The musky smell of his body after he played soccer on the quad. The way he looked at me. Sometimes, he would turn away from me in bed at night. With purpose. To hide.

I remember his hands.

It started in the Clark Theatre, in the arena bleachers, in the dark. A read-through I was supposed to be watching. He came with me, because he always did. And he threaded his fingers between mine, because he always did, but something about the friction of his hand against my palm was different. I remember my heart pounding, a lump in my throat. The panic running through my veins had an edge of excitement.

The theatre smelled like fresh paint and the stale tang of welded metal. Luca was wearing a flannel shirt, and the arms were too long on him. His cuff felt soft on my wrist.

I knew it was the end. I was powerless to stop it, because I wanted to feel his hip bones against mine. To know the smooth skin low on his belly. I wanted to push his hair from his face and kiss his lips and feel our connection in every way. I wanted to be alive for once.

Before the first act was done, he nudged me with his elbow, tugged at my hand. We snuck from our seats, and ran through the lobby, down the steps to the basement. He pulled me into the empty black box theatre, and as soon as the door shut behind us, his mouth was on mine. We'd kissed before. Politely. Sweetly. An act of love, not lust. But this time, we were insatiable.

I was on the pill. He knew. He saw me take it every night. Neither of us had done this before. There was no physical reason not to. No need to leave that room and risk the brisk air of early spring jolting us from this certainty.

We fumbled in the dark, looking for the risers. Shed clothes with purpose. I took off his shirt. He slid my pants from my ankles, the boundaries between our bodies becoming less and less clear.

I'd always heard that sex was supposed to be awkward the first time. New navigation. Learning parameters. But most of his body was as familiar as my own. We didn't have much to learn. It felt inevitable. Necessary. We pushed away the fear of what was next. The carpet on the risers burned my back. My body was present with his.

Even years later, even after all the hurt I held from losing him, that moment was the one I went to when I needed to remember something good. It was my touchstone for joy. The best anything could ever be. We were completely alive.

CHAPTER THIRTY-ONE

～～～～～～

Luca was still sleeping when I left to work the wedding party at Isaac's. I snuck down the hall to peek in on him. He was wrapped around the blankets, the way he used to wrap his body around mine. I wondered about women after me. If they shared the same closeness. Eric and I never took that kind of comfort in each other.

At work, I struggled to push thoughts of Luca's possible girlfriends from my mind. What were they like? Were they past or present tense?

The sound of a sewing machine is a peaceful hum to a calm mind, and a driver of repetitive thought to a chaotic one. But once the bridal party came in, their noisy bluster and relentless demands forced me into the moment.

When I got home, Luca and Nan were in the living room playing music and looking through records. They didn't notice Bark slip away to greet me. I whispered my hello to him, and watched from the hallway.

"I love this one," Luca said, smiling in recognition at a record with a white cover and a picture of a woman in a striped shirt. "My mother has a thing for Eydie Gormé. She had this one."

"Play it," Nan said, so eager to make him happy.

He placed the record on the turntable, careful to put the needle down exactly right. The cowbell started and Luca bopped his head in time with the music, wide smile on his face. "I haven't heard this in forever!"

"May I?" Nan offered her hand.

Luca bowed, slipped his hand into hers, and they twirled around the room as Eydie sang "Blame It on the Bossa Nova."

In college, Luca taught me how to waltz on the gravel roof of his dorm, after he confessed that his mother made him take ballroom dancing as a child. I watched the way he held his neck long and straight as he moved through the steps with Nan, and the wanting collected in my chest until it hurt. I snuck to my room so they wouldn't see me.

I was scared of so many things, but I'd never been more terrified than this. I always ruined everything, and Luca was too special to ruin.

A few songs later, Luca knocked on my open door. "I didn't know you were home."

"Just got in," I said, avoiding his gaze.

"I'm going to head out early tomorrow."

"You're leaving? Already?" I said, showing too many cards. I didn't know how to be around him, but I couldn't stand the idea of him leaving.

"Only for the day," he said with an inflection on *only* that suggested he knew it would calm me. "My friend Danny in Orlando has camera equipment to lend us."

"That's good!" I said, attempting to pull all my feelings back in.

"Would you— Do you want to come with me?" Luca asked, lifting his arms to stretch them against the top of the doorframe.

I tried not to look at the swath of belly he exposed. Toned, muscular, like maybe he exercised purposely now, not just the occasional soccer game.

My knee-jerk reaction was to say no, pretend Isaac needed me, but I made eye contact with Luca for a split second and saw my wanting reflected in the look he gave me. "Sure."

He drummed at the top of the doorframe. "Good!" He stood there for a moment, looking at me, like there was more he might say. Then, "I'm going to go clean up. For dinner. Are you going to Ruth's?"

I shook my head. "No. I need to get over to Bitsie's and work on the costumes." It felt like way too much to share him with the other ladies again, and I needed to store up my energy for our road trip.

"Oh," he said, face falling. "I'll—I can bring home a plate."

I stared at the doorway long after he walked away.

That night, at Bitsie's, working on costumes, the hum of the sewing machine seemed to be asking, *Why can't you? Why can't you? Why can't you?* A brave person would have grabbed Luca's hand and gone to dinner.

CHAPTER THIRTY-TWO

I was up before sunrise, trying to get ready for the road trip before Luca woke, so I'd have extra time. But when I got out of the shower, he was already in the kitchen making coffee. I could hear him humming, the way he always did. Low, atonal. Adaptive self-soothing, or maybe a song he couldn't quite remember.

I got dressed in the bathroom. Underwear sticking to my damp body, my dress not wanting to slide into place easily. I'd sewn a quick tank dress the night before from a few yards of heathered jersey I found in Bunny's closet. I left the edges unhemmed to make it look a little more casual. Even though I knew everything about me was the opposite of breezy, I wanted to look like I could say, *Oh, this? Something I just threw together*, and it might seem true.

"You guys don't even have eggs in there," Luca said, nodding toward the fridge as I walked into the kitchen. He poured coffee into two mugs and handed me one.

"I know," I said, sitting at the counter. "Crazy, right? I think the whole Vegan Nan thing is more shocking than the boyfriend."

He slid a plate with a breakfast sandwich to me.

"Whoa! Thanks!"

I'd stayed at Bitsie's long after she came home from Ruth's, using my work as an excuse to wait to go home until Luca was surely asleep. Luca, as promised, left a Tupperware container filled with some sort of casserole in the fridge, but I was overtired and I'd just gotten my period. My stomach seemed likely to revolt over anything stronger than cereal. Now I was starving.

"Tofu and avocado. Best I could do."

I took a bite. Luca had coated the slab of tofu in spices and browned it in the frying pan. "This is good!"

"Phew! I didn't know what I was doing. I pretended it was eggs." Luca sat next to me at the counter. "So do you like Nan's new boyfriend?"

"Oh my gosh, yes!" I said. "Isaac— That's my boss. I worked for him in high school . . ."

"Ohhh!" Luca said. "That's why I already knew Isaac. We went to his shop once when I was here."

"Yeah. He's wonderful."

"It's good when nice people find each other," Luca said, looking into my eyes.

I could feel my face flush.

As soon as I took my last bite of breakfast, Luca said, "We should get going. So we can make it back and put that camera to work!"

"Okay." I rinsed my plate in the sink.

I was confused over what he wanted to photograph right away. The costumes weren't ready. I'd finished Bitsie's top, but she'd gone to bed before I could get a fitting in. Nan's top was still in pieces. The tails needed a paint job and Mo was working on borrowing her friend's airbrush equipment. The other mermaids weren't due for almost two weeks.

I wanted to ask how long Luca was staying, but I didn't feel like I'd have enough control over my reaction to the answer.

"Great!" Luca said, patting his pocket for his keys.

"I just have to use the . . . restroom." I ran to the bathroom to change my tampon and wallpaper my underwear with an array of panty liners, in case this trip did not allow for enough pit stops.

I longed for normal periods. In my mind, other women, girls like Nikki, had cute little uteruses that left cute little spots on their menstrual products and housed cute little babies when they got pregnant without extensive medical intervention. I pictured my uterus like Oscar the Grouch's home. A trash can with a grumbly beast where a baby should have been.

When I was done, I went to the bedroom to say goodbye to Bark, but he wasn't there. "Bark? Barky?" I called, keeping my cool as much as I could. The panic felt like it was on the other side of a sliding glass door. It hadn't reached me yet, but I could see it. I started making the rounds of places to search for him. "Bark?"

"He's in the truck already," Luca said, walking back into the house as I rushed toward the living room. "I assumed you wanted to take him along?"

I looked out the window, and there was Bark, sitting happily in the driver's seat of Luca's truck. "Sure," I said, bewildered. Maybe the time with Althea and Nan was actually making him better.

Luca's red Ford pickup was old, but well cared for. His dashboard wasn't covered in dust like mine. Bark moved closer to me when Luca climbed in the driver's seat, his dog breath hot on my face. He snapped his head to look at any source of noise—the ding of keys in the ignition, the click of my seat belt—but he had a certain ownership of Luca's truck. He wasn't grimacing or trying to hide.

A raspy voice poured from the CD player, singing a song that flowed like waves hitting rocks. Full of longing. Nothing like the Top 40 stuff Luca listened to in college. It fit him better.

"I love this," I said, pointing to the radio.

"Chris Pureka," he said. "I want to use her music in a documentary someday. When I can find the right one."

"The right song, or the right documentary?"

"Both," he said. "But I feel like either the idea will hit me, and I'll know the exact right song, or I'll listen to one of her songs enough and the idea will appear."

"I get that," I said. "Sometimes I feel like I'm frantic for input, like I can't see enough or hear enough, and then when I hit overload, something suddenly makes sense."

"Exactly." His smile felt like recognition.

"I've been mainlining the B-52s while I work on mermaid costumes."

He took a second, like he was considering the combination, then smiled. "Yeah. It's in your sketches."

I smiled back.

He looked at me, then the road, then me. "It's weird, right? To be together again?"

"Yeah."

"Weird and then normal. Like I'm supposed to see your face. It feels good to be with you."

If he hadn't been driving, I might have thrown myself at him. Held him as hard as I could.

We both got quiet. I worried we were going to talk about what happened. I didn't want to be stuck in a car when we did, so I got chatty, asking him questions about his mother and Carla and Marco. I told him I thought Isaac was prepping me to take over the shop, that I was nervous about the responsibility. I asked him if he'd kept in touch with anyone from college. What was Sundance like? I filled every silence, blocking every chance for him to ask me why we lost each other. Maybe he already knew.

Bark spent the first half of the trip looking out the window, but then he stretched across my lap and dozed off. I ran my fingers through his fur as I talked. Whenever I stopped petting him, he'd wake up and look at me like I'd fallen down on the job.

I talked so much that we passed the WELCOME TO ORLANDO sign before I remembered I wanted to stop at a gas station before we got to his friend's house.

"Oh, hey, do you think we could make a pit stop?" I asked. Breezy. So breezy.

"We'll be at Danny's in two minutes."

"I think there's a gas station—"

"I swear, it's, like, two minutes. Promise."

I wished I hadn't said anything so I could ask him to stop on the way home instead.

Danny made a micro-budget film about a farmer who finds bones in his cornfield and suspects they are alien. It got a lot of festival attention and ended up making millions. I was expecting a hulking McMansion, with a shiny sports car in the driveway, but Danny lived in a tiny ranch house on the south side of the city. It was a little run-down. There was a rusty yellow Chevy pickup in the driveway that looked like the one in the movie poster picture Luca showed me.

"I'm so glad we caught him," Luca said. "He's hardly ever here. But he's got a couple months before his next shoot."

Luca backed his truck into the driveway. As he did, the front door to the house opened. Bark shot up, suddenly awake, hind legs shaking as he looked around. Luca didn't seem to notice his nerves.

Danny was over six feet tall, with a mane of curly brown hair, sun-bleached at the ends. He wore beige cargo pants so weathered they looked like they could blow away in a breeze, and the soles of his dirty checkered Vans had separated from the rest of the shoe so each step had an extra slap.

"Heeyyy, brother!" he said as we got out of the truck, his voice a lazy growl. He ran at Luca.

Bark, still in the truck, growled back at Danny. I climbed in again to grab his leash.

Danny hugged Luca around the waist and lifted him off the ground. Bark yelped a warning, hair on his neck standing.

Luca laughed. "Put me down! Put me down!" he yelled, legs wiggling. "You're upsetting the dog."

Danny put Luca down and poked his head in the truck. "Who's this guy?"

Bark lunged at him, yanking his slack leash hard against my hand. My skin burned.

Danny wasn't fazed. He offered Bark the back of his hand to smell. I held the leash tight. Bark sniffed carefully, backing away, then going in for another sniff. He looked at Danny's face, like he was taking careful measurements of his expression.

Danny grinned at Bark, flashing a slightly chipped front tooth. "You're working hard, aren't you, buddy?" he said. His smile took up most of his face, but it was easy, not intense. He seemed simply, clearly happy. I felt like I was seeing a unicorn.

Bark's hackles softened.

"Thank you," I said across the seat of the truck.

"Hey, no problem," he said, reaching over Bark to offer me his hand. "Danny."

Bark's hackles went up again. I heard his lowest-level growl, so quiet you might miss it.

I shook Danny's hand quickly. "Katie."

"Nice to meet you, Katie," Danny said, and then he was out of the truck, patting Luca on the back hard enough to throw him off balance. "So good to see you, man!"

I jumped out of the truck. Bark followed without protest, but stayed close, the ends of his fur brushing against my leg.

"Oh, hey," Luca said, "can Katie use your bathroom?"

I cringed.

"Sure," Danny said. "Go on in!"

I handed Bark's leash to Luca and started to walk toward the house. Bark ran to the end of the line to walk with me. When I kept walking, he squealed in panic. I heard Danny say, "Whoa."

"It's okay," Luca called after me. "I've got him."

But the further I walked, the harder Bark cried.

"You can take him with you," Danny called.

So I went back to get Bark, who happily followed me to the house without hesitation, walking so close he pushed me off the path. I didn't look back to see if Danny and Luca saw me trip.

Danny's house was a little run down on the inside too. Clean, but worn. Sagging brown couch. Cracked tile floors, the scent of stale pot smoke hanging in the air. There was a huge projection screen on the wall. Speakers that seemed way too big for such a small room.

I found the bathroom in the usual ranch house bathroom location and closed Bark in with me. It was clean and dirty at the same time. Scrubbed of immediate grime, but there were rust stains in the bathtub and hard water deposits on the faucet. I didn't feel confident about the plumbing. No trash can in sight. I checked under the sink, but there was only a plunger and extra toilet paper.

I dug a roll of blue dog poop bags from my purse. When I changed my tampon, I triple-bagged the old one and tucked it in my purse, hoping I could sneak it to the kitchen garbage before Luca and Danny were done slapping out their hellos in the driveway. But as soon as I flushed the toilet, I heard the front door open. Bark growled again.

There were dark sweaty crescents under the armholes of my dress. We'd driven with the windows open and my hair was frizzed and knotted. I wiped runny mascara from under my eyes. This was the opposite of breezy.

"Hey," Danny said as Bark and I left the bathroom, "you guys want a beer?"

"Naw, man," Luca said. "I want to get back on the road to get some shooting in today."

When we got close enough to Danny, Bark lunged, growling again.

"It's okay," Danny said, dropping to the floor, lying on his back to show Bark his belly.

Bark didn't know what to make of it. He inched closer. Danny swatted toward Bark, hitting the floor with his palm. I held my breath.

Bark wagged his tail.

"Yeah, buddy," Danny said. "I'm your friend."

Bark head-butted Danny in the gut. Laughing, Danny gave Bark's side a firm pat. Bark jumped, smacking his paws against the floor like he was bowing. Danny sat up, giving Bark's head a rough rub. Bark looked like he was smiling.

"He's a weird dude," Danny said. "I like him. Those eyes are crazy beautiful." He pulled his phone from one of his cargo pockets and snapped a picture of Bark. "Look at that!" He held up the screen of his phone.

I felt silly for leaning over to look, like maybe he thought I'd never noticed Bark's eyes before, but when I saw the picture, I had to admit that Danny captured the contrast between them in a way that made Bark look even more striking and a little bit wild.

"I love that," I said.

Danny typed something into his screen. "Sent it to you," he said to Luca as I heard Luca's phone ding. "Give it to her, okay?"

"Sure," Luca said, offering Danny a hand to help him up. "Should we get packing?"

Before they went outside, Danny got Bark a bowl of water. I stayed in the house with Bark, until he finished drinking. After I washed the bowl, I checked under the kitchen sink for a garbage can, but there was only a paper grocery bag with a receipt and an orange peel in it. Too conspicuous.

I ran Bark out to the truck and stashed my purse under the front seat so I could help Danny and Luca load the gear.

"This is a lot of equipment for a photo shoot," I said when they came out of the garage with a second dolly stacked with metal-edged road cases full of equipment.

"Didn't Nan tell you?" Luca asked, shock on his face.

"What?"

"We're shooting a documentary," he said. "Of the reunion show."

"Show?" I said. "It's just a calendar. I thought—"

"I can't believe Nan didn't tell you," Luca said, laughing. He didn't understand the implications.

Danny watched me carefully, like maybe he picked up on my weirdness. It was his job as a filmmaker to notice every last movement and tell a story with it. I didn't want to be the story, even if it was only in his mind.

"That's Nan." I forced a laugh. "She probably told Mo twice and forgot about me."

"Hey, is there anything I need to know about the camera?" Luca asked Danny. "I've never shot underwater."

"Here." Danny opened the top case on the dolly. "I'll show you . . ."

I looked over at the truck. Bark was in the driver's seat watching me, holding something in his mouth. It was blue. He wagged his tail. I waved my hand at him, flat palmed, the gesture command for *down*.

Danny stopped talking for a second and watched me. It probably looked like I was waving away a bad smell. I doubled down, doing it again, with more purpose, and then grabbed at the air, like I was trying to swat a mosquito. Bark disappeared from sight.

Danny went back to showing Luca how the waterproof case fit the camera.

I made a beeline for the truck.

Bark lay on the seat, the tattered blue bag with my tampon clutched in his teeth. I put my hand under his mouth. "Drop it," I hissed. He turned his head away. "Drop. It."

Bark started to shake his head violently, like he was trying to stun his prey. Luca and Danny started loading cases. Danny jumped up on the truck bed.

"Drop it," I whispered, prying the tampon from Bark's mouth. I dumped the mangled bag in my purse just before Danny looked in the back window of the truck. He waved at us. I waved back, and then, worried, checked my hand for blood. It was clean, but Danny caught me staring into my palm like a weirdo.

"Are you okay?" Luca called to me.

"All good," I said, slipping the strap of my purse across my body. I wore it the whole time we finished loading the truck, and prayed the bag wasn't leaking.

I was quiet on the ride home.

"Since *Durango*," Luca said, "I've been trying to find the next project. But everything that gets suggested to me is heavy, grim. *Durango* wasn't grim to me. It was about hope. I want my work to be about the human spirit. Not politics, not sadness. Not at the core."

"Yeah," I said, watching the white dashes on the road disappear beside us. Adrenaline overwhelmed my brain, forcing horrid thoughts of Nan underwater and the potential seepage in my purse.

"Their story is beautiful," Luca said. I could hear a hint of hesitation in his voice. "Older women get pushed toward invisible, and I want to show women who are still in full color. I've watched my mom—Carla—struggle with being treated like she's fading, when she's earned the right to feel powerful with all those mountains she moves. So the mermaid show hits good marks for what my managers want, but it also hits the right places in my heart."

His words felt like an apology, or maybe a pitch. I didn't have any enthusiasms to offer him beyond a smile that probably looked fake. I knew it wasn't fair of me to feel betrayed when I hadn't told him I was terrified of watching Nan and Bitsie swim. A reasonable person would assume I'd gotten over my fear of water by now. But I'd also had hope when it was clear I shouldn't have. Luca didn't come to Nan's for me. He was looking for a new story.

Bark slept soundly, worn out from the adventure, his head resting on Luca's leg. I tried to check my purse discreetly, but the bag with the tampon had fallen to the bottom. I didn't want to risk digging around when I couldn't see clearly. I put my purse on my feet so it wouldn't leak on the floor of Luca's truck. Every time I tried to tell myself I was being ridiculous, the images of disaster amplified. I pictured blood pouring from my purse onto my feet. I pictured Nan tangled in her air hose, Luca capturing it all on film instead of helping her. No matter how hard I tried, I couldn't imagine everything being okay.

When we got back, Luca ran inside to ask Nan where he should put all the equipment. I threw the tampon in the garbage can in the garage. It hadn't leaked in my purse at all.

CHAPTER THIRTY-THREE

After we loaded all the road cases into the dining room, Nan and Luca left to meet Bitsie at the community center. Since a large enough tank would be hard to find, Luca came up with the idea of underwater cameras and big screens to project the action. They were hoping to charm the community center manager into letting them use the pool for free, since tickets from the show would fundraise for the center.

Hannah and Woo Woo sent me measurements, so I needed to work on their costumes. I stole some of Isaac's good coffee and made the closest approximation of a frappuccino I could manage with almond milk and maple syrup.

And then Mo called. "Please, can you help? The unveiling is two weekends from now, and I'm totally behind."

"For a little bit," I told her, "but I need to work on costumes."

"You help me," Mo said, "and when we're done, I'll help you crank 'em out."

I knew it wasn't a fair trade. Mo didn't have patience for fine work the way I did. She was good with broad strokes. Large scale. What I did was slow and small and careful. But I said yes anyway, because it was Mo, and she needed me. And I needed the company.

*　　*　　*

I downed my coffee and changed my clothes, grabbing a pair of socks for those gross work boots. Bark followed me to the foyer. When I stepped into my flip-flops, he wagged his tail.

"Do you want to come with me?" I asked.

He reared up, waving his front legs in the air. I decided to go with it. Maybe the road trip and his time with Althea had made him brave. On the walk to Mo's, he trotted slightly behind me, barely pulling on the leash. He even sniffed a mailbox post like a normal dog.

"Hey, how was it?" Mo asked, voice muffled by her welding mask.

Bark was taken aback by her getup. But as soon as she lifted the mask, his legs stopped shaking. He pulled on the leash to bring us closer so he could say hi.

"I lived." I wasn't sure if I wanted to talk about it. I didn't want to hear that I was being silly.

"Alone in a car with your dreamy man and 'Oh, I lived,'" she said, scratching Bark's head, leaving soot behind his ears. He was wiggly and happy for her attention.

"I got my period yesterday. So, you know, awkward bathroom stuff." I told her about Bark's thievery.

"Oh! Worst!" Mo said. She got us beers and we sat on an old wood pallet. "You can let him off leash. I don't think there's anything at his level he can get into." She pointed to her eyes and pointed at Bark, like she was putting him on notice.

The garage door was wide open. I wasn't used to having Bark off leash in an open space, but I unclipped him because Mo seemed so sure it would be fine. I half expected him to run away from me, like this shot at a jailbreak was all he'd been waiting for. Instead, he walked around Mo's garage sniffing things, then plopped down on the floor at my feet.

"One time," Mo said, "I was sort of seeing this guy in college, and he lived in an off-campus house. I flushed a tampon and he had to call Roto-Rooter. I wanted to disappear. And the Roto-Rooter guy was all, 'If it doesn't come off the roll or out of you . . .' And I was like, 'Well, it did come out of me,' but I was way too embarrassed to defend myself."

I was shocked. Mo never seemed to get embarrassed by anything, but just telling the story made her face flush.

"And, like, if guys had periods, all plumbing would be able to handle tampons. You know it's true."

I laughed. "That sounds about right."

"But, that was in college. Luca is a man. I bet if you'd explained why you wanted to go to the gas station, he would have been happy to take you."

"Maybe," I said, knowing she was probably right. "I might have added an obstacle that wasn't really there." Worrying about a tampon was so much easier than worrying about everything else.

"So what's really bothering you?" she asked.

"Luca is staying."

"That's great!"

"To shoot a mermaid documentary."

"Whoa!"

"Because they're doing a reunion show at the community center."

I expected Mo to get excited about the idea of the show, but she didn't. Her face fell.

I looked away. Hot with shame. Eyes tearing. Bark came over to smell my cheek.

"Oh, hon," Mo said, wiping tears from my face with her hand. "Shit." She used the sleeve of her t-shirt to wipe the spot on my cheek she'd touched, and waved her sooty fingers at me. "Sorry. Got most of it." She wiped her hands on her shorts. "They're not going to drown doing this show. One, I go to mermaid class sometimes—"

"You do?"

"Yeah," Mo said. "It's a hell of a workout. Those ladies are strong swimmers. And two, I know all the lifeguards over there. They're awesome. And three, I'll go to as many rehearsals as I can. And I'll be at the show no matter what. Okay?"

I nodded.

We sat, shoulders touching, quiet.

"Maybe it'll all get better if you kiss that boy and tell him you love him," Mo said, nudging me with her shoulder.

"I think he's only interested in my grandmother," I said.

Mo laughed.

"You know what I mean. He came here for a new story. Not me."

"Couldn't it be both? Or even that he came for you and found an excuse to stick around?"

"Even if he did come for me—I can't do that to him, Mo. He's too—"

"He's too wonderful and I'm too shitty," Mo said, raising her voice half an octave to mimic me. "Stop. Seriously. Stop. You're good. I like you. I've liked you for most of my life now."

"I was gone for a lot of it."

"I didn't get stupid when you got married," she said, smiling. "I still liked you." Bark sniffed Mo's shoulder and pushed his head into her hand for a scratch.

"But Luca's been through so much," I said.

"So have you."

"Yeah, but there's something broken in me."

"The people who don't have broken parts aren't interesting," Mo said. "You're hurt and you hide it until you can't. It's okay. You're just human."

"It's not okay."

"I've seen you at your worst," she said. "It's not so bad."

I remembered the time I had a panic attack when her uncle came to visit and took us to SeaWorld. I screamed at her in the bathroom. *Leave me alone. Leave me alone.* Echoing in the cinder block walls. It was a big deal for her to get to take a trip like that. To have the attention of her uncle. And instead of leaving me, she sat on the floor of the bathroom with her hand under the stall door, waiting for me to hold it.

"You always made me feel like it was safe to show you the messy stuff," Mo said. Her voice cracked. "So don't you dare tell me you're no good for anyone because you fall apart sometimes."

I thought about fifth grade when we'd finally scored invites to Ashley Marshall's sleepover. We both declined because Mo still wet the bed. Sometimes I washed her sheets at Nan's when she smuggled them to our house in a backpack so her grandmother wouldn't worry about her. Maybe she wouldn't have been able to tell another friend.

Mo kicked her boot against the pavement. "The thing that makes me sad— You're friends with me, so I don't know why you feel like you have to be perfect."

"Because my mom left," I said, surprised by how close the answer was to the surface. "I wasn't good enough to save my dad, and my mom left me, and if I wasn't careful, Nan would too."

"Nan wouldn't," Mo said. "I won't either."

I took a sip of beer. She held the bottom of the bottle up, so I had to gulp. When she finally let go she said, "Do it!"

I stared at her.

"For me," she said.

I let out the loudest, longest burp ever.

Mo fell on her side, laughing and kicking her legs. "Hysterical!"

Bark licked her face until she was gasping for air.

*   *   *

Mo and I worked for three hours, but we got more done than we had on all the other nights put together. We'd developed a flow to our work. I knew how to read her gestures, to anticipate what she needed and have a tool at the ready.

When Mo said, "Alright, I'm getting bleary-eyed," Morty looked done to me. He was mammoth and serene. She'd captured the grace that made manatees so easily mistaken for mermaids by sea-worn sailors.

"I can get this done in about ten to twelve hours," she said. I think she read the panic on my face, because she quickly added, "Solo work. You helped me finish all the heavy lifting stuff. I have to work on the patina at the welds, tweak things here and there. And then I'm all yours for costumes!"

"Thanks," I said, hoping she couldn't read that panic too.

CHAPTER THIRTY-FOUR

〜〜〜〜〜〜〜〜

Bark lagged behind me on the walk home, sniffing spots on the ground for as long as I'd let him. Once we turned the corner, he decided to take the lead, pulling on the leash like we'd never make it home if he didn't apply force.

Two blocks from Nan's, there was movement in the bushes by the sidewalk. Bark froze. I did too, imagining a person lying in wait behind the gardenias. I could almost feel a hand over my mouth. A handkerchief doused with chloroform, like a bad guy from a Nancy Drew novel would use. Only real. And worse. I started to run, but Bark wouldn't budge.

"Come on," I hissed, tugging at Bark's leash.

His legs shook. He growled. The hair on his back stood up. I was terrified.

And then a cat darted from the shadows. I laughed even though my heart was still pounding.

Bark was not amused. He lunged toward the cat, but when the cat turned to look at him, he darted in the opposite direction, ripping his leash from my hands. He took off down the street.

I chased after him, kicking off my flip-flops so I could run faster. "Bark! Bark!" I yelled, bare feet smacking against the pavement. It was late. Rude to yell. I didn't care. It was Bark and I needed to get him back. A car could come at any minute.

I couldn't keep up with him. I tripped on an uneven seam in the sidewalk and cracked my toenail, blood gushing. When I crouched on the sidewalk, gasping in pain, Bark snuck back. Stealthy. Silent. He licked my cheek. Sniffed the blood on the concrete, looked at me, worried.

"I'm okay," I said, petting his head, grabbing his leash.

We walked back toward Nan's. I only found one flip-flop. When we got to where the cat had been, Bark's legs started to shake. Again, he wouldn't budge.

I picked him up, trying to get his weight balanced in my arms. His legs flailed. His body slipped. I had to keep hiking him up, straining the muscles in my back. I waddled home.

"Good lord," Nan said, opening the door. She must have seen us coming. "Have you been to war?"

I put Bark down in the foyer. His legs splayed out like Bambi on ice, as if he'd never walked on tile before. He scrambled to my bedroom.

"Fuck cats," I said, and hopped to the bathroom to bandage my foot, trying not to bleed all over the floor.

Once I cleaned up, I went to comfort Bark. He was already sprawled across my bed, feet paddling furiously as he chased the cat in his sleep. Maybe in his dreams he got to be the fierce dog he wished he were.

I ventured to the living room.

Luca had camera equipment spread across the coffee table.

"I heard you had an incident," he said, smiling.

"Sort of." My toe was throbbing.

"Want to see this?" He hooked the camera up to the TV, pressed a button, and there was Nan on the screen.

Bitsie's voice in the background says, "She's ready for her

close-up, Mr. DeMille!" Nan laughs, looks up at the camera, eyes bright. Elegance in her posture.

"So," Luca asks off camera. "How did you become a mermaid?"

"There was an ad," Nan says. "In the back of the newspaper. My father read it out loud to my mother at breakfast one day, because he thought it was a joke. 'Girls Wanted for Mermaid Show. Strong Swimmers Only.' I stole the paper when he left for work. I couldn't use the phone to call without my mother overhearing, so I walked all the way to the address on the listing. Miles and miles. The warehouse was in a bad part of town. As soon I got there, a man took one look at me and said auditions were the next day. Two o'clock sharp, in the parking lot. So I had to walk all the way back again. My feet were so sore."

The camera cuts to Bitsie. "I had a friend from high school, Meryl Stephenson, and she told me about it. She wanted me to go with her so she didn't get kidnapped or whatever they told us happened to girls back then. I was such a scrawny little thing," Bitsie says. "Not like I could have helped if anyone was going to try anything funny. But Meryl was the pretty one, and that seemed to need some sort of protecting. She looked like a Breck Shampoo girl, but she was a terrible swimmer. She thought she was so beautiful it wouldn't even matter. And I think we both thought I was too funny looking to get the job." She smiles, and her warmth, the red hair, her tanned skin, lines in her face, all come together to make her absolutely stunning. "So we got there, and they had this big tank set up in the parking lot. I mean—it was big for what you'd expect for a parking lot, but it was small for someone to actually get in. Like a long tube. We had to go down to the bottom, grab a rock they'd thrown, and come back up. Then we had to stay under and breathe air from a hose. That was the test. Meryl panicked. She couldn't do it, and she was so embarrassed that she wanted us to go home before I'd even had a turn. She didn't want to leave me there alone, but she didn't want to stay. And then I heard, 'I'll stay until you're done. We can walk together.' I looked over, and there she was." Bitsie's eyes sparkle. She ducks out of frame. Luca pulls the camera back so we see her reach to grab Nan's hand. Nan squeezes back.

"The other love of my life," Bitsie says.

I didn't even realize my eyes had filled with tears until one splashed on my cheek.

"I know," Luca said, laughing. His eyes were shiny. "I think if you listen closely, you can hear me gasp."

"It's gorgeous," I said, suddenly thankful for the chance to see this and hear stories they wouldn't think to tell me otherwise. As much as I was afraid, I wanted to know everything Luca would learn. I wanted to see Nan and Bitsie from his point of view. "Thank you."

Luca reached over and squeezed my hand.

CHAPTER THIRTY-FIVE

All of a sudden the mermaid reunion was a show and a documentary, and there was a firm timeline in place, and the pressure to get the costumes done was crushing me. For a photo shoot, I could use binder clips and safety pins to adjust fit. In a show, it all had to work. And whatever I did would be on film. Mistakes would last forever. Plus, I had no experience designing for water. Not many people did. After a ton of searching, I found an online forum for people who work and play as mermaids. It was a gold mine of tips about tail caulk, sequins, and waterproof makeup.

When I told Isaac what I was up against, he helped me between our tailoring appointments, but after a few days of frantic sewing, he told me he was giving me time off until the show.

"I don't want to leave you in the lurch," I said.

"What lurch? I can do this," he said with a look that let me know he meant it.

He lent me his extra serger so I could finish seams faster, and promised to keep sewing for me whenever it was slow at the shop. Even with all of that, I knew I was in trouble.

When I tried to talk to Nan about it she said, "You're so talented. You always make it work!" Like it was absurd for me to be concerned.

Bitsie offered to help, but I worried her help would make

more work. Mo was busy with Morty. Luca was busy filming. The person I needed most was Bunny.

I thought when I started sewing in Bunny's room I'd hit the bottom of the grief I would feel. But now the way I needed her cut so close to my core that it was an entirely new entity. Sometimes, when I was up late, sewing sequins on tops, I tried to talk to her in my head, hoping she'd arrive with words of comfort, or an answer to a question. But I couldn't summon her the way I had before. It felt like talking to myself, and I didn't have anything good to say.

I decided to nix tails for the women from the mermaid class, since they didn't have experience swimming in them and I didn't have enough time. They would be performing at the surface like synchronized swimmers anyway, so I decided on black 1920s bathing costumes with swim caps covered in multicolored plastic flowers.

I spent an afternoon taking apart fake leis from the party store. I stuffed the caps with newspaper and lined them up on the driveway to work them like an assembly line, gluing on the flowers with bathroom caulk. Toward the end, when my hair was a ball of frizz, and my arms were covered in drying caulk that looked like peeling skin, Luca snuck up on me with the camera to capture it all. I was still wearing the *Man of La Mancha* t-shirt I'd slept in.

"Hey!" I covered my face with my hand when I saw him, pretending to be playfully shy instead of horrified. When I stood up, I noticed that my legs were covered in bruises from working at Mo's.

He kept filming, smiling at me from behind the camera.

I was mostly done, but I walked to the far side of the row of bathing caps and pretended they needed extra preening. I fluffed flowers and hoped that in action I'd look better than I did just standing there.

Eventually, Luca put the camera down. "These are great."

"You don't have to film me," I said.

"But I do. You're part of the story."

"What if I don't sign a release?" I tried hard to smile, keep it light.

"I'll sic Nan on you," he said. His smile was actually light, oblivious to the fact that I was uncomfortable.

"You have to see the footage I got at the pool," Luca said in the house later, when I was done gluing flowers. He hooked his camera up to the television, and then there was water covering half the screen.

The camera pans up. Mo is poolside, connecting hoses to the scuba tanks she borrowed from a friend. She drops a hose on either side of the deep end of the pool so Nan and Bitsie can sip air and swim free. Everything shakes. Splashing sounds. The waterline waves across the camera.

The work of keeping my bad thoughts away made it hard to focus on the television. I fought the urge to reach for Luca's hand, like his camera self could be in danger. I wanted to call Nan and Bitsie. Hear their voices while I watched and know for certain they were alive. Breathing. Dry ground under their feet.

"Wow," I said, fake smile on my face, as I watched Bitsie and Nan holding hands underwater, descending to the bottom of the pool, bodies arching toward each other, tails fluttering. "They're so graceful!"

"Yeah," Luca said. "And their tails work so well. Look! Look at this!" He pointed at the screen.

Nan takes a breath from the hose and swims away quickly, the fin propelling her, while Bitsie does somersault spins for the camera. Three in a row before she rights herself, blows a stream of bubbles from her mouth, and uses her hands to shape them into a heart that perfectly frames her smiling elfin face. As soon as the bubbles dissipate, she is swimming away, faster than seems possible. Nan swims toward the camera with an old-fashioned bottle of Coca-Cola and a bottle opener. Another hit from the air hose as Nan displays the bottle like a sommelier. With the bottle opener, she pries off the cap. And then she drinks the soda underwater.

Luca laughed and nudged my arm. "Soda is not on her diet. She replaced it with iced coffee," he said. "Mo helped her reseal the cap."

"Amazing." I wiped my sweaty palms on my shorts. "Shoot." I stood up. "Bark needs a pee break."

Bark was snoring on the floor.

"It's two hours past his usual," I said, lying. "Hey, Bark! Barky!"

Bark jumped to attention, the fur on his face in disarray. "Come on, bud! Pee time!"

He stumbled toward me, gaining spring in his step as we ran for the yard.

While he sniffed around, trying to find the exact right spot to go, I sent Mo a text. "They're out of the water now, right?"

The white bubble with gray dots showed up on my screen. Disappeared. Came back. Disappeared. Came back. Then a photo: Mo's dive watch showing the current time. In the background Nan and Bitsie lounge on chairs by the pool, gabbing away, iced teas in hand, tails carefully hung over neighboring chairs. *They r fine k. Promise.*

Thank you, I wrote back.

She sent me an eggplant emoji.

"Do you want to watch more?" Luca called when Bark and I came back inside. He met us in the kitchen.

"I have to work," I said, which wasn't untrue.

He looked disappointed. "Those tails you made are amazing," he said.

"But they're still the color of baby diarrhea," I said. "I've got to clear out some other work so I'll have time to airbrush when Mo's friend drops off the machine."

"Can I shoot some of your work?"

I didn't want to disappoint him, but I didn't want to be around him with so much stress piling up when I was a sweaty, swearing mess.

"Have you interviewed Isaac yet?" I asked. "Nothing I have to do right now is interesting, but he's at the shop. I could call over for you."

Luca took the bait. Once I got him on his way to Isaac's, I went back outside to check on the caulked bathing caps. They'd have to cure overnight, but they were dry enough to move to the workbench in the garage. I needed to get them to safety before Nan got home and accidentally ran them over, or a bird pooped on them, or someone from the neighborhood decided to try one on and got it stuck to their head. I didn't have enough time to do everything once. I was in abject fear of having to redo something I'd already checked off the list.

CHAPTER THIRTY-SIX

Luca left early the next morning to fly to Atlanta to film Woo Woo in her own home. He'd go to Hannah's two days later, and be back in time to capture their arrivals on Nan and Bitsie's side of the story.

Nan did laundry for him, but he'd only taken what he needed. The rest of his clothes were stacked in a pile on top of the dryer. They smelled like our detergent, not like Luca. I brought them to the guest room and placed them at the end of the pullout couch bed. The blankets were rumpled. I lay on the bed, imagining that the sagging mattress still held the imprint of his body.

When I woke up, it was starting to get dark outside. Bark was snoring next to me. We'd both drooled on Luca's pillow.

Late that night, when I was in the garage testing the airbrush machine Mo's friend dropped off, my phone chimed in my pocket, but my hands were too messy to dig it out.

Mastering the trigger pressure was harder than I'd expected. I kept ending up with lines of paint that were thinner or thicker than what I wanted. Bark, banished from the garage for getting underfoot, whined on the other side of the door. I wanted to quit so badly, but the only way the tails would get done was if I did them. I sprayed a base coat on each one and hung them from the rafters to dry. Turquoise for Bitsie, fuchsia for Nan, gold for Woo Woo, and orange for Hannah. The garage looked like a cartoon fish market.

After I'd scrubbed the paint from my arms, brushed my teeth, and climbed into bed, I remembered to check my phone. I had a text from Luca.

Super late, but wanted to let you know I got in safe. Sleep well.

I wrote back: *You too.*

I watched my screen, hoping he was wired from traveling and still awake, but no response came through.

Nan and Bitsie went on a whirlwind tour, charming local media and peppering the town with fliers. The affiliate morning shows loved them. The first time Bark heard Nan's voice coming from the television, he stopped in his tracks, staring at the screen.

"My granddaughter, Kaitlyn Ellis, is our costume designer," Nan said.

They flashed my Facebook profile picture on the monitor behind Nan and Bitsie's heads. Me and Nan with our wine glasses, my eyes closed, Bark licking my chin.

The anchor gave a chuckle. "Well, it looks like you're having a ton of fun!"

"Oh, we most certainly are," Nan said.

Bark ran to look behind the television.

"I don't think she's hiding there, buddy," I said.

He ran around and looked from the other side. Just in case.

That night, when Luca texted—*Hannah's house tomorrow*—I responded right away.

How's it going?

Good. Then: *Looking forward to getting back.*

Me too, I typed, and waited. Letting him know I wanted to see him felt like walking out to the very end of a wobbly diving board.

But then he wrote: *I can't wait to see you.*

I felt wobbly in a different way. *Me too.*

My brain was too flooded to sleep, so I stayed up to disassemble thrift store costume jewelry. When the manager at the church store near Isaac's found out I'd take broken pieces, she sent me home with two grocery bags full for five dollars. I was planning to make Nan's mermaid top a gem-encrusted affair.

I rounded up pliers, an old toothbrush, and a bottle of Windex, spread everything on newspaper on the coffee table, and switched on the TV. Pickings were slim, but I found a 1960s flick called *The Girls on the Beach*. I wasn't keen on the idea of a beach movie, but I was only half paying attention anyway. The Beach Boys performed in a restaurant hangout. Fish nets and buoys and seashells galore, and I realized we needed to decorate the space around the pool. Mrs. Cohen could lend us her remaining flamingos. Marta had her husband's rattan tiki bar shoved in the back of her garage, and Ruth had some old crab traps I might be able to work with. I'd jogged past a pile of palm fronds stacked at the curb in front of Lester's house that morning. If I nabbed them before garbage pickup, I'd be golden.

I stayed up well into the infomercials, prying apart jump rings and unscrewing eye hooks.

Next morning, first thing, I put Nan to work calling neighbors to see what they would lend us, and went over to Lester's to haul the palm fronds to his backyard.

*   *   *

The night before Mo's unveiling ceremony, Luca got in past midnight.

He hugged me when I opened the door, slumping into my shoulder like he needed the hug. "Epic delay. The stuck-on-the-plane kind," he said, his arms still around me. "Hey, why is Bark blue?"

"Airbrush accident," I said as we pulled away. I scruffed up Bark's fur so the stripe was a little less obvious. At the time, painting my dog felt like one more thing spinning out of control, but Luca laughed like he was laughing *with* me, not at me, and I could finally see the humor.

Nan was already in bed. I heated up leftover vegan lasagna for Luca and we sat at the kitchen table, Bark snoozing on the floor. I sipped mint tea while he shoveled lasagna in his mouth, heaping forkfuls at a time. We watched each other, knees touching under the table. It was like a preview of what our lives could be.

"I could stay up all night with you," Luca said.

I blushed.

He set his fork on the plate after his last bite. "But I have to get the equipment set up early in the morning." He was going to film Mo's ceremony. He wasn't sure where it fit in the story, but it seemed like something to capture.

We brushed our teeth together again. He walked me to my room, like he was dropping me off after a date.

"Goodnight," he said. And then he leaned in and kissed me. It was somewhere between love and lust. Tentative. I wasn't sure if it was going somewhere. I wasn't sure if I wanted it to. Then he said, "Sleep well," and walked down the hall to the guest room. Door open a crack.

I left my door ajar too.

In the morning, I woke up alone. While I was sleeping, Bark had snuck down the hall and crawled into bed with Luca.

CHAPTER THIRTY-SEVEN

〰〰〰〰〰

"You're wearing *that*?" Nan said, walking into my room in a cute navy trellis-print tunic and orange leather sandals.

I was in jeans and a plain black t-shirt and thought I looked fine. My jeans actually fit, thanks to Nan's veggie fanaticism.

"It's an art unveiling," Nan said. "This is a big deal for Maureen. We should act like it."

All the clothes I'd made for myself were in a dirty heap on the floor. I hadn't had time to do laundry.

"I guarantee Mo doesn't care what I'm wearing."

"I do," Nan said.

I felt like I was sixteen again and Nan was telling me I should wear a dress to the school dance, when all the other kids would be in jeans and I'd just be hugging the wall with Mo anyway.

"I have something you can borrow," Nan said, scurrying back to her room.

As she walked away, I saw the outline of a microphone pack. She was already wired. I wanted to scream, but saying anything would only compound the situation. Luca didn't need to hear more of this.

Nan came back with a tunic almost exactly like the one she was wearing, but purple, with a floral print.

I gave her a look, trying to express what I didn't want Luca to hear.

"Wear it for me," Nan said in a tone so firm it couldn't be countered with an expression. I took the dress.

"You look nice," Luca said when I walked into the kitchen after I'd changed. He had a smirk that told me he'd heard Nan's side of the conversation. I gave him my best *don't start* look. He laughed, handing me the mic kit. I went into the bathroom to strap the battery pack to my leg.

And that's how I ended up at Mo's manatee unveiling looking like twinsies with my grandmother, recorded on film for posterity.

"Oh, you guys look so cute!" Mo said when we got to the park, giving both of us a kiss on the cheek. She gave Luca a huge hug. "So great to see you, buddy! Thanks for filming!"

"I can't wait to see the sculpture," he said, hugging her back. "And even if we don't use the footage in the doc, I'll put a clip together for your website."

Mo laughed. "I'll have to get a website."

"Get on that!" Luca said. "Katie showed me your postcards. Your work is awesome."

Luca went off to film the gathering crowd. Mo and I ducked into the park restroom to get her wired up. I switched my mic off just in time, because Mo said, "I like the way he looks at you."

"I do too," I said, clipping the receiver box to the back of her pants, inside the waistband. "You ready for this?"

Mo grinned. "I think I am."

"I think you are too," I said.

She was dressed in a pair of crisp high-waisted black slacks, a white collared shirt, and a chunky turquoise necklace. I'm pretty sure the pants were her grandfather's, and I knew the necklace was her grandmother's. She was rocking the whole thing.

Once I got the wire threaded through her shirt and clipped to her collar, I said, "Okay, I'm turning our mics on now. We'll be on record when I do."

As soon as I flicked the switch she said, "That Luca guy is kinda weird. But he has a cute butt." And then, laughing, she shouted, "Hi, Luca!"

I laughed too.

After setting Mo free to do her thing, I hung back to watch her navigate the crowd. Big smiles and gracious gestures. I could still picture her little kid self so clearly, and it felt like an honor to watch her flourishing as an adult, to be in it for the duration.

I'd expected a small ceremony with a few people, but this was a big deal. They'd wrapped Morty in blue fabric and a huge red ribbon. Local news trucks flanked the area, and a group of kids from the middle school chorus were lined up on bleachers, ready to sing the national anthem. There were at least a hundred people already, more trickling in, filling the massive span of folding chairs.

I found Nan in the front row. Bitsie chatted with Luca toward the back.

"Meggie and Ennis would be so proud," Nan said, welling up. She kissed her fingers and wiggled them toward the sky like she was sending a blessing to Mo's grandparents. Nan wasn't religious, but they had been.

The head of Parks and Recreation introduced Mo by saying she was one of the talented people who makes Port St. Lucie special. Then Mo stood in front of the microphone. Poised and loud.

"I want to thank you all for being here today and the Port St. Lucie Arts Council and Parks and Recreation for supporting my work and the addition of art to our parks. I'm proud for this piece to become part of our community. I'd also like to thank my dear friend Katie Ellis for her contribution to this project. She's a brilliant artist. Her camaraderie and perspective, and also her help lifting things, mean so much to me."

My nose stung and my heart thudded. Nan nudged my arm with her elbow.

"We get where we're going when we have great people to cheer us on," Mo said. "So thank you, all of you, for cheering this on."

The president of the parks board handed Mo a giant pair of scissors.

"I probably shouldn't run with these," Mo quipped, crossing her eyes and giving a goofy grin to the chorus kids on the bleachers. They erupted into giggles.

When she cut the ribbon, the fabric fell, making a puddle of blue below Morty. I was awed by the way he fit in the installation space. Too perfect to be anything other than Mo's vision in action. The arc of his body played with the horizon behind him like it was the surface line he swam below.

After, of course, there was a party at Bitsie's. Everyone was extra-animated in the presence of Luca's camera. I held a boom mic over the chaos, and even though my arms ached from the weight of it, I loved how the microphone kept me slightly to the side of the activity so I could officially be an observer.

Luca and I were the last to leave. Bitsie sent us off with a plate of cornbread and lipstick stains on our cheeks.

Luca slipped his hand into mine as we walked back to Nan's. The air was humid, with a breeze that gave the slightest hint that darkness might chase away some of the heat from the day. We didn't make eye contact. I couldn't. But I gave his hand a squeeze. I was glad to be holding it. His palm was warm, and rough from camera calluses.

"I missed you," he said, but he didn't look at me either.

"Yeah." I nodded, knowing if I said any more, it would all come rushing out.

Later, when we went through the footage, Luca showed me how he caught Bark sneaking around the party, sniffing people when they weren't looking. When Bark did accidentally trigger some-one's attention, he was polite about it. Like a little kid enduring a cheek pinch.

"Hey, did you get anything good on your trip?" I asked when we'd finished dog surveillance.

"No spoilers," he said. "It'll mess with your timeline."

"Nerd."

He smiled. "I don't want anyone else to see Hannah and Woo Woo before they get here, so everything they say is a surprise when it should be."

"They did have some phone calls," I said, and told him about the ridiculous FaceTime meeting.

"Damn! I wish I'd gotten that!"

"Maybe you could get them all on the FaceTime again to finalize plans," I said.

Luca shook his head. "I don't want to manipulate the way it unfolds. Even little things. It adds up. It'll start to feel false."

"That makes sense."

"But if you see them on FaceTime and I'm not there, you have to call me."

"Deal." I put my hand out to shake his. As a joke. As an ex-cuse to touch him.

He slid his hand into mine, leaned in, and kissed me. Then he pulled away, checking to make sure I was okay.

I kissed him back.

And then I panicked. This was too real. Too soon.

"I have to sew sequins," I said as calmly as possible. I didn't know how to stay in a moment with him without feeling flooded.

Luca's eyes flashed with disappointment.

"I'm going to put on a movie and sew. Do you want to watch with me?" I asked as an offering.

So he sat next to me on the couch while I stitched sequins and we watched *Mr. Smith Goes to Washington*. Bark sprawled across Luca's lap, demanding a belly rub. The storm in my brain began to shrink.

Luca and Bark fell asleep, snoring, before I finished Nan's tail. Luca looked worn out. I didn't want to wake him, there wasn't room for me to sleep on the couch too, so when I finished my work, I kissed them both on the forehead, tucked a blanket around them, and tiptoed off to bed.

CHAPTER THIRTY-EIGHT

~~~~~~~~~~~

Nan and Bitsie went overboard getting the word out about pool-side decorations, so Mo and I had a long list of houses to visit. Luca offered up his truck as long as we let him film. I'd hoped to be done before noon so I could get back to my sequins, but everyone wanted to feed us and share stories about the things we were borrowing, and Luca needed to capture all of it. By the time we made our last trip to Ruth's house, it was four p.m.

"Oh, I think I'm a natural performer," Ruth said, looking directly into Luca's camera when he asked her why she'd joined the mermaid class. "My father was in the Marine Corps, and my mother was a dance teacher before she married him. So when he came home on furlough, she'd have us do a show for him. All seven of us. Wearing little blue shorts she made. Lined up in height order. I was first, until Tommy had a growth spurt."

Mo and I left Ruth and Luca to talk while we loaded chairs into the truck. Six chairs. Three trips. When we got back to the patio, Ruth was tap-dancing for the camera.

"First to fight for right and freedom," she sang, belting the words, waving her arms in the air as she stepped in an exaggerated march, Keds hitting concrete with a dull slap. "And to keep our honor clean!" She had a childlike certainty to her performance. It was a flashback, unfiltered through the lens of who she was now. She was still a little girl who wanted to impress her daddy. "We are proud to claim the tiii-tle of United States Marine! Ten-hut!" She snapped to attention, eyes bright as she saluted.

I clapped. Mo joined me. Ruth smiled like a pageant winner, and I saw how much she needed that applause. Letting go of my need to have her like me, or pretend that I liked her, left me room to actually see her. She was brash because she'd had to be to get what she needed in a lineup of seven children. If she wasn't the tallest, she could be the loudest. If she wasn't right, she was wrong. That sad little girl never went away. It made me think that maybe everyone is just trying to figure out how to be a person. Maybe no one knows how to do it best. And maybe we don't have to like someone to be kind.

Mo and I ran a few crab traps out to the truck and when we got back, Marta had joined Ruth and Luca on the patio. She was talking to the camera, her arm around Ruth. "I've lived right over there"—she pointed to the blue house behind Ruth's—"for the past . . . What is it, Ruthie? Thirty-five years now?"

"Thirty-seven," Ruth said. "Because, remember? You moved in right when my Joey was cutting his first tooth."

"Thirty-seven," Marta agreed. "And every single time she goes to the grocery store, she calls to ask me if I need anything." She looked at Ruth with overwhelming affection.

"She's always running out of bread," Ruth said.

"It gets moldy too fast," Marta said. "The humidity. You buy the good stuff, and it only lasts a few days."

Ruth nodded. "Wonder Bread lasts forever."

Marta shook her head. It was an argument they'd probably had every single time Ruth went shopping. "I don't need it. You're always running to the store," she said, smiling.

I hurried to Luca's truck with an armload of twinkle lights so I didn't start crying. Ruth didn't have to be perfect to be loved. What if I didn't either?

"You're ready to feed an army!" Nan said when I dumped the treats we'd acquired on the kitchen counter. "They're not going to keep until the show." She eyed Marta's mini fruit tarts.

"Oh, these are everyday treats," I said, grinning. "The special mermaid show treats have yet to be made." I handed her a list I'd compiled of the food the neighbors promised.

"Well," Nan said, trying to pinch at Luca's waist, "this one looks like he never gets a real meal." She pulled back the wax paper on Ruth's rugelach. "But these are filled with saturated fat, so I don't know what's worse."

"Don't you dare throw those out, Nannette," Mo said. "I will fight you."

Nan raised her fists, throwing pretend punches at Mo. "I just want you all to be healthy."

"I'll run it right off," Mo said, grabbing a tiny pastry from the plate, jogging in place as she shoved it in her mouth.

The front door opened. "Here she is!" Bitsie called to us, half singing, half shouting, "Miss America!" She sauntered into the kitchen. Her short spiky hair was Raggedy Ann red.

"Bitsie Marie!" Nan shouted, laughing and laughing.

Bitsie broke into hysterics too. Tears streamed down their faces as their sides shook.

"You like?" Bitsie asked, her voice choked in giggles.

"How did you . . ." I asked, not understanding how she knew about the wigs I hadn't had time to procure.

"I loved your Pinterest picture of Kate Pierson and her beautiful bright red hair," she said, winking.

Nan cupped Bitsie's face in her hands and kissed her on the forehead. "Gorgeous," she said. "And loud. Just like you."

They gazed at each other with tenderness, eyes flashing like they were exchanging secret thoughts. The magnitude of their friendship hit me hard. I could see it from an adult perspective. Nan and Bitsie had gone through most of their lives as friends. They'd experienced all the big moments together—the joy and pain and heartbreak—and also the repetitive ins and outs of everyday life. It was an epic love story, free of romantic entanglements, solid in the places where romances can falter.

I stopped feeling sad for all the years Nan spent single after my grandfather died. From the time she met Bitsie, she'd always had someone in her corner.

"You are such a badass," Mo said, brushing her hand over Bitsie's head.

Bitsie wiggled a shoulder, raising an eyebrow. "I know it. I know it."

CHAPTER THIRTY-NINE

The next day when I came home from sewing at Bitsie's, Nan was in the kitchen mixing something in one of her stainless steel bowls, talking at Luca and his camera.

"I hope I'm getting this right," she said cheerily in her *company's here* voice.

I missed having her all to myself. Documentary Nan made me long for the times I'd sit on the couch with Regular Nan to watch *Wheel of Fortune* and rest my head on her shoulder and feel like I was nine again in the good way.

"Whatchya making?" I asked, hearing the weariness in my voice, trying to make up for it with a smile when I caught movement from Luca out of the corner of my eye.

Nan tipped the bowl in my direction. It was filled with bright purple goo.

"Frosting?" I asked, not allowing myself to get too excited. My guess was it involved tofu and one of Nan's other strange staple ingredients, like the liquid from a can of chickpeas or the gelatinous horror that was soaked chia seeds.

"Hair dye," Nan said. "Can you believe it?"

"For who?"

"Me," Nan said, patting at her hair. "Bitsie dared me."

I laughed. "You two are nuts."

"We're a couple of cashews." She was elated. Supercharged. "Wanna help?" She gestured to the back of her head. "I don't want to miss a spot."

"Now?"

Nan nodded. "It's ready to go." She gave the purple goo one more firm mix.

"We don't have to shoot this," I said. "Right?"

I could see the need in Luca's eyes. He wanted the footage. He wanted to be included. It was the same feeling I always had. *Invite me to your birthday party. Don't pick me last for your kick-ball team.* But all three of us in that damp little bathroom while I tried to dye Nan's hair would be sensory overload. It would be too hard to act normal.

"Kaitlyn! For posterity!" Nan said.

"I think maybe—" I said. "Maybe I could shoot this? It's a small bathroom and, you know, girl stuff." It made more sense than Luca having to perch on the lid of the toilet with his camera.

"I'll set up the tripod," he said, a hint of pouting in his voice.

"I'll get good footage," I said. "Promise."

Nan stood on her tiptoes and grabbed a stack of old towels from the top shelf of the linen closet. Luca came back with the tripod. "There's going to be echo. I should run out to get foam for the walls."

"Oh, no," Nan said. "We're doing this now! Before I lose my nerve. Bitsie would never let me live it down!"

Luca sighed. "Well, let's get the mics closer to your mouths, at least," he said.

"Tape it," Nan said, pointing to her chest. "I'm not going to keep my top on."

"Nan!" I shouted.

"Get creative with the angles, Kay. I don't want to get my shirt all dirty."

Twenty minutes later, Nan was wired up, wearing one of my theatre t-shirts inside out, to keep the Western *Annie Get Your Gun* lettering from mucking up the shot.

We lined the floor with towels and Nan sat on the edge of the bathtub. I took a look through the viewfinder and nudged the camera a little to cover where I thought we'd be.

Then, with sandwich bags on my hands, I used a paintbrush to slather her hair with purple goo.

When I was in high school, there was a girl a few grades ahead of me who had long black hair with a hidden rainbow underneath. When she put it in a ponytail, you could see all the colors. I longed for hair like that. Mine was baby fine, caught in an awkward state between curl and wave. Even if I'd had the guts to do the same, at the slightest hint of humidity, my rainbow would have frizzed to a jumble, like too many Play-Doh colors blended together. But I could have been happy with one crazy color. Blue or purple or hot pink. The chance to feel like someone else.

"You know," I said, painting the last section of Nan's hair, "I wanted to do this in high school." I wasn't used to sharing my inner life with Nan. I tried to keep my wants from becoming her problem.

"You did?" Nan said. "I never would have guessed! Why didn't you tell me?"

"It was silly." I wrapped Nan's hair with Saran wrap, like a turban. "How long do we wait?" I asked.

"Half hour," she said, grabbing her phone from the sink and setting the timer. "Now you. We have leftover dye."

"I think with darker hair you're supposed to bleach it first and I don't want to—"

"You just told me you always wanted purple hair. Now is the time." She grabbed the brush and swabbed at my head.

"Hey!" I said, ducking out of the way.

"We'll only do the ends. You can cut them off if you hate it. They're sun-bleached anyway."

I sat on the side of the tub, closing my eyes as Nan came at me with the brush.

"You don't have to make that face. It doesn't hurt!" Nan laughed, dye dripping on the tile.

When she finished painting my hair, I adjusted the camera, and we sat on towels on the bathroom floor with our backs against the tub.

"Why didn't you tell me you wanted purple hair?" she asked again.

"I didn't want to be a pain in the butt."

"I would have loved to do stuff like this with you," Nan said.

"Really?"

"I never knew what to do with you. I had a boy. In the seventies. I knew I was supposed to do things differently, but I didn't know how. You never asked for anything. You were always so agreeable. I felt like I was doing something wrong. Aren't teenage girls supposed to rebel?"

"It was never you," I said.

"But it was something?"

I nodded.

Nan watched me, waiting for an answer, her face full of concern.

I didn't want to say it, especially not on camera, but it bubbled up. "I worried you'd realize I was too much trouble. Like my mom did."

"Kaitlyn!" Nan said, her face blanching. "That was actually a worry you had?"

I nodded, choked with tears.

"Oh, honey." Nan pulled me to her chest, my plastic-wrapped hair sticking to my cheek. "That's ridiculous!" She kissed my forehead and I could feel the lipstick mark she left behind. "You can't get rid of me. Even if you try."

Nan wiped my face with the edge of her shirt. "What else did you want?" she asked when the worst of my tears had passed.

"I wanted a dog," I said.

"Done!" She pointed to Bark's paw, shoved through the gap between the door and the floor, like he was offering us a lifeline to the outside world. "Next!"

"I don't know," I said. "There wasn't much else." I couldn't bear to work through all the things I wanted. Most of them were impossible.

"You need a better bucket list," Nan said.

"What yours?" I asked.

"Well, I wanted to fall madly in love," Nan said. "That Hepburn and Tracy friendship kind of love."

"Done?" I asked.

"Yes," she said breathlessly. "When I was married to your grandfather, I spent so much energy trying to be the wife and mother he expected me to be. I loved him. I know he loved me. But our marriage didn't have room for friendship. Isaac is good at being my friend. He loves me right where I'm standing."

I squeezed her hand.

"And someday I'd like to ride in a hot air balloon," she said.

The alarm chimed, I unwrapped Nan's head. She sat on the edge of the tub again. I stood in the tub and used the showerhead to rinse the goo from her hair.

"Alright," I said when the deed was done. "I think we got it all!"

"This shirt is soaked!" Nan said, pulling it over her head.

"Nan!" I yelled. "Stop!" I pointed to the tripod, but it was too late, she'd flashed the camera. "I think you just made a nudie film!" I scrambled to wrap a towel around her.

"Oh, who cares?" she said, only blushing a little.

We dried her hair. Her pixie cut was a shock of bright purple. I positioned the camera to catch her reaction when she looked in the mirror.

"Look at me!" she said, turning her head from one side to the other. "Oooh, your grandfather would have hated this." She closed her eyes for a moment. When she opened them again, she grinned at herself, nodding.

She rinsed my hair for me, testing the water on her arm first to make sure it wasn't too hot, like she had when I was a little kid. The purple fringe at the ends looked like feathers from an exotic bird.

When we were done, the tub and the floor and Nan's towels were stained purple, but she was thrilled.

Later, when Isaac came over for dinner, Luca had the camera set up at the door to capture his reaction.

"Oh," he said, face flushing. "Oh my goodness, Nannette!"

Nan touched her head. "Too crazy?"

"I love it," he said, touching her hair. "You are stunning." And then he kissed her. Right there in front of us. Without hesitation.

Behind the camera, Luca looked up and smiled at me.

CHAPTER FORTY

The next morning, Bitsie came over at seven on the dot to get ready to pick up Woo Woo at the airport.

"Hey, buy a girl dinner first," she said when Luca used an elastic bandage to strap a microphone pack to her thigh.

"Yeah," Luca said, grinning. "As if a girl like you would ever go out with a guy like me!"

Bitsie tousled his hair. "You're a good one, you know that?" She winked at me.

Nan snaked a mic wire up her pink polo shirt and I clipped it in place, just under the edge of her collar.

"Your turn!" Nan said.

I was wearing a sundress I'd made with Bunny's fabric. Yellow flowered cotton that skimmed my curves. There was no good place to hide the battery pack.

"I don't think I need a mic," I said.

"If you're in the footage and I can't hear you, I can't use it," Luca said.

"But it's about *them*!"

"The world needs to see your beautiful face," Bitsie said.

"It's about the reunion, and you're part of it." Luca grabbed another mic pack.

"Give it," Nan said, taking it from him. She pushed me down

the hall to my room and helped me strap it to my lower back, running the bandage around my waist.

"Thank you," I said.

"I thought it might get awkward," Nan said. "Although, maybe that would be a good thing."

"Shit! It's not on yet, is it?" I whispered, pointing to her mic.

"I wouldn't do that," she said. "But he's great, right?"

I nodded.

"He thinks you're pretty great too."

"I don't know if—"

"You don't have to know," she said, clipping the mic to the neckline of my dress. "You just have to show up."

I drove everyone to the airport in Nan's car. Nan sat in the passenger seat chatting about her ideas for refreshments at the show. "I was thinking vegan rumaki, if I can figure out the bacon part. Stuffed mushrooms, of course. Do you think we should have mai tais or piña coladas?"

No one was answering, but it was rhetorical. If anyone chose mai tais when Nan wanted piña coladas, she'd be annoyed.

"Should we give people a choice?" Nan asked. "No! Wait! Blue Hawaiians! Who doesn't like a Blue Hawaiian?"

I watched Bitsie in the rearview mirror. She stared out the window, snapping her blue bauble bracelet against her wrist, oblivious to Nan's chatter. Luca sat across from her, filming as she fidgeted.

"Isn't Ruth allergic to pineapple?" I said loudly, hoping to get Luca's attention off Bitsie.

"She just says that," Nan said. "No one's allergic to pineapple."

"I think some people are actually allergic to pineapple," I said. Luca wasn't biting on the conflict.

"Well, maybe, but Ruth isn't. She just says that." Nan remembered the microphone and clapped her hand over her shirt collar after the fact. "We can do mai tais, I guess." She sighed, like it was an enormous compromise.

"People are coming to see the show," I said. "Not to eat."

"But we have to feed them!" Nan said.

"Do we?"

Nan laughed at me.

"Are you alright?" I whispered to Bitsie when we got to the short-term parking lot.

"It's stupid stuff," she said, squeezing my hand. "Worrying Woo won't like me anymore. What will we talk about? How many ways can I put my foot in my mouth? You know?"

"I do know." I gave her hand a squeeze. She linked her arm into mine and we walked around the car to Nan and Luca. Nan hooked her arm into my other one, and we set off to meet Woo Woo at baggage claim.

Bitsie swung her foot out in front of me, so I swung mine in front of Nan's. Nan picked up on what we were doing and did the same. Then we reversed it, walking through the sliding doors like a slower, more deliberate version of The Monkees. Bitsie hummed the theme song under her breath. We were a spectacle with our crazy colored hair. People stared, but I felt brave, sandwiched between Nan and Bitsie.

"Careful," Nan said, "one of us is likely to break a hip!"

Bitsie tugged my elbow. "My vote is on this one."

I laughed. "It's probably true."

We found the carousel for Woo Woo's flight and waited. Nan and I sat on a bench. Bitsie paced. Luca leaned against a pillar next to us, filming. He kept his actions so low-key that I had to keep reminding myself we were being observed.

"What's she on about?" Nan asked, nodding in Bitsie's direction.

"Nerves," I said.

"Oh." Nan clapped her hand to her mouth. "She's worried Woo Woo won't be okay with . . ." Her voice trailed off.

"Woo Woo doesn't know?" I said.

"No. Last Woo was aware, Bitsie was married to a man."

"I never thought about what a continual process coming out is," I said.

"I forget it's ever hard for her," Nan said. "She's Bitsie! She's inherently lovable. How could anyone have a problem with anything about her?"

"Do you think this could be a problem?"

"I won't let it." Nan patted my leg. She got up and went over to Bitsie. I couldn't hear what they were saying, but I knew Luca could. His camera was trained on them, and I watched his face. His eyes were wide, sad. He held his mouth tight.

Nan hugged Bitsie. Bitsie nodded and pulled away to wipe tears from the corners of her eyes. I hoped Nan was saying helpful things and not some variation of "You're fine! It's okay!"

The red light at the top of the carousel flashed and there was a loud buzz. We looked around. People trickled in from the flight, but none of them fit Woo Woo's demographics.

Nan and Bitsie came over to stand with me. I think, in part, to keep me in the shot. We waited and waited. Nan smoothed my hair. It didn't annoy me as much as it had when I was a kid.

An attendant pushed a wheelchair toward us. "*Whoo, whoo!*" the woman in the wheelchair yelled, waving. She was long and lanky, as her measurements suggested. Her hair, poofy like spun sugar, was brilliant white, gathered in a wispy knot at the top of her head. It looked perfect with Nan and Bitsie's bright colors.

"Woo Woo!" Nan and Bitsie yelled back, rushing to greet her. Nan looked concerned. She wasn't expecting the wheelchair. I realized Woo Woo had been sitting in all the photos we'd seen.

Woo grabbed on to Nan's arm as soon as she got close. "Help me out of this thing, will you?"

She plunked her cane on the floor with the other hand and Nan pulled her up.

"This is my daughter's doing," she whispered, then plastered a smile on her face. "Thank you, young man," she said to the attendant, pulling a ten from the pocket of her sweater and shoving it in his hand. "You were a delight and a careful driver."

When the attendant walked away, Nan grabbed Woo in a great big hug. "It's *you*."

"It's *you*," Woo said.

Woo turned to Bitsie. "What a marvel! I can't believe I'm actually here. Seeing you. This hair!" She placed her hand on Bitsie's cheek. "Perfection!"

Bitsie gave Woo's arm a squeeze, but I could see the worry on her face.

While Luca and Nan got Woo Woo's mic set up, Bitsie excused herself to use the restroom. I followed. When we were safely inside, I clamped one hand over her mic and the other over mine.

"If it's a problem, or you're uncomfortable at all, let me know, and I'll make up an excuse to give Woo Woo my room so I can stay with you instead."

"Nan told me it would all be fine . . ." Bitsie's voice trailed off.

"But she doesn't know."

"Exactly," Bitsie said. "She loves me, but that doesn't mean everyone will."

"If there's a problem, we'll fix it the best we can. You're not alone," I said, telling her the things I always wished Nan had said to me. "I love you no matter what."

"Thanks, kiddo." She gave me a huge hug, her strong arms squeezing tight. "I love you no matter what right back."

I left her to have a moment to herself and rejoined Nan, Woo, and Luca, who were red-faced from laughter. Luca was clipping a microphone to Woo Woo's shirt.

"What did I miss?" I asked.

"Woo told Luca he had to buy a girl dinner first," Nan said, cackling.

"Like Bitsie did," Luca said. He looked at me and mouthed, *I love them!*

"Cut from the same cloth!" Nan said.

Woo Woo looked at me. "You are the spitting image of Nannette back in the day," she said. "You have the same face. It's hard not to stare."

I blushed. "Thank you." I loved hearing that I looked like Nan. It made me so proud as a kid. Like a sign I belonged.

Bitsie rejoined us.

"Well, kids," she said, looking bright and brave. "We ready?"

Of course, we had a cocktail party. At Bitsie's house. Half the neighborhood showed up, because everyone was always invited to everything all the time. I worried about Bitsie having so many people in her space while she was already stressed out, but she seemed fine.

Nan and I made sure the food kept moving and the drinks kept flowing while Bitsie and Woo sat on the bench in the corner talking and laughing. At one point Woo wrapped her arms around Bitsie, planting a kiss on her cheek.

Later, in the kitchen, Bitsie grabbed my arm and pulled me

aside. She clamped her hand over my microphone and then her own. "Her nephew is gay," she said excitedly. "And he's her favorite one. She told me she thinks I was brave to follow my heart."

Nan had already gone home, but Luca stayed after the party to film Bitsie and Woo as they did the dishes. I ran around the living room collecting plates and glasses, to keep them at the sink in conversation. They were comparing notes on different stages of life like a movie they'd both seen.

"I didn't expect to feel that way," Woo said, "but it was important to me to work."

"I know," Bitsie said. "That first real paycheck with my name on it . . ."

"I cried," Woo said. "I actually cried."

"Me too," Bitsie said.

When we got back to Nan's, Luca commandeered the living room to watch footage from the day. I knew if I went in there to work, I'd spend more time watching than sewing. So I holed up in my room with Bark and five boxes of large gold sequin paillettes to finish Woo Woo's tail. The way I'd worked out the design, the tail didn't need to be covered in sequins entirely, but the patterning was swirling and intricate. I couldn't zone out and sew rows on top of rows. I sat on the bed, with my headphones on, and got to work, listening to the B-52s as I stitched. It was my favorite kind of work, focused and fine. I lost myself in the meditation of the task.

I didn't hear Luca in the hallway. I didn't hear him shut the door to his room. But I did hear a text from him chime through my headphones.

Sleep tight, he wrote. There was a video attached.

It was Nan.

Off camera, Luca asks, "What made you decide to become a vegan?"

I felt ridiculous that I'd been too focused on how her new diet ruined cookies to think of asking why.

"Well, I like animals," Nan says, smiling. She's being evasive. Looking off to the rest of the party.

"It's an interesting life change—" Luca says.

"At my age?" Nan says with a teasing bit of sarcasm. "Well, you know, heart disease runs in my family and I—" Her voice breaks. "I want as much time as I can have with that gorgeous granddaughter of mine. I'm being greedy about it." She looks at the ceiling for a moment. A deep breath, then Cocktail Party Nan returns. "And that man over there?" Luca turns the camera to Isaac for a moment, then back to Nan. "I wouldn't mind more time with him either." She gives Luca a dazzling smile.

CHAPTER FORTY-ONE

I woke up at five thirty in the morning, covered in sequins. When I pulled them from my skin, they left red marks.

I ran to Bitsie's, still in my pj's, tail slung over my shoulders like a shepherd carrying a lamb, my rat's nest of hair pulled in a ponytail. Bitsie would be up already.

I'd talked Woo's daughter through the measurements over the phone, and Woo explained the specifics of her partial mastectomy from years earlier. I found a tutorial on making a compensation form insert for the bra, but I'd never done work like that, and it raised the stakes for me. Woo had been self-conscious talking about it on the phone. I wanted to help her feel confident. I knew it wasn't fair to leave Luca out, but I needed to see if Woo Woo's costume would work, and I didn't want to handle my panic on camera if it didn't.

"You walked over here like that?" Bitsie asked, grinning, when I got there.

"It's nothing they haven't seen before," I said, smiling back.

"Why are you splotchy?"

"Sequins. It'll fade."

"Oh, of course," Bitsie said, laughing. "You've got a mean case of the sequins! I hear that's going around."

"Is Woo Woo up yet?" It was strange how quickly I'd normalized the idea of calling a grown woman Woo Woo. I wondered if anyone in her regular life called her that.

"She's in the shower," Bitsie said. "You want coffee?"

"I was hoping we could squeeze in the fitting now," I said. "And yes."

"I think Nan wants to do that tonight, when Hannah gets here."

"I know, but . . ." I was going to make up an excuse; instead, I told her the truth. "I'm nervous. Working from measurements I didn't take. I'll feel so much better if . . ."

Bitsie nodded. "Why not knock out a worry when you can? Go for it!"

I went into Bunny's room and got the top from the closet.

"Gosh, Kay." Bitsie traced her fingers over the swirls of tiny seashells and champagne-colored crystals I'd stitched to the top. "It's art."

The shower was still running. Bitsie knocked on the bathroom door, opening it enough to reach in and hang the costume on the hook inside. "Hey, Woo? Try this on, will ya?"

"What?" Woo shouted.

"Your costume," Bitsie shouted back. "Try it when you're done."

While we waited, Bitsie poured me a cup of coffee, and we sat at the kitchen table. She gave me a rundown of all the things they'd caught up on last night. I was interested, but it was hard to pay attention, like I was waiting for the grade on a final exam. I'd never been so nervous about a costume before. I'd never felt so much ownership over a project, and while Bitsie and Nan were going to love what I made them, because I made it, Woo Woo wasn't such a biased customer.

We heard the bathroom door open and the sound of Woo Woo's cane ticking down the hallway. "I don't want to poke a hole in this tail," she called.

"We'll come to you," Bitsie shouted, and we ran to meet her.

Woo Woo leaned on her cane with one hand, her other arm in the air, palm to the sky. "A pretty girl! Is like a melody!" she sang, twisting her shoulders from one side to the other, her smile wide. Her legs were free through the slit in the back, and the tail fell in front of her. The compensation form worked perfectly and the crystals added light to her décolletage. Her long neck arched gracefully. The flesh between her top and tail had a beautiful soft drape.

I held my breath, hoping Woo Woo liked it.

"Wow," Bitsie said. "You're a dream!"

"I feel like a dream," Woo said, beaming. "You are a treasure, my dear. I want to wear this all the time!"

For days I'd felt like a balloon about to pop. The pressure was finally dissipating. I tested the fit around her hips. I'd left myself some wiggle room in the sequin pattern in case I had to make alterations, but it was perfect on the first try.

"Do you mind if we pretend this hasn't happened?" I asked. "I think Luca is going to want to film—"

"Of course," she said. "Thank you for letting me do this without the cameras. I was nervous."

"Me too."

"This is more amazing than I could have imagined. I look better than I did when I was twenty!"

"You look regal," Bitsie said. "Queen of the mermaids!"

"If I swim now, will it dry before the fitting?" Woo asked. She looked like a kid who couldn't wait to play with her new toy.

She wanted to feel like a mermaid again. I knew it wasn't fair to let my fear keep her from the pool, but I didn't want to be there to see it.

"If it doesn't dry we'll tell everyone I had to water-test the sequins," I said, and made my escape as graciously as I could before the pressure started to build again.

CHAPTER FORTY-TWO

I spent the next few hours sewing orange sequins on Hannah's tail while Bark chased a fly around the room, snapping at it with his teeth. He was mostly graceful, but at one point he jumped on the bed and slammed into me. I poked the needle straight through an adhesive thimble pad to my index finger. "Hey, bud! Watch it!"

Bark slunk off the bed and pouted on the floor, until the allure of the fly got to be too much and he started the chase again. I opened the door, shooing both of them to the hallway.

Instead of attending to my puncture wound, I replaced the adhesive thimble with a new one to seal the blood in so I could keep sewing. It had been ages since I'd gotten enough sleep. As soon as I secured the last sequin, I decided a nap would be in order.

When I hung the tail in my closet and took my headphones off, I heard Mo in the kitchen, laughing.

Instead of lying down, I went to say hi.

I heard Luca say, "And then Bitsie shows me the scar on her leg."

"Oh," I said, joining them, "her alligator bite?"

"Yes!" Luca said. "It's amazing it didn't do more damage!"

Behind Luca, Mo had her finger to her lips, shaking her head. In reality, Bitsie tripped on a rake Bunny left wrong side up in the yard and ended up with a row of scars on her calf, but for some reason, maybe to make Bunny feel better, we all started calling it an alligator bite.

"Well," I said, trying to keep a poker face, "it was a very small alligator."

Mo snickered. Luca turned around to look at her and started laughing too.

"Seriously?" he said. "She looked into my camera and told me a made-up story?" He was laughing so hard there were tears in his eyes. "I totally bought it."

We were punchy and overworked. Our laughter got the air moving. It felt good.

"You gotta watch out for those ladies," Mo said.

"Apparently," Luca said.

"You ready to go?" Mo asked me.

"Shit." I clapped my hand to my mouth. We had to take all the stuff we'd borrowed from the neighbors over to the pool to decorate.

"Did you forget?" Mo asked.

"No. No," I said, suddenly acutely aware of the fact that I was still in my pajamas with disaster hair. "I'm running a little late. Five minutes!"

"Mo and I can do it." Luca gave my shoulder a squeeze.

"Don't you have to film?" I asked.

Luca shook his head. "I've got a few hours. The mermaids are at a spa and they told me I wasn't allowed."

I loved the way he called them mermaids, like it was normal.

"I can do it," I said, "it's fine. I just need—"

"It's gonna be more than one trip," Mo said. "Why don't we make the first one and you can come with us on the next." She gestured to her neck, like she was trying to tell me something without Luca seeing.

"Fine," I said, and turned away from them. "I'll be ready on the next one."

When I got back to my room and looked in the mirror, in addition to the horrible hair and worn-out pajama pants, I had a streak of blood from my pinpricked finger across the side of my neck. I inspected Hannah's tail, and once I was sure it was clean, I jumped in the shower.

Mo and Luca were back faster than I'd planned for. I threw on my ugly brown shorts and a t-shirt from a production of *Starlight Express* that had been done sans roller skates for insurance purposes. I left Bark in the bedroom and ran outside, hair dripping wet, to help load the truck.

Mo and Luca left me at the pool to arrange things while they went back for the last truckload. I hadn't been to the community center since I first moved in with Nan and she was convinced I was too young to stay home alone. She'd drag me with her while she swam laps, and I'd sit on a lounge chair in the corner, as far away from the pool as I could get, facing the fence, reading Harry Potter. I'd try to pretend I was at Hogwarts, not waiting for the only adult I had in my life to get out of the water.

I'd forgotten how big the pool was. Olympic-sized, three meters at its deepest. I tried to focus on hanging Lester Sam's old fishing nets from the fence, but I felt dizzy knowing the depths that were there. Even though I stayed several feet from the edge, I felt like a misstep or a gust of wind could push me in the wrong direction.

My phone rang. It was Nan.

Hannah got in at noon. She'd rented a suite at the hotel by the golf course, and wanted everyone to come by for champagne. "We can do the fittings over here," Nan said while I tried to figure out how to get Mrs. Cohen's flamingos to stand on concrete. "Come over when you're done."

"The sewing machine is at Bitsie's," I said.

"Well, bring it."

I sighed.

"Or don't. Pin everything and sew later," she said, like that didn't also add unnecessary steps.

"Fine," I said, but I felt like bursting into tears. I hated that I couldn't let go and have fun, but I was exhausted. The worst of me was starting to leak out.

When Luca and Mo got back, Luca left for the hotel in a hurry, frustrated, because Nan had promised to call him once she had an ETA on Hannah, not after her arrival. Mo stayed behind to set up the air tanks.

I ran to Nan's to pick up Hannah's costume, then Bitsie's to get Woo Woo's costume. At least Woo Woo's fitting was for show.

I was a flustered, sweaty mess when I got to the suite. Hannah's tail was in a garment bag, but I hadn't wanted to put Woo's damp one in with it, so I looped that tail around my neck. It left wet spots on my shirt.

I dropped a box of pins on the floor right after I knocked. "Come in, come in!" Hannah said when she opened the door, and then she had to wait while I picked pins out of the carpet.

Hannah was elegant, with shiny silver chin-length hair and soft pink cheeks. Her zaftig figure was beautifully draped in a magenta silk caftan. She was at least four sizes larger than her measurements had led me to believe. They'd seemed out of line with the pictures I saw on the internet, but they were old, so I assumed the discrepancy meant she'd recently lost weight. I'd cut the costume a bit bigger, and positioned the sequins away from the seams, so taking it in wouldn't be a problem. But even with the generous cut, there wasn't any way the costume would fit.

I would have to work straight through the night if I had any shot of getting a tail for Hannah done in time. And I couldn't call her out on it. How awful it would be to say, "You could have been honest!" But the truth was, she could have been. I loved the idea of making a costume that showed off her beautiful curves. I had a million ideas, and no time to execute them.

"I'm so sorry," I blurted, ignoring the fact that I had an extra garment bag with me. "I haven't gotten to your costume yet. But I can take your measurements and get it together tonight."

Luca was sitting on the corner of the coffee table, filming chatter between Woo Woo and Bitsie, so he didn't catch my lie.

"I sent you my measurements," Hannah said, filling a champagne glass and handing it to me.

"I know." I waved off the glass. "But since I'm here, let me just check them."

"Well, fine," she said with a bright smile, but enough edge in her voice to let me know she was irritated.

I pulled the tape measure from my purse and got started at her bust, typing the numbers into my phone as I went.

When I got to her waist I said, "Hannah?" as gently as possible. "I think maybe you're sucking in, and what I need is a true measurement. Don't worry. I'll make you look good."

"Okay," she said, laughing but keeping her voice low. "I'll let it all hang out."

And then she sucked in.

"Oh! I think you did it again. It's a costume that has to move with you, so I want to get an honest fit. I'm the only person who will see the numbers." I felt weird assuming that stance, like I was somehow telling her the size of her waist mattered in a greater way. It didn't. I just needed the facts so I could make a good costume. She didn't have to pretend to be smaller. And it made me sad, because I had this idea that by the time you reach your seventies, the superficial pressures of being a woman would dissipate, and health and happiness would be all that mattered. That was supposed to be the bargain you made with age.

"Sure, honey," Hannah said. And then she sucked in again.

I wanted to scream. It felt like a giant spoiler. I didn't want to know that I might still care about my stupid thighs in forty-five years. I turned away to catch my composure. Bitsie saw me and smiled. I made a face, hoping she'd come over to help me, but Woo Woo had a tablet on the table and said, "This one, here! That's my great-granddaughter's christening! Can you believe it?" Bitsie went back to oohing and aahing over pictures.

I tried measuring the rest of Hannah and then going back to her waist. I tried asking her questions, hoping to get her absorbed enough in conversation to let her stomach relax. Nothing worked. In the end, I had to estimate, which didn't make me feel great.

My head throbbed, my fingers stung, and I knew it was only going to get worse.

Back at Bitsie's house, I had to come to terms with the fact that there was no way to take those numbers and fix the tail I'd already made. I thought about using insert panels, but since Hannah seemed self-conscious about her stomach, I wanted to cut her tail a little higher than the others. If it ended right below her rib cage, the neoprene could arc over her curves instead of cutting into them. Part of me wanted to say, "Screw it!" and do a hatchet job on the old tail, but if I didn't make her feel good and look good, it would make me look bad. I'd put so much work into every other detail, I didn't want to ruin it all in the last lap. So I sewed my way through a new tail. I didn't have enough orange tulle to make a matching dorsal fin, so I used a mix of what was leftover from the three other tails. I was much more adept with the fabric, and I had a good system in place for assembly, but it still took me two hours to get the tail together enough to run back to the hotel for Hannah to try on.

"It's an interesting color," Hannah said, not trying at all to hide her disgust.

"I'm going to paint over it. It will be orange."

Hannah looked disappointed.

"Like the tail from *Splash*!" I said.

"I'm sure you have a vision," Hannah said.

I turned away and took a deep breath, hoping my face wasn't too flushed with anger.

And then, to keep Luca and Nan happy, I had to help a very tipsy Woo Woo into her costume so we could pretend to be thrilled and surprised when it fit.

Before I left, I pulled Nan aside. "Aren't you planning to rehearse?" I asked. Nan and Bitsie had their routine down, and the synchronized swimmers were well practiced. The plan was to use Hannah and Woo Woo sparingly, having them perform moves they could learn easily in a few hours, but they still needed to learn their parts and get a refresher on breathing air from tubes.

Nan looked at her watch. "We have to get going, girls," she announced.

"You shouldn't be swimming if you're drunk," I said.

"Oh, Kay. We just had a little champagne."

"It's not safe!" I whisper-yelled.

"We're fine. We'll sober up on the drive over."

"You can't *drive* like this!" I said.

"We're taking one of the hotel golf carts over there," Nan said, laughing. "It's fine." But the worry had started coursing through my veins, collecting more worry as it went.

CHAPTER FORTY-THREE

I spent the rest of the afternoon working on the tail. I worried the paint wouldn't dry in time to sew any sequins and the tail would look completely out of sorts. It's not like I could print an asterisk statement in the program to say it was Hannah's fault, not mine.

Once I had the tail stitched, I stole Bitsie's hair dryer. On the way back to Nan's to start painting, I remembered I knew the code to get into Mo's house, so I went over there and poked around. No hair dryer in Mo's bathroom, but in the master suite, I found her grandmother's old beige Conair and swiped that too. I didn't think Mo would mind.

Once I'd finished the base coat, I strung up the tail and Nan's hair dryer from the rafters of the garage and grabbed the other two dryers, pointing them like a double-shooting outlaw from an old Western. When it was dry enough to work with, I used dark orange permanent marker to draw scales, standing on a chair while the tail was still suspended. The markers didn't have as nice of an effect as the airbrush, but I couldn't risk adding more paint, and I couldn't deal with the frustration of it. When I'd drawn enough scales, I stitched sequins sparsely while it hung from the ceiling, hoping if I spread the sequins strategically, the sparkle would be distracting, and I could get away with fewer.

Even still, I ran out of sequins and had to cut some off the old tail to fill in the gaps, fighting tears as I undid my careful stitching. I was used to dismantling what wasn't working. It's par for the course in a costume shop. I prided myself on being able to hack away at what I'd done without too much angst, but this was different. When I re-sewed Edith's costumes, they weren't mine. And I wasn't also worrying the actors would drown on stage.

A familiar rusty yellow Chevy truck pulled into Nan's driveway, sending a cloud of diesel fumes into the garage. It was Luca's friend Danny, and I wished I could hide behind the garbage cans. I didn't feel like talking to anyone.

"Hey," he said when he got out. "Katie, right?"

Bark whined from behind the door. I heard a thud as he pushed his body against it.

"Yeah," I said.

"Nice tail," he said, and I felt my face get hot. I knew he meant the actual tail hanging from the rafters in front of me, and not my backside, but I had a hard time with compliments. I wished he were seeing one of the good tails.

"Thanks," I said, trying not to sound mopey.

"Luca around?"

"He's filming." I used my orange Sharpie to draw a quick map to the pool on a scrap of newspaper.

"Thanks! Hey," he said, "Luca told me I could crash at some guy's house. Moe, I think? Are you sure it's okay? I can grab a room at a hotel, if—"

"I'm sure it's okay," I said, suspecting Luca was plotting something I thoroughly approved of. "*She'll* be happy to have you stay with her."

"Oh!" Danny smiled. "Thank you for that."

When he left, I went back to sewing sequins. The brief break made the work feel even more laborious. My shoulders ached from holding my arms up as I stitched. The muscles in my neck clenched, and I couldn't get them to relax. I swiped a shot of whiskey from Nan's pantry, then another, hoping it would loosen me up, but it only fueled my headache.

Thankfully, Hannah's bust measurements weren't as far off as the numbers for the tail, so I managed to save the top by adding extension fabric to the sides and a ruffle of tulle across the bustline.

By the time I finished, I was sore, tired, almost in tears, and a little bit drunk. Instead of taking a hot shower or flopping in front of the TV, I searched Facebook for Nikki's profile page again. Like piling hurt on hurt on tired would erase all of it. Or maybe I wanted to feel worse.

Eight hours earlier, Nikki posted a photo of Eric holding up an ultrasound. Eric's eyes brimmed with tears as he pointed to the baby in the middle of the black static. Her caption read: *FOUR MONTHS ALREADY!*

"Kay," Bitsie called from the foyer. "Kay? Are you alright? You left the door to my house unlocked." I heard her footsteps in the hall. "That's like me, but it's not like you."

"Shit," I called. "I'm sorry. Hey, I left Hannah's—Hannah's costume is in the garage." I hoped she'd take it and go. My voice was thin.

"Are you okay?" she called. And then she was in my doorway.

I wasn't crying yet. I wasn't anything yet. But I must have been wearing the shock on my face.

"What happened?" Bitsie asked.

I pointed to the screen.

"Oh, kiddo," she said, hugging me to her chest.

"I don't want this to hurt so bad," I said, holding the tears in with such great force I felt like I was choking.

"Let it hurt." She wrapped her arms around me even harder. "I promise it won't kill you. I promise I'll pull you back."

I buried my head in her armpit and sobbed. She held me the whole time.

"I'm so sorry," I said when I finally came up for air, leaving wet blotches on her shirt.

"Are you kidding?" Bitsie said. "Don't you dare be sorry. Sure, technically you're Nan's, but you're my kid too, dammit. I'm here for this stuff."

"I feel so shitty."

"It's okay to feel shitty about what's shitty," she said, wiping my hair from my sweaty face.

The front door opened.

"We're in here, Nannette," Bitsie called.

"Nan hurried in, freezing when she saw my face and Bitsie's tearstained shirt.

"Where's Luca?" I asked, terrified this might be caught on camera.

"He's with Hannah," Nan said. "What happened?"

"Nikki is pregnant," Bitsie told her.

"Oh, that . . . fucker!" Nan said. They sandwiched me in a hug so strong I thought I'd be crushed. "I'd like to cut his balls off."

"You take the right one. I'll get the left," Bitsie said.

I pictured the two of them showing up at my old house in their matching mermaid t-shirts, pinking shears in hand. It didn't make me feel any better, but it was enough of a distraction to help me pull myself together.

CHAPTER FORTY-FOUR

I went to Bitsie's to put together a sewing kit I could take to the pool for last-minute emergencies. When I got home, Luca's truck was out front, but the house was quiet. I wondered if he was at Mo's with Danny. The ladies were ordering room service and spending the night in Hannah's suite.

Bark skittered across the tile, wagging his tail. I bent to press my face to his. "I love you, bud." He licked my chin. I got him some kibble and sat on the kitchen floor with him, digging into a ramekin of vegan shepherd's pie without bothering to heat it up. Bark kept trying to lick mashed potatoes off my fork.

He followed me to the bathroom and lounged on the bath mat while I brushed my teeth. When I headed to my room, Bark darted to the end of the hall, pushing the door to Luca's room open.

"Hey!" I whispered. At the sound of my voice, he slowed enough so I could catch up and grab his collar. In the dark, I heard Luca's breath, heavy and metered from sleep. His feet hung off the end of the pullout couch.

He slept on his stomach, making it harder for him to breathe. I wanted to flip him over. Clear the airways. I hated the fact that other people didn't look for the disaster in every damn thing and I always did.

I pulled Bark back to my room and closed the door behind us firmly like I was cementing a decision.

When I got into bed, I couldn't fall asleep. Bark snored while I lay there, trying to see the shapes in my room in the dark. And then I heard the first rumble. A flash. Tiny, but true. The tightness in my stomach started small, but it spread with each clap of thunder.

I snuck out of bed. Bark stirred, but didn't wake.

The rumbling got louder and the lightning got closer and I wanted Luca's arms around me. I tiptoed down the hall and stood in his doorway, waiting for him to notice. He'd been so busy and I'd been so busy, and suddenly the idea of how little time I'd actually spent with him seemed unbearable. We hadn't even talked about what would happen after the show. How long he would stay. Where he was going next. I'd been so scared of getting too close, and now I felt the loss of him before he was even gone.

I climbed into bed, slipping under his arm. He adjusted his body around mine, like a reflex. I listened to the whoosh of his breath until my eyelids felt heavy and I drifted into sleep. The storm didn't matter. I could ignore the thunder if I focused on Luca's breath.

A few hours later, I woke gasping, unsure of where I was.

Luca woke up. "Oh," he said, "I didn't dream that." He pulled me close and kissed the back of my neck.

I turned to face him, kissed his chin, his cheek, his mouth. He kissed me back. I was so aware of the angles of him pressing against me. His body harder than before, mine softer. He held me with ferocity, running his hands over my hips. He whispered in my ear, "You are beautiful." I bit his shoulder, hooked my legs around his. There was no division between us, only movement, skin, sweat. Everything made sense.

*   *   *

The night after I slept with Luca the first time, we were drinking at the quarry with friends. I had to be careful. Two drinks and I could forget things. Feel loose. Three drinks and I would spend the darkest hours listening to my heartbeat thumping in my ears, waiting for light. I observed my limit carefully, but everyone else was done for.

We'd lit a bonfire by the water, but it wasn't a healthy one. We kept it fed with twigs and damp leaves. The flame constantly threatened to die out and the smoke was terrible. I still hate the meaty smell of singed leaf mold.

It wasn't warm. But it was warmer. In Western New York, you celebrate the days that aren't brutally cold. We'd had a week of tepid temps, and there was more winter on the way. People were walking around in shorts and flip-flops, even though it hadn't broken sixty degrees. Forties of hard cider, the flickering fire, and the closeness of our huddled bodies made everyone think it was warmer than it was. Everyone swam naked in the quarry in actual warm weather, so the idea of skinny-dipping was already in the group subconscious.

A bunch of people went in from the shore. The girls mostly, yelping as they shed their clothes. Screams when the cold water inched up to their armpits. I kept my clothes on. I stayed on shore. I hated the quarry. Terrified of the depth that went far beyond what was normal for a pond that size. I hated how everyone ignored the NO SWIMMING sign. There were rules, they were breaking them, and even though intellectually I understood that breaking rules was part of the point of being young, it wasn't the reality I lived in.

I leaned against a tree, sitting on my heels, trying hard to disappear into my black puffy coat.

Anya, a theatre techie, called to me from the edge of the water. "Coming?"

"No," I said, shaking my head.

"You only live once!" she shouted.

I put my hand on my stomach. "Cramps," I said.

I'm not sure if she heard me. She ran into the water, screaming.

I was so focused on her scream and the splashing and the moonlit figures in the water, I didn't notice the group of guys making their way to the edge of the tall rocks on the other side.

The first two jumped with wild yells. Big splashes.

The next guy fell. Or tripped while he was jumping. He landed in the water with a huge sick slap. It hurt to hear. My stomach stung in sympathy.

One of the guys on the rocks yelled, "Holy shit! Holy shit! Where did he go?" Another yelled, "Luca!" And then there was nothing. Whispers from the girls at the shore. Murmurs of "Oh my god!" "What should we do?"

I was in the water immediately. I didn't even take my coat off. The down weighted me and my limbs were stiff in the freezing water. Each stroke took monumental effort. Moonlight made everything bluish gray. I could only see shapes. I followed voices, grabbing at bodies. A guy shouted, "Hey!" when I reached for his arm. "Hey!"

I don't think anyone else was looking for Luca. They were panicked in that thick, drunk-minded way, when time seems slower than it is, like there's ages to make decisions and anything important will wait for you to catch up.

Finally, I grabbed a leg, and heard only gasping in return. In the moonlight, I could see Luca's nose and chin above water. He was on the surface. He was still alive. I hooked my arm under his armpit and started swimming back to land, shouting, "Help me! Help!" but no one did.

I wasn't just hauling Luca's body to shore, pushing him into the dirt when we got there. It wasn't only his weight I carried.

Luca was fine. The belly flop had merely stunned him. Knocked the wind out. He coughed a bit and sat up and laughed at me for my seriousness. My "heroic rescue," he called it. He was still drunk. The other guys teased him about being a damsel in distress, and I could tell from the weakness of his laugh he was embarrassed. I tried to convince myself that later, sober, he would be thankful, realize his stupidity, convert to being a rule follower. But I still hated him, acutely, fiercely, because now I was thinking about blue lips and dead skin. I had to contend with a pounding heartbeat in my ears too intense to think and hear and feel anything that was actually happening.

The people on the shore were laughing and chatting, they thought I was ridiculous for jumping into the quarry in my jacket. Everything had worked out. Everyone was fine. They were oblivious to the ways people drown. Without me, Luca might not have snapped out of his shock. The breaths he took to refill his lungs could have been waterlogged. He might not have found his way back to shore before his muscles fatigued. Because Luca was fine after I saved him, they believed he'd been fine all along and my intervention was superfluous, absurd. So I hated all of them too.

I felt like I was hearing their idiotic banter from miles away, aware and unaware at the same time. "Fuck you," I said to the dark. To Luca. To all of them. I don't know if anyone heard me.

Everyone else was putting on clothes warmed by the anemic fire, but even on shore, I was stuck in water. The weight of my sopping jacket made it hard to breathe, but my frozen fingers couldn't get the zipper open. I stunk of winter rot and algae.

Instead of asking for help, I started walking. Away from the chatter. Away from Luca and the depths of the quarry. I don't know if they saw me leave, or noticed I was missing. If they stayed by the fire and kept drinking. I didn't care if they went back in the water and sunk to the granite floor. I walked two miles, through the woods, then along the side of the road, stunned by headlights, in heavy wet clothes with cold dead skin that was mine and not mine. Stuck with my heartbeat, and I couldn't tell if it was normal or not. Too fast. Too slow. Was my heart as weak as my father's? Did I need to be careful? I wasn't sure if I cared. And when I got back to my tiny damp studio apartment, it felt flooded by the unfailing hiss of Six Mile Creek rushing in the gulch just beyond the yard, swollen from snow-melt. I cut myself out of my jacket, even though it was the only one I had. I pulled my wet jeans from my bloated legs. Got in the shower, and tried to see my own skin. My own fingers and toes. But all I could think about was my father's blue lips and the hollow thud of my body hitting his chest. The breath that didn't come back. Cold, dense nothing.

I sat on the floor of the shower until the water ran cold, and I couldn't even cry. I sat there and tried not to choke from the pain in my throat, from the pain in my chest and the horrible feeling of how truly alone I was, and how truly alone I'd proba-bly always be, because the world is not made of people who find comfort in rules. Because college is not populated with kids who watched their father die on a dock in a thunderstorm. Because no one would ever understand me.

That night was the last time I talked to Luca. He talked to me. Tried to apologize. Followed me from class. Left messages on my voicemail. But I did not talk. I had already felt the loss of him, and the only way I knew to keep that pain from happening again was to keep Luca away.

I barely talked to anyone after that. No chatter beyond the necessary: classroom, costume shop, procurement of food. Even then, I kept it brief. When Nan called, I mostly listened and hoped she wouldn't ask much of me.

Then Eric, who had been the TA for media literacy the semester before, found me eating alone in the snack bar and asked if he could join me. "I wanted to ask you out after the last class, but I couldn't quite work up the nerve," he said with a sweet, sweet smile.

Even though I knew there was nothing about him that didn't have enough nerve, I chose to believe him. He was someone who colored completely in the lines, happy to adhere to the way things should be. He felt wonderfully safe. We would never be entangled in ways that made me ache or fear. We would stay above the surface together.

One night, Eric and I were leaving Simeon's restaurant after dinner. Eric took my hand and his fingers were so warm that I felt like the heat was traveling through me. Then there was Luca, getting off the bus, and he saw us. I leaned toward Eric, pretending I hadn't seen Luca, that he didn't even exist. I had compressed all that pain, the same way I'd stuffed my puffy coat in a grocery bag and thrown it away, ignoring the feathers that escaped.

I knew I should have given respect to the duration and intensity of our relationship by saying words back at Luca, telling him why I was hurt/sad/destroyed/done. But I couldn't. One day I loved him, and the next he felt like my enemy. Maybe he thought it was sex that drove us apart. Maybe it would have otherwise.

On Fountain Day, when all the seniors jumped in the fountain in front of the theatre building, I stayed home. I was officially done with water. Saving Luca was the last time I swam.

Sex with Eric was never anything more than what it was. Nothing was transcended. It was parts and the feelings from those parts. Sometimes it was good. Sometimes it was just friction. Once we started trying to conceive, it was a task, and then a painful reminder.

Sex with Luca was joy joy joy, until I woke up terrified.

Luca was still fast asleep. Bark had wedged himself between us, his wet doggy nose tucked under my chin. I moved slowly, deliberately, to sneak away from them. Bark woke and watched me go, but stayed with Luca, stretching to take up the spot I'd left.

In my room, I closed the door and sat in front of it, my nervous rabbit heart beating faster and faster. The smell of burning leaf mold. The way the air feels right before lightning. Cold skin. My bright blue bathing suit. The weight of wet down.

I lay on the floor, pressing my cheek against the metal air vent. *This is real*, I thought, trying to keep my focus on the cold metal, the scratchy texture of the rug. I didn't want to feel this way. I didn't want to treat Luca this way. I wanted to be more than my panic. I feared I never would be. The rattle of the air conditioner. The eggshell texture of the paint on the walls. The gap under the door. The worn wooden legs of my dresser. *This is real.*

Then I saw it: my dad's watch, all the way in the back, stuck behind one of the dresser legs, hiding in dust bunnies. Missing since a few weeks after I moved in with Nan the first time.

I stood up and grabbed my yardstick to push it out. Black with gold numbers. A brand called Raketa. Tiny Russian letters at the bottom of the face. My father was considered to be one of the leading authorities on Wassily Kandinsky. He'd gotten the watch when he went to Moscow to do research on Kandinsky's early life. No one in American art history had access to those archives before the dissolution of the USSR, so he had the chance to uncover details no other art historian had seen. He was so proud of that watch.

There were cracks in the leather, a few green mold spots on the underside of the band. I could restore it. I'd seen worse pieces in the costume shop and brought them back to life.

I wrapped the band around my wrist. The worn-out hole was two notches bigger than the one that fit me. I had cried every night, for weeks, over the loss of his watch. Nan and I tore the house apart looking. I wasn't sure if I believed in signs, but it felt good to think that maybe my father was telling me to be brave.

CHAPTER FORTY-FIVE

I heard Luca and Bark scramble down the hall. When their feet hit the kitchen floor, I snuck to the bathroom to take a shower before show day prep took over.

By the time I was out and dressed, Luca was lining up sound equipment on the dining room table, next to sticky notes with each mermaid's name. I watched him from the hallway, his back turned to me. I loved his careful movements.

"Shit," he said quietly to himself, and then reached into his backpack. He rifled around and came up empty.

"Hey. Do you need help?" I hoped maybe if I acted like everything was fine, it would be.

He smiled at me. "Hey, you," he said, and started to get up, maybe to kiss me. We heard Nan rush through the front door, and I turned away ever so slightly.

"I ran out of condoms," Luca said matter-of-factly. When what he'd said dawned on him, he blushed.

The condoms, I knew from my work in the costume shop, were to protect the mic box from sweat. It was such a common use that it was easy to forget there was anything odd about it.

"I can run to the store for you," I said, politely ignoring his fluster, even though I was not relishing the idea of buying condoms in a town full of retirees manning registers.

"Who's running to the store?" Nan called as she walked in to join us.

"Nothing, Nan," I shouted. "It's fine."

"Do you need something, Luca?" she asked.

"Thanks, Nan," Luca said. "I think it's okay."

"I'll be back in ten," I said. Luca nodded.

"What do you need? What's going on?" Nan could never let anything drop. She always needed to know.

"I just— The protective covers for the mic boxes," Luca said. "I need a few more, and Katie said she'd run to the store for me."

"Where do you even get something like that?" Nan asked.

"I've got it, Nan," I said. "It's fine."

She surveyed the stacks of equipment and picked up a condom packet. "Is this what you're using?" she asked.

Luca nodded.

"Oh, I have condoms," she said, putting the packet back on the table. "We're all adults here. Let's not be silly."

She left the room. Luca and I stood in silence.

"I'm not going to look at you," he said, and I could hear the smile in his voice.

"I appreciate that."

Nan came back with the largest box of condoms I've ever seen. "Here you go. Take as many as you want. No need to run to the store."

"Thank you," Luca said in a very metered tone.

"Thanks, Nan," I said, trying hard to be polite and mature. She'd been so worried about my acceptance of her relationship with Isaac and I most certainly didn't want to shame her.

"Oh," Luca said quietly, turning to me. "These aren't the right kind."

I nodded.

"Because of the ribs?" Nan asked.

"I'm going to run out for a sec, Nan," I said a little too loudly. "It's fine. I don't mind."

Nan looked hurt. Like her condoms weren't good enough.

Luca took a deep breath. "The lubrication—"

"Oh!" Nan said. "Of course! I didn't even think of that. What good is protecting it from sweat if it's going to be covered in—"

"Helloooo!" Bitsie called from the front door. She joined us in the dining room.

"Luca is using condoms to protect the mic boxes," Nan told her earnestly. "But mine won't work because of the lube."

"Well, you learn something new every day," Bitsie said, smiling. She understood the awkwardness and it delighted her.

"I'm going to run to the store," I said.

"I'll go with you," Bitsie said.

"Helloooo!" Ruth called.

"Okay, let's go now," I said, instead of arguing with Bitsie. I couldn't handle running through this whole conversation again with Ruth.

I mouthed, *I'm sorry*, to Luca as we exited. He smiled. There was more to the smile than the awkwardness. There was brightness. Knowing. He expected last night to mean something. We were supposed to move forward. And I wanted to. I wanted to. I didn't know how.

"Well, it's good she's practicing safe sex," Bitsie said as soon as we were in the car.

I nodded.

Bitsie laughed.

"I'm happy she's happy," I said. "And I'm totally pro . . . whatever. And I love Isaac . . ."

"But you don't want the details."

"I don't!"

"I think she's had a bit of an awakening," Bitsie said with a devilish smile.

I put my hand over my right ear and started singing, "Twinkle, twinkle little star."

Bitsie grabbed my wrist, laughing. "I promise! I'll stop!"

"Your grandmother had sex at some point too."

"Yeah, but she probably didn't enjoy it. My grandfather was an asshole."

"Ooh, I think that's worse."

"It's all awkward," Bitsie said. "Amazing, isn't it? We get so embarrassed about the human things we do." She patted my shoulder. "So when are you going to tell Luca you're in love with him?"

I forced a laugh like she was talking crazy. "What? Where are you getting this?"

"You kids are breaking my heart. I've never seen such longing looks."

"I don't know what you're talking about," I said, trying my best to sound lighthearted and quippy. I parked the car as quickly as possible so I could escape the conversation.

In the pharmacy, Bitsie loudly asked the greeter, "Where do you keep the condoms?" and delighted in the checker's discomfort as we paid for them. When he said, "Have a good day!" she lifted the bag and said, "Oh, I plan to!"

But as soon as we got back to the car, she was on me about Luca again. "That kind of love is terrifying, isn't it?" she said, as if there'd been no break in our conversation. "Like the world opened up and showed you another layer."

"Yeah. It is." I didn't start the car, fumbling with my keys. "I walked away from him once."

"I would have too," Bitsie said, "if I'd met Bunny when I was nineteen. I wasn't ready for that. But you're getting a second chance."

"It's still too much to feel."

Bitsie sighed. "You were such a lionhearted kid, and now you're walking around trying to pretend you need to protect yourself with three layers of bubble wrap? You don't. You can handle it."

We watched a mom and her toddler leaving the store. When the toddler got to the edge of the curb, she jumped, throwing her arms up in triumph as she stuck the landing. Her mom threw her arms in the air too, and they both cheered.

Bitsie patted the dashboard. "Whoo, it's hot in here! Let's go bring that boy his condoms."

"I'm giving you that job," I said, starting the car.

Bitsie took the box out of the bag and read the back as we drove home. "In my day, a woman buying these . . ." She shook her head, grinning. "It was considered untoward."

"I think it's still your day," I said.

"Huh." She looked at me like she was thrown by the thought. Then she nodded. "Well, I am a mermaid." Her phone chimed. "Ooh! Nannette says we should just go to the pool. They're all there."

"I have to go get the costumes."

"She says they have them."

Everything was starting and I hadn't had a moment to collect myself. I'm not sure what I would have gathered up in that moment, but the absence of it made me dizzy.

CHAPTER FORTY-SIX

I dropped Bitsie at the front door to the community center.

I parked the car. I sat there. Hands still on the steering wheel, willing myself to take the key from the ignition. Move my legs. I tried to think about what I needed to do. Get the ladies dressed. Check the seams. Make sure no one was losing any sequins. But I kept thinking of underwater. Of Nan and Bitsie underwater. I tried to remind myself this was a happy thing for them. I was proud of what they'd done. I was proud of the work I'd done. This was good. It was good. It was good. But I didn't feel good. All I could think about was underwater and it hit my heart with a jolt. My stomach twisted. Sweat beaded on my upper lip. I took a deep breath. Another. Again.

"You can do this," I said out loud. "You can. Do this." I pried myself from the car with a bargain. I'd go straight to the clubhouse. I wouldn't even look at the water. I'd stay in our makeshift dressing room for emergency repairs. After the show, once I knew everyone was safe, I'd watch the footage, so I'd still get to see the performance.

I kept my head down as I passed the gate to the pool, trying not to look at the water, but then I heard a scream.

Over by the deep end, Mo chased Luca, pushing him in the pool. There were two huge projection screens set up at the far side. One feed came from a camera at the surface, the other from Danny filming underwater in a dive suit. On the screens, I saw Luca hit the water and go under. Bubbles. Arms paddling to bring himself back up. It felt so close. I saw him reach the surface and gasp for air. Nan was sitting next to Althea in a lounge chair at the shallow side, laughing.

I tried to breathe harder, deeper, to calm myself, but I couldn't get the air in. Each breath was more shallow. I felt the panic rise.

"Ha," Mo shouted. "That's what you get!"

Luca threw a beach ball at her head. "*Bam!* Got you!"

She dove in and dunked him under. I held my breath until they both came up safely. And then I noticed Bark running along the far edge of the pool, watching them, leash trailing. He could so easily trip. I pictured his body, floating, limp, dappled fur waving in the water.

"Why is he here?" I yelled to Nan. I called to Bark, but he was too fixated on Mo and Luca.

"Oh, he's fine, Kay," Nan said. "He likes all the ladies."

"He could drown!"

Mo climbed the ladder. As she got to the top, Luca pulled her back in. They were like kids, wound up in play, existing only in that moment. Bark howled.

If I called to him again, he might jump into the pool instead of walking around. If I didn't, he might anyway. My knees were wobbly. I worried I wouldn't make it over to grab him. I gasped, out of air. Dread filled my body like a current.

"Bark!" I yelled as my head swirled.

"Oh, hey, Kay!" Luca called, waving.

I didn't want Luca to see me. Bark was too close to the edge. My heartbeat pounded in my ears. I couldn't stop thinking of the two gray hairs on my father's chest. The dull thud when I heaved myself on his body. The silence that followed. Cold skin. Blue lips.

It was eighty degrees. I was covered in goose bumps. I got closer to Bark. Almost there.

"Kay!" Mo shouted once she'd climbed out again.

I felt her hand on my back, and I thought it was there to steady me, but then the pressure grew and I realized what was happening. "No!" I screamed. "No!" and my voice sounded far-away, like it was someone else, somewhere else, so when I hit the water, it was a shock to feel the slap against my body, the sting in my nose. My leg scraped the side of the pool as I slipped below the surface.

There was a splash. Loud. A churning current. Mo's arm hooked under mine.

I coughed as we resurfaced. Trying to rid myself of water.

"Shit! I'm sorry! I forgot! I'm so sorry!" she yelled, dragging me toward the ladder.

"I know how to swim!" I shouted, trying to shake her off me. "I know how to swim!"

Bark jumped in the pool. I screamed, and twisted away from Mo, elbowing her in the chin as I freed myself from her grasp. I swam toward Bark, lungs still burning from the chlorine, arms aching. I threw him over my shoulder and tried to climb the ladder, but he wriggled around and his weight out of water was too much to carry that way. I kept falling back in the pool, try-ing again and again. Cold skin. Thunder rumbling. Dark water. Cold skin. That dull, dull thud. This time, I'd be fast enough. I'd be strong enough.

"Bark knows how to swim," Nan called to me. "I taught him. He's fine, Kay." Her words sounded muffled, like I was still un-derwater.

I couldn't breathe. I couldn't breathe. "He's not fine," I screamed when I finally had enough air. "It's not fine!" I inhaled water, again, coughing to get it up, but it didn't matter. I didn't matter. I had to save Bark. I couldn't let him go. He writhed in my arms.

Finally, I boosted him high enough and he scrambled out of the pool on his own. He cried until I climbed out too. Collapsing at the edge, I couldn't catch my breath. My head throbbed. Bark licked my face. I wrapped my arms around him, sobbing. Feeling his body against mine—breathing and alive—didn't stop the feeling that everything was going wrong. My heart raced like I would still fail. Like I couldn't save him.

I heard Mo's wet feet slap against the concrete, louder and louder. I wanted to run away. My father's watch was still on my wrist. Water pooled under the glass. The second hand had stopped moving. "No," I sobbed, trying to shake the water out.

"I'm so sorry, Kay," Mo said, resting her hand on my back. "I forgot. For a second. I forgot."

"It's not okay," I yelled, standing up to get away from her. "It's not okay!"

Bark cowered. His legs shook, water dripping on the concrete. I was making him worse. He was fine and I scared him. When he was with other people, he was okay. I was the one making him nervous. I looked around, searching for Althea, and saw myself. All of it—every last moment—had been broadcast on the big screens, for all the people at the community center to see. Everyone around the pool was staring. Beyond them, people on the golf course were standing at the fence, watching me lose it, larger than life.

I grabbed Bark's leash and trudged toward Althea with him in tow. "Oh, honey," she said, "why don't you sit down?"

"I can't." I was crying so hard my words were only small squeaks. I handed Bark's leash over to her, and walked away.

Luca followed me to the parking lot. "Katie," he said, reaching for me. I twisted from his grasp.

"Don't!" I yelled. "Don't! It's too hard. I can't love you like that."

"Kay!" he called.

"Don't follow me," I yelled without even looking back.

I kept walking, past the parking lot, away from the community center. Down the street. Further and further from all of them.

CHAPTER FORTY-SEVEN

I needed to be alone. I couldn't trust myself with the people I loved. In my head, with each step, I heard my words: "I can't love you like that." By the time I walked all the way to Mo's house, I'd worn off the worst of the adrenaline, and it left me shaky and weak. I typed F-U-C-K into the keypad to let myself in. The garage looked empty without Morty. The workbench was cluttered with sketches of a giant squid that looked like a play structure, slides built into the tentacles.

There was a six-pack of PBR in the fridge. I grabbed it and crawled under the workbench into the bomb shelter, pulling the pallet door shut behind me. The air felt dusty and scarce. I opened the first beer, drank it in gulps, pacing the tiny stretch of floor between the two cots. I didn't know what to do with myself. I couldn't stand my own skin. I wanted the pulsing thump in my veins to stop. It felt like my life could only run on that rhythm, and it was offbeat from everyone else.

My phone had been in my pocket when I fell in the pool, and the screen was hopelessly black. I sat on a cot and dropped my head in my hands, covering my eyes. Trying to breathe. I'd forgotten how normal people take in air, worried I might never remember. I couldn't even cry. My shorts were still soggy, and even though it wasn't cold in Mo's garage, I kept shivering. I wrapped one of the army blankets around my shoulders, but it smelled like mildew, and the wool scratched my skin. I threw the blanket on the other cot and drank another beer. And then another. I drank until my fingers felt numb and my breathing became less of an effort. The details of what had happened at the pool were starting to feel far away, like they were at the end of a long, dark tunnel. I couldn't remember what I'd said, if everything I'd thought had come out of my mouth, if words came out without any thought. What was still clear was the memory of the weight of my wet dog on my shoulder and handing his leash to Althea. I'd failed Bark most of all.

Lying on the cot, staring at the ceiling, I noticed a box on the top shelf. Plain cardboard, because we thought that would draw less attention. Held shut with a collection of rubber bands running in both directions. We'd believed the effort of removing them would deter any adult from trying to open our treasure chest. As if anyone besides me and Mo even went in the bomb shelter anyway.

I got up. The cot had a damp imprint of my butt, back, and hair, like I was made from disconnected parts. I climbed on one of the water drums, my brain struggling to find equilibrium. The drum wobbled under my feet. I stood on my tiptoes. As an adult, I was the same height as Mo at twelve; I could finally reach the box on my own.

I wanted the box to be full of the kind of mementos that would push me toward being a whole new person. I'd open it and something in there would suddenly twist my mind into the right shape and the world would make sense. I climbed down with the box and rested it on the cot. The rubber bands were disintegrating and broke when I stretched them.

It was just a box of junk. Some seashells, smooth stones, little green army men with plastic bag parachutes, the Barbie who'd suffered a buzz cut at our hands, a bunch of Atomic Fireballs, a pack of playing cards, some SpongeBob stickers, and a stack of Mo's uncle's old Spider-Man comics. No magic answer to be found.

I sat on the cot, opened another beer, and tore the wrapper off an Atomic Fireball with my teeth. I couldn't trust myself with the people I loved. All I did was fail them, and it was probably better if I stayed away. So instead of going back to the pool to apologize, I read Spider-Man comics and tried to dissolve the fireball in a mouthful of beer.

Two fireballs and three Spider-Mans later, I finished my last beer just as I heard Mo's car in the driveway. Maybe she wouldn't even find me. She probably came home for a snack or goggles or aspirin or sunscreen. I lay very still on the cot and wished I could turn the light off with my mind. I closed my eyes like maybe that would help me stay undiscovered. But she opened the garage door and went directly to the bomb shelter. I heard her moving the pallet door away. And then I felt her standing over me. I kept my eyes closed.

"I thought I'd find you here," Mo said. "The show's about to start. We can still get there in time."

"I can't." I rolled on my side toward the wall. My bladder was full and my stomach felt empty.

"Kay. I'm so sorry. I was wound-up like a puppy dog. I wasn't thinking."

"Yeah." I opened my eyes and stared at the cinder block. I knew she hadn't pushed me on purpose. She would have done the same thing to any of her lifeguard friends with no consequence. But I couldn't find the warmth in my heart that belonged to her. I couldn't feel much of anything, like I'd overspent my emotions.

"Nan, Bitsie, they're about to do something amazing, and you're going to miss it?"

"I can't," I said, my throat constricting. I picked at a glob of grout between the cinder blocks with my fingernail, trying to break it and leave a smooth edge. It wouldn't budge. "Are their costumes okay?"

"They're perfect, Kay. They look incredible. I checked the hoses. All of them. Four times."

I nodded. All of me hurt. There was still water sloshing under the glass of my father's watch.

"Let me take you home at least. Before I go back."

"I don't want to go home," I said a little too loudly. "And I don't want to talk to you."

"Okay," Mo said, sighing. "At least go in my room and put on some dry clothes, okay?"

After she left, I crawled out of the bomb shelter, ran inside to the bathroom, and peed for what seemed like an hour. In Mo's bedroom, I found a wad of clothes that smelled pretty clean in a laundry basket at the foot of her bed. Her room hadn't changed since we were kids either, but she'd been living in it this whole time. She still had a Bart Simpson poster hanging on the ceiling over her bed, and a giant stuffed snake wrapped around her headboard. I changed into a pair of powder blue Bermuda shorts and a Hawaiian shirt covered in a print of hibiscus flowers and vinyl records. It smelled like Tide and had been washed so many times it was soft as silk.

Pops wasn't a drinker, but I found a dusty old bottle of Drambuie in the living room hutch. I poured it in a coffee mug. It was sickly sweet and smelled like licorice, but it burned my throat enough to make me think it would do a good job of keeping me from sobering up. That was all I wanted, to not feel anything.

I ate an entire box of Cheez-Its and watched a million episodes of *Law & Order*. I thought maybe Mo would come back after the mermaid show. That she'd check on me before going to the cocktail party at Nan's house. But she didn't.

When the eleven o'clock news played on the TV, there was a clip from the show. The four mermaids, underwater, smiles on their faces, arms around each other, the sequins on their tails shimmering in the water. Nan and Bitsie's students in their matching bathing caps, kicking their legs in unison behind them. A brilliant spectacle. When the segment was over, I turned off the TV and sat in the dark in Mo's living room, wearing her enormous old man clothes. Finally, finally, the tears came, and all I wanted to do was find Bark.

CHAPTER FORTY-EIGHT

I cut through yards to get to Althea's house. My legs were not up for collaborating with my brain, and I tripped running through Lester's lawn, sliding on my knees. I could smell the grass, the way I'd bruised it, and knew my legs would be stained with green.

I knocked on Althea's door and then remembered the doorbell and rang that too. I realized all the lights were out. Maybe she was still at Nan's. Had she left Bark inside? Was there a way I could get to him?

I had my hands cupped around my face at the entryway window, trying to see in, when Althea came to the door.

"Are you okay?" she asked, tying the belt of her bathrobe in a bow.

I nodded, feeling terrible for waking her up. I hadn't even thought about how late it was. I didn't know how long it had been from the end of the news until I actually got off the couch.

"Don't worry," she said. "Bark's fine. We went for a walk, split a hamburger. I dropped him at Nannette's. He's been a happy boy."

"I didn't mean to— I shouldn't have—"

"One of the things I learned with my girls is that sometimes you need to hit pause. Do you know how many times I dumped them at Marta's? I'd call her from the end of my rope. And then I'd take myself out for ice cream, like I wasn't a grown woman."

"Thank you," I said. "I'm so sorry. For everything. Before." The haze of Drambuie was starting to wear off. I could feel the tears and the headache coming.

"I know, honey. I never thought you weren't." Althea yawned. "I've got to get to bed."

I think she read the panic on my face. "Do you want to stay in Cara's room? Nan's probably got a crowd over there," she said. "And maybe you need to sleep it off?"

"I'm so sorry," I said. My eyes welled up and I felt my drunkenness again, like a pendulum swinging back. Bark was safe and happy with Nan, and it was probably better if he didn't see me this way, or maybe I was still being a coward because I didn't want Nan to see me this way. I didn't want to face her. Or Luca.

"Sometimes," Althea said, "it's nice to have other people breathing in this house at night."

She made me drink a glass of water and take two aspirin before I went to bed. She even had an extra toothbrush. She said, "Sleep tight."

I soaked it up. Althea was the kind of mom I'd always wished I had. She knew how to set rules. How to cheer her kids on. How to stay.

I climbed into Cara's four-poster bed, under sheets covered in pink cabbage roses, and wished everything about me was different.

I woke to chatter in the kitchen. Nan's company voice. The pillowcase smelled like lavender, a scent Nan hated because she said it smelled like "old ladies." I sat up, my brain lurched in my head. Cabbage roses. Cara's room. Althea's house. I remembered. I remembered all of it. My eyes teared until the inner workings of my head settled into place again. The headache was manageable as long as I didn't move.

The actual details from the pool were swirled together with what happened to my father. Jumbled, as if everyone had watched me fail to save him on a big projection screen. I knew what wasn't real and what was, but the thoughts wouldn't stay separate. I did know for sure I scared Bark. That was real. It was horrible.

There were footsteps in the hall. The cadence of Nan's walk. Heavy on her heels. I slunk down to pretend I was sleeping, movement making my eyes tear again.

She opened the door. I lay very still. She sat on the bed and leaned over me. She never believed my fake sleep.

"Are you okay?" she asked, brushing hair from my forehead.

"I'm fine," I said, not turning toward her. Not moving at all. I kept my eyes closed so she wouldn't see how puffy they were. "I'm sorry."

I heard her breathing. Not saying anything for the longest time. It was unbearable.

"I see you differently now," Nan said finally.

The rush of shame that flooded my system made my face hot, my limbs frozen.

Nan took a deep breath. "I used to be afraid of how fragile I thought you were. Bitsie always yelled at me, 'Stop worrying a stiff breeze will blow that kid over! She's tough!'" Nan said in her Bitsie voice, and I realized that what I'd thought she was saying was not where she was headed. "Bitsie always said you had a lion heart."

It was strange that Bitsie had used those words for me before and it wasn't just something she thought up when we were talking at the drugstore. They were her label for me. The blood stopped rushing to my face so quickly, pressure in my head fading enough to be bearable.

"I couldn't see how you were tough," Nan said. "I saw your panic. The way words could break you. But when I watched you swim across that pool to save Bark, I understood what Bitsie meant. I saw your lion heart in action. It's not about the fact that you're scared. You were terrified and you did it anyway. You thought Bark was drowning and you were determined to save him with all you had. The same way you saved my son."

"I didn't." My voice barely worked. "I didn't save my dad."

"Oh, Kay," Nan said.

"I'm sorry," I said, because I didn't save her son. Because I ruined her big day. I made her worry about me. "I'm so sorry."

"Kay." She lay on the bed, wrapping her arms around me. "No one could have done more for your father." I felt her body shiver, and realized it was a sob. "Not a grown-up. Not a doctor. No one could have."

I held my breath, trying to stem the tears.

Nan said, "I see it now. The way you are—the worry and fear—that's the price you pay for that lion heart. You're always on guard to save the ones you love, aren't you?"

I reached for her hand and held it to my chest.

"We would all save you too," she said. "Don't forget that."

Althea made us oatmeal and picked a pile of kumquats from the tree in her yard. She didn't drink coffee, but she gave us steaming mugs of jasmine green tea, and slid a bottle of aspirin across the table before I even had to ask. None of us talked much. Polite words. The silence was kind. My head was too full.

"Well," Nan said when we were done eating. "I have to meet Bitsie and Mo at the pool to clean up."

"Okay," I said, getting up to rinse my bowl in the sink.

"Not you," Nan said. "If anyone deserves a day off after all of this."

I didn't want to go back to the scene of the crime, but I wanted to be busy. I always hated the days after a show ended under the best of circumstances. All that work, and time, and purpose, and then, nothing. The cleanup was a process for letting go of the ideas that had been turning in my mind for months. "I can—"

"Kay, no," Nan said, smiling. "We're strong. We'll manage."

"I think that dog of yours is probably waiting to see you," Althea said, in a mom tone, the way you offer a consolation prize to the kid who doesn't want to leave a playdate. But I did want to see Bark. I needed to know he was okay. I needed him to know I was too.

CHAPTER FORTY-NINE

Bark was the only one home when I got to Nan's. I opened the door. He let out a long, desperate whine when he saw me. I bent to pet him and he knocked me over, frantically licking my face. He sniffed at my hair. Pushed his head under my hand. Maybe he'd thought I wasn't coming back for him. Maybe he thought he'd done something wrong.

"Oh, buddy. I'm so sorry. I'm so, so sorry." Fat tears ran down my face. He shoved his head into my armpit.

"Barky," I said, kissing his head. "I'm not going to do that again. I'm not going to leave you."

When he was done inspecting, reasonably certain I had come home in one piece, he ran from the hallway and came prancing back with Murray dangling from his mouth. He looked at me and stepped toward the living room, and then looked back at me. A few more steps. Another look. Like he was trying to use Murray to lure me into following him.

Bark settled on the couch. I sat next to him, tugging at Murray's leg as Bark tugged back. I felt forgiven. I knew there was more work, that it wasn't as easy as Murray and kisses and a good scratch behind the ears. But he didn't hate me. He wasn't afraid of me.

"You're a good boy," I said. He watched me with his mismatched eyes, soulful and sweet. Then he shook Murray to get me to tug again.

When Bark was done playing, I searched for the remote and noticed Luca's camera, hooked up to the TV. I got up and turned it on.

The footage was queued to the start of the show, but I went back further. This was the camera at surface level. Toward the beginning of the file, I found myself. No one was manning that camera when it happened, so I was spared a close-up view. I was a screaming figure at the side of the pool, but it was clear enough to see the terror in my eyes, even from a distance. I yelled at Mo. My voice sounded hollow, unfamiliar.

When I attempted to lift Bark out of the pool I was singular in focus. Fast. Strong. Even in the struggle. What had felt like ages only lasted forty-three seconds.

I rewound, and watched the moment when he jumped in. Forty-three seconds. Rewind. Watch again. Before I got to him, Bark was fine. Swimming to me. He wasn't drowning. But when I got him out of the pool, his legs shook with fear.

I did that to him. I turned what was okay into something that wasn't.

The front door opened, but I couldn't stop watching. Horrified. Aching.

"Hey." It was Luca.

I'd worried so much about what I would say to Luca on the way home, but the first thing that came out of my mouth was "You're not going to use this, are you?"

"Of course not," Luca said, kneeling on the floor next to me. "Of course not. I was going to delete it, but when I saw it—your fear was so primal—I thought maybe if you saw that, you'd be more kind to yourself. Mo said you were embarrassed. But what happened, it doesn't look like something you could help." He touched my arm. "Like when you tried to save me?"

I turned away. "You knew. You were the only person at school who knew what happened to my dad. And then you jumped in." I felt a twinge in my bottom lip, and willed myself not to cry.

"But I didn't die."

"You could have."

"I didn't."

"You didn't even care. When I pulled you out, you didn't even care." I remembered that there'd been a pack of peppermint gum in the pocket of my puffy coat. When I walked home, hands in my wet pockets, the gum made my fingers sticky and my eyes stung when I wiped tears away.

"I was embarrassed," Luca said softly. "I didn't need saving."

"You can say that for sure, because I saved you. You were so drunk. I thought you were dead. When they called for you, you didn't call back. I thought you were dead." I couldn't shake the feeling of being trapped in wet down.

"I didn't do it to scare you." Luca's voice was heavy and careful. "I felt like the other kids. For like five minutes, I felt like a normal kid." He sniffed. Ran his hand along the stubble on his cheek. "I could help. I would do anything to help. But you can't expect everyone to sit vigil for your fears, Katie."

"That's not— I don't—" I thought about all the people dressed in black at my father's funeral. No one else mourned him long enough. No one mourned me. I stopped being normal and no one ever mourned for me.

"So that's why we ended?" Luca asked, rubbing at his forehead with his palm. "Because I jumped in the quarry?"

"I couldn't stand how much I loved you." My voice sounded hollow, like it had in the video.

"That's stupid," he said, a flash of anger in his eyes. "That's so stupid. You loved me so much you had to marry someone else? I thought you didn't love me. I always thought that was the problem."

"I'm not good enough," I said. I could almost smell wet feathers. "I wasn't then. I'm not now."

"Don't."

"What am I supposed to do, Luca? I just got divorced. I lost two babies. I wasn't okay to begin with. I'm not going to suddenly be fine now."

"Twice now," Luca said quietly. "Twice now, we slept together, and I thought it was the beginning of something."

"I'm sorry." I wanted to cling to him for comfort, but that wasn't fair. His hurt lived in the back of his eyes. Like mine. It could get worse, it could wane, but it would never go away. I didn't want him to pay the price of me on top of everything else. "I'd love to believe you can come along and fix me, but you can't. And I can't get better by dragging you down."

"I thought I got you back," Luca said.

"I'm going to go," I said, holding back sobs. "I don't want to watch you leave."

Luca sighed. Tears in his eyes. "If that's the way you feel about me leaving, how . . ." His voice trailed off.

He hugged me, and I hugged him back, for a moment, then I pulled away.

I whispered, "I won't be gone long!" to Bark, so softly that only he would hear it, and walked out the front door without stopping for my shoes.

I ran to Bitsie's and hid in Bunny's room, sewing scrap squares together to make a quilt. The rhythm of the sewing machine told me over and over that I'd made a mistake.

CHAPTER FIFTY

The front door opened. Before I could hide the quilt squares, I heard the jangle of dog tags. Bark nosed his way into the not-quite-closed door to Bunny's room. He jumped up, paws on my lap to lick my face. I pressed my forehead to his, whispering, "Hi, Barky! What are you doing here?"

His whole body wagged.

"Hey, Kay," Althea called, joining us a moment later. "I thought you might be here."

Bark searched the room, smelling everything.

Althea pointed to the quilt pieces. "That's beautiful!"

"It's a surprise. For Bitsie."

She touched a square of light gray gingham. "I remember this skirt," she said with a sad smile. Then she pointed to a square of purple broadcloth. "And that. Bunny wore the heck out of that shirt." She worked her jaw, like her muscles were talking her out of a good cry.

I remembered her husband Sam's red flannel shirt. He wore it on cool Sunday mornings in the winter, and you could tell it was his favorite.

"I stopped by Nan's to take Bark for a walk and thought you might want to join us for a lesson," Althea said.

I worried if I left the safety of Bunny's sewing room, I'd run into Luca. I'd see him. I'd cave. I'd ruin his life. "I don't—"

"Luca left," Althea said. "Right after I got there."

I nodded. It was for the best, but that didn't stop my heart from falling. I had to fight the urge to run outside and sprint top speed to catch him at a stop sign.

"His face looked kinda like yours," Althea said, sympathy in her eyes.

She picked up a quilt square from the stack I hadn't sewn yet. A Brunschwig & Fils leaf-patterned chintz. "I was so jealous of Bunny's kitchen curtains."

"She used to get every fabric catalog known to man," I said. I'd spent so much time at the kitchen table with Bunny, over milk and pretzel-shaped butter cookies, dog-earing pages to mark the prints we liked best.

"You honor her well."

I shook my head.

"The things she taught you are still with us," Althea said. "That makes me feel good." She studied my face carefully, like she wanted to read my reaction. "Can I ask a favor?"

I tried to keep my expression even, but I worried whatever she might ask would be beyond my capacity. One of the reasons I had a hard time asking for help was that I never felt like I had enough to offer in return.

"Can you teach me to sew? Bunny said she'd teach me, but we never made it happen."

"I would love to!" I said, relieved for something I could give her with confidence.

"Can I teach *you* something?" Althea asked, shaking Bark's leash.

"Alright," I said, standing up. "But I'm much better at sewing than walking Bark."

"Well, you've had practice sewing. Did you expect to wake up one day and you and Bark would magically be in step?"

I laughed. "It did feel a bit all or nothing."

"It's not going to happen all at once," Althea said. "We'll fix this a little bit every day."

"The first time I tried to walk him, he was such a nervous wreck. So I got nervous and now . . ."

"He's a dog, you can't pull that *well, he started it* stuff." She gave me the same kind of look I'm sure Cara and Sophia got if they tried to wheedle their way out of eating peas. "You're the person. He's a big heart with a tail. Bark doesn't care what you were feeling yesterday."

The first thing Althea taught me was that if Bark wanted something, we had to make him sit to tell us. "Nothing's free anymore," she said. "He has to ask for it."

She held up his leash and he wagged his tail. "Do you want to go for a walk?" she asked. He jumped toward her. She stepped out of his range. "Ah! What do you do?" He looked at her. He looked at me. And then he sat. His tail wagged across the floor, making a *whish-whish* sound.

"When I try to get him to go, he runs away. Or he wants to go, but the first stiff breeze ruins everything."

"When he can be the follower, he's ready," Althea said, clipping Bark's leash to his collar. "He reads your nerves. If he feels like he has to be your protector, that's when he'll freak out."

We stepped outside and I locked Bitsie's front door. Bark looked to Althea for cues. She handed me the leash.

I took a deep breath.

Althea smiled. "With Jax, it felt like he was trying to fill Sam's shoes. He was so crazy about protecting me. One day, when I was out with him, there was a dog across the street. Jax started to lose it, but I caught him before he could lunge, with about three inches of leash between my hand and his collar." She pinched the spot on Bark's leash where she wanted me to hold. "I held it tight and kept walking and something clicked for both of us. Holding his leash like that reminded me of holding Cara or Sophia's hands when they were toddlers and they wanted to get into everything. You're not messing around, but you're on their side, you know? That's the right mindset. Bark will read you."

I had painfully little experience holding a toddler's hand.

"Okay, I see that storm crossing your face," Althea said, nudging my shoulder. "Push it away, like a cloud in the sky. You can have your feelings later. This is meditation. Find a mantra if it helps."

I couldn't think of a good mantra, so I cycled in my head, *I know the way. I know the way. You don't have to lead.*

Bark's posture changed immediately. He was subdued. Instead of rushing ahead of me or hiding behind me, he walked close to my thigh. He still surveyed our surroundings, but he was a passenger on our walk, not the leader.

Althea walked beside us and we made it down the driveway. A car passing by barely garnered a look from Bark. I made eye contact with Althea and smiled. "Is it really this simple?"

"Well, you want to build up from here. Keep it short. Only walk him for as long as you can keep your head in that good place. Stop before you're done. End on a high note."

Halfway to Nan's, my mind wandered to Luca leaving. Bark started tugging on the leash. I tried to get my brain back in line, but I couldn't kick the sadness.

"Tomorrow," Althea said, taking the leash from me, but keeping our pace, "I'll stop by and walk you two to my house after work. We'll have tea, and you can walk him back. The next day, maybe we'll go to Mo's."

"I don't want to be a burden," I said.

"What's this burden bullshit? That's life, Katie. When Homer had dementia, you sat at his house with him after school. You drove him to appointments and listened to his stories. Did you feel burdened?"

I shook my head.

"You had a way to help and it felt good, right?" Her eyes welled up. "I never would have gotten past the worst of losing Sam without Jax. He kept my heart together. I would like to pass on what he taught me."

I put my arm around her and gave a squeeze, the way Bunny always used to with me, shoulder to shoulder. "I'm so sorry I yelled at you when Bark was gone. And that it took so long to— I should have apologized a long time ago."

"I'm going to tell you what I used to tell Sam. You're not your anxiety. You are a person who *has* anxiety. I watched you take care of Homer, and I watched you helping Nan and sewing with Bunny and dancing with Sam and the way you make Bitsie laugh. I'm certainly not going to take an anxiety attack as the symbol of all you are as a person. And I don't think you should either."

"Sam had anxiety?"

"When Sam was just out of the academy, new on the job, he and his partner were breaking up a fight and a stray bullet hit him in the leg."

I thought about standing on Sam's shoes, dancing around Nan's living room to Astrud Gilberto. He felt so safe and calm. His smile made me feel better. "I didn't know."

"Well, it wasn't something he talked about. There's this idea that if you picked the job, you're supposed to be able to handle that stress, but no one is prepared to get shot. And working on the force can leave a person with a whole chain of things they can't shake. Sometimes that stuff would flash back on him. He said it was like a lens he had to look through to see everything else. It was so much work to pretend to be normal. And when he couldn't actually get to normal, he felt like he was letting us all down. That's how you feel, right?"

I nodded.

"Sam got a lot better. He went to therapy, we started yoga, he got really good at paying attention to himself. It can be better than it is now, Kay. I promise. It's not your spine. It's not all of you."

After Althea left, I checked the guest room, my room, the living room, hoping Luca had left something behind. A note. A t-shirt. A sign of some sort. There was nothing.

Everywhere I checked, Bark followed, bright-eyed and interested. When we were done with our search, I filled his Kong with treats to keep him busy. I found Nan's eyeglass screwdriver from the junk drawer and sat at the kitchen table to take my father's watch apart.

I'd managed to get the back panel off, and was using a cotton swab to soak up moisture on the gears, when Mo came in without knocking, carrying an armload of Chinese food.

"Peace offering." She lined up the paper containers on the counter. "I can fix that watch," she said with absolute certainty, like sheer will would make the difference.

"Thanks," I said. "I don't actually know what I'm doing."

"Do you hate me?" There was a bend in her voice I'd never heard before. She was actually afraid I did.

Bark pushed his head under her hand. She scratched his ears absentmindedly.

"No," I said. "I know you didn't mean to— It's not your job to hold my fear at the front of your mind."

"But I want to," Mo said. "I don't want to hurt you." She

opened the containers and put the one with dumplings on the kitchen table next to me. "You're my favorite person."

My eyes stung.

"Aw! Don't cry on me!" she said, hugging me to her chest way too hard. "I swear to god, Kay. The only thing in the world I'm not tear-proof against is you crying."

"I'm not crying," I said, trying hard to stop the flow. "You have onions in your armpits."

"Weirdo."

I pulled away and wiped my cheeks. "Someday, I'm not going to cry eight times a day."

"Maybe four?" Mo said, grinning.

"Shut up."

She put me in a headlock and rubbed her fist into my skull. I fake-elbowed her in the gut. She pretended to go in for a body slam, lowering me gently to the floor. Bark jumped in, yelping, stepping on my leg.

"We're just playing!" I shouted.

Bark knocked Mo over and licked her face.

CHAPTER FIFTY-ONE

Two weeks later, when I finally replaced my phone, I had three voicemail messages from Luca.

The first one was right after I left the mermaid show: "Are you alright?" he said. "Come back, okay?"

The second: "Hey, Katie. You didn't come home and I—I want to make sure you're okay. I'm here for you."

The third was only hours old: "Hey, Katie. Thinking about you." And that was it.

I sat in my car in the parking lot of the phone store and tried to think of what I would say if I called back. I didn't know how to trust myself. I wondered if there'd ever be a point where I knew for sure I could be someone who would make Luca happy. If I could be someone who *was* happy.

I remembered when Eric slunk into the basement after our first miscarriage, saying the furnace smelled funny and he had to change the filter. I heard his sobs through the floorboards. I wished he would come up and comfort me, but I should have tried to be his comfort too. He was a man who'd lost his child, crying in the cold, damp basement alone. Somehow I expected him to be my hero when I couldn't be his. We didn't show up for each other. We'd thrown too much blame when I couldn't get pregnant, and we never took the time to fix it. By our second miscarriage, we were barely speaking. Not angry, but quiet. He'd come home late. I'd go to bed early. Or I'd offer to do all the costume repairs after a performance, to have an excuse to stay at work. When I found him asleep on the couch, I convinced myself that pulling a blanket over him counted as care. I didn't want to wake him up. I didn't want to see his sadness when I was still stuck in mine. I left our marriage before he did, or at least at the same time. He wasn't the only one who failed us.

When I got home, I went to Nikki's Facebook page. I stared at the picture of Eric holding the ultrasound photo, feeling joy for him and sadness for me, and realized those things could exist in the same place. I didn't want him to be unhappy. I didn't want Nan and Bitsie to cut his balls off. I wanted to move on and heal, and it was okay for him to do that too. I took one last look at his red-rimmed eyes and the way his smile stretched across his whole face. I saw the wrinkles and the touches of gray in his two-day beard. We'd come a long way together. Or at least we'd tried. I touched the screen, tapping his chin with my thumb, right on his dimple, the way I used to back when we were crazy college kids who thought we knew what we were doing. Then I blocked Nikki, and went to Eric's profile and blocked him too. Not out of anger, but so I couldn't see their lives anymore. So I could move on.

Bark followed me to the kitchen. I gave him a dental bone and made myself a cup of tea. He followed me into the living room, bone gripped in his teeth. I took one of Nan's blank note cards from her desk, sat on the floor in front of the coffee table, and wrote. Bark leaned against me as he chewed.

Dear Eric,
   I heard the news, and while I hold my own sadness, I am also grateful for your joy. I'm sorry about the way we ended. I'm sorry

for how things fell apart. I wish you happiness. Thank you for the
time we spent growing up together.
With love,
Katie

I addressed it and stamped it, and stuck it in the mailbox.
And then I took Bark for a walk, clearing other thoughts from
my head like wind pushing clouds away until all that was left was
this: *I don't know what will happen in the future, but right now, we*
get to walk together. And we did it well, keeping time with each
other. I breathed in the scent of gardenias and fresh-cut grass as
we walked up one street and down the next, trying to make the
good moment last.

CHAPTER FIFTY-TWO

I rented Althea's friend's house for the summer. Cheap, because Althea's friend wanted a caretaker more than she needed the money. I had to tend the yard and three tanks of tropical fish, but it allowed me to live well beyond my means. It was a cute cottage with exposed beams in the living room, ceiling fans with paddles shaped like palm fronds, a white picket fence, and a kidney-shaped pool.

I suspected Nan and Isaac's future included marriage, or at least cohabitation, and I wanted to give them space to decide without feeling like I needed to be figured into the arrangement. Plus, I wanted my own space. I hadn't lived alone as an adult. It was time to try.

Nan swiped boxes from the liquor store so I could pack. I didn't have much more than I'd brought home, but I'd made enough clothes for myself that I felt okay getting rid of all the theatre t-shirts. I dumped them in the rag bin in the laundry room.

Elvis was playing on the stereo. Nan was in the living room shaking her hips to "Hound Dog" as Bark pranced around her. I joined them, jumping in the air.

We switched albums every few songs. Bark eventually gave up and crashed on the couch with Murray. Our dancing got slower and lazy, until we were sitting on the floor looking at records. I loved the sharp scent of the stained pine record cabinet, the snap of the magnet on the door, the rustle of cellophane still covering some of the cardboard sleeves.

Nan started making a pile of records. "Do you have an extra box?" she asked. "You should take these with you."

They were the albums Nan bought for me at rummage sales. Outdated for my timeline, the way yard sale records would be, but they were strange choices for Nan too: Kate Bush, Cyndi Lauper, Pat Benatar, Blondie, Joan Jett, Patti Smith, Heart.

"Why did you buy me these?" I asked, flipping to my favorite Blondie album.

"They were so different from the music I grew up hearing, like 'Chantilly Lace,' and all those songs about being someone's girl or wanting to be someone's girl. These ladies were changing what being a woman meant." She reached over to touch Cyndi Lauper's face on the cover of *She's So Unusual.* "I remember the first time I saw her on television, with that crazy hair, singing about upsetting her parents. I wish it was the version of girlhood I'd heard. I wanted you to have that."

My eyes teared. "Thank you."

"It's just a silly little thing," Nan said, messing up my hair.

"It's so kind," I said. "How much you thought about me."

"Well, *of course* I was going to think about you! You're my granddaughter!"

"You had to take on a lot more than a normal grandmother," I said, flipping back through the pile of records so I wouldn't have to make eye contact with Nan. "I know I cramped your style."

"You weren't dumped on my doorstep. It was my choice to spend my life with you," Nan said, tears in her eyes. "I lost my husband. I lost my son. But I got you. We kept waking up every morning. And look at all we have now."

She wasn't offering a platitude. She meant it. She'd said sim-

ilar things a million times before, but finally I had room in my
brain to believe her.

Nan reached up to grab a photo album from the shelf next to
the record player, opening it on the floor in front of her. "Look
at these nice times we've had!" she said, flipping the page.

I scooted closer. She'd already printed out the picture of me
and Mo posing like the Hulk and Wonder Woman before we
went out prowling. It was toward the back of the album, but we
had many pages left to fill.

Nan flipped to the front and pointed to a picture of me and
Mo playing Wiffle ball in the yard, my eyes closed, swinging the
bat. The ball was already well past me.

I laughed. "It drove Mo nuts that I was so bad!"

We spent the next hour thumbing through all the old photos. Cocktail parties and canasta games, twenty-pound turkeys
at Thanksgiving. Nan and Bitsie blowing paper horns on New
Year's Eve. Nan holding my newborn father in her arms outside
the hospital, ready to take him home. In another picture my father is asleep on Bitsie's shoulder, her ponytail draped across his
bald baby head like hair. Nan and Bitsie were younger than me
when my father was born, and it was strange to know that I had
two years on the women in those photographs.

There were pictures of my father in a cowboy hat and diaper,
playing on the front lawn. In another, he's grinning to show the
camera his first missing tooth.

A few pages later, there was a picture of Bitsie with short
hair like Twiggy, wearing a National Organization for Women
t-shirt, painting a placard on someone's kitchen floor.

"It made me so nervous when Bitsie went off marching," Nan
said. "I brought her casseroles so her husband wouldn't go without
dinner and get angry. As if chicken surprise could save a marriage."
She turned the page and pointed to a picture of Bitsie holding the

sign. It read: *I AM A HUMAN BEING. ERA NOW!* "I think I was most worried because my life felt set in stone after I had your father, and if Bitsie's changed too much, maybe she'd outgrow me."

"But she didn't."

"No," Nan said. "She didn't. We had times when we felt a little further apart. She had school and then work and I had your dad and Gramps, but eventually . . . Oh, when she and Bunny bought their house here, I was so happy." She grinned. "I may have pushed them into it a little."

"You," I said in fake disbelief. "No!"

Nan laughed.

On the next page there was a picture of my dad, at about seven or eight, pushing an old canister vacuum cleaner.

"I got in so much trouble for that!" Nan said, flipping the page. "And this." She pointed to a picture of my dad standing on a step stool washing dishes at the sink.

"For what?" I asked, sure I was missing something.

"For making him clean the house," Nan said. "Ruth told me I would turn him into a sissy. Her boys"—she mimicked Ruth's accent—"didn't lift a fing-ah in her house." Nan's face flushed, she clenched her hand into a fist. "Oh, I got so mad! I remember I yelled, 'Better a sissy than a jerk!' We didn't talk for months."

I'd never heard about more than light bickering between Nan and her friends. We'd never had discussions like this. It felt like our world was starting to tip a bit sideways, but I was happy for it. Nan had been a young woman once, and it wasn't a storybook tale. Her young womanhood had all the complexity mine did.

"It seems so insignificant now," Nan said, "but at the time, sneaking Bitsie casseroles and making your father dust the bookshelves felt like my own little revolution. I was proud of Bits for marching, for naming the wrongs we faced, and I was determined to make your father an equal partner when he got older.

I already had to defend it to your grandfather. Like hell I was going to hear it from Ruth too!"

"My dad always did the dishes," I said, remembering him scraping our plates into the compost bin after dinner. He always said that the cook shouldn't have to clean.

"I wish it had mattered more." Nan flipped pages without looking at them. "What does it even matter in a world that didn't value your mother's work enough?" She pressed her hand to her cheek. "He would have loved being home with you instead. And I know it broke your mother's heart to give up on her career."

"It did?"

Nan never talked about my mother. As a rule. So I'd always felt like I shouldn't ask questions. I knew my mother had been "in school" when I was a toddler, but I didn't know any of the details.

"She was All But Dissertation on her PhD, you know. She put her work aside to support your father while he finished his PhD. Someone had to." Nan shook her head. "He couldn't do it alone. They had you, and quite frankly, he was going to make more as a professor than she would."

"And then he died and she didn't have a PhD or a husband," I said, understanding something I hadn't before.

Nan nodded.

"I don't even know what she studied."

"Art history, like your dad. Do you remember that book he wrote on Kandinsky?"

I nodded.

"That was going to be your mother's dissertation."

"He plagiarized her work?"

"She's the one who gave him the idea," Nan said. "It's not like he stole it from her. She felt like she'd never get taken seriously without the PhD, so the research she'd done would better serve your family if she gave it to him."

My version of my mother had been someone who bitched about things. She never had fun with us. She kept order. She had a hard line where her smile could have been. And then, when she left me, she was all light and wide grins, perfume that made my throat itch, gauzy white cotton shirts. She talked about auras and the universe's path for her. It made more sense now. She'd given up everything for the betterment of a family that no longer existed. Maybe she needed to believe it had all been for a reason. It would have hurt too much otherwise.

"I wish your mother could have handled her pain in a way that didn't hurt you," Nan said, hugging me with her strong arms, "but I'm happy we got to have all this time together. Don't you ever think for a second that you cramped my style, okay?" She pointed to her purple hair. I'd helped her re-dye it the day before. "We've got style for miles, kiddo."

Of course, the whole neighborhood came to help me move. And, of course, there was a party.

"It's not really my house," I said when Nan wheeled her drink cart three blocks over. "And it's only temporary."

"Oh, like we need a bigger excuse for a party," she said, kissing my cheek. She also brought grilled vegetable canapés topped with herbed cashew cream, and carob macadamia nut cookies.

Isaac brought me a bottle of good scotch.

Ruth brought me a huge bouquet of roses from her garden. Marta gave me a stack of homemade dinners. "Who wants to cook, right?" she said, sticking them in the freezer.

Bitsie gave me Bunny's sewing machine.

"I can't," I said. "I can't—"

"You are always welcome at my house," Bitsie said. "But someone with talent like yours should be able to sew whenever she wants. Just . . . bring it back to visit, okay? I like it when you're in Bunny's room."

"That I can do," I said, hugging her. Isaac set the sewing machine up on a desk in the guest room for me.

Althea brought Bark a calming pheromone collar in case he got new home jitters. She gave me a smooth gray stone with the word *Breathe* carved in the surface. She'd helped me find a therapist who was teaching me to use deep breathing to calm my frantic thoughts. "Sometimes, it helps to have a touchstone," she said. "Literally."

I slipped the stone in my pocket and rubbed my fingers over the letters. "I have something for you." I ran to my bedroom to get the tail I'd made for Althea, wrapped in kraft paper. "Open it," I said, handing it to her.

Althea ripped the paper open. "Oh, Kay," she said, holding it up to show everyone. I'd covered the tail in a rainbow of sequins that flowed from bright to pastel in an ombré pattern. "It's beautiful!"

"We're going to make the top together," I said. "Sewing lessons."

"Thank you!" She hugged me. "I get to be a mermaid!"

"Now," Nan said to her, "you'll have to come to class."

"I think you need to add a class for people who sleep until normal hours," Althea said.

Mo arrived, covered in soot, Luca's friend Danny in tow. Danny was wearing Mo's favorite sailboat shirt. He wasn't as dirty as she was, but not exactly clean. He'd never gotten around to leaving after the mermaid show, and Mo seemed pretty happy about it. I don't think Danny knew anything bad had happened between me and Luca. Whenever I saw him, he'd bring up things we could all do the next time Luca came to visit.

"Where have you guys been?" I asked.

"A chimney?" Nan asked.

Danny laughed. "Something like that."

"I've got a new project," Mo said. "I'll show you later."

She handed me a wadded handkerchief. Inside was my father's watch. Ticking.

"I can't believe you did this!" I said, strapping it to my wrist. She'd even polished the leather and sanded the corrosion off the buckle.

"I told you I would," she said, shrugging, like she was determined to keep the moment from getting sappy.

We sat around the kitchen table and drank and talked, and ate terrible cookies, and I felt like I belonged on my own merits. Bark worked the room, trying to con food from our guests, succeeding a little too often.

Once the housewarming committee had filed out, I was thankful that my version of alone included Bark. The quiet was staggering.

I didn't have a bathing suit. I changed into running shorts and a t-shirt and walked out to the pool, Althea's touchstone in hand. I rubbed the letters over and over again.

"We're doing this," I said to Bark, standing at the edge of the pool, breathing deep to keep the anxiety from taking over my body. I dipped my toes in the water. Bark jumped in, swimming circles in front of me.

I made it in up to my knees, and then went inside to dry Bark with the hair dryer and watch *Golden Girls* reruns.

The next day I made it waist deep.

The next, after work, I turned the pool lights on, and lay back in the water, floating, straining my eyes to see the stars.

"I did it," I said to the sky, tears running down the sides of my face into the water.

CHAPTER FIFTY-THREE

<hr>

"Close your eyes, close your eyes, close your eyes," Mo said as she drove. "Don't look until I tell you." The car swerved. I worried I might vomit.

"Okay," she said when she finally stopped the car.

I opened my eyes. She clapped her hand over my face. "Don't open yet!"

"You said, 'Okay!'"

"I meant, 'Okay, we're here.' Not 'Okay, open your eyes.'"

"Well, I didn't know."

"Keep 'em closed. Stay put. I'll come get you."

She helped me out of the car and put her hands on my shoulders to steer me. "Okay, step up."

I lifted my leg.

"Not that high," she said, laughing. "Like the normal height that anyone would ever step."

A few more steps and then the ground went from pavement to grass. "Can I open my eyes yet?"

"No."

"Come on!"

"Stand still." She let go of me and I heard something scraping. Then her hands were back on my shoulders. We walked a few more feet.

"Okay, step up."

I did, lifting a little less high than before. My foot caught on something and sent me hurtling forward, but Mo steadied me.

"Higher," she said, laughing. "Hysterical!"

We took a few more steps.

"Okay, sit down."

I reached behind me for a chair.

"On the ground!" Mo said.

"In movies this kind of thing is much quicker, and way more romantic."

"Yeah, well, I only like you as a friend," she said, helping me find the ground.

I stumbled.

"Can you even move like a normal person?" She laughed. "Alright, lie down."

"Really?" Around me I felt dirt and pokey pieces of grass.

"Lie down."

So I did. And she did. Her arm against mine.

"Okay," she said. "Look!"

I opened my eyes. All I saw was blue sky, the sun streaming down.

"We're under the sea!" she shouted.

"What?" I sat up.

There was a huge metal circle surrounding us, and a construction fence beyond that. We were at the marine park, where Morty lived.

"Ready to work?" she asked, pulling a pair of gloves from the pocket of her overalls and tossing them in my lap.

"What is this?" I asked.

"A mermaid tank," she said, standing up.

"Are you serious?"

"Yeah," she said. "Jen Gonzalez from the park board came

to the mermaid show. She's madly in love with Morty. So I had lunch with her and pitched this."

"That's amazing!"

"The only thing—I hope Nan isn't mad . . . I told her Nan and Bitsie would teach two mermaid classes a week," she said, picking at a scab on her elbow. "I want to surprise them with the tank, so I didn't clear it with them first. It's an adult class and then one with kids. And then some shows." Mo wrinkled her forehead. "Do you think they'll do it?"

"Absolutely, they will," I said. A few nights earlier, Nan, Bitsie, and I had a martooni-fueled brainstorming session about starting a business called The Mermaid Experience, where clients could have a costume custom-made and learn some moves from the pros. By the end of the evening, Bitsie and Nan had all but planned an empire.

"I'm making a rock formation in the shop," Mo said, drawing a picture of it in the dirt with a twig. "Kind of like the tunnel you'd see in an aquarium. So it's going to look like a great big fish tank, and we're all so small."

"What will you do for the glass?" I asked, taking the twig from her. I drew a mermaid swimming through the tunnel.

"Danny has a friend who does plexiglass art. Like thick installation pieces. So he'll get co-credit, and half the grant. Totally worth it. I don't know shit about plexiglass."

I could picture all of it. I drew air bubbles rising from the mermaid's mouth.

Mo drew a face in one of my bubbles with her finger. "Luca helped me."

"Oh," I said, trying to keep my feelings off my face.

"He sent me footage of the documentary so I could show it to Jen. She thinks when his film comes out it will be fantastic for tourism." Mo shielded her eyes from the sun with her hand.

I drew another mermaid.

"You'll help me?" she asked. "Because I've totally overpromised on this."

"Yeah," I said, leaning against her. "I'll help you."

I knew she was already sure I would help when she asked. I hoped when we were seventy-five, we would still have crazy projects to work on together. Our own mermaid show, in whatever form it might take.

I studied her sun-bleached hair and peeling, sunburned nose, the way her eyes squinted in the late afternoon light. I wanted to cup her face in my hands and tell her I was going to love her forever, the way Nan loved Bitsie. I was going to be the person who showed up for her, because friendship is a love story too. There were so many things I couldn't figure out how to commit to yet, but I could commit to Mo. I could show up for Mo for the rest of my life. I could have faith in myself about that.

"Why are you looking at me that way?" Mo said, crossing her eyes at me.

"Because I think you're amazing."

"Good," she said, blushing. "Can you help me bring that beam over to lock into this one?"

CHAPTER FIFTY-FOUR

I'd managed to smuggle the quilt from Bunny's room to the cottage. A week after the move, in the wee hours of the morning, Bark asleep on the floor next to me, I finished sewing the last bit of double-fold binding around the edge.

When the orange glow from the coming sunrise started to show at the horizon, I folded up the quilt and tied it with a ribbon of extra binding.

"Hey, Barky," I whispered, and watched his ears twitch. His eyes opened and drifted shut again. "Do you want to go for a walk?" His eyes snapped open. He jumped to his feet, tail wagging. Then he sat to say yes.

We walked to Bitsie's, the quilt under my right arm, Bark's leash tight in my left hand. I used my key to open the door and left the quilt in the foyer without even setting foot inside so our footsteps wouldn't wake her up.

As soon as we made it back to the sidewalk, I heard the door open.

"Are you kidding me?" Bitsie called. "Get in here!"

Bark and I jogged up the path to her house.

Bitsie hugged me, kissed both my cheeks, and then my forehead. "You can't leave me something like this and walk away. It's the best gift I've ever gotten! I want to look at it with you."

She spread the quilt out on the living room floor. "It's like our whole life together," she said, crying, but smiling too.

I'd alternated rows of large blocks with strips of smaller ones so I could get pieces of all the important fabrics in, even when I only had tiny scraps. It was colorful and chaotic. A piece of the red-flowered clown costume Bitsie wore to the NICU on Halloween, right next to a swatch of Bunny's favorite yellow tablecloth. Green plaid salvaged from the Christmas tree skirt Bitsie accidentally set on fire when she knocked over Bunny's Swedish candle chimes. There was a square of leftover fabric from the curtains Bunny was making when she died, and one from the white skirt she wore to the courthouse when she and Bitsie made their marriage legal. There was fabric from the kaftan she always wore that Bitsie hated, and from the kaftan she made Bitsie for her birthday as a joke.

"I don't even know how to thank you, kid," she said, wiping her eyes. "But I've got coffee. You want coffee?"

We brought our mugs out to the front step to watch the sun rise. Bitsie had already watered the roses, droplets still falling from the leaves. Bark rolled around on the lawn. Everything felt quiet and clean, like we were above the day, not in it yet.

"I was rooting for Luca," Bitsie said out of nowhere. "Not that it's any of my business. But you two seem to find nourishment in being near each other. That's how I felt around Bunny." She shook her head. "Maybe I'm projecting."

"I think it might be better to start fresh," I said, willing myself to believe it.

"What are you scared of?"

Bark rubbed his chin into the grass, butt high in the air. We laughed.

I hoped Bitsie would move on to a new topic, but she said, "Huh? What is it?"

"Losing the people I love," I said. The sky was broadly orange now. Bunny's roses looked like they were glowing.

"The secret isn't to love them less," Bitsie said. "You're going to lose most of us. Eventually. And there's nothing you or I can do about it. That's what happens. But wouldn't you rather spend that time together?"

Her honesty slowed the frantic feeling in my chest.

"Love is always a brave act, kiddo." She cupped her hands around her mug.

"I don't want to make Luca's life harder—"

"Do you love him?"

"I think so."

"So love him."

"It's more complicated than—"

"You're trying to make permanent decisions when nothing is permanent. Once you start to see the years on someone you love, the thing you fear most is not loving them hard enough. If love goes well, we don't decide when we say goodbye, it's something that happens to us. So the best you can do is love the crap out of the people you love." Bitsie squeezed my arm with her freckled hand. "You're an old soul anyway. Love like an old person."

She raised her mug and blew into it. "Right now, we have coffee. I can smell Bunny's roses, and I get to share my thoughts with you, and hear your thoughts. I love you, and I know you love me. Simple, right? That is all this moment has to be."

I felt my heartbeat quicken. "I have a hard time with good moments," I said. "I catch myself changing songs on the radio when I'm listening to one I like. What is that? 'Oh, I like this, let me get rid of it.' I do it with everything." I tapped my feet on the ground. "I feel like that now, that I should flee. Like I'm not supposed to enjoy things or let people be nice to me."

"Your signals got crossed, Kay," she said, as if it was something she'd known for a long time. "That day when you were swimming with your dad . . . That was a good day, right?"

I remembered raspberry jam and butter on whole wheat toast for breakfast, the jam dripping on my fingers in globs. I loved my blue bathing suit, and we had new red and purple beach towels that were soft like velour. I'd read three chapters of my Babysitters Club book before I'd even gotten out of bed. And when I started racing my dad in the water, I thought I was winning. My heart was full. Maybe it did make me nervous about having good things. Maybe I wanted to stop them before the bad came.

"The day Bunny died, we'd had the best . . . relations," Bitsie said, smiling. "Bunny made French toast and good coffee. Before I went out, she read me a Mary Oliver poem she'd read the night before and couldn't stop thinking about. There's no foreshadowing in real life. We had thousands of mornings like that."

Bark flopped over in the grass again, belly to the sky, head back, legs flailing, like it was pure ecstasy.

"You can't stop enjoying the good stuff because life is random," Bitsie said. "I'm seventy-five years old. I am going to die. Hopefully, very long before you. You'll lose me, and it'll be sad, because I'm a lovely human being. But don't you love this moment? We don't get this moment if all we think about is how I'm going to die. We have to live in it to keep it good."

"But how do I do that?" I said, because in my head, I was already trying to save Bitsie from every scenario that could be her end.

"Maybe we need to see the bad things as a passage, not a failure. I couldn't have saved Bunny even if I had been there when it happened. But I loved her well. She had a wonderful morning. That's the comfort we get in our losses. It's the only part we can plan for." Bitsie took a sip of her coffee. "I know being okay is work, and there's chemical parts and physical parts and it might be a long fight. But it's a fight for something worth it, right? Look at that big colorful life Bunny and I had!"

She pointed toward the house, and I had a flashing image of the quilt I could make myself one day, with snippets of chambray from the dresses I'd sewed, the pink sheets Nan bought for my room when I moved in, a panel of sparkling paillettes, a Hawaiian shirt I'd steal from Mo, swatches of Bark's blanket, and maybe, maybe some squares from Luca's faded blue jeans and his favorite flannel shirt.

Bitsie's eyes gleamed and she pushed a little further. "Don't you want Luca to know how loved he is? What else are you doing with your time?"

I smiled. "So I'm supposed to call him and be like, 'Hey, in case you die today, I want you to know I love you?'"

"It's as romantic as anything else, if you think about it," she said, laughing.

"That's terrible advice." I grinned and reached out to squeeze her hand.

"Sometimes I hit. Sometimes I miss."

I laughed.

"You know what I mean," she said.

"I know what you mean," I said.

She squeezed my hand back. "You always were a smart-ass."

When Bark and I left Bitsie's, we walked to Nan's. She was outside watering the crown of thorns.

"Did you come over for breakfast?" she asked, and her voice was hopeful.

"Sure," I said, walking up the driveway.

She leaned over to scratch behind Bark's ear, and then put her arm around my shoulder. "I'm making omelets. But with chick-pea flour instead of eggs."

I groaned.

"Oh, hush. It's better than you having to cook, right?"

"It's not better than cereal," I said, laughing.

Nan laughed too. "Try it at least. Two bites."

Inside, Isaac whistled as he scooped coffee into the percolator. He smiled when he saw me and whistled a little louder. I think it was a riff from a Frank Ocean song.

The sun was over the horizon now. Pink-bellied clouds taking over the sky. The patio doors were open. Bark ran outside to pee on his favorite canistropsis.

When I got home, I went on Facebook.

Luca's profile picture was one I'd taken. He was wearing a gray flannel shirt that was threadbare at the elbows, holding the boom mic over his head, laughing so hard at one of Bitsie's jokes that he was blurry with movement.

His cover photo was a picture Mo took two days before the mermaid show. Me, Nan, Luca, and Bitsie in a row, arms linked, walking like The Monkees across Bitsie's lawn.

I sent him a message: *There's more to shoot. Come back.*

EPILOGUE

Isaac cut his hours so he could spend more time with Nan. He was training me to take over. He came in mornings, while Nan had swim class, and left to spend afternoons with her. We'd been working out the details. My ideas were bigger than my fears.

Marta hired me to create her granddaughter's wedding dress from scratch, and I was at the shop early on Sunday to put in time on the beadwork.

The doorbell rang. Bark ran to the front of the shop, growling. "Hey, bud," I said, following behind him. "That's not good for business!" I pointed to the CLOSED sign, but then I looked up. It was Luca.

I opened the door.

Bark wagged his tail.

"Hey," I said, moving aside to let Luca in. He'd cut his hair. It was wispy around his face.

He gave me a hug. I hugged him back. My heart pounded, but it felt different. Good nerves.

"It's great to see you." And I felt clear when I said it. I was seeing him in the moment, not through a haze of our past.

"It is?" he asked, and his voice was bright with hope.

"Yeah."

"It's good to see you," he said.

"I have to finish this one thing." I gestured for him to follow me to the back room so I could secure a row of beads. I couldn't abandon the work mid-strand. The fabric was too delicate to leave the needle hanging for long.

"This is beautiful." He pointed to the gown.

"Thanks," I said, sitting again, gesturing to Isaac's chair.

"I ran into my friend Lacey when I was in New York." He sat, and kicked his legs to wheel himself closer.

"Oh," I said, holding the string of beads in place, stitching between each one. I felt a flash of jealousy, and tried to let it pass through my brain like clouds on a windy day. My hands didn't even shake.

"She's making a movie. It's like a throwback 1950s beach flick, but about what was actually happening at the time, not the shiny Annette Funicello version."

"That's really cool," I said, picturing high-waisted bikinis and rompers with plunging necklines.

"She wants to work with you."

"Don't—don't do that," I said. "Don't try to get me a gig because you feel sorr—"

Luca laughed. "Seriously, Lacey has no interest in pity. She's a perfectionist."

"But you told her about me?"

"I showed her some footage," Luca said. "I was, like, fishing for a compliment about my camerawork. There's a shot of Bitsie and her bright red hair in the blue water. She's floating on her back, laughing. It's the best shot I've ever gotten, and two seconds into it, Lacey was asking me who made the costumes."

"I mean, I'll talk to her. I can try to pull together a portfolio," I said. I hadn't gotten pictures from the show. I hadn't even seen any more of the footage. "But I'm kind of busy with all this." I pointed to the stack of slacks on the workbench. I was looking for a high school kid to help me after school, but I hadn't found one yet.

"The film was your portfolio. She wants *you*. Call her. She'll kill me if you don't." He stared at me for a second. "You should do this. It's not a small deal. Her last film premiered at Cannes."

"And she wants me?"

"She's in awe of you."

"That's . . . terrifying," I said. I finished the row. Secured the thread.

"Right? I spend so much time in this business shaking in my boots."

I was shocked. "You're not scared of anything."

"I'm terrified right now," he said, and when I looked at him, I could see the fear in his eyes. The tightness in his brow.

"Why?"

"Kate," Luca said. "I don't want to lose you again."

"I don't want to lose you either." I stood up and hugged him. His back was damp. His breath was hot. I kissed him. "Can we take it slow?" I asked. I wanted to learn how to live in moments with him, to love him bravely.

Luca nodded. "No matter what, we're friends, okay? That part doesn't end for anything."

"Yeah," I said. "Good."

Bark pushed himself between us, shoving his head under Luca's hand.

"Clearly, you're not paying enough attention to him," I said.

"Clearly." He crouched to scratch Bark's chest. Bark licked Luca's face. "I missed you, buddy."

"Hey, the mermaids have rehearsal in a few," I said, grabbing my duffle bag. "You want to come? I have something to show you."

"Can I film?" Luca asked.

"Sure," I said, knowing it would be okay with the ladies.

"I don't have an ending yet," Luca said.

"Wait until you see the tank."

"It's done?"

"Yeah. This is their first time in it."

There was a small crowd at the park already, even though it was only a rehearsal. Mo was on the platform hooking up the air hoses. Nan, Bitsie, and Althea were already on the perch in their tails.

"I've got to go over there for a sec," I said, and dashed off toward the cabanas with Bark.

While I got ready, Bark chased a fly around the stall, jumping and snapping his teeth when he got close to catching it. Like a normal dog. Even though we were out in the world, he wasn't on high alert, because I wasn't on high alert either.

I leaned against the wall for balance and slid into my tail. It was silver at the waist, transitioning into bright blue, with a feathery green dorsal fin. I slipped my legs through the slit in the back, and kept the monofin separate. I'd attach it when I got to the perch. Aside from trying something on for functional reasons, this was the first costume I'd made that I actually wore. I made clothes, of course, but a costume for performance is something different. It's a tool. And mine was beautifully engineered. I was proud of myself every time I put it on.

I slid my arms into the shell top. A confluence of blue sequins, molded foam, and neoprene. Cut wide in the back to allow full arm strokes, with a hook to attach the air hose so it wouldn't get lost. I dug my bright red waterproof lipstick from my purse. It was only a rehearsal, but I couldn't help myself. I twisted my hair back with a plastic sea star barrette that clipped in strands of blue tinsel.

Then I knelt down. Bark ran over, tail wagging. "Do you

want to go swimming?" I asked. He yelped, jumped in the air, and then sat emphatically. I slipped his legs into his life vest and snapped it closed. I'd added a neoprene shark fin to the top. It cut through the surface when he swam.

"Look at what a good shark you are!" I said so he could hear the calm, happy tone of my voice. He was a wonderful shark, and a wonderful dog, and the very best of friends. He wagged away, the fin flapping back and forth.

At the tank, Mo hoisted Bark up to the platform, and I climbed the ladder. Mo's next project was a ramp to allow for greater access so anyone who wanted to could be a mermaid.

Luca was setting up his camera in front of the glass. "Hey!" I yelled, and he looked up.

"You're going in?"

"I'm a mermaid!" I said.

I could see him bite his lip, holding back tears. He gave me a thumbs up. I looked away so I wouldn't cry.

I sat at the edge to slide the monofin into the tail, and tucked my feet in. "Okay, Barky," I said, and pushed off into the water. Bark took a running jump and leapt in next to me. Mo threw a tennis ball for him, and he swam away to retrieve it while I dove through the sun-streaked water to join Nan, Bitsie, and Althea at the bottom of the tank. I took a long drag from my air hose and watched the bubbles rise to the surface as I exhaled.

The sounds of the outside world were muffled. The water was mine again. I belonged there, under the surface with Nan and our friends, Bark's legs churning up waves above us. Through the glass, I could see Luca's camera lights, or maybe it was the reflection of all our sequins, but I knew he could see me, so I waved. Then I took a deep breath from the air hose, and started to dance.

—Fin—

ACKNOWLEDGMENTS

To my friend-family, thank you for helping me build the palette of emotions I needed to be able to write this book. Everything I know about love and the healing powers of belonging comes from having the privilege of being your friend.

Extra thanks to:

Linda and Roger Bryant and the Titles Over Tea book club, the Fiction Writer's Co-op, and my Rochester writing group.

Michele Larkin, for your patience and love. My books never feel done until I know what you think. Ingrid Serban, for your beautiful magic. Sarah Playtis, Matthew Andreoli, Amy Franklin-Willis, Therese Fowler, Jan O'Hara, Sarah Callender, Jeanne Kisacky, Greer Macallister, Ann-Marie Nieves, Dana Spector, Marty Heresniak, and Matt Weatherbee for advice and support right when I needed it.

Ann Mah, Regina Marler, Renee Swindle, Julia Whelan, Lisa Brackmann, Melanie Krebs, Therese Walsh, Bethany Chase, and Brantley Aufill for sharing your brilliant writerly opinions.

My social media buddies for chatting at the internet watercooler, and especially my hilarious Facebook friends for answering all my weirdo research questions about life, intoxication, and language use.

Kaitlin Olson, my editor, and also Tara Parsons, Isabel

DaSilva, Megan Rudloff, Tamara Arellano, and everyone at Touchstone and Atria, for your enthusiasm and care in ushering this book out into the world.

To my intrepid agent, Mitch Hoffman, thank you for your patience, logic, and remarkable kindness. You brought me back to the meaning of the work and I am eternally grateful. And special thanks to the lovely people at the The Aaron M. Priest Literary Agency.

Cassandra Dunn, thank you for sharing your vast and careful wisdom, ferocious friendship, and all those glorious miles. I look forward to the mountains we will climb.

Caroline Angell, you brilliant soul, I will introvert with you anytime. You are a spectacular writing partner and you ask the best questions. Thank you for holding me accountable to this book and to myself.

This book would not have been possible without the love and friendship of my fearful, faithful dog, Stella, who has taught me, among other things, that sometimes bravery can be measured in the distance between fear and action.

And thank you, thank you, thank you to Jeremy Larkin for being my best friend and love of my life, and for hugging me when I cry about imaginary people.

Allie Larkin is the internationally bestselling author of the novels *Stay* and *Why Can't I Be You*. Her short fiction has been published in *Summerset Review* and *Slice*, and her nonfiction in the anthologies *I'm Not the Biggest Bitch in This Relationship* and *Author in Progress*. She lives in the San Francisco Bay Area with her husband, Jeremy, and their fearful, faithful German Shepherd, Stella.

SWIMMING FOR SUNLIGHT

Allie Larkin

This reading group guide for Swimming for Sunlight *includes an introduction, discussion questions, ideas for enhancing your book club, and a Q&A with author Allie Larkin. The suggested questions are intended to help your reading group find new and interesting angles and topics for your discussion. We hope that these ideas will enrich your conversation and increase your enjoyment of the book.*

INTRODUCTION

Aspiring costume designer Katie Ellis is at the end of her rope—her marriage has ended in a messy divorce and she's just agreed to give her ex-husband everything so she can keep their fearful, faithful dog, Barkimedes ("Bark"). Katie packs up a few remaining belongings in her beat-up old car and drives to Florida with Bark to live with her grandmother, Nan. She reconnects with her childhood best friend, Mo, and Nan's circle of colorful friends.

Buoyed by the support of people who love her, Katie begins taking her mental health seriously. She reconnects with her love of costume design, fights her long-held fear of water, reignites a past romance, and finally finds the right way to be Bark's best friend.

TOPICS & QUESTIONS FOR DISCUSSION

1. Throughout the first half of the book, there is not much description of what Katie looks like, although she observes a lot about what her grandmother and her friends look like. What does this say about Katie's perception of herself?

2. In Chapter Eight, Katie reflects on how her smaller income created stress in her relationship with ex-husband, Eric. How do you view money in the context of long-term romantic relationships?

3. Nan and Katie begin to bond as Katie helps Nan reach out to old friends via Facebook, something Nan hasn't previously used. Have you noticed a generational difference in how your friends and family use social media?

4. Have you ever reunited with a long-lost friend? Was your connection still there? What changed since the last time you saw them? Have you kept in touch since your reunion?

5. The mermaid show gives Nan and Bitsie a chance to reclaim an activity they loved when they were younger. Is there something you loved doing that has fallen by the wayside? Is it something you'd like to try again?

6. In Chapter Twenty-Two, Mo encourages Katie to see a therapist, but Katie doesn't take it well. Has anyone in your group ever tried to help connect a friend with mental health resources? How did it go? How do you think Mo could have done things differently, or do you think she did a good job?

7. Throughout the book, Katie has panic attacks when she can't control certain things. Can you think of times when she tries to micromanage aspects of her life that she *can* control?

8. What do you think of Katie's relationship with Bark? How is her attention to Bark's needs helpful, and how is it a coping mechanism?

9. Katie's marriage to Eric was a mismatch. How do you think Luca would differ as a partner? What kind of partner do you think would be ideal for Katie?

10. Nan and Bitsie have fun telling Katie about their time as mermaid performers. Have any of your loved ones surprised you with an unexpected story from their past? Do you have stories people in your life would be surprised to hear?

11. In Chapter Forty, when Woo Woo arrives, Bitsie worries about coming out to her. How do you think the experience of coming out later in life might differ from the experiences of people who come out at a younger age?

12. In Chapter Forty-Two, as Katie is trying to get Hannah's measurements, Hannah seems insecure about her weight and keeps trying to "suck in." Katie thinks, "It made me sad, because I had this idea that by the time you reach your seventies, the superficial pressures of being a woman would dissipate, and health and happiness would be all that mattered." How has your perception of your appearance changed over time? Do you think you'll feel differently

about your body in the future? Growing up, how did the women in your life shape your ideas about body image and aging?

13. At the end of the book, Katie has learned to be more comfortable in her own skin. What changed to make this possible? What has she had to let go?

ENHANCE YOUR BOOK CLUB

1. Set up drawing or collage supplies (complete with sequins!) and have everyone design their own mermaid tail. Ask each member to talk about how their design represents aspects of their personality.

2. Read "The Last Mermaid Show" from the *New York Times Magazine*: https://www.nytimes.com/2013/07/07/magazine /the-last-mermaid-show.html. Discuss the allure of being a mermaid, from the early years until today.

3. Have a cocktail party that would make Nan proud! Serve "martoonis," vegetable sushi, and vegan canapés. Look for recipes on sites like https://itdoesnttastelikechicken.com and Engine2Diet.com.

BITSIE'S RECIPE FOR THE PERFECT EXTRA-DRY DIRTY MARTOONI

Dash of dry vermouth
1½ oz. gin
Cocktail olives + juice

Swirl vermouth in a martini glass. Dump the excess. Vermouth is not the star of this show. Pour the gin into a cocktail shaker filled with ice. Follow with a generous splash of olive juice. Shake and strain into a glass. Garnish with three or four cocktail olives. Don't skimp. You deserve a snack.

A CONVERSATION WITH ALLIE LARKIN

What was your inspiration to start writing _Swimming for Sunlight_?
I was doing writing exercises every morning to generate ideas. I can't remember the specific exercise that led to it, but the line "My husband brought a date to our divorce" popped in my head and I was hooked. Katie and Bark showed up soon after, and I couldn't stop thinking about them.

Where did the idea of writing about mermaid performers come from?
As a kid, I obsessively loved swimming underwater, and I was fascinated by mermaids. The movie _Splash_ was a big deal at the time, my local video store had an anime retelling of _The Little Mermaid_ that closely followed the Hans Christian Andersen story, and I fell madly in love with a book called _The Search for Delicious_ by Natalie Babbitt that had a mermaid named Ardis who lived in a lake.

I first read about mermaid performers at Weeki Wachee Springs at some point in my twenties, but if I had known about them as a child, being a mermaid would have been my ultimate aspiration.

When I started writing Nan, I had the idea that she'd become a fitness enthusiast, but it didn't feel like enough of a story for her. I wanted to give her new endeavor deeper roots. Suddenly, Nan's mermaid past started spinning in my mind, and it felt like something I've been gearing up for my whole life. I truly loved writing about women who found a way to return to their love of mermaids and underwater performance. Possibly, in part, because I'd like to believe it's something I can still aspire to.

Who is the character of Nan based on? Did that person also go through a major health kick?
None of the characters I write are based on real people, but Nan's health kick was inspired by my own quest to protect my heart health by switching to a whole food, plant-based diet. I've

been eating this way for several years now, and it has drastically changed my life and health for the better, but I also know how eye roll–inducing people talking about their diets can be. I decided to have a little fun at my own expense by turning Nan into a militant vegan and making Katie very frustrated by this change. That said, I do take great joy in hacking recipes to make them meet my dietary needs, and I've made most of the foods Nan serves. Except for those terrible cookies.

Did your dog inspire any of Bark's personality?
Stella, our German Shepherd, came to us at thirteen months and was an absolute terror. Through a lot of hard work, she eventually settled in and became a functional member of our family.

Then, over the course of a year, we lost our other dog to cancer, our elderly cat passed away, and we made a cross-country move. The ways we'd taught Stella to cope were dependent on having animal buddies, a big yard, and a regular routine. Suddenly, we were living in a different environment with different parameters, so Stella and I had to go back to the drawing board to figure out how to help her function in our new life. It also forced me to confront my anxiety issues, because she picks up on my nerves. I wanted to be better for Stella and it made me better for myself too.

Stella has taught me so much about bravery. She still has her jittery moments, but she's gone from being afraid to leave the house to nudging me out the door for our two-mile walk every day.

How did you approach writing a community of characters in their retirement years?
I realized in an early draft of the book that to write Nan and Bitsie and their friends, I needed to cultivate a greater understanding of their formative experiences. I never had the opportunity to take women's studies in college, so I decided to engineer my own crash course. I spent a summer reading and researching the history of the women's movement and the ways

women have been represented in pop culture over the years. It was fascinating, maddening, enlightening, heartbreaking, and deeply inspiring.

Katie seems to have shied away from the things she wanted most in an attempt to create a sense of safety. Can you relate to the way fear navigates her choices?

When I was in college the first time around, I was so afraid of failing. The idea of trying for something I might not get felt so horribly shameful, and I got very good at aiming just below what I thought I could achieve. Then, after my sophomore year, I dropped out of college and promptly went out into the real world, where I fell flat on my face. It was the life events equivalent of doing a belly flop when there had never even been a pool. At the time it was horrible, but in the overall trajectory of my life, it was the best thing that could have happened to me. I failed and I survived, and I didn't have to pretend to be perfect anymore. On the other side of that failure, it seemed way less scary to start trying for things that felt out of reach. Rejection didn't scare me.

Katie is just at the edge of that experience; she's starting to get comfortable with the fact that playing it safe hasn't gotten her the things a person needs to thrive.

As the story progresses, we learn that Katie is afraid of a lot of things. Do you identify with her struggles on a personal level? How did you figure out what Katie's healing process should be?

I was a nervous little kid, and I headed into adulthood with anxiety issues. I think it's one of the things that made me a writer, but training your brain for writing doesn't necessarily help. Once you've taught yourself to always think about the what-ifs, it's hard to stop. I finally got to a point where I was uncomfortable being uncomfortable and started seeking better ways to manage my mental health.

I consulted therapists and read as much as I could on trauma and anxiety. *The Body Keeps Score* by Bessel van der Kolk is brilliant. I found *The Antidote: Happiness for People Who Can't Stand Positive Thinking* by Oliver Burkeman so helpful on a personal level, and it sent me down a rabbit hole of stoic philosophy (which probably inspired some of Bitsie's worldview).

Toward the end of *Swimming for Sunlight*, Bitsie says to Katie, "I know being okay is work, and there's chemical parts and physical parts and it might be a long fight. But it's a fight for something worth it, right?" There are so many variable personal elements involved in mental health issues, which means there aren't cookie-cutter answers. I wanted to be careful not to prescribe anything too specific for Katie's recovery. It felt right to leave Katie at a place where there's still work ahead of her, but she's set up to succeed, and she's finally fighting for herself.

The setting for *Swimming for Sunlight* is in Florida. How did that come about, and what kind of research did you do to get the Florida vibe just right?

I spent time in Florida as a child, and was back a few years ago on vacation. I have a soft spot for that particular brand of suburbia and palm trees. Also, when we lived in Rochester, we were the newcomers in a neighborhood full of people who had built their houses in the fifties and sixties, and that was certainly an inspiration.

This is your third book! How did writing it feel different from writing your first two?

This book feels very special because I'd had the idea and a vague outline for a while, but when it came time to kick it into gear, my friend Caroline Angell (author of *All the Time in the World*), suggested we do a weekly call. We reported in on our work, talked through narrative problems and character development, and set goals for the next week. We called our calls "Introvert Happy Hour," even though they very often strayed far beyond the hour mark. There's something so meaningful to me about the way our friendship grew through nurturing each other's work, and how that celebration of female friendship is echoed in the book.

How did you get your start as a writer? What specific moments and people along the way have encouraged you to keep going?

I grew up performing in summer camp plays and community theatre and first went to college as a drama major. I loved the work, even though I wasn't always thrilled about being on stage. When I went back to college in my twenties, I took a few writing classes and felt like I'd finally found the right medium for my interests. But I draw on my theatre training constantly, especially when it comes to character development. I'm so thankful for that foundation, even though I didn't realize what I was laying the groundwork for at the time.

After college, I joined a writing group in Rochester, and the camaraderie, the feedback, and the deadlines were vital to helping me stick with it. I also had the pleasure of attending the *Titles Over Tea* book club at the Greece, New York, Barnes & Noble. *Titles Over Tea* is open to the public, which results in a group of book lovers of different ages who have had very different life experiences. I read novels I would never have read otherwise, and also had familiar books opened up in new ways through our discussions. It made me a better reader and a better writer. And I think also influenced some of the multi-generational relationships in this book. Moving away from my writing group and book club is one of the hardest things I've ever done.

Now I'm in an online group of novelists, I have critique partners who are constructive and inspiring, and I take weekly writer hikes with my friend Cassandra Dunn (author of *The Art of Adapting*). Since the actual writing process is so solitary, connecting with the community of writers around me is vital. It truly is an honor to get to work with and root for other writers on this level. It's an experience I cherish.